END OF
SECRETS

END OF SECRETS

RYAN QUINN

THOMAS & MERCER

Published by Thomas & Mercer, Seattle

www.apub.com

Amazon, the Amazon logo, and Thomas & Mercer are trademarks of Amazon.com, Inc., or its affiliates.

ISBN-13: 9781477825525
ISBN-10: 1477825525

Cover design by *theBookDesigners*

Library of Congress Control Number: 2014938730

Printed in the United States of America

For the creative.
Never stop thinking.

gnosis \ ˈnō-sis\ n. knowledge of spiritual mysteries [from Greek: literally, "knowledge"]

—*New Oxford American Dictionary*

The challenge of modernity is to live without illusions and without becoming disillusioned.

—Antonio Gramsci, philosopher

PROLOGUE

Washington, DC

Kera Mersal was pounding pavement by 5:59 AM, one minute ahead of schedule. She liked to beat the heat, of course, which settled thick over the Beltway earlier and earlier this time of summer. But she also liked to catch the District's wide thoroughfares, blocky marble structures, and out-of-scale monuments in their eerie magnificence as the first sunlight hit them from low, aspiring angles.

As her legs warmed to the task, her eyes focused, embracing the discomfort she sought from the city's streets and paths each morning. Though she hadn't competed since high school, her middle-distance runner's build was intact, a lean but sturdy five feet eight that in her jogging outfit turned the heads of early morning motorists. She had maple skin and wavy Earl Grey hair pulled back tight in a ponytail. As she ran she listened to a BBC News podcast. She liked to know what the world was being told about what was happening in the world.

She ran along Embassy Row and into Rock Creek Park, where she could stick to trails all the way to the Potomac. It was usually when she hit the Mall that the buildup of lactic acid in her calves and quads tipped the scales toward discomfort, and she became aware of her pulse pounding in her chest and at her temples. She lifted her head as she rounded the World War II Memorial and then slowed abruptly. She would have completely missed the man sitting on the park bench except that he'd lowered his newspaper and looked directly at her. She stopped in front of him and tugged the earphones from her ears.

"Morning, Kera."

"Lionel. Hi." Her first thought was that this was some kind of test, and she felt her flushed cheeks warm a few degrees for having not noticed him sooner. He was not in disguise. Half a lifetime earlier, Lionel Bright had known three-dozen ways to alter his appearance on short notice. But for every day of the six years Kera had known him, he had always looked the same: like a middle-aged bureaucrat, with gray-white hair and beat-up glasses resting on his thin, angular nose. He'd once been in fierce shape, though impressive physical stats had never been among his genetic gifts. He was an inch shorter than average and as prone as he'd ever been to gaining weight if he neglected exercise.

Kera was breathing heavily. Out of instinct, she looked around. There was a black SUV parked on Seventeenth Street. Otherwise, nothing out of the ordinary. "A newspaper. How quaint. You know, the only people who read newspapers on public benches anymore are spies."

"Busted," he said, attempting to fold the paper. The broadsheet resisted stubbornly. He stood, giving up, and stuffed the rumpled sections into a trash can.

"That your ride?" she said, meaning the SUV but not looking at it.

"Not usually, no. But there's someone in there who'd like a word with you. Want to take a drive?"

"I prefer to run, actually. That's kind of the point."

"I never got that. Come on. This won't take long, and we can't do it at the office."

They'd been tracking a group of Chinese bankers suspected of plotting a cyberattack on the New York Stock Exchange. There were also the antisecrecy hackers who kept publishing classified documents online. And, of course, there were any of a dozen hot spots being closely monitored in the Middle East. There was always shit flaring up in the Middle East. She made a silent bet that this was about a new intercept from a target there. But what couldn't be discussed at the office?

As they approached the SUV, the driver got out and came around to open the rear passenger-side door.

"Can you turn that off?" Lionel asked, holding out his palm.

Kera looked at her smartphone, which was still playing the BBC podcast. She powered it down and handed it over to him. Then she climbed into the vehicle. There was a woman seated opposite her in the backseat.

"Good morning, Kera. I'm Gabrielle di Palma."

"I know who you are, ma'am. It's an honor."

Kera had not seen the Directorate of Intelligence's deputy director this close before in person. Di Palma had collar-length blond-white hair that shot back from her forehead. Shallow tributaries of wrinkles at the corners of her eyes and mouth were visible in the low light coming through the tinted windows. Di Palma was thin—bony even—and an inch or two taller than Kera. She wore a blazer with a silk blouse and skirt; the whole ensemble came together with a commanding elegance that made Kera self-conscious of her own sweaty running clothes. She felt even worse when she remembered that she'd dashed out the door without brushing her teeth.

"Lionel tells me you've come up under him in CSAA," di Palma said, referring to the agency's Office of Collection Strategies and Analysis. Kera nodded and glanced quickly at Lionel, who had climbed into the front passenger seat. The driver, Kera noted, remained outside. Di Palma switched on a tablet and pushed it across the seat toward her. "I'm going to offer you a job, Kera. But before I do, I need you to agree to keep this conversation between us. Please sign and fingerprint this NDA after you've read it carefully."

Kera moved her eyes over every word of the agreement, but she was too distracted to absorb more than a quarter of them. Using a finger, she scrawled her signature on the touch screen and then pressed the flat tip of it to the print scanner at the bottom of the display.

"Thank you," di Palma said as she tucked away the tablet. "As you know, the new frontier in our field is all-source data mining. The problem we've run into at the agency is not our technology. We've got that; we're ahead of the curve, even. As a result, though, we're absolutely buried under mountains of signals intelligence data that is piling up in servers much faster than we can make any sense of it. It will take a decade to address these problems institutionally. And that makes us vulnerable. Very much not ahead of the curve."

Kera tried to appear as if she were listening patiently, but she couldn't guess why she'd been pulled off the street so that the DI's deputy director could tell her what she already knew.

Di Palma paused as if reading Kera's mind. "I'll be direct. I've been cleared to field an elite team for a black op, code-named Hawk, to operate a more flexible and efficient cyberintelligence platform. I want you on that team."

Kera looked to the front seat to gauge Lionel's reaction. His expression gave her nothing. "I—"

"Hold on. I haven't given you the most difficult thing you need to consider before making your decision. The mission of Hawk is to master information. To gather it at its source, to analyze it, and to act upon it at the precise time it is needed. The scope of this work may extend into areas many of our citizens and lawmakers would consider unacceptable. As a result, most of our missions will require us to operate completely off the books. That means we have to get all of the personnel for Hawk out of the agency. The team will be structured like a private contractor."

"Is that merely a technicality, or are you asking me to leave the agency?" Kera looked again to Lionel. There was no way he approved of this. She'd only ever heard him curse agency people who defected to the private sector. His eyes urged her to keep listening.

"Both. It's a technicality, but it has real consequences. If you're not comfortable with this, you're welcome to walk away. If you accept, you will have to resign from the CIA and apply for a job at the *Global Report*, an online news organization that went live two days ago. You will then relocate to our offices in Midtown Manhattan. Your cover will be as an investigative journalist. Stories will be created and published in your name, but you will have nothing to do with those because you'll be carrying out a variety of covert cyber-intelligence missions under my direction and the direction of Dick Branagh, who's joining us from NSA."

"Ms. di Palma—"

"Gabby, please."

"Gabby . . . ma'am . . . if I may. I didn't come to Langley and go through years of taxpayer-funded training just so that I could bail for the private sector at the first opportunity."

This produced the first tangible reaction out of Lionel, who let a proud smile curl the corners of his mouth.

"This won't be bailing, Kera. Quite the contrary. It's still an agency op, we just have to run things more independently than we're used to," Gabby said. "Everyone from the White House down is desperate for an elite unit like this. To develop it inside the agency would take a culture shift and a bureaucratic shuffle that we don't have time to wait for. Besides, some of the talent we need has already gone private, and they're too hard to pull back."

"When do you need my decision?"

"By the end of the week. Think about it carefully. And let me be very clear about one thing. Hawk will be secret and autonomous not only so that we can pursue the most advanced cyberintelligence operations ever conducted, but also so that the agency will have plausible deniability if anything goes wrong. Do you understand? If Hawk fails, they will disavow us."

Kera heard herself say, "Yes, ma'am."

"Lionel, will you get my driver back in here?" Gabby said. Then she turned to Kera as Lionel stepped out, scanning her from head to toe as if noticing for the first time what Kera was wearing. "Would you like a ride?"

"No, ma'am. Thank you."

The driver opened Kera's door, and Lionel must have seen the conflict on her face. He leaned past her and told Gabby to go ahead without him. "I think we'll take a walk."

When the SUV had pulled away, they strolled across the open field that gradually sloped up to the Washington Monument. For several minutes neither of them spoke. Lionel Bright was the director of the Office of Collection Strategies and Analysis. His job title made him Kera's boss. His conviction in her potential had made him her mentor. He was in his midfifties or thereabouts and claimed—correctly, as far as Kera knew—that no one in this world knew his real birth date. What did it matter? Kera doubted that *any* of his official biographical information was accurate, including his name.

"You put me up for this?" Kera said. He nodded. "Why?"

"Because you're the best." She gave him a cut-the-bullshit look. In response, he tipped his angular nose down so that he could meet her eyes over the rims of his glasses. "You are. And also because I need you there."

"You need me there because of me? Or because you don't trust di Palma?"

"Don't ask questions you know the answers to."

He was right. Of course he didn't trust Gabby di Palma. Distrust had been a cornerstone of his instruction. *Trust only your instincts and your training. Make an exception only when your instincts tell you it's worth the risk. As for really trusting someone, that may happen only once or twice over an entire career.* Kera had asked him once, "Has it happened to you?"

"What? Trusting someone?" After a moment he'd nodded and said, "Twice."

She'd wanted to press him further then, to ask him who, but she didn't.

"I need you at Hawk, yes. But I'll miss you around here," Lionel said, changing course slightly to keep them out of earshot of a family of tourists. "You can't think about me, though. You have to choose what's best for you."

"What about what's best for the country?" she said before she could stop herself. "I meant it when I said I didn't go through the Farm and spend all these years working under you just to coast into the private sector." She did mean it. And she hated that needing to prove her patriotism was ingrained in her DNA.

He shook his head. "This won't be a pleasant job, Kera. Think about it. They're going private with this because things are going to get dirty. Nothing you'll do with them is going to be by the book."

"In other words, it'll be real intelligence work?"

He chuckled, but his expression was sober. "Yes. And that's a strong argument for why it's the most effective way you can serve."

"Would you do it?" Kera said, searching his eyes. Aside from her parents, Lionel Bright was the only person she had ever trusted.

He exhaled deeply. "It's certainly where the action is headed. You'll have access to technology the rest of the world won't see for years. But as far as job security, I don't know. You heard Gabby. If something goes bad, you're done. You won't be able to come back."

Kera nodded and sat down on a bench. "Leave me here, OK?"

She watched Lionel trek across the lawn and disappear into the blocks beyond Constitution Avenue. She sat for a long time, savoring the views of the White House and the institutional buildings that flanked the Mall. They felt different to her than when she'd started her jog—there was something about them that was different from every other morning she'd been here. It took her a few moments to understand what it was.

I'm going to New York, she thought.

ONE

Manhattan,
Two Years Later

The man at the table was her source. She saw that immediately. He had chosen the darkest booth, the one with high wooden seat backs—for privacy maybe, or as respite from the harsh glow of daylight, which is always a little sad to see in a bar. He was watching the door when she came in, and from the shadows his eyes widened slightly.

Neither of them belonged in a place like this before noon on a Wednesday. The location had been his call. It made her wonder now if he'd turned to drinking. He was thirty-three and rich, but the way he slumped in the booth made him look like an awkward college boy—spotty facial hair, a worn hoodie hanging off his slender frame. He was MIT-educated, with a wife of two years, a newborn baby girl, and a condo in Tribeca. She had never met him before this moment, but she knew all that. That and, of course, that he was newly unemployed. They were here to talk about his former employer.

"I shouldn't be talking to you," he had said over the phone a few days earlier.

"And yet you called me," she had replied, her attention divided between the call and a database on the screen in front of her that was sorting through a list of IP addresses in Tehran. The man had apparently called the *Global Report*'s newsroom the previous day. Nothing unusual about that; the newsroom received calls like his constantly. Few of them were even potentially worth following up on. They all went into the system and, unless a computer flagged the message, it was ignored or deflected by one of the newsroom staff. Her computer had not flagged his call, but that was no surprise either. Her casework was related to foreign threats, and his was some sort of domestic matter.

Someone's computer had flagged it, though, because this guy's message had gone up the chain as far as Gabby, and Gabby had turned it over to Kera to see if it checked out.

"How can I help you?" Kera had said when she called him back to follow up.

"I saw your story."

"I've written a lot of stories, Mr.—what's your name?"

"No names. If I talk to you at all, it has to be on deep background."

"Mm-hmm." She sounded bored. It was only half an act. They always wanted to remain anonymous. A startling percentage of the callers were certifiable nut jobs absolutely sure that they had evidence of some newsworthy conspiracy—a secret murder, innocent death-row inmates, political crooks, the government spying on citizens. *If they only knew,* she thought.

"The ONE story."

"I'm sorry?" She pried her eyes from her other work and pulled up the *Global Report*'s website on a new monitor.

"Your story about the ONE Corporation. The one about the Wall Street bankers."

So that was why Gabby had stuck her with this—it was related to a story that had run under her byline. In the *Global Report*'s search bar, she entered the keywords he'd just provided along with her name. *ONE Wall Street bankers Kera Mersal.* The headline popped up: RISING I-BANKERS DECAMP FOR ONE.

"Sure," she said, skimming the first paragraph. The article reported that, in an unusual move, the ONE Corporation had poached twelve men from Wall Street banks in the last year. She remembered reading it now. Couldn't have been more than two or three days earlier. There were at least one of these articles per day with her name on them, and although many were much less interesting than this, the banker piece hadn't particularly stood out. Not with everything that was going on with her actual casework. "What about it?"

"I have information about ONE that people should know."

"What kind of information?"

"Information that ONE doesn't want you to have."

"Why should I trust your information if I don't know who you are?"

"I was one of the bankers."

This checked out. The number she'd reached him on belonged to the cell phone of one Travis Bradley, formerly vice president of Project Analysis (whatever that was) at the ONE Corporation, and before that a vice president at Goldman Sachs. Bradley had no criminal record, was in good standing with the IRS, and owed no debt other than a monthly balance on three credit cards. She listened to as much as he was willing to say over the phone, which, in her professional opinion, was more than he should have said into any electronic device. She said she'd get back to him, a promise she had no intention of keeping.

She wrote up a report for Gabby, filed it electronically, and had forgotten all about Travis Bradley by the time she returned her attention to the batch of IP addresses located six thousand miles away.

An hour later she got an e-mail from Gabby. The subject was "Bradley." The entire message was two sentences: MEET WITH HIM. SEE WHAT HE KNOWS.

Which is how, two days later, Kera found herself in that Upper East Side dive bar doing the first fieldwork she'd done since joining Hawk.

"I quit," Bradley told her.

"Why?"

There were a handful of people in the bar, none of them within earshot. Bradley had chosen the site—far from his home and far from the stomping grounds of any of his ex-colleagues on Wall Street or at the Midtown headquarters of ONE. Pool balls clacked on a scuffed table in the back. A few patrons chatted up the bartender, their wandering eyes cutting between televised baseball games. There was a jukebox, but no one had bothered to feed it any money at this hour. Instead, a Tom Petty album played low from the speakers.

"I couldn't do it anymore. I've made too much money to claim to have a conscience, but that's the closest thing to it. Can you turn that off?" They both stared for a moment at her phone on the table between them. After she'd switched off the mic and dropped the phone back into her bag, he spoke quickly. She didn't have to ask him many questions to keep him talking. The gist of his intelligence was this: ONE had hired the bankers to develop sophisticated algorithms that could mine huge amounts of data and deliver precise predictions about consumer behavior.

"So what?" Kera said. "Don't all smart companies do that, or at least try to? I search for something online, the search engine uses all of my recent web activity to get me the best results. I buy music or a book, the retailer tells me what other titles I'd like. How is what you're talking about different from that?"

"Those are very two-dimensional examples. What ONE is actually able to do is more like this: ONE gathers up a record of all the entertainment you consume, and the entertainment your friends consume, and how close you are to each of those friends. Most of that stuff is trivial, of course, and consumers are just giving it away anyway. But ONE also is gathering up data on the jobs you've held, and your educational background, and your medical history, and the medical history of your relatives, and your driving record, and most of your financial transactions, and a thousand other factors you'd never even think about."

"But how could ONE get all of that?"

"You mean, how is the data collected?" He shook his head. "I knew better than to ask that."

"You think they're getting it illegally?"

"Would there be a legal way?"

"I hope not. But then *why*? ONE is a media company. Why do they even want data like that, especially if they have to break laws to get it?"

"They're not just a media company. Not anymore. Their ultimate objective—the arrogance of it—is staggering. It would have been laughable to me before I got to ONE, especially coming from the Street, where I thought arrogance had been perfected. But I've seen these models work, and—"

He hesitated, and she sensed he was holding something back. "And what?"

"With data on this scale, yes, they can tell you what book you might want to read next. But they can also tell an insurance company your likely medical future, including the age and cause of your death. Or they could tell an employer whether you are the best candidate for a job you've applied to. Or supply a university's admissions committee with a report that details not just whether you're a qualified candidate, but what you're likely to do with the degree they give you, and how much you'll be making ten years from now."

"It's hard to believe it could be that precisely predictive."

"Believe it."

"And this data is for sale?"

He nodded. She saw his eyes scan to the door. "That part is secret. Well, everything's secret. They have a whole new facility full of servers—they call it 'the bunker'—that no one is allowed to see, just churning out these calculations. But they're most secretive about the fact that they're selling the information."

"Selling it to who? Insurance companies, employers?"

"Yes. And other clients."

"Like who?"

This time he shook his head. "Use your imagination."

"No," she said. "I hope you'll forgive my skepticism, but extraordinary claims like this require extraordinary evidence. And you're hardly making sense. You've got to give me something more concrete."

He shifted awkwardly in his seat. Again, his gaze darted around the room before it returned to a point on the table between them. "I think I better not say anything more."

"Have you been threatened? Why not go to the cops first?"

He shook his head as though frustrated with her. "This is a little outside their jurisdiction."

"The FBI, then?" she asked, reaching.

His eyes caught hers and then he looked down. "That isn't an option."

"OK. Then why'd you call me?"

"I told you. The article you wrote. I thought maybe you'd turned up something about ONE on your own that I could help confirm. But if I'm the only source, they'll know it was me."

"Who will know? ONE?"

"Yes. And . . . their clients."

She gave him a few beats, a final chance to elaborate, but he didn't jump at the opportunity. "Well," she said, standing to leave. "When you're prepared to say anything more specific, you know how to reach me." Gabby had been vague about what Kera should hope to learn from this meeting, and Kera had exhausted her patience for fishing around in the dark. She made it only a few steps across the room when he said something more. It was the way he'd said it, like a confession made on an impulse, that urged her to stop and look back at him. "What?"

"The end of secrets," he repeated.

She returned to the table. "OK," she said. "That was portentous. Now what the hell does it mean?"

He waited a few moments for her to sit, but when she didn't, he began to talk again. "When the other quants and I started at ONE, the first thing we did was have a private lunch with Keith Grassley, the company's CEO. Well, the first thing after we'd signed a bunch of nondisclosure agreements to ensure we'd never repeat anything like what I'm telling you now." He swallowed, and again his eyes worked the room. When they returned to her, there was something like anger in them, as though she were forcing this from him.

"At the end of that meal, Grassley stood up and told us why we were there. 'ONE is no longer just a media company,' he said. 'We are an information empire.' I know, I rolled my eyes at first too. But it wasn't hyperbole. He told us that in the future, perhaps the near future, power in the world would lie with those who could amass the most information and have the ability to organize it with a few strokes of a touch screen. 'Perfect information about the past and the present contains the very instructions to build the future.' That's another quote I recall. This information was out there, he said, as it had always been. It just needed to be collected. When ONE accomplished that, he said, it would be the end of secrets."

"He's a quotable guy."

"Yeah, well, when you have a minute, think about that last one," Bradley snapped. But then, just as quickly, the anger washed out of his eyes, and they flooded with desperation and fear. "Will you write something?"

She shook her head. "You're an anonymous source with no evidence. Give me a call when you're ready to go on the record and have some proof to back it up. Until then, you're just a coward with a conscience. And that isn't news."

The way she walked away, backlit by the blinding daylight coming through the windows near the front, she must have looked to him more silhouette than woman.

TWO

The premise of the exercise was simple: notice something new about the neighborhood. An architectural detail, a storefront, a billboard, a pattern in the flow of pedestrian traffic. Lionel had taught Kera the game early in her training. He'd insisted that it was a crucial exercise, both to help maintain observational fitness and to understand new environments. She found that it was most interesting to play the game in places she thought were most familiar. A startling array of things was always there and never seen. Most days, like today, a perfectly new detail in the landscape revealed itself to her in plain sight and reminded her of the extraordinary vastness of the ordinary world. It was a beautiful thought, but it was also evidence of a weakness, a vulnerability.

The words caught her eye by chance. Technically, this violated the spirit of the exercise, which called for deliberate observations. Nevertheless, there they were—six words where she had never noticed them before. She'd just disembarked from the downtown N train, and the bottleneck in the stairway drew her gaze upward over the hats and hair and bald heads toward the freedom of the sidewalk. The words were made of small letters—the entire phrase stretched at most four feet—painted on the underside of a scaffold landing that shielded pedestrians from the persistent construction along Houston Street.

HAVE YOU FIGURED IT OUT YET?

She cleared the bottleneck and climbed the stairs with her face tilted up, studying the phrase. The vandal's penmanship was plain, unlike the stylized tags graffiti artists threw up on walls and train cars and mailboxes across the city.

Have you figured it out yet? The words were close together, each one nearly running into the next. It might have been the work of a bored construction worker in broad daylight. It might have been someone high or drunk, claiming a small corner of the city in the night. It might have been anyone. The city was dense and unfathomable.

Kera moved with the flow of commuters, the words passing overhead, and then she was on the sidewalk.

She scanned the intersection at Broadway and Houston. The streets and subway tunnels roiled with the citywide migration from office to apartment, career life to family life, from museums to Broadway theaters, cocktails to dinner, from daylight to twilight. Leashed dogs, freed from a day's captivity, splashed urine at the base of walls and planters and parking meters. Bareheaded cyclists dodged fares climbing out of open cab doors. Banks went dark and sports bars ran specials. It was rush hour and happy hour.

It was early for Kera to be off work. Normally, she stayed at Hawk's Times Square offices until after dark. But today coordinated raids in Sweden, Germany, and Russia had resulted in the arrests of anarchist hackers that her team had been homing in on for months. Gabby had congratulated them and sent everyone home early, reminding them that there would be many late nights to come. Kera had no intention of taking the evening completely off. She had other cases. But she could do that work from home via the secure connection to Hawk's network while she waited for Parker, who was in the air over the Atlantic and due home in a few hours. She would have dinner waiting for him, she decided. Her fiancé. She had cooked rarely since she moved to the city, and even less since they moved in together. Preparing a meal would mean an inventory of the cupboards and refrigerator, and then a run to at least two of the narrow-aisled groceries in the neighborhood. All of that, just to cover a simple recipe. Maybe she would just order out something nice.

She paused at the edge of the intersection, anchored against the humanity seeping up from the subway tunnels and receding into the buildings. She liked to absorb the chaos of the city at the end of the day, to measure its unsteady pulse against her own. She had heard that this city was unforgiving, that the people here were cold, or greedy, or lonely by the millions, that life here was gritty and hard. She had ignored these warnings when she'd accepted the job. She wanted to see for herself. She had lived here now two years, two years exactly to the day. She was unnoticed and underestimated and underpaid. But she was underway.

On the sidewalk nearby, a homeless man sat patiently watching his coffee cup fill with change as the stuffy transit system drew breath through the grate beneath him. She did not avert her eyes, though the city's beggars still disturbed her more than DC's had. Gabby, who was a New Yorker by birth, had assured her that she would get used to the homeless, just as she would get used to the other extremes that in the city were routine, like the absurd monthly apartment lease payments or the trash bags piled to shoulder height along the streets and the rats that darted from beneath them. Kera had no intention of getting used to any of this. Routine dulled the senses. Her training had taught her that people saw only what they wanted to see and what they happened to see. A good agent must see everything else. She was only an analyst now, but she knew that taking the job with Hawk had put her on track to make agent and could eventually lead to a long career as a case officer.

Her eyes lingered for a moment on the beggar's cup. Emblazoned on its side, with the logo of a popular coffee chain, was a colorful graphic promoting the release of a forthcoming movie. *Apocalypse*, it said. *May 22.* A pair of pretty actors clutched each other, witnessing some unseen horror that was suggested by orange fireballs reflected in their widened pupils. This same advertisement glowed—on a much larger scale—from the side of a five-story building across the street. The electronic billboard lurked over the intersection, dominating the canopy of the neighborhood's tangled commercial jungle. A few seconds later, the board served up a new ad, this one featuring a naked model, artistically obscured in shadow, pitching a men's fragrance (with dubious effect, given the palette of smells—garbage, bus exhaust, urine, the overcooked meats sizzling on vendors' carts—all competing for attention at street level). And then the giant LED screen flashed back to the Hollywood production, invading sight lines in every direction.

She skirted the bum's outstretched legs and crossed Broadway toward Lafayette. She knew all she needed to know about *Apocalypse*. First, that the film was crap and she had no intention of viewing it. And second, that she didn't matter; the movie was predestined for box-office glory with or without her approval. But mostly, she was aware that the studio that had produced the film was owned by the ONE Corporation, the world's largest media conglomerate.

After the meeting that morning with Travis Bradley, Kera had gone directly to Gabby's office. Although Kera now considered Hawk's deputy director approachable, she was as aware as she'd been at their first meeting—in the back of that SUV on the National Mall—that this was a shrewd, impatient woman who was difficult to please. Kera knew nothing about Gabby's personal life but assumed it was impossible she was married.

"You look flushed," Gabby said when Kera was escorted in by her boss's militant gatekeeper of an assistant. "What've you got?"

One thing Kera had learned through a half-dozen embarrassing reprimands over the preceding two years was that the deputy director loathed having her time wasted. Kera spoke without sitting down.

"ONE Corp. hired a dozen investment bankers from prestigious Wall Street banks over the last ten months. All men, of course. Quants—the math guys on the Street who turn market data into money."

"And Bradley was one of them?"

"Yes, that's confirmed."

"What does he want?"

"He's doing the whistle-blower dance. The charges are a little foggy, but he claims ONE is running some sort of Total Information Awareness data-mining project and selling off the consumer data."

"Selling it to who?"

"He wouldn't give any specifics."

"Do you believe him?"

"I don't know. ONE isn't an investment bank. Hiring a dozen of the best quants in the world does strike me as odd." But that wasn't the main thing about the meeting with Bradley that had stayed with Kera. "His fear was real. Whatever he thinks he knows, he's not comfortable talking about it. Then again, he said he wouldn't go to the Feds, so maybe he knows his story isn't credible. Want me to look into it?" she said, hoping Gabby would say no.

"No. Forget it. Go home. Go to the park. Go to a museum. I don't care. Pretend you enjoy having an afternoon off. That's an order."

"Yes, ma'am."

· · · · ·

She'd lost all track of time when she heard the key in the lock. She met Parker at the door and embraced him before he could pull off his shoes, lifting herself a few inches to his height by going on tiptoe. His familiar smell was layered with a stale whiff of recycled airplane air. His youthful, all-American handsomeness was textured with an extra day's scruff. When his cheek brushed hers, she felt a warm, satisfying shiver. It reminded her, in the way that only a touch, smell, or song can surface a memory, of the first months she'd spent with him. The months when she'd first detected the symptoms of love.

"I brought us something," he said, unveiling a bottle of wine from a paper bag.

When she saw the label, she smiled. "You already proposed to me, remember?"

"I want to hear your answer again. The first time I was too nervous to take it all in."

She mussed his sandy-blond hair and then stood back and made a show of contemplating the question posed by the bottle. Finally she said, "Well, all right, yes. I will spend the rest of my life with you if you keep turning up with bottles of wine and that sweet look on your face." And then she leaned in to kiss him.

The night Parker had gone shaking to one knee to utter his blur of compliments and confessions and, finally, the proposal, they had been right here in their new living room with an identical bottle of wine—the winery was called Eons; he was prone to gross sentimentality—and a too-expensive dinner they'd ordered for takeout to avoid paying extra for a tip.

"Oh, shit. Dinner. You're probably starving," Kera said, remembering now with a pang of guilt. "I got distracted with work. What are you in the mood for? I'll order us something." She made a move to carry the wine to the kitchen, which, like most of the apartment, was only a few feet from the front door.

"Big news day today, huh?" Parker said, watching her with his gray-blue eyes and a big grin.

"Hmm?"

"Your story. This spy business with Iran."

"Oh, that," she said, struggling to remember what she had supposedly written about Iran. Iran and China had become her main fields of expertise, first at the agency and now at Hawk. But she couldn't remember what latest piece of the international saga had been released by the Pentagon or uncovered by an actual reporter somewhere that would have triggered a story today under her byline in the *Global Report*. She'd read the brief at the office, and she must have glanced through the copy—she always did—but her mind had been preoccupied after her meeting with the ONE whistle-blower, and she'd failed, apparently, to retain even a few conversational details about the latest Iran headline.

"It was hardly a scoop. I'm not exactly reporting from the front lines," she said.

"At my job it might matter who gets there first. But at yours it only really matters who gets it right," he said, opening his laptop. "Look, your piece has dozens of shares on Facebook. Almost a hundred tweets." He looked up at her. "My fiancée's famous."

"Hardly. And don't say that. Fame ruins careers in my business," she said, kissing him playfully and pushing him toward the bedroom. "Get out of here. Make yourself at home. I'm going to order Thai."

The moment he disappeared into the bedroom, dragging his suitcase, she spun his laptop around and started reading. There was her name under the headline MALWARE CRACKED, SHEDDING LIGHT ON IRAN'S AMBITION. She was doing some real multitasking now, one hand in and out of a drawer with the takeout menu, the other scrolling the web page as she read through blocks of copy.

"The story's published now. You still can't talk about it?" Parker said from the bedroom.

"Order for delivery," Kera said into the phone, loud enough for him to hear. The details came back to her as she skimmed through the article. The virus had targeted British, Israeli, and American intelligence assets in the Mideast. As a countermeasure, the CIA had exposed the malware to disinformation, feeding it data that could be traced back to the virus's creators. It was a classic trapdoor, only in reverse. The trail led to a bundle of servers in Tehran. Busted.

By the time she'd placed their order and hung up the phone, she'd absorbed enough to carry on a conversation.

"The cyberattack originated in Iran, but we turned it against them?" Parker asked.

"Yes, essentially."

"And in the process, we discovered that they're selling nuclear weapons?"

"Correct. Except we don't think they actually have the capability to make nuclear weapons. Not yet."

"Whoever's buying them must think they do."

"Maybe. It's more likely the weapons deals are fake. It's disinformation designed to provoke Israel. They like to provoke, the Iranians."

An ambulance or fire truck raced past the end of their block, and the room swelled with noise. Then the siren trailed off, leaving a silence. Kera found that she couldn't get Travis Bradley out of her mind. Even if she'd at first been annoyed that Gabby had sent her to the meeting with the ex-quant, and even if she was still skeptical about Bradley's credibility, his allegations were unsettling. Out of curiosity she'd done some research into ONE that afternoon. The company's stock price, which she'd been studying when Parker arrived home, had closed the day in record territory. Other than hiring the twelve quants, however, she saw no indication that ONE was branching out into anything beyond the entertainment industry. In a decade ONE had patched together a gargantuan media empire by gobbling up every small magazine, newspaper, TV station, record company, and film studio on the map. They were buying competitors and start-ups at a rate of a half dozen a month. It was impossible to walk down the street or turn on the TV without encountering ONE's influence. They seemed to control every third billboard in the city, every third song that played on the radio, every third movie opening in every megaplex. What was this need to own *everything*?

She put on music and rinsed two dusty wineglasses while she watched Parker struggle to ease the cork from the bottle with a tool she knew had been designed to make the task much simpler than it appeared to be for him. While they sipped wine and waited for dinner, Parker told her about Dubai. He had traveled there for something called a global social networking conference.

"The place is unreal. The whole time I was thinking about how much you'd love it. I'll take you with me sometime. If we pick up this business, I'll have to travel there once a month." Parker worked at a peppy start-up firm that specialized in digital marketing and that was owned by a distant friend of a family friend. "Remember that thing I was telling you about with the shoe designer app? We're pitching a soccer brand for a campaign that will lead up to an international tournament they're hosting . . ."

Kera did remember him telling her about the shoe app. And no matter how much she tried to prevent it, her reaction now was as it had been the first time he'd brought it up: her eyes glazed over and her mind drifted back to her own work. She wondered whether the hacker arrests overseas had been made public yet. With any luck, data on hard drives had been recovered in the raids that would lead her team to additional hackers in the network.

"I'm boring you," Parker said.

"No, babe," she said, though they both knew she'd been caught with her mind wandering. She slid a hand up the back of his shirt and spread her fingers across his lower back. "I'm glad it went well."

Another siren crescendoed on the street, momentarily drowning out the Internet radio.

"Can you believe all that?" Parker said.

"What?"

"She lived a few blocks from here."

"She who?"

"You didn't hear?"

"I've been doing work stuff."

"And you call yourself a newswoman," he joked.

"What happened?"

"Rowena Pete."

It took Kera a moment to place the name. The singer. Yes, that was right. Kera liked the music of Rowena Pete. "Dead?"

Parker nodded. "I read about it on my phone. And then it turns out she lived so close. They shut down a whole block, and the cab had to go around. It's a complete circus."

Kera poured them more wine and sat on the couch next to him. He was on his computer now.

"Gnos.is?" she said disparagingly.

"They're the fastest. Look," he said, opening the *Global Report* in a new window for comparison. He was right. *TGR* hadn't yet published any reports on the death of Rowena Pete. Neither had the *New York Times* or any other serious news organization. She rolled her eyes as Parker, his point made, clicked back to Gnos.is. "They think pills."

"Who thinks pills? How would anyone know something like that already? There used to be a time when people preferred a medical examiner to make that call."

"And a medical examiner will have his say. But people have always wanted information as fast as possible, even if that information is imperfect at first. The only thing that's changed is that now they can have it almost immediately. Look at the way Gnos.is works. Maybe a cop leaked something, or a resident working at the coroner's office. Whatever the source, a new fact makes its way online and Gnos.is verifies it to the degree it can in that moment. It's doing the work of a dozen reporters in a fraction of the time."

"It's not journalism."

"Sure it is. Journalism's changing. You're as aware of that as anyone."

What she wouldn't let Parker know was just how much Gnos.is baffled her. The site had appeared three years earlier and, after a slow start as a hard-news site, it increased its offerings in entertainment news and started to gain real traction. While that trajectory wasn't unlike any number of other Internet start-ups, one thing set Gnos.is apart: the owners of the site were anonymous. No one knew who they were or where they operated—or why. At first, the site's top-level domain—".is"—was thought to be a clue, an indication that the site was hosted in Iceland. But the CIA's cyberspies had determined that the site was in fact hosted by a complex network of servers around the world, bouncing from one to another randomly to prevent hackers or government agencies from sabotaging the site or identifying its owners.

Gnos.is created no revenue. It simply used high-powered computing to assemble and publish news. The anonymity was irregular enough in a world where successful high-tech entrepreneurs typically flaunted their egos along with their sudden wealth. But what was first believed to be a gimmick on the part of the site's unknown owners quickly became something more ominous. No one could crack Gnos.is. Even chat rooms frequented by the hacker community began to buzz about the mysterious site. And still, no one came forward with any credible insight about who was behind Gnos.is, nor how they kept the site's operations secret.

The obsession over Gnos.is in the intelligence community took the form of panic. Many analysts concluded that the site was a front for a foreign, state-sponsored intelligence-gathering program. Gnos.is didn't exist to make a profit, so their intentions must be hostile. Or so the argument went. Some of that paranoia found its way to Hawk, and Kera had briefly been assigned to a Gnos.is task force. Like everyone else, though, the Hawk hackers failed to locate the site's owners or to decode the algorithms that made Gnos.is work. But they also failed to come up with any evidence that Gnos.is was sponsored by a foreign state or that it was collecting the data of users and storing it for illegal or otherwise suspicious purposes. Eventually, funding for the task force was pulled and, embarrassed, everyone turned their attentions elsewhere. To Kera's knowledge, it remained the only case that Hawk had failed to deliver on.

"See, more sources are contributing. Gnos.is is saying it's a suicide."

"You mean, some idiot on the street is tweeting that," she said.

The buzzer rang. For twenty minutes Kera and Parker sat across from each other sharing pad thai and curry out of plastic containers. Afterward, Parker opened another bottle of wine, and they sat on the couch with dueling laptops. Kera browsed a few news sites, looking for early reports of the hacker raids. When she came up empty, she closed her laptop and leaned her head on Parker's shoulder. He was reading Gnos.is's coverage of the Rowena Pete story. Other news sites had begun to report rumors of the singer's death, but few claimed to be able to confirm anything. Local television stations and even CNN had perched correspondents in front of the singer's apartment building, but none of them were going live with new details. The *New York Times* had posted only a brief, bare-bones mention of the tragedy on its website, a sort of preobituary that had come from the AP. Meanwhile, Parker gloated, Gnos.is had pages and pages of information, including dozens of photos and videos uploaded from smartphone users on the street.

"Pills were found in the apartment, but a cause of death has not been determined," he read from the text in its current form. The paragraphs updated themselves, sometimes more than once a minute, as new reports were uploaded and confirmed. Parker frowned. "Hang on. Several sources also report that a knife has been found on the scene. There is at least one report claiming that the singer hung herself in a closet."

"See, no one knows anything, so they just publish everything," Kera said, standing to clean up from dinner. "What's to keep me from submitting my own made-up version of the story? These quote-unquote reports could be coming from some bored idiot at work on the West Coast—or in Tokyo, for that matter."

"The reports are filtered against each other and against established facts," Parker said. Kera listened, assuming a layperson's understanding of the site. "False reports are discarded, and the users who submit them are flagged. I'm not saying it's a perfect system. But it's still a useful tool."

"Useful for what? The latest celebrity gossip. What Gnos.is provides is hardly news."

Parker shrugged. "It's what people want. It's entertainment."

"I've never understood what's entertaining about what most people call entertainment."

It was not the first time they'd had this conversation. Parker came down on the side of technology's inevitability and its uncanny knack for improving, on balance, the lives it inevitably disrupted. He usually seemed more enthusiastic about the conversation than Kera, who secretly liked to see his passion stoked. She envied him this outlet, to be able to discuss openly what he did at work.

Parker got up to pour another glass of wine. Minutes passed without any update. The image he'd left on-screen was a photo of Rowena Pete taken at a show earlier that year.

"What was she, twenty-eight?" Kera said, studying the photo. "A few years younger than us. I always wanted to see her perform live." She entered "Rowena Pete" into the Internet radio player and sat for a moment, her glass of wine in hand, listening in the way you do only when it's too late to not take something for granted. There was a raw quality that Kera liked about Rowena's music that was missing from most other music she listened to. Something honest and present. The year before, she'd almost bought them tickets to see Rowena Pete at the Bowery Ballroom. She remembered now why she hadn't. During her first months in the city, she'd been tempted from all sides by concerts and museums and Broadway shows. So much happened in this city every day of the week, and the chance to see a Rowena Pete show had felt, like everything else, as if it would always be there.

Kera's phone chirped to life on the counter. She looked at the time. It was after ten.

"Shit. It's Gabby."

Parker looked up at her for a moment with raised eyebrows, but then returned his attention to his computer.

"Are you at home?" Gabby said over a background din of voices and vehicle engines, the occasional bleat of a car horn.

"Yeah, what's up?"

"Can you join me at a fresh scene at Fourth and Bowery? Branagh himself sent me out here, and I want you looped in," she said, referring to Dick Branagh, Hawk's reclusive director and the only person higher up the chain than Gabby.

"A scene?" It was unusual for Hawk personnel to be present at a physical crime scene. Hawk agents lived almost exclusively in the digital world, and for good reason. It was a vantage from which they could access any crime scene report they needed without the nuisance of having to get a human being on-site under false pretenses. Human intelligence was viewed by Director Branagh as not only fallible, but the greatest source of vulnerability to the operation. Anytime they worked in the field, they risked blowing their cover. It was a risk that was judged, more times than not, to be unacceptable.

What struck Kera as even more unusual than that, though, was Gabby's location. Fourth and Bowery was only blocks from their apartment. She stepped into the bedroom with her phone. Through the open door she could see the screen on Parker's laptop, still open to Gnos.is.

"That was my reaction too. Until I saw it for myself," Gabby said. "I need you to get over here, Kera. I want you to take this case."

"A *case*? This thing with the singer? How is that a case for us?"

"I'll show you when you get here. Use the back entrance. The front is a total shit show. Cameras everywhere. Oh, and Kera?"

"Yeah?"

"Don't take any shit from these cops. We're here with permission from the mayor's office, and nobody's happy about it."

Kera exhaled, rousing her body from the sleepy buzz of wine. "All right, I'm just a few blocks away. I can be there in ten minutes."

She hung up and retrieved her shoes and jacket from the closet.

"Something urgent?" Parker said from the doorway.

"I'm sure she's overreacting."

"Breaking news in Iran?"

"I can't say." She wanted to listen to him talk more about Dubai. She wanted to curl up next to him in bed. Anything but have to lie to him. She flashed him a look they both hated: *don't start this now.* She'd been up front about her job when they first met. She worked a lot. She couldn't talk about much of it because she had sources to protect. He'd known what he was in for, and he'd agreed to tolerate it. It would not always be like this, she promised. Just a few years. Then her career track at the *Global Report* would be made, and she could choose her own hours. She could work from home and have kids, if that's what she wanted, though she didn't want them now and suspected she might never. "Look, I gotta go."

"Of course. Your editor calls. The news cycle must go on."

"Don't wait up for me. You're exhausted," she said, feeling for her *TGR* media credentials in her pocket.

"Babe?" Parker called out to her when she was at the door. She turned. "Be safe."

She blew him a kiss and then she was gone.

THREE

Red and blue light bathed the entryway of Rowena Pete's three-story town house. A half-dozen cruisers flanked a waiting ambulance, poised at the curb below the singer's front door as if a lifesaving dash to the ER might still be in the cards. The town house's facade looked surreally familiar to Kera. The fire hydrant on the sidewalk, the thin trees planted along the block, the tips of their branches sprouting May buds. The wide maroon steps and solid white banister that rose to the landing outside the open front door. Kera recognized it all from the Gnos.is coverage.

Onlookers persisted well past nightfall. She swung wide of a gaggle of bored paparazzi, telescopic lenses swinging from their necks, and cut down a narrow alley. She was stopped before the rear entrance by a pair of cops who took turns scrutinizing her credentials.

"You're with the *Global Report*?" one of them asked.

"That's what it says."

The cop shook his head. "No media. You can wait out front with the rest of 'em. There'll be a news conference soon enough."

"Check with your supervisor," she said. "I have clearance through the mayor's office. We're doing an exclusive, behind-the-scenes-with-the-NYPD's-finest kinda thing."

The cop flashed his partner a look that said, *What the fuck? Do we really have to do this?*

The other cop shrugged. "Call it in." The first guy got on the radio, and within a minute he was stepping back and gesturing a sarcastic welcome with one arm as he lifted up the tape for her with the other. "Hopper's gonna love this. Good luck in there," he said.

She was asked to produce ID twice more between the perimeter and the entryway, where Gabby was waiting for her with an NYPD spokeswoman who didn't seem too happy to be working overtime on account of a media request from the mayor's office. The spokes-woman waited downstairs while Gabby led Kera through the town house.

"What are we doing here?" Kera whispered as soon as they were alone.

"An all-access piece on forensic evidence. Everything we see tonight is on background." Kera hadn't really been asking about their cover, but she heard Gabby's response loud and clear: *shut up and go along with it.* "Come on, everything's on the middle and top floors."

Kera followed her up the stairs. She had to jog the final steps to keep up. The second floor was an open, loftlike space stretching from large, street-facing windows past a living area, dining table, and then finally to a spacious kitchen. She was now in unfamiliar territory. The cameras uploading footage to Gnos.is had not penetrated this far. Kera shut her eyes for a moment to focus. *See everything,* she reminded herself. *Keep an open mind. You can only see a scene for the first time once.*

Gabby pointed out clusters of evidence as she walked through the room. A translucent orange prescription bottle lay lidless on the rug by the coffee table. Small red and white capsules dotted the couch, collecting near the cracks in the cushions. It felt a little staged,

Kera thought, a little cliché, like the opening scene to an episode of *Law & Order*. Deeper in the room, a cop with a video camera was shooting something on the kitchen counter. Gabby paused, allowing him to finish before they approached. "Here's the note," she said.

Kera stared down at the message, scrawled in fat blue marker on the back of an opened envelope: *I dream every day of flying off the Brooklyn Bridge.*

"A little precious, if you ask me," Gabby said.

Kera reached for the gloves she carried in her pocket and looked around to make sure the NYPD spokeswoman hadn't followed them upstairs. "May I?" she asked Gabby.

"Go ahead. Everything's already been photographed and dusted."

Kera flipped over the envelope to check the return address. A talent agency in Midtown.

"Mean anything to you?" Gabby asked.

"Her managers," Kera said. "Probably routine correspondence. A royalty statement, something like that."

Gabby raised an eyebrow. "Should I ask why you know who Rowena Pete's managers are? You a fan or something?"

"Something like that," Kera said. She'd come across a mention of the singer's manager in the Gnos.is coverage she'd read back at her apartment. The coverage had also mentioned that both the talent agency and the recording label that Rowena Pete was signed to were owned by the ONE Corporation. "Could mean something that she used this particular envelope," Kera said. She looked around until she spotted the neat stack of mail—mostly envelopes and magazines—slanting out of a bowl perched atop a nearby credenza. "Or it could have just been the closest piece of paper to write on."

"Wait till you see the rest. This is a girl who thought things through."

In the master bedroom on the third floor, Gabby showed her the space in the walk-in closet where hanging skirts, jeans, and T-shirts had been parted to make room for a nylon cord secured tightly around the hanger rod. The noose was as crude as the act it suggested: a thin, simple loop formed by a series of inexpert knots.

Kera wondered whether it was too obvious to ask where the body was. Their tour had featured pills, the note, and now the noose, but still no corpse. Its absence grew more distracting with every room they entered.

"There's more in the bathroom," Gabby said.

Two NYPD detectives huddled outside the threshold of the master bath. They glared territorially at Kera and Gabby, but they'd gotten word to let the two women in for a look. When Kera stepped into the large bathroom, her eyes went immediately to the floor. At some point hours earlier, a pool of pink bathwater had splashed from the tub and dried against the white tile, leaving a papery, mortal pink dust. It would have been this very spot, Kera guessed, where Rowena Pete might have stood, unclothed, testing the water's temperature with a hand, her toes curled against the cool tiles, until finally she slipped into the tub.

The knife was at the bottom, shimmering through the pink water.

"What do you think?" Gabby asked after she gave Kera a minute to take in everything.

"I'd say she's trying to send a message."

"Not a very clear one. A normal suicide letter would have been more helpful."

"Where—" Kera began, but then stopped. There was writing on the mirror behind Gabby. She'd noticed it as she turned, and then the rest of the room disappeared. She stared at the words for a long, blank moment.

"You with us?" Gabby asked.

"Yeah, sorry. I was just wondering." She pulled her eyes away from the mirror. "Where's the body?"

She felt the detectives look her way. Kera glanced back at them and then looked to Gabby.

"There's no body."

Kera's lips parted slightly to take in a breath. Her mind raced backward, back through the apartment—to the pills, the note in the kitchen, the nylon cord, and the knife in the tub behind her—but her eyes remained level, staring past Gabby to the short string of words on the mirror.

"What about the bridge? The note downstairs mentioned—"

"NYPD has frogs in the East River. But I don't expect they'll find anything," she said quietly so that the detectives couldn't hear. "Do you?"

"No forced entry?"

"Nope."

Kera's eyes scanned the counter around the sink, taking inventory of the toothbrush, makeup, blow-dryer. Gabby seemed to understand.

"Wherever she went, she took nothing with her. Her phone, tablet, wallet, keys—it's all downstairs."

Kera nodded.

"You two, time to clear out," one of the detectives said. Kera glanced at the badge hanging around his neck.

"Detective Hopper. I'm Kera Mersal." She didn't bother with a handshake. Instead, she held out her business card. The detective took it. "I'd love to see the lab results from the blood in this bathwater. I'm also curious how you process smartphone, tablet, and computer data as evidence in a case like this. In the meantime you can call me anytime if you get word about the girl."

The detective held up her card between two fingers as if he might fling it aside. "My advice, don't wait by your phone. Someone down at City Hall owes you favors, not me."

Aware that Gabby was watching her, Kera kept her eyes level on Hopper's. "Look, mayor's orders. You can take it up with him, if it's worth your time. But it seems like you've got bigger problems than me. You're one body short of a crime scene, and pretty soon someone's going to have to tell that pack of reporters outside that you have a missing celebrity on your hands. You keep me in the loop, I'll stay out of your way, and we can both keep the mayor out of it." Kera gave the detective a cooperative smile, but he only moved aside to let them leave.

"All right, we'll get out of your hair," Gabby said. "It looks like you're in for a long night. When you find the girl, or come up with a good reason why you can't, please let Kera know."

Kera let Gabby get a few steps ahead of her before she paused at the bathroom door and glanced back at the mirror. The words were clumped in two slanting lines near the base of the glass. They had been written in the same blue marker and the same lowercase handwriting that had crafted the vague note on the envelope in the kitchen. The words said: *Have you figured it out yet?*

. . . . .

Parker awoke as Kera got into bed.

"Everything OK?"

"Yeah."

"Want to talk about it?"

"You know I can't."

"I know."

She laid her head on his chest. Parker resented the secrecy. She knew it. He took it personally. He had asked, "Want to talk about it?" but what she heard in his voice, even through the half-sleep haze, was, "We're engaged. We're going to spend our lives together. Is there really something—anything—you can't tell me?"

You don't trust me. Wasn't that what he was saying?

She'd learned to live with this guilt, both with Parker and with her parents. It was unavoidable, but it was supposed to be manageable. *Never forget there's a difference between your undercover life and your real life,* Lionel would say occasionally when he recognized that guilt in her eyes. *They are not the same. Your real life matters more.*

Maybe, she thought. Either way, it seemed impossible to earn complete trust in one without betraying it in another.

She lay on her back, listening to Parker's breathing and thinking too much about the sleep that would not come.

FOUR

Kera tapped her ID badge and pushed through the security turnstile in the ground-floor lobby of the steel and mirrored-glass skyscraper where Hawk leased office space under the name of the *Global Report*. Exiting the elevator on the twenty-seventh floor, she waved hello to the receptionist, who sat behind a sleek metal counter imbedded with a wide flat screen displaying the *TGR* logo and a digital news ticker that announced headlines as they went live on *TGR*'s site. Two sides of this room were glass, providing views straight into the open-plan newsroom behind the receptionist. On Kera's first day at Hawk, she had sat in this very waiting room and noted the ironic transparency evoked by the office's open design. The appearance was of a busy, high-tech newsroom; what couldn't be seen beyond the newsroom's walls did not exist.

The waiting area was empty at this hour, as it was most hours. But the newsroom itself, which Kera entered through glass doors that slid open after another tap of her ID badge, maintained a staff around the clock. This staff consisted of copyeditors, headline writers, and a few senior editors who processed the unclassified reports fed to them from servers programmed to aggregate content for the *Global Report*. They assembled the reports into news stories and prepped them for publication. In addition to the editorial staff, a lean but highly capable department of web designers and IT personnel kept the news site updating constantly.

There was a cubicle in the newsroom with Kera Mersal's name on it. The desk had pictures of Parker and her family, the drawers contained binders with notes pertaining to stories filed under her byline, and the phone rang there when someone called the number on her *TGR* business card. Kera had sat at this desk only a few times—when Parker had visited the office, for example, or when she met with anyone who did not possess a high enough security clearance to be inside Hawk's secure quarters. Kera walked past the cubicle now, as she did every morning, and turned down a short hallway that branched off the newsroom and led to a conference room, kitchen, copy room, and bathrooms. At the end of this hall was a solid, nondescript door. Kera waved her ID badge at an unmarked reader built into the wall next to the door frame. Inside she greeted the three security guards by name and unloaded her bag and phone onto the X-ray machine's conveyor belt. Making small talk with the guards, she steadied her face in front of the retinal scanner that hung at face level in the center of the room. She waited, unblinking, for the approving beep that came a half second later. The display next to the scanner read:

KERA MERSAL, INTELLIGENCE ANALYST
CLEARANCE LEVEL: TS/SCI

Beckoned by one of the guards, she passed through the metal detector and collected her things. It was eight thirty. A typical start to the day.

Kera noticed the light on in Gabby's office, which was several doors down and across the hallway from her own, much more modest work space. It was rare that Gabby beat Kera into the office. Kera set down her bag, turned on her desktop computer, and went across the hall to say good morning. Gabby wasn't at her desk. Nothing unusual about that, though. Hawk's deputy director was constantly in meetings, often with Director Branagh, whose office was next door and whose door was always shut. Kera had met the director only once, and on that occasion—her first day at Hawk— they'd hardly exchanged more than a few words in greeting. She got the impression Branagh was an old-school spy, antisocial unless it served whatever mission was at hand, and protective of the inner bubble he created around himself. Gabby operated as his enforcer and, internally, as the face of the higher brass for Hawk employees. As such, she spent a good deal of her day in the Control Room, the windowless chamber at the center of the floor plan where agents monitored data collected by HawkEye, the firm's proprietary sur- veillance software, and created reports that were disseminated to clients throughout the intelligence community, including—not infrequently—analysis that made its way into the president's daily briefing.

Kera had never been inside the Control Room. It was a restricted area that required need-to-know clearance for a particular clas- sification of sensitive compartmented information code-named UNIVINT, or universal intelligence, which was the sort of all-source intelligence that was HawkEye's specialty. UNIVINT referred to a form of supercomputing that combined all available surveillance methods to construct a comprehensive, unifying understanding of a target or an evolving situation.

When it pertained to her work as an analyst, Kera had been granted access to raw reports generated by HawkEye, and she'd occasionally filed intel requests that were fulfilled by agents in the Control Room, such as obtaining IP addresses or tracking the pre- cise movements of a hacker or suspected terrorist. But she had yet to work a case that required her to set foot in the room herself.

Gabby had e-mailed Kera early that morning to call her to a ten o'clock meeting. Kera could guess what that meant. Gabby wanted an update on the Rowena Pete investigation. What was there to report? She still wasn't sure why she'd been assigned to the investigation, or even what they were supposed to be investigating. It didn't seem clear to anyone that a crime had even been committed. It was even less clear to Kera why any of it was Hawk's concern.

After a detour to the kitchen for her first cup of coffee, Kera retreated to her office to start prepping for the day. She began with the intention to start digesting what little she knew about Rowena Pete, but when she sat down at her desk, there was an e-mail from Travis Bradley, the ex-ONE quant. It was two sentences: I CAN GET EVIDENCE. WHAT DO YOU NEED FOR A STORY?

There's no story, Bradley, she thought, closing his e-mail without responding to it and wondering how long it would take before he gave up on her and sought out a real journalist.

She was halfway through the cup of coffee when an e-mail came in from Detective Hopper. It was terse. The prints on all the evidence were a match to Rowena Pete. The town house had been examined top to bottom, and there was no sign of forced entry. There also was still no body. The NYPD was classifying Rowena Pete as a missing person. The detective's tone seemed to imply that the singer had simply run away, an interpretation that made it seem like she didn't want to be found, as opposed to the alternative—that the detective was too incompetent to find her. This irritated Kera. The runaway theory didn't make sense. Run away to where? And why? And, OK, say for a moment Rowena Pete *had* run away; why go through the trouble of staging multiple, symbolic suicides? Why leave behind her phone and wallet? Kera felt torn. A missing persons case seemed insignificant compared to the global threats of cyberwar and terrorism that she was accustomed to monitoring. But she couldn't suppress her curiosity. "Where did you go, Rowena?" she whispered aloud to herself, letting her eyes drift over the scissoring intersection of Broadway and Seventh Avenue below her window.

She needed to prepare for her meeting with Gabby. Normally, the first thing she'd do with a new subject was put in an intel request. But she'd only ever been assigned cases that unfolded on foreign soil and involved non-US citizens. She suspected that it wouldn't be so easy to pull HawkEye data on Rowena Pete. Not without a FISA warrant, which wasn't even worth pursuing at this stage in the investigation. She wondered again why Gabby wanted her on this case—and why Hawk was even involved at all. She would get started soon, she told herself. But first, just for a minute, she allowed herself to gaze out the window, to be pulled into the patchwork panorama of billboards and flashing screens and ticker symbols ascending the vertical steel and glass that scraped the sky.

A three-story portrait of a young pop singer hung across the facade of a building with words announcing: *JW. New music from Jalen West.* An ad on a smaller scale made a pitch for a documentary film called *America. The search for the average American begins May 19*, the billboard said. The *America* ad was dwarfed by another ad for *Apocalypse*, this one the length of a tractor trailer, which offered one-word excerpts from unnamed critics—"Thrilling!" "Terrifying!" "Blockbuster!"

Soaring over this commercial thicket was an ad that was visible from every vantage in Times Square. It was a broad white billboard stretching across the facade of a skyscraper, perched high above the pitches for soft drinks, Broadway shows, and television programs:

ONE
There are 7,369,090,938 people in the world.
Soon they will all be connected.

The string of giant electronic digits at the center counted faster and further into the billions. Ever since the billboard had appeared months earlier, Kera often caught herself mesmerized by the number, watching it grow relentlessly, one digit at a time, turning over slightly faster than twice every second. The billboard began to unnerve her whenever she stared at it for too long. Is that what people wanted, to be connected?

Bradley's words rose up in her mind: *the end of secrets.* Across Times Square the number hit 7,369,090,967. And then 7,369,090,968. She turned to face her computer before the population clock could update again and began to look into how to handle intel requests for American citizens.

A few minutes before ten, she took her tablet and phone and approached Gabby's office. She felt unprepared. Looking into the intel request had been a mostly symbolic gesture meant to signal to her boss that she wasn't just sitting in her office staring out the window. The only actual development since last night had been Detective Hopper's benign e-mail.

"Come in. Shut the door."

Kera did as requested, sitting but not quite settling into one of the leather chairs facing the desk. Gabby's office was neat and sparse. There were no pictures of family, only a few framed photographs of Hawk's deputy director shaking hands with familiar politicians and Washington bureaucrats—the current and former directors of the CIA, NSA, and FBI, a couple of presidents, the attorney general. Hawk operated completely without paper files and Gabby's office reflected that. No file cabinets lined the walls, no folders stamped CLASSIFIED cluttered her desk. Just a thin, sleek computer, a tablet, a flat-screen television on the wall, and an STE—or Secure Terminal Equipment—desk phone for encrypted calls.

"I got a briefing from Hopper an hour ago," Kera began, opening the detective's e-mail on her tablet. "NYPD is classifying this as a missing person, possible abduction. They collected prints, hair, and fabric samples from Rowena Pete's town house. Forensics all came back negative for an intruder. No demand for a ransom—so far. And no other sign of foul play." Kera looked up from the e-mail she was summarizing aloud. "Except, of course, for the missing woman."

Gabby leaned forward and put her elbows on the desk, tenting her hands in front of her mouth. She seemed to be thinking for a moment. Then she smiled. "It's much stranger than that. Come on. There's something I want to show you."

Kera followed her boss into the hallway. They walked past Director Branagh's office and then continued on, traveling a quarter of the way around the floor. It wasn't until Gabby slowed to make the left-hand turn down a short side hallway that Kera understood where they were going. At the unmarked entrance to the Control Room, Gabby stopped and gestured for Kera to step in front of the retinal scanner. Kera flashed Gabby a quizzical glance, but then she did as ordered and stood, unblinking, while the scanner matched her retina with her identity and security clearance. The scan was followed by a soft beep. She jerked her head back and looked at the adjacent screen, confused. It said:

KERA MERSAL, AGENT
CLEARANCE LEVEL: TS/SCI-UNIVINT
PLEASE WAVE ID CARD FOR ENTRY.

Kera looked at Gabby.

"Well, try it," Gabby said.

Kera waved her badge over the card reader. When she did, she heard a dull click within the heavy door. The screen displayed a new message: AUTHENTICATION CONFIRMED. THANK YOU. HAVE A NICE DAY.

Kera stood dumbstruck as Gabby submitted her own retinas for scrutiny and waved her badge.

"Congratulations, Agent Mersal," she said, holding the door for Kera as they entered. Kera started to say thank you, but it came out as only a whisper. She was already looking past Gabby into the windowless room beyond.

The Control Room was a galaxy of screens. Overhead lights had been dimmed to make the environment ideal for viewing digital images. Men and women sat at multiconsole workstations in the semidarkness, pale light from the monitors washing over their faces. Directly ahead, the front wall was dominated by a massive tactical display—a large screen flanked on either side by columns of smaller screens. Above these, a row of digital clocks ticked off the local time in cities around the globe. At the front of the room beneath the main tactical display was a shallow pit where a half-dozen people huddled in discussion around a sprawling command station. Their heads shifted in unison, tilting up at the big screen and then back down at the monitors and touch screens in front of them.

Gabby led Kera to a pair of semicircle workstations that sat on a plateau overlooking the rest of the room.

"Wait here," she said.

Kera watched Gabby go down to the pit at the front of the room and get the attention of a man who was leaning over an analyst's workstation and gesturing about something on one of the screens. Gabby exchanged a few words with the man, who glanced up at Kera and nodded. Then he went back to what he'd been doing.

Kera studied the big screen. It displayed a giant map that spanned from East Asia, across the Americas and Europe, to the Middle East as far as Saudi Arabia. Color-coded dots marked a handful of geographic locations. She couldn't begin to guess what the map or the dots were meant to illustrate, and she was too far away to overhear the discussion in the pit.

After a few minutes, Gabby approached with the man she'd been talking to.

"This is J. D. Jones," Gabby said. Kera recognized his face. Perhaps they'd shared the elevator one or twice, though they'd never met. His name meant something to her, though. She knew that J. D. Jones was the designer of HawkEye. Kera was thirty-one. Jones couldn't have been more than two years on either side of that. He had wavy black hair that guarded his face and glasses with thick black rims. He was wearing a black T-shirt and jeans. He might have been handsome, but she didn't notice that at first. He was mostly just plain, the kind of man who would stand out in a crowd like a blade of grass on a golf course. Jones shook Kera's hand, but his eye contact was fleeting. By the time Kera introduced herself by name, he was already seated at his workstation in front of a large touch-screen keypad surrounded by an array of screens.

Jones laid a hand flat on the touch-screen pad and the main screen flashed to life. Beneath the Hawk and HawkEye logos, his picture and full name appeared next to two entry fields. The initials stood for James David, Kera noted. Could that be any blander? She doubted it was his real name. With a quick, fluid blur of finger activity, he entered two passcodes and then tapped the log-in button. Within seconds, the screens around him flashed to life. Controlling them with a combination of efficient swipes and taps, he called up a series of files. Kera immediately recognized images of Rowena Pete on one of the monitors. There were hundreds, maybe thousands of images of the missing singer. They came and went across the screen quickly, one after the next. It took Kera's eyes a moment to register that these were not just photographs. Most of the images were video files.

"Any luck?" Gabby asked, eyeing the screens over his shoulder.

"Luck's for Vegas. This is actual data," Jones said. "And we have a lot of it." He made a few deft strokes on the touch-screen keypad and two rows of photographs materialized on one of the screens. The images resembled something between head shots and mug shots, but more candid than either. Kera scanned them, not recognizing any of the faces until she picked out Rowena Pete's, which was displayed last. "To answer your question, yes, I found the others."

"How many are there?" Gabby said.

"Leaving out abducted children and runaway teenagers, New York City reported just three missing adults last year. So far this year there have already been eight. Of those cases, six remain open. I think we can remove these two," Jones said, pointing at a pair of faces. "This guy had a gambling problem his family didn't know about before he buried them all in debt. And the woman here had been in and out of mental health facilities for a decade before she vanished." He keyed a few strokes on the keypad and their photos dissolved. "That leaves four that fit our profile."

"What do we know about them?"

Jones clicked through their files quickly. "Craig Shea, a waiter at Otto in the Village. Also a novelist. He'd had two novels published before his thirtieth birthday, which he celebrated by renting a sail-boat in Newport, Rhode Island, and hasn't been heard from since. Next is Cole Emerson, thirty-four. He's an investigative documentary filmmaker. Disappeared from a boat off the coast of the Horn of Africa while shooting a film about Somali pirates. And as of last night, we can add Rowena Pete, who is the most well-known of the missing. The fourth subject, Caroline Mullen, abandoned her bike on a path leading to the George Washington Bridge. The cops concluded she jumped, but no body's washed up. The thing with her is, she was a law associate at an estate-planning firm, not an artist, so she doesn't exactly fit the profile of the others. But on second glance she has more in common with them than not."

"Like what?" Gabby said.

"To start, she was young, just twenty-nine. And single, so she left behind no significant other. But what's most odd about all of these subjects is the lack of an obvious motive—either for suicide or running away. Usually, adults who go missing are dodging debt or a failed relationship. But not these people. Legally and financially, they had their lives in order."

"What about suicide? You never know what goes on in someone's mind," Gabby said. "Plenty of people—especially creative people—appear normal to friends and family one day and then kill themselves the next."

"No, he's right," Kera said, feeling like she should jump in. "Separately these could each easily be explained by suicide. But together? If no bodies have been recovered? Something's off." She couldn't get the odd scene in Rowena Pete's apartment out of her mind.

"Have you run the names through the watch list?" Gabby asked.

"Of course. There's nothing there."

"None?"

"Not a single match," Jones said.

"The terror watch list?" Kera asked, confused. "I thought we were talking about artists. Why would they be on the watch list?"

"We don't know what they are. We have to start with what we know and check everything. What we know is that they were young and passionate."

"That doesn't make them terrorists."

"It makes them idealists, which makes them prone to extremism," Gabby said, not without disdain. "Has Branagh seen this?"

"Not yet."

"All right, I'm headed to a meeting with him now. I'll fill him in. In the meantime, Jones, get a code name assigned for this case. Kera, this will be your priority, starting immediately. Here's your new workstation." Gabby unlocked a drawer under the desk and retrieved several items from it. "This is your secure phone and tablet. Both automatically sort incoming and outgoing calls and data as either classified or unclassified. You won't be able to access anything classified when you're outside of Hawk's walls. Jones has already transferred all of your current data over. Your phone number will remain the same, and you're to keep the phone on you at all times. Is that understood?" Gabby paused as if considering whether she'd covered everything. "I'll need you to give me your old phone and tablet."

Kera hesitated, not realizing at first that Gabby meant now. But after a moment she acquiesced, handing over the old devices and reaching for the new, which to her looked identical.

Next Gabby pulled a thin strip of glass out of a small case and held it out to Kera. It was about the size of a Band-Aid and completely transparent. "Here are your access codes for HawkEye. The memory will wipe clean at 1200 hours. OK? You two need to learn everything there is to know about these people. Their routines, their work, their friends—everything. And, most importantly, what the hell happened to them."

Gabby pivoted to leave, and Jones turned back to his monitors as if Kera wasn't standing there.

"Gabby?" Kera said, hurrying to catch up. "I—I'm a little confused. I'm grateful for the promotion—thank you—but this is a missing persons case. I've been tracking major cyberthreats coming out of China and the Mideast. Aren't I a little overqualified for this?" Gabby stopped her right there with a look of reproach. Kera tried to backpedal. "Don't get me wrong, I'm not questioning you—"

"That sounds like exactly what you're doing."

"I'm sorry, I didn't mean that. I'm just—"

"Do you remember what you said when we were in Rowena Pete's bathroom last night? You said, 'She's trying to send a message.'"

Kera nodded slowly.

"You think you're overqualified? Prove it. Figure out what message she's trying to send."

"What about my other cases?"

"We'll find someone else to cover your caseload. This is your only priority. Is that clear, Agent Mersal?"

"Yes, ma'am," Kera said, but Gabby was already walking away.

· · · · ·

Kera's new workstation was adjacent to J. D. Jones's. Their dueling banks of monitors angled toward each other at ninety degrees so that Kera and Jones also had clear views to the big screen at the front of the room. Kera sat in the swivel chair at the center of her work space and laid a hand flat on the touch-screen keypad the way she'd seen Jones do. The center monitor came to life immediately, displaying her photo, name, rank, and a prompt for the two passcodes. For a moment she savored this. *Agent Mersal.* She liked the sound of that. There was a bitter irony, though, in being promoted in a job that didn't exist. Later, when Parker asked her about her day, she would say it was fine or busy or just all right. She wouldn't be able to tell him that she'd made agent. Celebrating or in any way acknowledging the promotion to someone outside Hawk would amount to a felony offense that would, among other inglorious consequences, jeopardize her security clearance.

She looked at the piece of glass that Gabby had given her and turned it over in her palm. It looked like a microscope slide. She held it up to the monitor, hoping the backlight would reveal the passcodes. Nothing. Her cheeks and forehead flushed. It had been a long time since she'd experienced any form of helpless panic in front of a computer. Maybe it was supposed to plug in like a USB drive, she thought, feeling like an idiot for not thinking of that first. She put the side of her head to the desk, her hair falling onto the keypad as she scanned the side and back of the touch-screen apparatus for a slot that looked like a promising fit.

"What are you doing?"

Kera sat up, startled. Jones was looking at her over the rims of his glasses as though she were an idiot.

"I was . . ." She held up the glass slide. "I've never seen one of these before."

Annoyed, he held out his hand. She got up, walked around the end of the desk that separated their stations, and handed him the glass slide. "It's like this." Using both hands, he pressed each end of the glass between a thumb and forefinger. Then he gave it back to her. She held it the way she'd watched him do. Instantly, two strings of blue digits appeared within the glass. She released a finger and the digits disappeared just as quickly. Simple as that.

"Thanks," she said. Jones ignored her; he was already back to work.

She returned to her seat and studied the passcodes. Because the slide required simultaneous fingerprint readings from both her thumb and forefinger on both hands, she couldn't type while the digits were visible. She had to memorize the codes before she could do anything else.

Once she was in the system, she faced a new obstacle. The interface had been customized for Hawk and was entirely unfamiliar to her. Having made up her mind not to ask Jones for help again, she waded into a trial-and-error tutorial on her own. She got only as far as the list of files that she could access from the server before she realized this wasn't going to work. Every case appeared to have been assigned a code name at random, probably by a secure computer program. This was no doubt meant to add a layer of security to the classified information. It was effective; none of the words in front of her made any sense.

"It's ATLANTIS," Jones said, interpreting her confusion. "The code name for the case. I've already attached our case files to it in the system."

"Thanks," Kera said to him for the second time in ten minutes.

She opened the ATLANTIS files to see what she had to work with. The better acquainted she became with the system, the more she began to appreciate its intuitiveness. It was an elegant interface that seamlessly integrated information across many files at once. And, unlike at Langley, where everyone had separate computers for classified and unclassified information, HawkEye was one interface. Behind the scenes it sorted out the classified information and kept it firewalled from access to any Internet connection. This might have only been a cosmetic improvement, but it made data much more readable to the human trying to understand it.

Kera found it both thrilling and a little intimidating to be working alongside the mind who had created this software. She also felt aware of how much catching up she had to do. Jones had programmed HawkEye to build a digital dossier for each of the four people who had vanished. These files were packed with intimate biographical detail—photographs, employment histories, smartphone records, maps that tracked movement, charts that illustrated social networking activity, and even credit card and bank statements. After an hour spent immersed in the lives of the missing, Kera sat back.

"How long have you been working this case?" she asked Jones through the gaps between their respective banks of monitors.

"Since this morning," he said without looking up.

"You collected all this today?"

"Not me. HawkEye," he replied.

Risking embarrassment, she had to ask, "Where does all this data *come* from?"

Jones exhaled in a way that suggested she was a growing nuisance. She took this as confirmation that human interaction was something that required special effort for him. Whether that made him a computer genius or just an asshole was yet to be determined.

"Come here. Pay attention. I'm only going to explain it once." His attitude was undercut by the thick band of pride she detected in his voice. Clearly, he took her awe for HawkEye's capabilities as a personal compliment. "HawkEye relies on a very simple premise: that data exists. The problem HawkEye solves is how to unite data from many sources and apply it in an efficient way. People create floods of data, right? Every time you use a credit card or phone or swipe your ID badge at work. Whenever you log into a social network, save a file, send an e-mail, or stream a film on your computer. Even just walking down the street or into a building—it's nearly impossible to dodge all the surveillance cameras operated by both law enforcement agencies and private businesses."

Kera nodded.

"As our daily interactions and transactions become more digitized, our behavior becomes increasingly datatized. It's nearly constant, this generating of data we do. And viewed as a whole, it's like a trail of digital crumbs we leave behind us wherever we go. The problem, before HawkEye, was that we couldn't always see all these crumbs at once. There were too many gaps in the trail. Your phone company might know you made a call in Central Park, but it wouldn't know you went to SoHo and bought shoes an hour later. Only your bank and the shoe retailer would know that. And neither of them would know what you did between the park and the shoe boutique, even though surveillance cameras along the way captured your every movement. HawkEye pulls in data from all of these collection points and links them to the individual. The result is this."

He pulled up a map of Manhattan and started a time-lapse sequence. "This is all the activity that HawkEye was able to collect on Rowena Pete the day she vanished." A yellow dot appeared at the singer's address. On the side of the screen, a clock displayed the time of day. The dot had appeared around 0720 hours. After a few seconds, it started to move, leaving a faint line behind it. The dot crossed to SoHo, then retreated back to the town house. In the afternoon it snaked over to Washington Square Park. Kera noticed that the trail was not constant; there were a few gaps. In the park, for example, and around the middle of some blocks. The dot returned to Rowena Pete's building shortly after 1600 hours, and then it disappeared. Kera eyed the time-lapse clock. Another hour swept by. The dot blinked on and off several times between 1700 hours and 1830 hours. At 1844 hours it vanished for good.

"Those gaps, what happened there?" Kera asked.

"HawkEye can only track activity that is digitized. If there is no positive facial recognition ID from surveillance footage, no phone or computer use, no credit card transactions—we can't account for it."

"What about after the dot went dark at 1844 hours? The police didn't arrive until just after 2100 hours. How did she leave without the neighborhood surveillance cams picking her up?"

"That might require some old-fashioned police work," Jones said. "She could have left from an underground garage in a vehicle that wasn't hers. Or she might have been in disguise. If her face was obscured, the facial-recog software is pretty much useless."

Kera nodded. "It's only a two-hour window. I can check the tapes manually. I'm assuming we have access to individual cameras?"

On-screen, Jones dragged a box around the city blocks immediately surrounding Rowena Pete's apartment. Then he tapped a button on the side toolbar and a few dozen camera icons appeared on the map. "These are our eyes in the area. Just tap one of the icons to view footage. Like this." A box popped up with a black-and-white feed showing the entrance to a building. On the sidewalk, in view of the camera, a young woman had paused to finish a phone conversation.

"This is live now?"

Jones nodded. "If you want to play back archived footage, just select the time frame on the side here."

Kera studied the black-and-white surveillance feed. The woman on the sidewalk stood there, sometimes gesturing, sometimes smiling, but all the time oblivious to the fact that Kera was standing in a dimly lit room across the city watching her.

"You go to law school, Jones?" she said softly.

He turned his head toward her and eyed her then as if really looking at her for the first time. "No," he said, closing out of the live surveillance feed with the tap of a finger. "I dropped out of college as an undergrad."

• • • • •

She worked through lunch and deep into the afternoon. There were clocks all over the room, but without daylight, the passage of time was surreal. Hours passed without her acknowledging them. Meanwhile, HawkEye's power grew more exhilarating to her. Every day Great Lake–sized floods of information were being dumped into the oceans of data that hurtled through the world's communications networks. And HawkEye was there to collect it all, like a rain catcher the size of the rain forest.

And yet, four human beings had slipped through the cracks.

"What if they *are* dead?" she said aloud at one point, leaning back in her chair to stretch her arms overhead. She'd worked some bizarre cases, but usually the simplest explanation for any human event was the most likely.

"They're not dead." Jones sounded annoyed. "Don't confuse a reliance on electronic technology with life itself. Just because they ditched their cell phones and hunkered down somewhere where there aren't surveillance cameras doesn't mean they no longer exist."

The verdict was in; genius or not, Jones was an asshole. *Gabby's testing you*, Kera thought. *Just get through this case quickly, and she'll put you on a real assignment.*

At dinnertime she blinked away the screen glare. She'd been studying the life and times of Craig Shea, the waiter/novelist who had been the third of the subjects to disappear. Kera walked over to tell Jones she was stepping out to get food and to see if he wanted any. She hesitated when she came up behind him and peered over his shoulder at the large center monitor. The image on his screen was abstract and colorful, like artwork. After a few seconds he zoomed out. From this new perspective, she could see that he was looking at a mural painted on a billboard. He zoomed in and out on different sections of the painting and then suddenly tapped his keypad and a new piece of art lit up on an adjacent monitor. At least "art" was the word that came to her, though it hardly seemed adequate. The second image was of a sculpture made from street objects—a mailbox, a fire hydrant, and a bicycle—twisted and mashed together to create the visual effect of violent motion. It appeared from the photo that the sculpture had been erected in the middle of an intersection. Jones zoomed in. Kera leaned forward, squinting. Every square inch of the sculpture had been painted in the same pattern as the billboard mural.

"What's that?" she said.

"Fuck," Jones said, startled. "Goddamn it. How long have you been standing there?" He swiped his finger, and the images vanished. She watched him, eyebrows raised. "It's nothing." With his back to her, he pulled up a HawkEye database and scrolled through the latest query results.

"I'm going downstairs for some food. Want anything?"

"Just some peace."

She made a move to go, but then stopped. "Did I do something?" she said, a little more confrontationally than she'd intended. She hadn't eaten all day, and it had put her on edge. Jones didn't look up; he just kept staring at his screens. "I know we just met, and it's too soon to expect you to trust me. But a little civility might be a better way to get this partnership off the ground." She thought his shoulders had recoiled slightly at the mention of a partnership.

He looked at her finally, but as soon as they made eye contact, he turned back to his screens. "I like to work alone."

FIVE

It was nearly ten when she left the office and got on a southbound F train. At her stop she climbed from the subway platform to the street, feeling with every step the stuffy warmth of the underground give way to a mild spring evening. Under the scaffolding at the top of the stairs, she pulled her phone out of her bag and aimed it overhead at the words she'd discovered the previous day. *Have you figured it out yet?* When the phrase steadied on-screen, she snapped the picture.

On her walk home, she detoured several blocks out of her way so that she could pass by Rowena Pete's town house. The street had been reopened, but there was still a police cruiser parked at the curb and yellow tape slung between the railings of the front steps. Ever since she'd left the night before, she'd half expected to get word that Rowena Pete had returned home and admitted that the whole incident was just a bad prank. But no such word had come.

"You made a risotto," Kera said, inspecting the pot on the stove after Parker greeted her at the front door with a kiss. He'd cooked the meal, cleaned up the kitchen, and gotten through half of a bottle of red wine waiting for her. Confronted with this visual evidence of her absenteeism, she felt the familiar touch of guilt, silent like a draft caressing the back of her neck. But there was no point in an apology. Work was work. Parker knew nights like this came with the territory. "You didn't have to do all this. I told you I'd be late."

"I wanted to do it. How was your day?"

Kera exhaled, tipping her head forward and massaging the back of her neck with one hand. "It was a blur. Gabby put me on this new thing, and I've got a lot to do to get up to speed." She changed out of her work clothes and washed her face while Parker filled their bowls and glasses.

"The new Natalie Smith movie is coming out in a few weeks," he called to her from the kitchen.

"Who's Natalie Smith?"

"You know. She's made a few other documentaries. *Faux Ed*, the one about higher education. That was her most famous one. Remember?" Kera didn't recognize any of the words he was giving her as clues. "The new one is based on her travels around the country in search of the average American."

Kera now thought she remembered seeing advertisements for the film, though she didn't know what to make of them. It was an odd subject for a documentary. "Did she find him?" she said, coming out of the bedroom.

"Who?"

"The average American."

"Who says it's a man?"

"Most men seem pretty average to me. I was playing the odds."

He laughed and pulled her to him, kissing her neck. "Gambling. God, I love your feisty side. Will you go with me?"

"What?"

"To see the movie."

"Oh. Sure."

"I know it doesn't look like much. But it's a Natalie Smith film. I promise it will be interesting."

"I'll go. I'll go."

He paused. "Babe, we're supposed to be planning a wedding, and we hardly even see each other."

"I know." She wanted to add that they'd merely hit a busy stretch this last week or two, with her work and his travel to Dubai, but she wasn't sure that long workdays like this weren't going to be the norm for a while.

"I thought it would be fun. Like a real date, with dinner and everything." Sweet Parker. It was because of him that their relationship survived. They wandered off into their separate worlds for most of every day, and then he brought them back together.

"Yes. Of course," she said.

"You don't have to."

"I'd love to."

After dinner she tried to watch TV with her legs in Parker's lap and his laptop resting on her shins. But she couldn't quiet her mind. She remembered that she needed to follow up with Detective Hopper. She hadn't heard from him since his e-mail that morning. There must be some evidence, some lead the police were pursuing. A woman can't just vanish from the middle of a city.

"Did you see this?" Parker asked, tilting his laptop in her direction.

"Please," she said. "I'll bleed from my eyes if I look at another computer screen."

"It's not Gnos.is, I promise. It's the *Times*." She waved it away because she could guess what it was about. "Here, I'll just read it to you. 'AFTER SUICIDE RUMORS, NYPD SAYS ROWENA PETE IS MISSING.'"

Kera let him read the article aloud. For now, the angle of the story that gripped the media's imagination focused on the staged scene in Rowena Pete's town house, rather than on the fact that there was no body. No stomach digesting the pills, no wrist draining blood into the bathwater, no neck swinging from a rope in the closet. Kera's mind wandered as Parker read on. Of the four missing people, only one name besides Rowena Pete's had been familiar to her. It was that of Cole Emerson, the investigative documentary filmmaker who had gained moderate notoriety with a film about income inequality a few years back. As she'd learned today, he'd been shooting a new film about Somali pirates when he disappeared from a boat off the coast of the Horn of Africa and was presumed drowned. That word— *presumed.* She'd never thought much about it, but now it suddenly seemed ridiculous. Could a life simply be presumed one thing or another? It seemed like something that ought to be more knowable than that.

ATLANTIS was getting to her. And, Kera realized, she welcomed the feeling of being consumed by it. The important cases for her had always started this way: with a confusing blackness and an intense curiosity that drew her in.

"I don't understand the confusion," Parker said, coming to the end of the article. "Did she kill herself or not? How can that be so hard to figure out?"

"I don't know," she said, and she wasn't lying. "What does Gnos.is say?" This she had meant as a joke. But Parker was already reading the latest Gnos.is coverage.

"They say Rowena Pete went underground."

SIX

Kera looked up at the four note cards on the wall of her office. One for each of the missing. The cards were a minor rebuke to Hawk's paper-free policy, but Kera had decided they were necessary. HawkEye, helpful as it was, generated flat-out too much information. The digital ATLANTIS files expanded faster than she could digest them, and her mental picture of the case was losing focus. Thus, after a morning spent blinking at her monitors in the Control Room, delving deeper into the dossiers that HawkEye had stitched together, she felt a need to be in a space where she could do some clear thinking. Computers might not need sunlight, but brains do. She told Jones to text her if he found anything and went back to her office for the first time since she'd been put on the ATLANTIS case.

There she sat at her desk and copied down on the note cards only the most basic information from each dossier: the subject's name, age, occupation, and a brief note describing how that person had disappeared. Then she'd taped the cards to the glass wall opposite her desk, arranging them in chronological order by date of disappearance.

She half leaned, half sat on the edge of the desk, staring up at the cards. Although few scenes were as dramatic as the one in Rowena Pete's town house, the cards did tell her something immediately: it was impossible to confirm that any of the four missing people were dead. This left three possible scenarios. One, the least likely, was that all four had died, and none of their bodies had been recovered. Two, some of them were dead, and some of them were alive. Or three, that all of them were alive.

Coincidences are illusions, Lionel had taught her. Four inconclusive suicides and no bodies—that was a hell of a coincidence. Too much of one. But just believing that brought her no closer to pinning down where these people had gone or why.

It's in here somewhere, she told herself. *You just have to see it.*

On her tablet she pulled up the picture she'd taken under the scaffolding on Houston Street. Next to that she displayed a photo of the mirror in Rowena Pete's bathroom, snapped by one of the crime scene investigators. She studied the phrase that appeared in both photos. *Have you figured it out yet?* She'd heard the phrase before and had noticed, with some bafflement, the way it had started to make its way into the lexicon. Lately she'd heard people utter it more and more frequently. She thought it meant *Get with the program!* or *Don't you know?* But it was more than that. There was something about it that she couldn't put her finger on.

Out her window the ONE billboard overlooking Times Square counted further into the billions. *There are 7,369,362,375 people in the world. Soon they will all be connected.*

A thought surfaced that brought her bolt upright in her seat. She paused for a moment to process the legitimacy of the idea, and then she reached for her tablet and pulled up Rowena Pete's dossier. Using HawkEye, she created a map from the singer's file the way she'd seen Jones do. The lower half of Manhattan appeared, followed by the yellow dot and then the line tracing the singer's movements around the city. Next to the time-lapse clock at the top of the screen, the date was listed as May 2, the day Rowena Pete had disappeared. Kera tapped the date display with a finger. This intuitive act was rewarded with the appearance of a pop-up box that displayed a calendar. She exhaled, unaware that she'd been holding her breath.

She changed the date on the map to May 1. Immediately, the map refreshed and the clock reset. Then it began counting through the hours of May 1. At 0702 hours, a dot appeared at Rowena Pete's town house. Kera watched the dot traverse the city and eventually return to the town house after a late dinner. The presentation of the full twenty-four-hour day played out over just sixty seconds. After it finished, she tapped the date display again to access the calendar. This time she scrolled back through six, seven, eight months—the calendar didn't seem to have a limit. Finally, she chose at random the third day of September nearly two years prior.

Again, the map reset itself and began the twenty-four-hour time lapse. The difference this time was that on that particular September 3, Rowena Pete had been on the West Coast leg of a performance tour. Rather than lower Manhattan, the map that appeared was of Portland, Oregon. The yellow dot illuminated over a hotel at 0817 hours, when the singer had turned on her phone to check her e-mail. Throughout the morning and into the afternoon, the dot made appearances at various points along Interstate Highway 5 between Portland and Seattle. There were many gaps in the line along the highway, some of them stretching for dozens of miles. But that made sense. Surveillance cameras in and between Portland and Seattle two years ago would not have been as pervasive as they were now in Manhattan, where digital eyes were virtually everywhere. It was also likely that the Rowena Pete of two years ago left behind fewer digital crumbs than the contemporary version.

Kera had an idea. She set off for the Control Room, resisting an urge to break into a jog.

"I have a question," she said to Jones, who was looking at artwork again on one of his monitors. She ignored that and didn't wait for him to acknowledge her presence. "These HawkEye maps can be created for any day or range of days I want, right?"

"Of course," Jones said.

"What about maps for more than one person at a time?"

"HawkEye can be programmed to do anything you want it to do. What are you getting at?"

"I want to know if any of our four subjects were ever in the same place at the same time. Can we write a program that would lay maps over each other to see if their paths ever crossed?"

"We?"

"You," she said. "Can you do it or not?"

Jones seemed to be thinking hard about it for several seconds. Not a good sign. Kera had yet to come across anything, computing-wise, that he wasn't able to do in a matter of seconds. Finally he said, "Sure, that'd be easy." She didn't expect him to admit that her idea was a good one, but she could tell he thought it was because of the way he spun away from her quickly to get started on the project.

"I'll have to write some code. And then it'll take some time for the system to process all the data across four profiles simultaneously. It might take me a few hours."

She laughed and told him that a few hours would be fine.

• • • • •

It took him one hour and forty minutes. And then, "Bingo."

She was at her own workstation when his voice broke through the Control Room din. She rushed over to see what he was looking at. His main screen displayed a map of Manhattan and Brooklyn crisscrossed by dozens of blue lines. A group of blinking yellow dots was concentrated on a city block near the West Side Highway.

"Look at this. All four of our friends were in this neighborhood after eleven PM on the night of June 12 of last year."

"Doing what?"

"I'm not sure." Jones rolled his cursor over one of the yellow dots, and a window popped up with Rowena Pete's head shot and the exact time that the computer had identified her. "This surveillance camera captured her near Hudson and Fourteenth Street at 11:38 PM and then again a few blocks north at 2:15 AM." They watched the two video clips. Rowena Pete was alone and on foot, dressed in a dark skirt and slender, dark jacket. She walked purposefully, but was unrushed. "That means she was somewhere in this neighborhood for nearly three hours. Same with the others." He rolled over each of the other dots. As he did, windows popped up to identify them. Besides the city's surveillance cameras, which had captured at least one shot of all of them, two of the subjects had also used their phones while in the neighborhood, though not to call each other.

"It's pretty industrial over there, isn't it?" Kera asked.

Jones nodded. "There are a few nightclubs nearby, but if they were meeting for drinks, we'd know it. Nightclubs have security cameras. And drinks cost money. There's a good chance someone would have used a credit card." He rolled over each of the dots again, studying the time stamps and shaking his head. "It could just be a coincidence. Stranger things have happened in this city."

"No," Kera said. "If we caught all four of them passing through Grand Central Station within a few hours of each other, that would be a coincidence. But not in that part of town, not at that hour."

"I also found this." Jones pulled up a new map, this one covering a small knot of red dots that hovered over a building across the street from Lincoln Center.

"Tell me that's a direct hit."

"Yes and no," he said. He sounded excited, which was a new emotion for him, at least in Kera's presence. "The building right here near the intersection of Broadway and Columbus is the Empire Hotel. We have confirmation that all four of our subjects were inside the hotel at least once in the months before they vanished. Probably at the rooftop bar, judging from nearly a dozen credit card transactions.

The catch is the timing. I can't put any of them there at the exact same time. Sometimes they show up within an hour or so of each other, but never overlapping."

"Huh," Kera said, thinking about this. "Forget the timing for a minute. You're saying that this is the *one* place in the city where all of them visited at some point in the months before they vanished?"

"Yes."

"There's no other place where all four of them happened to pass through on the same day?"

"Not even a subway platform or a Starbucks," he said. "Not even Grand Central, for that matter."

Kera looked at the map while she thought about this. On the screen the red dots continued to blink.

"OK. I've got my phone with me. Call if you come up with anything else."

"Where are you going?"

"If they all went to that bar, they were there to see someone or something. I'm going to have a look. It's just about happy hour."

She was headed uptown—provided the cab ever made it out of traffic in Times Square—when she pulled out her phone and placed a call to Parker.

SEVEN

Parker Cahill walked with his head down. He didn't feel like acknowledging the city tonight. The city was bleak and immovable. It felt too often like a heavy jacket he couldn't shrug off. He'd get a panicked, overheated claustrophobia that made him want to dive into the cold silence of a lake, lakes being something he associated with carefree childhood summers. Tonight he was an adult. There was no reason he shouldn't be content. He'd contributed ideas that were going to be implemented half a world away, and a feeling of achievement put the pesky city at bay.

They'd won the Dubai job. He'd received word of it this morning, and the day had rushed by in a blur of company optimism and personal rededication to the mission. His high waned slightly with Kera's voice mail: something had come up at work and she was calling to say that she couldn't meet him for dinner. So he joined his colleagues on the Dubai account for happy hour on the company's dime. When happy hour ended and his colleagues retreated to their families in the suburbs, he found himself still in the mood to celebrate.

He set out walking. He had no particular destination in mind. He was simply in search of a setting in which he could enjoy this feeling, this sense of freedom to possess a future he desired. This was really big, he told himself, the idea still sinking in. He glimpsed the years stretching out ahead of him. No longer would his days be filled with nine hours at a tedious desk job sandwiched between two ghastly commutes. He was now a businessman, a business *traveler*, with responsibilities and ideas. Ideas that mattered, ideas that were shaping the world, if only in a small way. Though he'd never possessed such an ambition, he felt tonight as if he'd conquered the city. This city that so many tried to conquer. He thrilled in that irony, that in his own small way, he'd beaten what he hated most about this city: that it was a place where no one rose above it all. Here was Manhattan, that sliver of an island that corralled the toughest and brightest like cattle being led to slaughter. He thought of the city as a murky, polluted ocean that drew in big fish from thousands of small ponds and mutated them into a school of ferocious minnows. Because when you came here, you became obscure and anonymous, you ground out sixty-, seventy-, eighty-hour workweeks just to turn the corner at par, just to have your office light on when the boss left for the day, just to outpace the cost of living. Plop down any Midtown skyscraper into any other city in the country, and it'd become the architectural landmark of the region. But build it side by side with four-dozen competing towers, and none of them stand out. They block each other's sun and step on each other's shadows.

It was the same way with people, and this made him worry about Kera. Already she was succumbing to the undertow of long hours and clawing ambition. She was not one of them, he knew. But she was a survivor. She would do whatever it took to succeed, and he worried that she might not notice if the summitless climb approached a point when it was no longer worth it.

He walked on, hands thrust in his pockets, head bowed toward the sidewalk. Much of the day had consisted of reviewing contractual documents related to the Dubai project. They were all dated May 3, today's date, and suddenly the number hit him. May 4, tomorrow, was the day they had planned to be married. Parker didn't know why he thought of that now—he hadn't thought about it in months, not since they'd decided to push back the wedding to August—but there it was, the date feeling somehow momentous again. Out of nowhere he faced in his mind's eye a clear picture of how this weekend might have played out. And then what inevitably followed was the stark contrast between the two Parker-Kera timelines—the original, abandoned timeline versus the real, revised timeline—and he was overcome with anxiety.

That would only spoil his mood, he thought, performing a mental ducking maneuver in his head. Why was it so hard to let go of everything else and celebrate for a night? He thought of calling Kera, but she had sounded distracted and busy with work, though God knew what was keeping her this late on a Friday. Wasn't Friday the slowest day in the news cycle? He knew too little about how she actually spent her workdays to even speculate. He called his parents' home instead. He had an unspoken obligation to his parents to go through the motions of a weekly phone call. Just the one call. No more or less seemed to be necessary.

His father answered in a low voice. Parker had to plug his non-phone ear with a finger and raise his own voice to communicate over the taxis flowing past on Broadway. He told his father about the Dubai account, explaining how he would travel one week out of every four and that the project would really get going in the fall, and ahead of that, he'd probably spend three straight weeks over there during August. He realized that mentioning this had been a mistake only after it was too late.

"I thought you were getting married in August," his father said.

"We are. We are." His parents expected the wedding to be a huge production, but Kera had made him promise that it wouldn't be. They had even put off plans for a honeymoon until winter, when work for both of them would slow down. "Can we not talk about that tonight?" He would be the bigger man, he decided, and rushed to wrap up the wasted conversation amicably.

He walked sidewalks blackened by shuttered storefronts, sidewalks yellowed by dim streetlights, and sidewalks whitened by glaring billboards. He realized he'd reached Houston Street, and the sidewalk took him around the corner to a bar called L@Ho. Immediately he liked the low ceiling, the long bar, the inviting stools. It wasn't too crowded; he hated crowded bars. Televisions lit the room with colorful flashes from a basketball game in Cleveland, baseball games in the Bronx and Milwaukee, and a soccer match from a crowded Barcelona stadium.

He settled onto a stool. The bartender looked up, lifting his pen from the napkin he was drawing on. Parker ordered and told him to keep the tab open. "Great place," he said, tasting the first crisp swallow of his gin and tonic. The bartender nodded, and Parker interpreted it as an invitation to talk. "I live a few blocks away. Don't know why it took me so long to come in." He didn't feel lonely; he was just talkative. It seemed right that a guy could wander in off the street and find a place to sit and think and talk things over with a stranger. "I was supposed to meet my fiancée for dinner, but she has to work."

Parker had begun to wonder whether they should have been married immediately, the very weekend he'd proposed, as had been Kera's instinct. She'd suggested that they drive to a beautiful place upstate, get married, make love in a bed and breakfast, and take the scenic way back in time for work Monday morning. "What are we waiting for?" she asked, as if it wasn't obvious. They were lying on the couch in their new apartment in the city, their noses inches apart, and all he could see was her marbled black and amber eyes. Oh, God, if getting married was as simple as that.

The soccer game on the corner TV reminded him of the Dubai project. Every player on the field was outfitted by the shoe company his firm was partnering with to create a global social campaign designed to determine communities most in need of shoes. During each day of the upcoming Dubai tournament, a cargo plane would take off from somewhere in the world, and fan posts on Twitter, Instagram, and Facebook would be collated in real time to steer the branded aircraft to what was deemed the worthiest drop point. It had been his idea. Gimmicky, yes, but it'd both put shoes on feet in desperate need of them and remind oblivious sports consumers the world over that something other than the World Cup standings required their attention. The firm had let him pitch it, and the client had loved it immediately. He should feel more celebratory, he thought, though having no one to celebrate with made the work victory seem illicit. He could feel it in his lawyer-father's cool indifference, and in his reporter-fiancée's distracted voice mail. *Good for you, Parker Cahill. You get to travel the world, but the rest of us have shit to take care of right here. Mind leaving us the fuck alone?*

He chatted with the bartender about the city's best neighborhood bars and sports and the shit economy and why things were the way they were even though they didn't have to be, not really. Parker found himself doing too much of the talking. When he wasn't pulling a draft or mixing a drink, the bartender listened contentedly while he doodled on his napkin. At eleven he assured Parker that he wasn't kicking him out, he just had to close the tab because his shift was over. "Really, stick around. You want another on me?"

A fresh glass atop a napkin, another crisp bite of booze and carbonation at the back of his throat. Left alone with his drink, Parker faced sudden gloom. He felt exhausted, too tired to shoot the breeze with the new guy across the bar. He hadn't eaten. His stomach had soured to its contents—an empty slime of unabsorbed gin and syrupy sugar. He would pick up two slices of pizza on the way home, he thought, feeling sad that the evening was coming to an end like this. He gulped at his drink, in a hurry now to get out of this place, but at the same time happy to have discovered it.

His glass left a ring of condensation on the napkin and he noticed something dark bleeding through. He peeled the napkin off the counter and held it up. The other side was covered in blue ink: stick figures, geometric designs, a crowded assortment of meaningless squiggles and symbols. He remembered the bartender scratching away at a napkin while he talked. The ink had run together as it bled through the wet fibers, and Parker had to turn the napkin 180 degrees to make out the short phrase that snaked along a white space between the figures. It was something he'd heard people say lately. It was just a saying, he thought, though something about it made him uncomfortable. Tonight it made him think, not pleasantly, of the wedding and Kera and Dubai and his father: *Have you figured it out yet?*

EIGHT

The bar at the Empire Hotel was on the roof with a view up and down the seam of Broadway. To the west, the sun set over the Metropolitan Opera House and, farther in the distance, the New Jersey horizon. At five thirty, the bar was only beginning to show signs of a busy Friday night: suits wound down with scotches and loosened ties, underdressed tourists rested their legs and crooked necks, and couples began dates that would eventually move across the street to the opera or ballet.

Kera circled once through the bar's seating areas, first indoor and then outdoor, looking more like a businesswoman searching for a friend than someone reconnoitering the place. Figuring that any bartender established enough to work the lucrative Friday-night shift was as likely as anyone to know the regulars, Kera returned to the main bar inside.

The bartender was a woman in her late twenties dressed in a collared maroon shirt under a black vest. She was shaking a martini as the lights of the Upper West Side twinkled through liquor bottles displayed on ledges behind her. She approached Kera within seconds, smiling professionally as she peeled a cocktail napkin from a stack and laid it on the bar. Service happened fast around here.

"Want to see a cocktail menu?" the bartender asked.

Kera said she would. When the woman stepped away to retrieve it, Kera opened a copy of the *Post*, which she'd bought in the hotel's lobby.

After leaving her voice mail for Parker in the cab, she realized she'd rushed out too quickly and had to call Jones to ask him to look up a few things. Running data-intensive HawkEye queries on her tablet generated reports that were classified and were therefore not accessible on the device outside Hawk's secure offices. She wanted to know if there were any patterns in the time of day or day of the week that the four subjects had visited the Empire Hotel. The answer was yes: mostly early evening, almost always on weekdays, usually Friday. She also wanted to know specifically when Rowena Pete had been at the hotel. As a minor celebrity, she would be the most conspicuous in the minds of any of the staff that worked at the hotel bar. Jones told her that the singer had made two appearances in recent months. Kera copied all this down in cryptic shorthand and thanked him.

"Great view," Kera said, glancing out the window when the bartender returned. She'd left the tabloid in front of her open to a prominent headline over three photographs: LAST KNOWN PICTURES OF ROWENA PETE. The bartender nodded politely, neither closed off from nor inviting conversation. "How long have you worked here?"

"A year, I guess."

"I mean this as a compliment. You look like the kind of person who isn't just a bartender. What else do you do?"

This question earned Kera a cautious glance, followed by a slight smile. "I'm an actor . . . sometimes. Tonight I'm a bartender. What can I get you?"

"I'll have a chardonnay."

The bartender headed for a rack of wineglasses. There were two cameras on the ceiling behind the bar, one in the corner overlooking the seating area, and there had been one in the elevator on her way up. They were all part of the hotel's private, closed-circuit surveillance system, off-limits to HawkEye without a warrant.

The bartender returned with a glass of wine, and Kera looked up from the article to thank her. She caught the bartender glancing at the photographs. This was her opening.

"Bizarre, isn't it?" Kera said. "I always wanted to see her in concert."

"I saw her a couple of times. It was a really great show. And—" She hesitated, as if deliberating whether it was appropriate to divulge what she had been about to say. Kera kept her eyes on the photographs, feigning nonchalance. "She's been in here before. Just a few weeks ago, actually."

"Oh, yeah? That's cool." Kera had learned from Jones that Rowena Pete used her credit card at this bar on a Tuesday evening exactly twenty-four days earlier. "Was she nice in person?"

"Yeah, totally." She grinned. "Well, I didn't really talk to her, but she wasn't rude or anything."

Kera leaned in, affecting mock shame for wanting to gossip. "Who was she here with?"

The bartender flicked her eyes to meet Kera's briefly, and then she looked away. "No one important," she said. Perhaps the bartender was just afraid of getting in trouble with management for discussing clientele, but Kera's instinct told her that the question had struck a deeper nerve.

The bartender made a show of glancing down the bar, where stools were starting to fill and a few pairs of eyes were trained her way, pleading for drinks. "I gotta get to these people. Let me know if you need anything else."

Kera finished the last of her wine and paid in cash. Ten bucks for a glass of chard. A waste of money, but maybe not a waste of time.

The bartender's name was on the receipt. Erica. This Erica knew more about whomever Rowena Pete had met with at the bar, and there was something overriding her human instinct to gossip about it.

Kera rode the elevator down to street level and stopped on the sidewalk in front of the hotel. She glanced around until she made the two surveillance cameras—both operated by the NYPD—that had captured the subjects entering and leaving. One was across Columbus Avenue above the Lincoln Center taxi stand. The other was attached to the hotel itself, mounted on the corner of the building nearest Broadway. She called Jones on her way to the subway and told him about her conversation with the bartender. "Whatever this girl knows, she's holding it close to her chest."

"You coming back to the office?"

"Nope. Don't wait up for me."

Jones was silent on the line for a moment. "You're going to scout the other location, aren't you?"

She smiled. There was no point in lying. "I want to get a look at what the surveillance cameras couldn't see."

"Wait until tomorrow when there's daylight."

"Are you worried about me, J. D. Jones?"

He hesitated. "You're not authorized to work in the field. Gabby was clear about that, Kera."

"Your concern is noted."

"The subjects were out there months ago. Even if we knew what to look for—and we don't—it's probably gone."

"I'm just doing my homework. I won't sleep if I don't check it out." She'd reached the stairs to the 1 train. "Speaking of sleep, do you ever go home, Jones?"

"Home is boring compared to what I get to do all day in this room."

She noticed a security camera across Broadway, mounted on a little arm jutting out from the corner of the Time Warner Center. The lens was directed at the plaza where she was standing.

"Jones?"

"Yeah?"

She paused. "Never mind. We'll talk tomorrow."

"Be safe," he said, but she was already descending the stairs toward the screech of a breaking train.

Boredom turned out to be a bigger obstacle than safety. The industrial blocks by the West Side Highway were deserted. She spotted a few homeless people, a few intoxicated revelers who had stumbled west from the Meatpacking District, and a night jogger coming off the bike path that ran along the Hudson. She took a few pictures of the empty streets and then walked east until she could flag down a cab to take her home.

NINE

The following Tuesday, the rooms of their apartment were filling with first light as Kera tiptoed from bed to bathroom to kitchen, a dance just delicate enough to keep Parker from waking. She skipped her morning run, swearing it would be the only time this week. It was counterintuitive that she ran more when she was engrossed in a case, but it had proven to be so. Her body seemed to crave the morning exertion. Today, though, she was on a mission to beat Jones to the office, just once, and the run was sacrificed.

When she pushed through the Control Room doors a few minutes before seven, there he was at his workstation, every screen around him lit as if he were a stockbroker hours into the trading day. He was exactly as she'd left him the night before, except he was wearing a different T-shirt.

"Have a look at this," Jones said by way of a greeting.

"What time do you get here every day? I've never seen your workstation empty."

"Missing people don't find themselves," he said, not looking up.

"Is that what gets you out of bed?" She'd meant it as harmless ribbing, but Jones fell into a tense silence. She realized she didn't know anything about him other than what she'd gleaned from their interactions in this room.

The moment expired when, without looking up at her, he said, "I think I found something." Except for a HawkEye map of the city on his center monitor, all his screens were filled with images of murals and sculptures. "I've been looking for additional cases of missing people who fit the profile of our ATLANTIS subjects. I haven't found any of those yet, but every time I run a new query, I stumble across these."

He leaned back to let her get a look at all the monitors. She recognized the colorful billboard mural and the odd sculpture bolted to the pavement at the center of a city intersection. She'd seen him looking at those before. But now, in addition to those, there were other murals, sculptures, and even video projections. She counted nine of them total.

"What are they?"

"They're the work of an anonymous street artist called It."

"It?"

"That's right. Ever heard of him? Or her?"

Kera shook her head. "Him or her?"

"No one seems to know. There's quite a bit of chatter about it online." He moved one of the images aside and pulled up a list of articles and blog posts about the artist.

"What's the connection to the ATLANTIS case?"

"I didn't see it at first either. That's why I kept dismissing these every time they popped up. But then I saw this." He tapped on a link to a *Village Voice* article titled WHO IS IT? "I'll spare you the artsy bullshit. What caught my attention is that nobody knows who the artist is. I don't mean that the artist keeps him- or herself anonymous, you know, as some sort of gimmick. I mean that there is no earthly evidence that this person exists, other than these works of street art that seem to just appear. At least, that's what this article claims. Obviously, that didn't sit well with me. I don't believe in ghosts, and that's because I believe in cameras. I take it kind of personal when HawkEye can't ID someone."

"You used HawkEye to look for the artist?"

"Yes. And it turned up nothing. There's no trace of this person," he said, as though hating each of the words as they came out of his mouth.

"Except for the art itself," Kera said, admiring it. "You think this artist might be connected to the others?"

"That's what I was thinking. But the timeline doesn't fit. The first person we know of to go missing disappeared eleven months ago. The first piece of art like this appeared a year and a half ago." He pointed to the billboard mural.

"Are you sure it's the same person creating all of these?"

"I'm not sure of anything. But look at them and you tell me."

He was right. The nine works of art were nothing alike in medium or size, but they did possess an unmistakable singularity, a bold and fearless quality that went beyond what most graffiti artists did to texture the city. This case had challenged Kera's instincts almost constantly, but on this account they felt solid: the nine installations had been created by a single mind.

"It," she said, shaking her head.

• • • • •

Kera left Jones in the Control Room and went back to her office, where she stood for a few minutes studying the note cards on the wall. They'd been hanging there for a few days, and now when she looked at them, she realized that they had become too familiar. She'd originally arranged them chronologically by date of disappearance, and that perspective had gone stale. She needed to look at them in a different way. She took down all the cards and thought about ways to reorder them. She started with age—Rowena Pete, at twenty-eight, was the youngest; Cole Emerson was the oldest at thirty-four. But what did that tell her? Next she thought about the ways they had disappeared. All could have been described as staged suicides, though Emerson, the filmmaker, and Shea, the novelist, could have been categorized as boating accidents. But she didn't think there was anything accidental about any of their disappearances.

The last criteria she'd written onto the cards referred to the subjects' occupations or otherwise notable hobbies. This was the one area where there was a clear separation: three artists and a lawyer.

TEN

The law offices of Milton & Booth sat in a cozy five-room suite on the seventh floor of an aging building on lower Broadway. Most of the walls were obscured by file cabinets, bookshelves, and other relics of the declining printed-word era. Any free wall space was jammed with framed plaques and law school diplomas.

When Kera was led by a secretary into the corner office, Raymond Booth was behind his cherrywood desk, frowning at the file his paralegal had created for their appointment. Booth was a presence, a human backstop of broad shoulders topped off with a head that seemed a scale or two larger than the rest. The temples of his eyeglasses disappeared into bushy gray hair on their reach for his ears.

"I understand you made an appointment with me, Ms. Mersal, but I don't see any of your paperwork. No matter, we can address that later." He was kind, almost jovial. "What can I do for you?"

Kera introduced herself as a journalist from the *Global Report*. Booth glanced again at the file, understanding now why it was empty. This did not dampen the warmth of his smile.

"Unless you're here for legal advice, I'm afraid I won't be of much help to you. I don't talk to the press about my clients. I'm sure you understand."

"I'm not here about any of your clients. I wanted to ask you a few questions about Caroline Mullen."

"Caroline," Booth said. His sadness was real, even touching, though appropriate for a colleague. "You're doing a story about her?"

"Perhaps. She was an associate here?"

"That's right."

"What was she like?"

"She was first-rate," he said without hesitation. "We lucked out with her. She was a class above us, I'm not ashamed to say. We never get associates of her caliber."

"What did she do around here?"

"Nearly everything. We're a small firm, as you can see. She wore more hats than anyone, and if she complained, she did it the right way—behind my back."

"You specialize in estate law?"

"Yes."

"Which means what?"

"Families today are as unique as ever. We help couples, married and otherwise, structure their investments, their property, their taxes and wills so that they can grow and protect their wealth over the course of their lives and beyond."

"Do you remember what Caroline was working on when she disappeared?"

"I remember exactly what it was because as soon as she was gone, it nearly ruined us trying to pick up all her casework."

Kera waited, hoping that he would elaborate, but he didn't. "Can you give me an idea of what that casework involved?"

"I really can't get into any details that involve our clients."

"I understand. But, generally, what was her role?"

"Like any associate, Caroline drafted and filed documents with the courts and the state. But she picked things up faster than most. It wasn't long before she was handling all the due diligence for new clients. She was extremely good at it."

Kera nodded. "She was good at her work. Do you think she enjoyed it?"

"Well, I wasn't close to her. I was just her boss—" he said, launching into the safe, automatic answer. But then he stopped himself on second thought. "Actually, yes, I'm confident she did like it. She had a passion for the law that can't be faked. It certainly can't be taught."

"A passion?" Kera said. "What do you mean by that?"

Booth's eyes narrowed as he searched for the words. "Caroline was . . . idealistic." Kera wrote that word down. "She was young, of course. And most young people are idealistic. But this was more than that. Fresh lawyers with her intelligence and Ivy League pedigree head straight to the big firms. Corporate finance, M-and-A, big-time employment law. But not Caroline. Her curiosity about the law was more grounded than that. She was interested in people and what they wanted to get out of life. I've seen a lot of associates come through here. Very few make an impact like she did. Especially in the short time before her passing."

"Before she went missing, you mean."

"Yes, I'm sorry. It's been long enough that, well, I guess I'd forgotten that they hadn't recovered her body."

"But you believe she's dead?"

Kera could see the answer within the internal struggle that was all over his face. "I see," he said softly. "That's why you're here."

"Do you have doubts about what happened to her?"

Booth shrugged. "The cops say they found her bike on the George Washington Bridge."

"Yes," Kera said. "And do you think she jumped?"

Booth hesitated. "I don't. No. Not Caroline. But what does it matter what I think? She's certainly gone. If all the evidence points to her jumping, well, at some point that reality must be faced."

Kera nodded. "Mr. Booth, can I ask you a professional question? For your legal opinion, that is."

"I'll give you one freebie. After that I'll have to bill you. Talking to reporters is not what keeps the lights on around here."

"I understand. What I'm wondering is whether someone like Caroline, being an expert in estate law, would know the sorts of things one would want to get in order if they planned to fake their own death."

* * * * *

The Control Room was never empty, but after business hours it set-tled into a productive peace. Rarely anymore were there overnight teams tracking real-time surveillance targets on the other side of the world. J. D. Jones looked around the room and pondered this, not for the first time. It was half past nine, and he was sitting at the center of his semicircle workstation, surrounded 180 degrees by eleven large LED screens. The monitors ran off a computer linked to Hawk's network, which had access to hundreds of public and private surveillance networks around the globe. During the first year that Hawk had been up and running, it was common to have one of the Mideast task forces working into the small hours. Two, sometimes three times a week, a group of men and women spent a night in the pit monitoring some action in Syria or Iran where it was daylight, local time. But not lately. Lately he'd seen less and less surveillance from overseas. It made him uncomfortable.

Jones loved the ambiance of a room lit by LED screens. He'd never watched much television growing up and watched almost none now, but he would have bet there weren't a hundred people in history who had spent more time than he had in front of screens.

Television was for passive audiences; computers were for builders. Even when he was just watching his screens, like he was now, it was an interactive experience.

He had two screens up, one for each of their live HawkEye profiles. She was on a downtown N train, reading unclassified e-mails on her smartphone. Jones noticed the way she took different trains each day, and sometimes cabs, and how she never walked the same route two days in a row. But however she got there, she almost always went directly home after she left the office. There she would usually log back into the Hawk network to do more work. The fiancé typically left his office much earlier in the evening and killed a few hours at a bar before going home.

Jones didn't like watching her, yet he couldn't always help it. A camera in the Prince Street station captured her disembarking from the train, and another showed her come up onto the sidewalk and turn east. There were no more cameras between the subway and her apartment, but ten minutes later the yellow HawkEye dot confirmed that she'd reached her address. The fiancé, HawkEye told him, was already home.

Jones turned his attention to the fiancé's profile. It was a familiar compulsion, one that his smoldering resentment permitted him to indulge. He selected the date field and scrolled back to the previous week. He found the videos from the cameras at the Hotel Grand International in Dubai. He watched them in sequence, as he had many times since he'd first happened upon the footage. The cameras showed the fiancé leaving the ballroom with a young woman. They walked together to the elevator and then down the hallway to his room. When the door shut behind them, Jones killed the feed and closed out of HawkEye. He sat there for several minutes, letting the peaceful quiet of the Control Room calm his anger.

ELEVEN

First word of the mural came just before sunrise three days later. A jogger paused on the sidewalk and snapped a grainy, low-light picture of the side of the building, which was tweeted along with the words, LOL. MORNING, NEW YORKERS! Minutes later, a few more pictures emerged on Facebook news feeds and Twitter streams, and an initial report was established on Gnos.is. Within a half hour, the uploading of pictures to social networking sites had become nearly continuous, spurred on by a swelling group of commuters who had gathered on the sidewalk beneath the mural. Bloggers supplied web page upon web page of commentary. The Gnos.is report grew, becoming richer and richer with photos, videos, and user-generated copy. Then it began getting serious traffic. By eight the mural was the top-trending story on the site.

Kera stepped onto an uptown R train at 8:17 AM and stood against the doors so that she could check her e-mail on her phone without anyone peering over her shoulder. There was a message from Gabby requesting that Kera and Jones set aside time for a daily meeting with her to provide updates on the ATLANTIS case. There was a reply from

Detective Hopper, in response to an e-mail Kera had sent asking for an update. His message—that Rowena Pete's bank accounts had been quiet since her disappearance—was predictably useless. Nice of him to send that along a week into the investigation. It was the sort of thing HawkEye could determine in a fraction of a second. But then again, Hopper didn't know about HawkEye, and he thought Kera was a journalist who was too clueless to track down information on her own. The detective also confirmed that the NYPD had received no word from any captor about a ransom, adding that they were now well outside the crucial forty-eight-hour window in which they had their best chances of finding a missing person. The only thing Kera found interesting about Hopper's e-mail was that he did not seem to presume that Rowena Pete was dead. There apparently was too little evidence even for that. As he always did, he echoed the little phrase that had appeared in all his communications with her and that she thought was plainly ridiculous, given the circumstances: *there is no sign of foul play*.

A fragment of conversation from across the car reached her ears and pulled her attention away from Hopper's e-mail. She looked up. The two men who were talking stood braced against the doors directly across from her. Both wore skinny jeans and T-shirts. One had a tattoo on his neck and piercings in his ears, nose, and over one eye. They were huddled together around a tablet. It was difficult to hear what they were saying over the cacophony of ads that, for a few prime hours each morning and evening, assaulted rush-hour commuters with a ferocious cross fire of flashing screens synched with voice-overs and music. She slid between two commuters to get closer, still pretending to be engrossed in her e-mail as she eavesdropped.

"It's gotta be It, right? Anyone else would claim credit."

"That thing looks massive. It can't be one person."

"Who knows."

"I'm sorry, but is that a new one?" asked a girl nearby who had also picked up on their conversation.

"Yeah, just this morning," said the guy holding the tablet. He tilted it so that she could get a look.

"Where is this?" she asked.

"Hold on a second. I just read that . . ." The guy began scrolling. Kera waited. She couldn't see the screen.

"Looks like Franklin and Varick. In Tribeca."

The train decelerated and lurched to a stop under the Flatiron building at Twenty-Third Street. A fresh hoard of commuters pressed in on them. Kera hesitated, walking herself through the motions of having second thoughts. But she knew she would go. She'd known it as soon as she'd heard them speak of the new mural. She pushed shoulder-first through the onboarding crowd and, moving with difficulty against traffic, broke free onto the platform just as the doors slid shut.

The 1 train was two blocks west. She covered the distance at a near run and stood on the downtown platform, winded, peering up the tunnel and willing the headlights of a train to curve into view. After two minutes light played against the tunnel walls, and then the train swung into sight. She rode impatiently near the door, gripping a handrail as the train lurched its way toward the southern tip of Manhattan. The crowds thinned below Houston Street. She got off two stops later, at Franklin. A bottleneck slowed her on the stairs, and it was then, even before she reached street level, that she first sensed the pandemonium above.

Car horns and sirens echoed through the canyon maze of buildings overhead. When she finally reached the sidewalk, her eyes easily found the source of the commotion.

The mural covered the middle three floors of an eight-story apartment building kitty-corner across the intersection. She wasn't an art critic, but if she had to categorize the style of the mural she was looking at, the words that came to mind were "provocative mock realism." The image made it appear as if a large swath of the building's outer wall had been blown away, exposing what lay within. In the foreground was a network of crisscrossing septic pipes, clearly burdened with a heavy load. Kera thought they looked a little like prison-cell bars. Trapped beyond the pipes were individual apartment units, in which people ate and bathed and defecated and fucked, one on top of the other, a compartmentalized tower of humanity imprisoned within its cage of piped sewage. There was something both playful and profound about the depiction, and Kera, standing in a crowd on the sidewalk with her head tilted back, was surprised to hear herself laugh out loud like some sort of madwoman.

The mural had thrown half of lower Manhattan into chaos. Mobs of onlookers swelled against hastily erected police barriers, crippling the intersection. Cops waved furiously at the jammed traffic, ushering rubbernecking motorists through and hollering empty threats at streams of jaywalkers. Kera skirted the mob at the base of the mural and stood farther back to take in the scene from a wider perspective. There was the painting itself, striking in its vivid detail and amusing in its voyeurism. But what she'd really come to examine was the feat of the production. Where had this mural come from? Its existence felt like a taunt.

The building, Kera began to see, was a perfect target for the stunt. There were no windows on the wall, which had previously butted up against an adjacent structure, long since torn down and replaced with the small, fenced-in parking lot that charged twenty-two dollars an hour for valet parking. The windowless wall provided a clean, vast canvas, and the parking lot provided a buffer between the wall and the street, where at night curtains of light must have hung from the infrequent street lamps, cutting off a view of everything in the shadows.

Kera shifted her eyes between the corners of nearby buildings. She could see just three cameras, all of them trained on the buildings' entrances. The awning of the parking lot's valet hut also sported a low-budget camera, but it was aimed at the cash register. Drawing her eyes to the roofline, she swept them back and forth. No obvious sign of how the artist might have suspended him- or herself into position. She could speculate about rappelling devices, but it would be only that—speculation. Without surveillance footage or physical evidence, looking at the mural provided her with no greater insight about its origins than if she'd come upon Michelangelo's ceiling— had it appeared suddenly overnight and without the permission of the Sistine Chapel.

She pulled out her smartphone and took a dozen pictures of the scene. Then she dialed Jones's workstation in the Control Room. "Have you seen this?" she said when he answered.

"Seen what? Where are you?"

"It. The artist. A mural appeared overnight on the side of a building in Tribeca. I thought I'd come by and have a look for myself."

"Forget the mural, Kera. Get back here. HawkEye identified a POI."

• • • • •

Gabby stood over Jones with folded arms. He was showing her the HawkEye map with the clusters of dots when Gabby turned to acknowledge Kera's arrival with a look that was one part concern for her disheveled appearance, and two parts scorn for her being late.

"Everything OK?"

"Eventful commute. What's up?" Kera said.

"J. D. was just walking me through a very detailed explanation of how our computers recognize patterns. He was, I hope, about to get to the point."

Kera could see Jones clench his jaw, but he continued. "Using HawkEye, we discovered that all four of our missing subjects were at the Empire Hotel in the weeks leading up to their disappearances. But we don't think any of them were there at the same time. Which means . . ." He looked at Kera.

"They had to have been there for something—or someone—else. That's what I was hoping to find when I went up there last night," Kera said.

She braced herself for a reprimand from Gabby. Venturing into the field without permission was prohibited. But Gabby only said, "And?"

"I looked around, talked to a bartender named Erica." Kera shook her head. "She knew something. She was working when Rowena Pete was in there last month, and I think she was being coy about who the singer was having drinks with. But my gut says she doesn't know the full picture. What've you got?"

"While you were at the bar last night, I reprogrammed a few of the queries I use to pull data out of HawkEye," Jones said. "You both know the basics of our surveillance software. It can identify faces as well as flag specific objects or traits, like a piece of luggage left alone for too long on a subway platform or, say, people wearing blue shirts, that sort of thing. But it can also be programmed to detect more abstract patterns. For example, you can isolate a single camera and look at, say, weekdays from 0800 hours to 0900 hours. The software begins to recognize people over time and can sort out who's there routinely and who's never been ID'd there before." Jones looked up to see if they were following. They both nodded. "Between our four subjects, we had fifteen confirmed sightings at the hotel. And we have this." On a different monitor, he pulled up the feed from a surveillance camera. Kera recognized the location immediately. It was a clear view of the sidewalk outside the main entrance of the Empire Hotel. "Using the time stamps from those fifteen confirmed sightings, I wrote a quick program that would look for general facial-recog patterns across a period of one hour on either side of each of those sightings."

"Any hits?" Kera asked.

"Yep. The Empire Hotel has three full-time doormen. Our camera here became familiar enough with them to know when they worked overtime or missed a shift." Kera's heart sank. They weren't looking for doormen. "It also identified three front-desk attendants, a concierge, and a dozen bartenders, chefs, waiters, and cleaning personnel."

"Can I see some of the footage? I can ID the bartender I spoke to," Kera said. It was unlikely that any of the doormen or lobby staff had a connection to their case, but she couldn't shake the feeling that her questions about Rowena Pete had meant something to Erica.

"I think the bartender's only role here is that she shows up for work like all the rest of the staff."

"You said you had a person of interest," Kera said.

"We do." Jones was not someone who grinned, but Kera could hear the equivalent of that in his voice. He pulled up a series of screenshots from the surveillance cameras. The same man appeared in each of them. "Here's the needle HawkEye lifted out of the haystack. He was at the hotel each time one of our subjects was spotted there."

"Holy shit," Kera said.

"Can you ID him?" Gabby asked.

"Of course. The software builds a 3-D faceprint using hundreds of different identifying values, such as the distance between the eyes, or the depth of hollowness around the eyes and cheeks, and even something as nuanced as skin tone. If the camera can catch a clear view of a subject's face, it compares that to faceprints in our available databases—"

"For Christ's sake, spare me the details," Gabby said.

"The ID is a match for a guy named Charlie Canyon."

"Not staff?" Kera asked.

"Definitely not staff."

"Not missing?"

"Nope. Mr. Canyon is alive and well at last check. He's an account director at a boutique PR agency in Hell's Kitchen. Interestingly, personal details get sketchy beyond that. He's gone pretty far out of his way to lighten his digital footprint. No social networking, no search engine results other than his employee profile on his firm's website. It's redaction city when it comes to his online identity."

"That's not easy to do," Kera said, glancing at Jones.

Jones shrugged. "Privacy's not a crime. I actually kind of admire the purity in that."

Kera stared at the frozen image on-screen, wishing she had a better view of the man's eyes behind his sunglasses. "So this Canyon guy covers his tracks pretty well. And yet you still found him."

"Well, it's the twenty-first century. A guy walks into a bar, he's gonna be on camera."

Gabby jumped in here. "What are the chances this is a coincidence? That he's not just a frequent patron of the hotel bar?"

Kera shook her head. She didn't even need to do the math. "No chance at all. Not if we can put him there for every single one of these visits."

Jones looked up at Kera. "Want to hear the best part? Guess where he was on the night of June 12 of last year?"

"You're kidding," Kera said, seeing in his face that he wasn't.

"Where?" Gabby said. "What are you talking about?" Using the map, Jones explained how the four missing subjects had been detected in the industrial blocks between the Meatpacking District and the West Side Highway—all on the same night back in June. Jones pulled up the map and pointed to two new yellow dots, representing the points where Charlie Canyon was ID'd entering the neighborhood and then exiting it several hours later.

Gabby stood thinking for a moment before she said, "OK, that's good enough for me. I want you to start round-the-clock surveillance on this guy. For now, just use the computers. No stakeouts or tails, and not a word gets out to NYPD or the Feds. Understood? Just use HawkEye to track him. We can't have this guy disappearing into thin air like the others."

Jones nodded. Gabby turned to Kera.

"Get into this guy's life. Find out who he is, where he goes, what he spends money on, what connection he has to our subjects—everything. OK?"

"I can do that, yes. But this guy, Charlie Canyon, he's an American citizen."

"So what? What are you saying, Agent Mersal?"

"Just that, well, I'm not sure a FISA judge would agree that we have probable cause that justifies this level of surveillance."

"We haven't asked a judge," Gabby said, clearly offended more by the insubordination than the basis of Kera's complaint. "And I haven't asked for your legal opinion. Your job is to analyze data available to you. If you have access to surveillance of Mr. Canyon, I damn well expect you to use it."

"I understand. But, with respect, we're talking about an investigation of missing persons, not counterterrorism. Do we even have reason to think a crime has been committed?"

"You haven't the faintest idea of the full parameters of this investigation. That's why you take orders from me. And I've just ordered you to carry out full surveillance of this target, indefinitely, until I order you to stop. Is that clear, Agent Mersal?"

"Yes, ma'am."

"Good. The three of us will meet with Branagh at the end of the week. Find me something worth talking about in that meeting."

Kera watched Gabby go. She didn't exhale until the Control Room door shut behind her. Gabby wanted them to meet with Director Branagh? About *this*?

"Was I out of line?" she said to Jones.

"I'm not a lawyer, remember?"

"Yeah, but you have common sense, don't you? And decency. You're not here for this kind of thing, right?" When he didn't answer, she turned to look at him. "Jones? Did you take this job—did you develop HawkEye—to spy on Americans who haven't been charged with any crime?"

Jones didn't look up, but he'd stopped working. For a long moment he was silent, his hands hovering over the keypad. Finally, very calmly, he said, "You have no right to question why I'm here." Then he added, a little more softly, "Do me a favor and don't get yourself fired, OK?"

· · · · ·

Later that afternoon Kera came back to Detective Hopper's e-mail message, which had been neglected in the wake of the mural's appearance and then the discovery of Charlie Canyon. She now thought it worth following up on. She called the detective on his direct line.

"Ms. Mersal . . . Ms. Mersal . . ."

Kera thought it was probably to her advantage that Detective Hopper didn't immediately remember her. "You e-mailed me this morning. About the Rowena Pete case."

"Yes," he said, first with minor triumph in his voice at remembering the name and then, using a much lower tone when he realized who she actually was, "Oh, yes. I'm sorry this case is turning out to be such a dud. And after starting out with so much potential for sensation. I understand you're frustrated, but I can assure you again that I have nothing new to report."

"I suspected as much. I was just wondering. You wrote in your e-mail that your investigation has turned up no sign of foul play." She expected the detective to become defensive or to at least toss in a "so far" or some such qualifier that promised future leads. But he said nothing. "How, then, would you classify the bizarre scene that was discovered in her apartment?"

"A person is free to do whatever she wants in her own home, so long as it doesn't break a law or harm anyone else. I've seen things a lot kinkier than that."

"So what happens now? You just stop looking for her?"

"If she doesn't want to be found, Ms. Mersal, I'm not going to spend taxpayers' money dragging out a search. I have real crimes to solve."

Kera thanked him halfheartedly for his time and turned her attention to the surveillance photos of Charlie Canyon. In most of them, he was seen at a distance, but she could tell he had dark hair and a handsome, boyish face. He usually wore sunglasses and his blank expression gave away less than his body language, which was calm and confident, an upright posture with shoulders back and chest out slightly as he walked. The electronic dossier, which HawkEye had begun to assemble rapidly, said that Canyon had recently turned thirty.

A few moments ago, Charlie Canyon had been an anonymous citizen, one of millions who set foot on the city's streets every day. But a computer linked to a handful of cameras had singled him out because he had a habit of having drinks with people who later went missing. Now he was about to get the full HawkEye treatment. In Kera's experience with surveillance—which had until this week included only foreign targets—when an individual's identity was investigated at this level, their lives ended up irrevocably changed.

TWELVE

That night, when Parker asked her if she'd heard about the mural in Tribeca, Kera admitted she'd been there and had seen it in person. He looked at her in that pleading, heartbreaking way he did sometimes in moments when his understanding of her work—of *her*—was exposed as superficial.

All she said was, "I was in the neighborhood for a work thing."

If that answer bothered him, he let it go. He was far more curious about the mural. He wanted to know how big it was and if it looked as real in person as it did in all the web photos. She said it did, realizing now that although she'd been preoccupied at the scene with a search for clues about the artist, the painting had transcended the mob and the cops and the sirens and her bizarre investigation. It had reached her; it was the kind of image that would come flashing across her mind's eye, at times, for the rest of her life.

"You should go see it for yourself," she said.

"Too late. The city's painting over it as we speak."

This shouldn't have come as a surprise. Of course they would paint over the mural. From their perspective, it was the work of a vandal who had trespassed and defaced private property, not to mention the disturbance it caused to the intersection below. But something in Kera, something beyond the instinct to preserve evidence, resented the idea that it should be painted over so hastily. "Had you seen any of the previous murals or sculptures?"

"Not in person," Parker said, disappointed. He had never mentioned It before, though she figured he must have been aware of the artist before she'd been. She didn't watch TV, or read popular blogs, or listen to the newest music. She was consumed by work.

Parker had reclined on the couch with his laptop, the dregs of a gin and tonic mingling with melting ice in a glass on the coffee table. She was on her own computer, perched on a stool at the bar that divided their kitchen from the living room. Like every other night since he'd returned from Dubai, she'd come home after nine, they ate dinner together, and then they sat and talked while browsing online. It had become a routine. A rut, maybe, was another word for it.

She typed the URL for Gnos.is into the browser's address bar, angling the screen self-consciously away from Parker so that he couldn't see it. If he caught her reading Gnos.is, he'd never let her hear the end of it. The coverage of the Tribeca mural was thorough. One art critic, treating the mural as serious art, wrote that it illustrated how the basic human functions were simultaneously harmonious and hypocritical. "The artist exposes how tenuous the true relationship is between our compartmentalized, outward lives and our filthy reality, at all times only inches apart." Other critics dismissed the mural as a depraved stunt and pleaded for the public to stop giving the artist attention.

Like Jones's unsuccessful search on HawkEye, Gnos.is had nothing to report on the artist's biography. Their coverage focused on the art itself, as well as the public's growing intrigue. With each new installation, people seemed to embrace the mystery of the unknown artist more deeply. It had become a living urban legend. Kera didn't care for mysteries, and she didn't believe in urban legends. She believed every case was solvable. She had to.

Parker was already in bed when she slid between the sheets next to him. A few minutes later, he startled her when he said, "You're thinking about your story, aren't you?" She couldn't tell whether he'd been awake the whole time or if she woke him when she got into bed. She nodded in the darkness, her chin brushing up and down against his shoulder. "Does it make you happy?" he said.

"What do you mean?"

"You seem so serious. Distracted. I worry that you're not happy here, doing this."

"Of course I'm happy," she said quickly, stroking his hair. "I'm sorry. You've been incredibly patient and sweet, and I'm off in another world. But yes, this is what I want to be doing. I love it."

Parker turned toward her. "Really?"

"OK, most of it. Sometimes it's frustrating. And sometimes . . ."

"What?"

"Nothing. I just hope it matters."

"Matters how?"

She exhaled. "I'm sorry, I really can't talk about it."

He didn't say anything to that. She was just glad he didn't draw away from her.

I hope it's worth it, was what she was thinking. *I hope that we at least do more good than harm.*

She thought about Jones's map and the layers and layers of data that had led them to the surveillance images of Charlie Canyon. At that very moment, computers were searching for and saving information about this man, a man who would wake in a matter of hours in a world that seemed to him the same—only something would have changed. His every move would now be watched.

Some time passed, and Kera fell back into a half-sleep world in which she was pursuing leads that darted for cover into dangerous alleys. She did not know how much time had gone by when a thought punctured her sleepless trance.

"Parker?" she whispered. "Are *you* happy?"

But Parker was asleep.

THIRTEEN

"I haven't found one suspicious call or charge in any of these records." Kera pushed away from the screens and leaned back in her chair with a cup of coffee. "If we were spying on my fiancé, he'd probably look more suspect than this. How can that be?"

Jones, who had been immersed in his own work, swung his gaze from the screens in front of him and aimed it directly at her, his eyes burning into her. After a moment he relaxed and dropped his gaze. "Canyon's covering his tracks."

"No, wait. What was that?"

"What?"

"That look you gave me."

Jones shook his head. "Nothing. I had something else on my mind. You were saying?"

"Canyon. He uses his cell phone regularly. He uses credit cards and e-mail. But all of it's clean. Work stuff, mostly—correspondence with clients and photographers and directors. The rest is calls to his mother in Tucson or short text messages when meeting up with a friend or something. Even his Internet searches are clean."

Jones shrugged. "He's careful."

"Careful? I can think of other words for it. Paranoid. Suspicious."

"Just because he's conscious of his privacy doesn't automatically implicate him in anything criminal. There could be a dozen motivations for that."

"I guess you would know."

"When did we start talking about me?" Jones said. He glared at her through the tension that had risen up between them.

"Just now," Kera said, returning his stare. Surely he must have expected that she would try to look into his background. It would have been negligent of her not to. She never would have brought it up, though, had her research turned up even the most basic information. Her searches into the life of J. D. Jones had been exercises in frustration. The only thing she'd gotten out of him directly was that he'd dropped out of college. She had no way of confirming that, and anyway, she doubted he was a dropout if he'd come from CIA, NSA, or some other government agency, which was another thing she'd been unable to verify. She didn't even know if James David Jones was his real name. It didn't sound real. In any case, the name hadn't gotten her anywhere. The only place she hadn't tried to search for Jones was on HawkEye. She was too afraid that such searches were recorded and that he'd be able to tell. "Charlie Canyon's records might be spotless. But yours don't even exist. What's that about?"

"Privacy. Job security. You're not exactly an open book either. It comes with the territory."

She was surprised to find herself so angry that he'd also been prying into *her* background. Given the effort she'd put into trying to violate his privacy, resenting him for doing the same to her was irrational. The difference, she realized, the true source of her aggravation, was her suspicion that he was probably more successful at prying than she'd been. *What might he have found?* she wondered. Her school and CIA files had been watered down and obfuscated to serve the purposes of whatever cover she had assumed. Her mind went to her adoption file. It contained nothing compromising, but it was just . . . private. In a way, it was the one thing that was most *her*.

Kera had tracked down the adoption file herself, years ago, while she was at Langley. It contained a name, ignored by her adoptive parents—her adoptive mother, an eccentric anthropology professor at the University of Washington, and adoptive father, an Egyptian immigrant who owned a news and shine shop in downtown Seattle. Kera knew only what her parents told her, and all they knew was that she had been born in a small coastal town in El Salvador. The mirror told her that one of her birth parents had likely been Salvadorian and the other likely hadn't. The date of birth in the adoption file was believed to be approximate.

Kera had felt no personal attachment to any of the file's data. There was only one artifact in the file that had surprised her and that she found significant. It was a photo of her infant self, cradled by a woman whose face was unseen. Kera had taken the photo and kept it for herself, though she later wondered why. Whatever life or name the woman in that photo had given her was not the life she had gone on to live.

Jones was still looking at her. Perhaps as a concession or an attempt to build trust, he interlocked his fingers in front of him and looked at her pleasantly. "What is it you think you need to know about me?"

"I don't need to know anything. I'm just curious."

"What are you curious about?"

"Where were you before Hawk?" Kera asked.

"Austin."

"Austin, Texas?"

"Yes."

"I meant, who were you working for?"

"Lone Star Communications."

"That a cover?"

"For what?" he said, his confusion sincere.

"Never mind. You did what for this Lone Star outfit?"

"Installed security software."

"You were an *installation* man?" She almost laughed.

"I didn't excel at school. It's amazing what talents get ignored when a person doesn't thrive in a typical education setting."

"You couldn't have been ignored completely. How did you wind up here?"

"I was recruited. Same as you," he said. "Same as all of us."

"How?"

"They found me online."

"So you do have a digital footprint?"

"In some circles, sure. I did, anyway."

Kera waited. When he didn't say anything more, she said, "You from Austin originally?"

"No. Fredericksburg."

"That in Texas?" He nodded. "So why Austin, then? Other than the blue-collar job."

"I was married."

"What happened?"

"You don't need to know that."

"Fair," she said. She had picked up on the gap in his résumé—there must have been five or six years between high school in Fredericksburg and marriage in Austin—and she considered whether she should question him about it now. She decided against it; he'd given her a lot suddenly, and she didn't want to test his patience. "Canyon, then. It's not as if he's just wiping his feet on the doormat to keep his online house tidy. This is like wiping away fingerprints every time he touches something. Why does a PR man like Charlie Canyon go through so much trouble to keep such a low profile?"

"Maybe you're asking the wrong question. Why don't the rest of you?"

Kera thought immediately of ONE. If Travis Bradley was right, there were math whizzes sitting at terminals across town scooping up these digital footprints and mapping them out into digital DNA that ONE intended to mine for profits.

Sure, Jones had a point about being protective of privacy. But it didn't necessarily explain what Charlie Canyon was up to.

"Didn't you build HawkEye around the idea that people are putting more and more of their personal data online?" she asked.

"Yes, and they are. But HawkEye doesn't get to know people. It just knows where they are. Getting to actually know Canyon is a job for a human. Like you."

While Kera thought about this, her eyes drifted to one of her screens, where a photo of the recent Tribeca mural was displayed.

"I want to find It," she said suddenly.

"What?"

"The artist."

Jones smiled. "If we learn only one thing from this case, it will be the immense value of gender pronouns to the English language."

"Exactly. Have you tried to run a Google search for 'It'? We're relying too much on computers. We need a witness. There's got to be one out there. Probably several. I mean, we're in the middle of a city. Have you ever been out on the streets, I don't care what time of night, and not seen other people? I want to talk to someone who saw that mural go up." What she really wanted was some insight into the artist's motive. Motive is what usually busted her through dead ends in a case. What was It getting out of this? Attention? Fame? Money? It was hard to cash in on any of those anonymously.

"If someone had seen something, we'd have heard about it," Jones said. "It's been days. No one's posted a picture of the artist. No one's tweeted about seeing the artist. No one's come forward to the police."

"Forget the cops. We're not talking about a homicide here. Maybe the menacing painter strikes again, maybe not. Who cares? It's a waste of their time."

"And it's not a waste of ours?" Jones said, turning back to his screens.

"You're the one who brought It into this case to begin with."

"That was before I heard of Charlie Canyon. The artist is a sideshow. Maybe he—she, It, whatever—is connected to the case. Maybe not. But Canyon is our best lead."

Without admitting aloud that Jones was right, Kera lit up her screens to see if she'd missed anything important in the life of Charlie Canyon.

· · · · ·

Late that afternoon Kera left the Control Room and walked the hall to her office. Using the web browser on her tablet, she visited the website of Lone Star Communications in Austin, Texas. It was a small cybersecurity firm that had been founded in 1999 by a Silicon Valley refugee who'd returned to the Lone Star State after the dot-com bubble burst. Lone Star's website proudly listed two-dozen local businesses that had been clients for more than ten years.

Kera reached for her phone and dialed the number she found on their CONTACT Us page.

"Hi there." She laid on the charm thick, but knew better than to attempt a Texan accent. "I'm calling from the law firm of Miller and Weston over on West Sixth Street," she said, referencing the name and address of one of the more innocuous of Lone Star's loyal clients. "I'm a new clerk here for Mr. Miller, and I'm hoping you can help me. We had our firewall upgraded a few years ago by one of your installation men, and Mr. Miller had a few follow-up questions."

"I can help you with that. Do you think you've experienced a breach?"

"Oh, no, everything is working wonderfully. The guy you sent out here was just a really big help to Mr. Miller, and he wanted me to give you a call and see if he could chat with the man about a few tips he'd mentioned. I know it's been two years, so I understand if—"

"You must be referring to J. D.," the woman said.

"Is he available?"

"I'm afraid he quit two years ago. We had people calling and asking about him for months after he left. But you're the first to call in a while. Can we send someone else over to help Mr. Miller?"

"No, no. It's OK. I wonder, though. You don't have any contact information for J. D., do you?"

The woman first thought that she did, but after she went to look it up, she came back on the line to say that he had not, in fact, left any contact information. "You might try looking him up. His last name was Jones."

Kera thanked her and then sat, looking out the window and thinking. The phone conversation with the woman had confirmed that Jones had worked at Lone Star Communications and that he'd used the same name then as he was using now. But that didn't give her anything new to go by. What she needed was some record of Jones, or whatever his real name was, that had been created before he became interested in wiping away his past—and that he could not have eliminated since.

She turned back to her tablet and searched for high schools in Fredericksburg, Texas. Mercifully, there was only one. She thought about using HawkEye to search the school's records for a J. D. Jones, but decided against it. It was too risky, and she doubted that that had been his name as far back as high school. She checked the clock and subtracted for the time difference. It was just after two PM in Texas; the school would still be open. She dialed the number and queued up her charm.

"Can you tell me which faculty member oversees the yearbook committee?" she asked the secretary, who proved to be very helpful.

· · · · ·

That night—in fact, early the next morning—Kera stood on a sidewalk beneath a street lamp squinting into the shadows. Beyond the curtain of light was only darkness, and nothing of that darkness distinguished itself from the rest. She moved several paces in each direction and looked again, scrutinizing the shadows for details that did not materialize. It was four AM on a Wednesday, two weeks to the day that the mural had appeared.

She retraced her steps to the intersection and turned left on the cross street. There, adjacent to the parking lot, she found a short length of sidewalk, maybe ten yards that fell in the gap between lampposts, from which she could make out the broad, colorless mass of the building. She spun around to scan the structure across the street; it was half car garage, half warehouse. All the windows were dark.

At four thirty she went around the corner to the Village Tavern and spoke to the bartenders winding down from the Tuesday-night shift. They all knew about the mural, and two of them figured they must have walked right beneath it, oblivious, after closing down. A few others had seen it Wednesday afternoon when they came back into work. But nobody had noticed anything suspicious early Wednesday morning.

At five thirty she was back on the street and approached a vendor setting up his cart for breakfast. Kera bought a coffee from the man and asked if he'd been here at the same time two weeks earlier.

"Sure. Made a killing that morning. I ran out of doughnuts and muffins by nine. Never seen anything like it. And then they paint over it same day and no more crowds."

"When did you first notice the mural?"

"I don't know. It was just getting light, like now. I went to the corner to buy a paper, and I saw it on the way back. The lights," he pointed up at the streetlight. "They clicked off and then I notice. The whole building—alive like an explosion!"

"Did you see the painter?"

He gave her a look. "No, no. The whole wall painted. No people."

"You don't remember anyone suspicious coming or going that morning?"

He shook his head. "I notice nothing until the lights go off. And then the crowds start coming."

Sipping her coffee, Kera walked across the street to get a closer look at the lower reaches of the building. The streetlights clicked off, and she made a note of the time—5:49 AM. She wondered what the building's owner planned to do with this wall. There was enough light now to see what had become of it. The city's whitewashing job had turned it into an ugly rectangle of uneven white paint framed by dirty bricks. She wondered whether they would repaint it to match the street-facing facade. It was probably only a matter of days before they got an offer they couldn't refuse from an advertiser looking to cash in on the site's new allure. She saw the irony in this, thick as the white paint that had started to reflect the first light seeping out of the navy sky. The city would tolerate an ugly white wall, and it would tolerate a wall dressed with brand names worn by airbrushed models. But the mayor himself had mobilized a crew to paint over the artist's mural.

Kera had turned for the subway to head to work, her head down, thinking, when she noticed the writing on the lip of the sidewalk. The phrase ran parallel to a crack in the concrete, the last three words rolling over the curb and into the gutter.

Have you figured it out yet?

FOURTEEN

A long, sleek table ran like a spine through the center of the secure conference room. The two interior walls dividing the room from neighboring offices were made of opaque frosted glass. The outfacing walls, which formed one corner of the building's twenty-seventh floor, were made of pristine sheets of one-way glass that came to a point like the bow of a ship sailing into the heart of Times Square. The view out the conference room windows was almost entirely of enormous, flashing advertisements. Inside, a half-dozen flat screens were mounted on slender posts around the perimeter of the room. In addition, a screen folded up out of the tabletop.

The director and CEO of Hawk sat at the head of the table, his back to the view. Dick Branagh had been a three-star army general with a reputation for operating so discreetly and efficiently that the only time anyone thought of him was each time the latest of his swift promotions was announced. Today, he was jacketless and tieless, his collar open at the neck. His hair was receding and going a little gray and thin, but he was handsome for sixty, despite the fact that he never appeared to be having a good time. At this moment, his expression fell on the displeased side of blank. Kera and Jones had taken up straight-backed positions to the director's right; Gabby sat across from them and to Branagh's left.

Behind the director, in the distance across Times Square, the population clock on the ONE billboard read 7,374,169,448.

Then 7,374,169,449.

Then 7,374,169,450.

"We've identified a person of interest," Gabby said. "We believe this man, Charlie Canyon, seen here on street surveillance cameras, met with each of the missing subjects in the months leading up to their disappearances. Our lead agent on the case is Kera Mersal. She can summarize what we've learned since we started tracking him last week."

Kera lifted her shoulders an inch higher and swiped her tablet to life. When Director Branagh looked at her, she nodded, trying to appear more confident than she felt. With all Hawk did in the service of homeland security, it was hard to imagine Branagh's interest in this case. She certainly had not expected her first meeting with him to be about a handful of artists who had gone missing on American soil. To steady her anxiety, she reminded herself to just focus on what she had prepared. For the past five days, she had lived not her own life but Canyon's, observing him in real time as he moved about the city. She had examined his routines, his purchases, the company he kept, the moments when he thought he was alone and unwatched.

"The subject is extremely private. He has no presence on any social networking sites, and his name returns no major search-engine results other than his employer's directory. He keeps to himself and rarely indulges in nightlife. The exceptions to this are semifrequent appearances at the Empire Hotel's rooftop bar, where we believe he rendezvoused with our missing subjects. Otherwise, Mr. Canyon spends as many as twelve hours a day at the offices of AM + Toppe, a powerful PR agency, where he appears to be something of a prodigy. His job description is a little vague, but the best I can gather, he consults brand campaigns in the entertainment, tech, and fashion industries." She set down the tablet. "What we don't know is why he appears to be the only person to have met with our four subjects. We could speculate—"

"Let's not," the director said. Kera was taken aback by the softness of his voice. She'd expected it to have a gruffer quality. She understood now, though, that he was a man who rarely needed to raise his voice. She'd yielded to him immediately. "Go back to the missing people for a second. What are your working theories there?"

Kera and Jones exchanged an uncertain glance. "There are none that we're comfortable with, sir."

"But they're alive?"

"It's possible, yes. If that's the case, they're living entirely off the grid."

"Are they fanatical?" the director asked. "What were they doing before they vanished?"

"They're not religious, if that's what you mean. In fact, I couldn't find an example of religious expression among any of them. They're creative types—" Kera started to say, realizing that a meeting with the director was not the place to try to articulate something for the first time. She had, in fact, noticed a similar quality in all of the missing people, the lawyer included—not in their title or day job, but in the dedicated way they pursued the work of their choosing. "They're passionate, I guess you could say."

"Extremist is another word for it," Gabby said. "Passionate people have hobbies. These people have either killed themselves or they've abandoned their lives and gone into hiding. That's something entirely different."

"We don't know *what* they've done," Kera pointed out.

"What *do* you know?" Director Branagh shot back.

"Well, three of the subjects were connected to the ONE Corporation," Kera said. She saw Gabby and the director exchange a glance, but she couldn't interpret it. "Rowena Pete was signed to

ONE Music. Cole Emerson, the filmmaker, had his last documentary distributed by a ONE subsidiary. And the novelist, Craig Shea, was published by ONE Books. The lawyer has no connection to ONE, as far as I know."

"What about Canyon? Is he connected to ONE?"

"Not in any way I know of, sir."

"You said Canyon met with the subjects before they vanished, but you have not said that he is responsible in some way for their going missing."

"It would be speculation—" Kera started, but then stopped herself. He wanted proof, and she knew they didn't have it. "We believe, sir," Kera said, feigning confidence, "that those meetings are related to the disappearances."

"And you've deduced that from these images?" the director said, gesturing at the flat screen.

Kera felt her face flush. "That's right."

"Because all I see is a guy going to get a drink after work." The director's graying eyebrows underlined his forehead, that great canvas of expression, expansive now in middle age and wrinkled most deeply in the areas that illustrated displeasure. He leaned forward as if he'd heard enough, and pressed both of his palms flat on the table. "I don't care about these artists. And I don't care whether you care about them either. But one thing we should all care about more than anything else is our reputation. We cannot afford to look incompetent because we're unable to locate not a solo terrorist hiding in a hole in Yemen—which, by the way, we're pretty good at doing—but four human beings who were essentially our neighbors. What happened to them? The answer cannot possibly be this difficult to figure out."

Kera withered. Humiliation burned her cheeks. She felt as if she'd been jerked out of orbit and now faced the scalding friction of reentry. She was angry for letting herself walk into this meeting with so little to show for her work. She might have said, "Yes, sir," or at least nodded, but in any event, the director stood up to leave, and then Gabby followed him out the door.

When they were gone, Jones let out his lungs next to her.

Kera looked out the window. The population clock ticked over to 7,374,171,852. She didn't know why the numbers made her uneasy; it was just a stupid advertising gimmick. She looked away, thinking. There was something else that made her uneasy too. She had an urge, one she wasn't proud of, to be back in front of the surveillance monitors in the Control Room. She wanted to know what Charlie Canyon was doing. Being away from him was like leaving the room for too long during a television commercial break; she felt anxiety for some unknown, breaking development she might be missing.

It was 11:18 AM. Canyon typically took lunch well after noon, usually takeout that he brought back to the office. But he often came down to the street about this time late in the morning for a second cup of coffee.

"I don't think we should assume that Rowena Pete was the last," Kera said.

"The last?"

"The last person to go missing. What if there are going to be more?"

Jones looked at her. "Why do you sound hopeful?"

"Because it could help us. If we can figure out who's next, it might lead us to the others."

Jones leaned back in his chair and rubbed his temples as if this, finally, was the thing about this case that he couldn't wrap his head around. "It's one thing to look for missing people. It's something entirely different to look for missing people who aren't even missing yet."

"True. But now we know at least one place these people might go before they disappear."

He nodded, though not optimistically.

"I know, it's a needle in a pile of needles, coming at it like this. But we can do it the old-fashioned way."

First, he gave her a look that said, *What are you talking about?* Then his face went blank, and she recognized the moment when her idea caught traction.

"I want to talk to him," she said.

"You want to approach Charlie Canyon with this list of names and ask him where they all went?"

"Not exactly. Look at this." She picked up her tablet. "Judging from Charlie Canyon's credit card statements, he goes to that bar most Fridays after work, right? This time, I want to be there. And I want to get close enough to see and hear what the surveillance cameras can't." She was on her feet suddenly, her tablet and phone tucked between her hand and her hip. "Just like you said, the computers can't tell us everything we need to know. I want to get in there close."

"You want to go *tonight*?" he said, but before he'd finished she was already in the hallway. "Wait. Kera?"

She didn't stop, only looked back over her shoulder to say, "I don't know about you, but by the time we meet with Branagh next, I intend to have something to tell him."

He watched her walk away until she'd made the turn at the end of the hallway and was out of sight.

FIFTEEN

Across the street from the entrance to the Empire Hotel, a small park sprung up between the colliding six-lane slabs of Broadway and Columbus like a blade of grass that had slithered through a crack in the sidewalk. Kera sat on a park bench and watched limousines and taxis glide up to the curb in front of the hotel. Across Columbus, the fountain in Lincoln Center Plaza danced, backlit by the giant chandeliers of the opera house.

She felt completely in the dark without HawkEye. Every fifteen minutes Jones sent her a text to say that Charlie Canyon was still at work. An hour passed. She stood up and walked the short perimeter of the park and then sat back down. Another half hour passed. When her phone buzzed to life, she sat up, alert.

"He just left the office," Jones said. "He's on foot, headed north on Broadway. That should give you about seven minutes."

Two minutes later Kera stepped off the elevator and onto the top floor of the Empire Hotel. By now it was after ten, and the crowd leaning into the bar was two deep. There were three bartenders. One of them was Erica. "Chardonnay?" Erica asked, remembering.

Kera took the glass of wine and sat on a bench of low cushions that wrapped around a cocktail table. From there she had a view of both the door and the bar.

Charlie Canyon entered alone. He was shorter than she'd imagined, but he had a commanding presence, in subtler ways, to make up for it. He wore a black shirt, dark jeans, and a black leather jacket. When he crossed the room he moved confidently, his shoulders square, his eyes steady. Kera looked down. She texted Jones to say she had established visual contact.

Canyon made his way to the far end of the bar. As he did, Kera shifted her gaze back to Erica in time to see the moment when she spotted him. Dispatching the customer at hand, Erica approached Canyon with a smile and made him a drink he had not ordered. After a short exchange, she returned to her other thirsty, paying customers. Charlie Canyon did not appear to be self-conscious about standing alone in a bar on a Friday night, and this gave Kera hope that he was waiting for someone. She kept an eye on him and on the door, all the while pretending to be busy on her phone, which she hoped would lessen the chance that she'd be approached by some tipsy banker or lawyer. She loaded the Gnos.is home page and scrolled through the top stories. The Tribeca mural was still trending, although now vivid images of the mural were displayed side by side with photos of the whitewashed wall.

At ten thirty a new bartender relieved Erica, who disappeared for fifteen minutes. When she reemerged, her maroon shirt and bartender's vest had been traded in for a skirt and knee-high boots. She joined Canyon in the corner at the end of the bar. Kera watched them closely. They spoke; Erica laughed a few times. Canyon checked his watch. Their alliance appeared friendly but unromantic. They did not interact with anyone around them, nor did they seem to be waiting for anyone else. Kera thought about trying to move in closer to hear what they were saying, weighing that opportunity against the risk that Erica might notice her loitering nearby.

She never got the chance. As soon as she'd made up her mind to move in, Charlie Canyon looked directly at her. The eye contact lasted only an instant, far shorter than many of the random, curious glances that pass between men and women at a bar like this on a Friday night. But Kera, who felt the fine hairs lift between her shoulder blades and on her neck, was certain it had been deliberate. Erica was standing with her back to Kera in such a way that Canyon's face was visible just over her right shoulder. Erica had said something to him, then Canyon's eyes shifted suddenly, met Kera's, and then swept away. A few moments later, the two of them made a move for the door, Canyon guiding Erica through the crowd with a firm hand on her lower back. Neither of them glanced once in Kera's direction.

She was on her feet the moment they disappeared into the elevator. She rushed through the crowd and, instead of waiting for an elevator, pushed through the heavy door to the stairs. She descended all fifteen flights two steps at a time, cornering with her inside hand anchored hard against the railing. With her other hand, she extracted a wireless earpiece from her pocket and called Jones by voice command. He answered just as she emerged from the hotel.

"Which way?" she asked, looking up at the camera. He didn't miss a beat, as if he'd been sitting there watching the feed the entire time.

"Uptown. Toward the Sixty-Sixth Street subway."

She spotted them on the crosswalk at Sixty-Fifth Street.

"What's the plan here, Kera?"

"I don't know yet. For now I just want to see where they're headed."

"Kera, you heard the director. We're supposed to be finding missing people, not tailing Canyon while he goes barhopping on a Friday night, which, by the way, I can do from right here."

"We've been tracking him with HawkEye for a week and it's gotten us nowhere. I want to get close." She knew she should have told Jones that Canyon might have made her at the bar. But she didn't.

She kept a half block between them until they descended into the subway station. Kera swept her Metro card at the turnstile in time to see them cross under the tracks and head up the stairs toward the downtown platform. An express train exploded through the station with a force that rattled her brain. When she reached the platform, she searched in both directions, finally spotting Erica leaning over the tracks to get a look up the tunnel. Kera edged closer, taking cover behind a group of Juilliard students. She wanted to be no more than one car ahead of Canyon and Erica when their train came.

On the opposite platform, a bum played a flute, its woody notes echoing off the tile walls in unflattering pools of sound. Finally, another rumble, low at first, then piercing, and the headlights of a downtown 1 swung into view. Kera waited for Erica and Canyon to disappear through the doors before she boarded the adjacent car. Through the smudged windows, she could see Erica sitting midcar, her head thrown back against an ad for the new Jalen West album. Canyon was standing in front of her, leaning against a vertical bar.

"I'm on a downtown 1," Kera said in a low voice.

"I can see that," Jones said in her ear.

She glanced up. There was a camera at each end of the car.

"Perfect. How 'bout letting me know when it looks like they're about to bail." Kera turned her back and sunk down in her seat so that she wasn't visible through the windows between cars.

After Twenty-Eighth Street, Jones told her that the girl was standing up. "They're getting off at Twenty-Third," he said thirty seconds later. Kera stepped through the doors at the last second and shuffled streetward, spotting them just before they disappeared into the city at the top of the stairs. She picked them up again aboveground and allowed some distance to open as she followed them west. They were headed into the industrial blocks adjacent to the West Side Highway.

"All right, Kera, how far are you planning to take this? You know I don't have eyes on you once you get past Ninth Ave."

"All the more reason for me to stay on them."

Though it hadn't achieved any special reputation for crime, this part of town was abruptly darker and quieter than the arteries of Chelsea that throbbed with nightlife only a few blocks to the east. She wondered briefly if she should stop. She tossed a wary glance back at Eighth Avenue before hurrying across the street to keep Erica and Canyon in sight.

Jones's voice was in her ear again. He seemed to have accepted that she wasn't turning back. "What do you see?"

Kera stopped.

"Hang on," she said. It was quiet enough to whisper now and still be heard. Erica and Canyon had disappeared midblock. They were no longer in front of her. They had traversed the island to within ear-shot of the West Side Highway, and now suddenly, Kera was alone. She stepped across the street, slowing as she came even with a door she thought they might have entered and then finding cover in the shadows of a construction site.

"What's going on?" Jones wanted to know.

"I lost them outside a building on Twenty-Second. It looks like an auto body shop." A pale orange fluorescent light flickered and buzzed over an aluminum door set into a brick wall soiled by layers of graffiti.

"We'll check it out tomorrow, OK? Don't go in there alone." It went without saying that they couldn't call for backup on an unauthorized tail. Gabby had been clear: no NYPD, no Feds. Jones was right. The only reasonable thing to do was to hustle back to Tenth Avenue where she could flag down a vacant cab. Then she could come back during business hours and get a good look at the place. She sat thinking for a minute, hoping a better plan would come to her.

A figure approached on a bicycle. Kera watched from the shadows, intending to let the cyclist pass before making a break for more civilized streets. But the cyclist hopped the opposite curb and braked to a stop at the corner of the brick building. It was a young woman—Kera noted the ponytail under the cyclist's baseball cap as she dismounted, locked her bike to a chain-link fence, and entered the building through the aluminum door. Kera exhaled, unaware she'd been holding her breath.

"Kera?" Jones said.

Punches of laughter burst from down the block in the opposite direction. She turned to see two young men spilling out of a cab at the corner, walking toward her. They crossed the street and disappeared into the building. Like the woman on the bike, they hadn't used a key to get in. The door was unlocked.

"I'm going in." She felt her legs carrying her across the street.

"Kera—"

"And I'm getting off the phone. I can't be seen with this earpiece. I'll call you when I'm out." She hung up before Jones could protest. And with a quick, right-left glance to check that the street was clear, she reached for the doorknob.

. . . . .

She found herself in a near blackness defined solely by two opposing exit signs. The room was large. She smelled car oil and dusty concrete. Over the sound of her own heart came another noise, another rhythmic thump, which took her a moment to understand was a bass line. The music drifted from an opening somewhere on the far side of the room. She squinted, impatient for her eyes to adjust. Gradually, she discerned the outlines of what appeared to be a large garage housing a half-dozen taxi cabs in various states of disrepair.

Then she noticed the painting.

The canvas hung over an open doorway directly across the room. Dark red, blue, and green brushstrokes swirled around a darker core resembling, she thought, either the Milky Way or a human eye decorated with heavy makeup. Kera moved toward the painting, stepping silently between two cabs. The thump of the music grew louder, and she could feel the driving beat tickle the concrete underfoot. Her senses worked double-time, taking things in, identifying them, entering them into the matrix that informed her decision to keep going or to retreat. She picked up cigarette smoke, fragments of a garbled conversation. She kept moving. The voices grew louder. There were people just around the corner—two female voices and a male voice. They were discussing Background Noise Pollution, which had to be the name of a band or else their conversation was completely unintelligible.

She peered through the threshold. The smokers were standing on a steep stairwell that disappeared beneath the garage. The guy, spotting her, waved a casual welcome and then returned to his discussion. Kera nodded as she squeezed by and started down the steps, descending farther into the building as if she'd been invited.

She entered a cavernous basement space that made no sense in the context of the grungy auto shop overhead. The wall through which she'd entered was exposed, rust-colored brick. The remaining walls were constructed of smooth concrete. They all featured wide, floor-to-ceiling paintings that matched the style of the piece over the doorway upstairs. In one corner a short-haired DJ spun dance music from an elevated booth. A keyboard and drum set rested on a platform extending from the far wall. Two bars stocked with liquor were arranged between flickering tea candles.

Kera moved along the edge of the room, getting a feel for the space while she considered the paintings. The van Gogh swirls gave them life, but it was not clear what they were meant to depict. At first she thought she was looking at human features. But the longer she looked at them, the more abstract the paintings became. They seemed to mock scale the way a picture of the inside of an atom can at the same time look like an unbound galaxy.

"Figure it out yet?" The voice came from over her shoulder.

"Excuse me?" she said, turning. "Oh." His shirt was unbuttoned at the neck where smooth flesh pulled against the sturdy contours of his collarbone. Dark, meticulous hair shot up from his forehead. What startled her were his eyes—a moody hazelnut color of uncertain depth. The surveillance footage had not been able to pick up on that. He was looking past her, up at the wall. She followed his gaze back to the painting, assessing the shapes and colors. "I think it's an ear canal," she said. "Or a wormhole."

"Those are very specific interpretations," said Charlie Canyon.

"I didn't mean to project. Don't tell the artist," she said, and then caught herself in time to play it off. "That is, I'm sorry, you're not—?"

"God, no. The artist is the girl over there by the yellow canvas. Marybelle Pickett. Sort of improbable, isn't it, a girl so tiny churning out these massive works?"

They were standing close enough to the canvas that color filled Kera's vision from one side to the other. "I think I like it. Whatever it's supposed to be."

"She's an important artist," said Canyon.

"Why's that?"

"Because her paintings expand our awareness of the world, rather than distract us from it. She's going to be famous."

Kera didn't know the art world from molecular biology, but her gut told her there wasn't a chance in hell the paintings hung around this basement would ever enjoy a wide audience. They seemed precisely the sort of indie achievements that would be destined for obscurity. Kera searched his face for any sign of irony, but found none. "I'll have to take your word for it. I'm no art critic."

"The opinions of those who call themselves critics matter the least." When he looked at her, his gaze was piercing, like he knew she didn't belong here, like he knew everything. "What do you do, then?" he said.

"Huh?"

"The drinks were better at the Empire Hotel. If you're not an art critic, what brings you all the way down here?"

"I'm a journalist." She didn't like how this was going. After watching his every move for a week, she'd assumed she was walking into this with the advantages of surprise and information. And yet she felt like he was a step ahead of her.

"Are you here on a professional basis?" he asked.

"Tonight? Yes. I'm researching a story." *Stick to the truth*, she reminded herself. *As close as possible to the truth.* Her training had taught her that, when working undercover, it was important to tell as few lies as possible. Especially about the big things, like her name and occupation. Necessary as they were, lies had a way of becoming very slippery once you started making them up on the fly.

"About?"

"About the city's underground art scene."

"Taking a pretty literal stab at it, aren't you?" he said, looking up at the ceiling.

"I guess I am." She smiled and turned toward Canyon, positioning herself so that she could perform a sweeping glance around the room. Erica stood chatting in a group by the small stage.

"What do you think?" he said.

"About what?"

"The underground art scene. For a journalist, you don't ask very many questions."

"Are the paintings for sale?"

"Of course they're for sale. What else would they be for?"

"How much does something like this go for?"

"That's the fun part. The market will decide."

She laughed.

"What's funny?"

"The market? Most of these people look like they couldn't afford a cab fare to get over here."

"These people don't want to own the paintings, not most of them, anyway. They want to enjoy them. See? They're having a good time."

"You said the point was to sell them."

"It is. But the paintings need to acquire value first."

"The artist hasn't given them enough value?"

"Oh, they're most valuable to the artist. But what does that matter? They need to become valuable to others."

"And what makes them more valuable to others?"

Canyon never got a chance to answer her because just then, the energy in the room shifted abruptly. It was nothing overt—no applause, no announcement, no gasps. Just a shift, subtle but unmistakable. Kera looked to the door. The man who had just entered was tall and lean, and his dark hair curled out in waves from underneath a beanie cap. The dim light in the room seemed to be soaked up by his olive skin. His fingers, she noticed as she watched him greet people, were long and beautiful. Bystanders hovered close, their bodies leaning slightly toward him, as if trying to catch a word or two of what he was saying. If he enjoyed the attention, he didn't show it. His limbs were loose, his back straight—not like someone who was acting proud, but like someone for whom pride was a baseline. His expression was open and radiant. She could not pull her eyes from him.

The basement was crowded now, and traffic throughout the room spun on two orbits. The man who had just entered was the gravitational center of one. A cinnamon-skinned woman with dark curly hair stood at the center of the other, her thin shoulders thrown back, her fingers pinching the stem of a wineglass. A trio of oversized bracelets slid up and down her forearm whenever she lifted her hand to drink. She wore jeans and a spaghetti-strap top that revealed an inch or two of flesh above her studded belt; a small tattoo peeked out from her abdomen as if it had been tucked into the waist of her jeans.

"Who are they?" Kera asked.

Canyon looked at her. When he saw that she was serious, he laughed.

"He's Rafael Bolívar."

Kera held the name in her mind. She'd heard it before but could not assign to it any meaning. "Is he a celebrity?"

"Only of the tabloid sort. It's refreshing, actually, to meet someone who doesn't know him as that."

"And the woman?"

"Natalie Smith."

"The filmmaker?" Kera said, picturing the *America* ad visible from her office overlooking Times Square and remembering that Parker had wanted to take her to see the film. She wondered if there was a way to tell Parker about this without jeopardizing her security clearance. There wasn't. Instead, she said to Canyon, "I'm going to see her film next week."

"It won't make it that far," he said.

"What does that mean?"

"The studio is going to kill it."

"Why do you say that? I just saw an ad for it today. It releases next week."

"Wait and see. They'll pull it."

"How do you know?"

"Because I've seen it."

"It's that bad?"

"It's brilliant. It might have given a real, nonpartisan meaning to the word 'values' again. But that, of course, scares the hell out of a lot of religious and right-wing groups. They'll mobilize. And in a few days, the first reviews will start coming out, and they'll be horrendous. The studio will get phone calls and e-mails. And because they're a bunch of pussies, they'll feel compelled to pull it. You ever notice how the people who most need to see or read something are the most oblivious or resentful of its existence?"

"Yes," Kera said quietly. She and Jones had gotten Canyon wrong. They might have proof that he met with the people who had gone missing, but she saw something now that was impossible to see with HawkEye. Charlie Canyon was the kind of guy who *would* meet with up-and-coming artists at a rooftop bar. He saw the world in the way that an artist did, or at least in a way that was compatible. Which is to say that he saw the world in a way Kera did not, at least not automatically. It was like the paintings. She looked at them first for the literal, surface truth. But after taking a few moments to look at them in a different way, it was possible to see that something both simpler and more complex was going on.

She shifted her gaze between Natalie Smith and Rafael Bolívar. They were on separate sides of the basement, entrenched in separate conversations, but there was a current suspended between them, unbroken by the intervening crowd. "They're together, aren't they?"

In Canyon's laugh was a hint of genuine surprise but also something darker, as if he both appreciated her and despised her for noticing.

"You mean, are they fucking? Jesus, is it that obvious? I underestimated the degree to which they were flaunting it."

"I didn't mean to imply that they were flaunting it." In fact, they weren't. They hadn't even come near each other. It just seemed to be a natural fact one noticed when seeing them together in the same room: these two are fucking.

Canyon, she noticed, was staring at Bolívar, his eyes sharp.

"You're jealous." It was something she probably shouldn't have said. She braced for blowback, for some sign that she'd crossed a line. But when he turned to her, his eyes had transformed. They were bright with laughter and a little wild.

"I suggest you stick to reporting and drop the speculation."

"I'm hearing that a lot lately. Excuse me a minute, I need to use the ladies' room."

She left him staring down at the shrunken ice cubes in his glass. But she made it only a few steps before he called after her. "Who do you work for?"

She turned. "The *Global Report*. We're a digital news organization that curates an—"

"Curates an insightful blend of the world's best original and aggregated news stories," he said. Then he shrugged. "I've heard of it."

She nodded. "I'm flattered."

She went in search of the ladies' room and found instead that there was one cramped, unisex restroom fitted with a urinal and two narrow stalls. She let herself into the farthest stall and pulled out her phone to text Jones. The strength-of-signal icon indicated that the phone had no service. That was a first. No device issued to her by Hawk had ever failed to achieve an uninterrupted signal, including while in the subway tunnels, which crawled much deeper beneath the city than this basement. She slid her tablet from her shoulder bag and sat down on the closed lid of the toilet. No cellular or Wi-Fi signal on the tablet either. There wasn't time to fiddle with the devices. Instead, she took a few minutes to enter her notes about what she'd just witnessed in as much detail as she could remember. She noted the approximate ages of people in the room (early twenties to late thirties), what they were wearing (casual, trendy), the ratio of male to female (close to even), and recorded the names of the people she'd identified (Canyon, Erica, Bolívar, Natalie Smith, Marybelle Pickett). Then she typed Canyon's name at the top of a new note and, using shorthand, recorded everything she could think of from their conversation.

She was in the stall six, maybe seven minutes. She stretched her cramped fingers and considered what to do next. It was well after midnight, she'd been out of communication with Jones for more than an hour, and her objective for being here in the first place was at best vague. But she felt sharp and wide-awake. She could feel each moment come into focus and then fly past, as if she were leaving them behind and not the other way around.

She noticed the wall markings on the stall as she was putting away her tablet. *Let's smoke drugs. Call me 917-214-7512. Janey is a bitch. I let him rape me. Have you figured it out yet?* A few heartbeats ticked off while she stared at the last etching. The words, scratched into the paint, curved around the circular knob that worked the lock on the stall door. She reached for her phone and clicked a photo.

When she emerged from the restroom, Canyon was talking to someone near the bar.

"Will you introduce me to the artist?" Kera said, interrupting.

Canyon excused himself and scanned the crowd. His eyes popped a little in his head when he spotted Marybelle Pickett, who was across the room, just visible through a break in the crowd. He said, "Oh, shit."

"What?" Kera said.

The artist was on her toes, whispering something into Rafael Bolívar's ear. Bolívar was hunched over, listening. But he was staring directly at them. Or, rather, at Canyon.

"What is it?"

Canyon didn't respond, he just returned Bolívar's stare. Bolívar glanced at one of the paintings on the wall, and then he swung his gaze back, locking it again on Canyon. Suddenly, he was coming toward them, maneuvering his way through the crowd with a dark smile that made Kera's skin crawl.

Bolívar stopped in front of them. He nodded to acknowledge Kera's presence, but only barely. His interest was in Canyon. "Can we talk?" he said, and turned for the exit without waiting for Canyon to respond. Canyon disappeared after him.

Kera allowed a few seconds to slip away. She might have taken a longer moment to weigh what to do next—interview the artist? Keep an eye on Erica?—but she already knew. She had to follow them. As she struggled to squeeze through the bodies, she caught a glimpse of Bolívar's beanie just before he and Canyon disappeared through the doorway. She reached the top of the stairs and stopped, her head cocked as she listened. Nothing. Just the din from the party downstairs, underscored by the soft punches of the bass line. Out of the basement, the comparative silence made her alert. With her eyes still

adjusting to the darkness, she felt her way around the decommissioned taxis and pushed through the aluminum door.

The West Side Highway hummed a half block away. The bike was
still locked to the fence at the building's corner. The pale fluorescent
light buzzed overhead.

But the street was empty in either direction.

She walked a block before she pulled out her phone and checked
for a signal. The bars indicated full strength. She rang Jones to say she
was safe and sound but couldn't talk. He was irritated with her. "Did
you see my texts? You could have at least checked in to let me know
you were OK." She couldn't talk, she told him again. The streets were
too quiet. Someone might overhear their conversation if she tried to
explain everything now. She told him that she'd fill him in tomorrow.

Parker answered almost immediately when she called him. She
said she was on her way home. He didn't ask from what. The quiet
blocks creeped her out, and she stayed on the line—without telling
him why—until she'd walked several blocks east and was climbing
safely into a cab.

At home, after saying good night to Parker, she Googled Rafael
Bolívar.

· · · · ·

J. D. Jones was furious with Kera. *She'd fill him in tomorrow?* What
she should have done was come in right away, tonight, and explain to
him what had happened. Then they could file the case notes together.
What she should have done was not go into that building in the first
place.

After a few minutes fuming by himself in the Control Room,
though, Jones realized that none of that was why he was angry with
Kera. In fact, he was angrier with himself. The feeling had snuck
up on him suddenly while he waited to get word from her after
she'd disappeared into the building and slipped out of contact. The

minutes had passed. Then an hour. And all he could do was sit there in front of his screens, worrying. The problem was what he was worrying about. He should have been worrying about whether her cover had been blown, or whether the information she brought out of that building could be trusted, or whether *she* could still be trusted after pulling such a hasty move. But as each minute went by, he worried only about her.

Instead of logging out and going home, he sat at his workstation and thought about how dangerous this feeling was. He was too self-aware not to contemplate it, but contemplating it seemed to lend it credibility. And that threatened to spoil the cut-and-dry professionalism he brought to his work.

He thought briefly of Annie, his ex-wife. It seemed to be the only reference point. He had loved her, whatever that word had meant to him then. But in the three years that spanned from date number one to divorce, he was never sure that he'd truly understood her. He knew for certain that he had never let her understand him. In a marriage emotional delinquency like that signaled a character flaw. That's how it must have looked to everyone else, anyway. He was just a computer nerd whose paycheck came from installing software that he would have been able to crack in under a minute. When he wasn't at work, he spent hours at his home computer. That had been where he was most productive. But no one, including his wife, ever cared about that. Not once, as he'd struggled through high school and menial computer jobs, had a teacher or colleague ever suggested that there were important, meaningful careers for someone with his talents.

At his job now, the ability to isolate himself and avoid close personal connections almost seemed noble. It was a sacrifice he made in order to serve his country. And that had been why he'd taken this job, hadn't it? To sacrifice and to serve. To do something that would have made his brother proud. The job with Hawk was, for the first time in his life, something that Jones recognized as having real meaning. It had been both a higher calling and a refuge. And it kept his personal life simple.

Until Kera Mersal had walked into the Control Room.

Watching her now, Jones noticed that Kera had called her fiancé immediately after she'd gotten off the phone with him. Jones stayed at his workstation until he saw on HawkEye that Kera was safely home. Then he left, hating himself for wondering whether Kera and Parker's relationship would prove to be as impossible as his own marriage had been.

SIXTEEN

"Where have you been?" Gabby wanted to know the next morning when Kera appeared in the conference room thirty minutes late. Jones, who was slumped in a chair across from her, looked up when Kera entered. As usual, his eyes did all of the talking; he'd been worried about her. Once he saw that she was OK, he looked away in anger.

"At an auto body shop on the West Side Highway," Kera said.

"You drive a car in the city?" Gabby said.

"No. It was—I was there last night. I wanted to go back and check it out."

"And?"

"I don't know what to make of it. Today it's—it's like it's just an auto body shop. The basement is full of tires and car parts."

Gabby gave her an odd look, and Kera realized that what she'd said wasn't as strange as her tone implied.

"Last night everything was different," Kera said softly. "It was completely transformed."

"I see," Gabby said, though it did not sound like she did. She looked down at the screen of her tablet. "I saw your report here, and I have to say it doesn't make much sense to me. You were at this auto body shop . . . for an art show?"

The three of them were seated around one end of the long table. Gabby was at the head seat, between Kera and Jones. A pop-up flat screen at the center of the table displayed its default image, the *Global Report*'s home page. Kera kept staring at the small type under the masthead.

THE GLOBAL REPORT
THE DIGITAL NEWS ORGANIZATION THAT CURATES
AN INSIGHTFUL BLEND OF THE WORLD'S BEST
ORIGINAL AND AGGREGATED NEWS STORIES.

"I'm sorry. What?" Kera said.

"It was an art show? This thing last night?"

Kera nodded. Gabby clearly had not read her report.

"What exactly were you doing there?"

"I was following Charlie Canyon and Erica Foster, a bartender who works at the Empire Hotel."

"Jesus Christ," Gabby said. Jones said nothing. "You followed them in?"

Kera nodded. "I made a judgment call."

"You made the wrong call. Where were you during all this?" she said to Jones.

"The Control Room."

"Where you both should have been. Did you advise her to go into that building?"

Kera didn't look at Jones. She didn't want to see him cover for her—or betray her. "No. I told her to get out of there."

Gabby turned back to Kera. "And you didn't listen, placing yourself in danger and the investigation at risk. I specifically said no tails. Digital surveillance only."

"There's a blind spot," Kera said.

"A what?"

"There are about twelve blocks on the west side where we don't have video surveillance," Jones said.

"A blind spot," Gabby muttered, as though frustrated that this couldn't be blamed on Jones and Kera.

The mention of the blind spot reminded Kera of how she couldn't get a signal on her smartphone or tablet while she'd been in the basement during the party. This morning, though, when she went back and was given a brief tour by the confused manager, the signal had been strong. She knew this because she'd snapped a few photos and they'd uploaded immediately to HawkEye over the network.

"There was no way to see what they were doing in there without following them," Kera said.

"Who's 'they'? Who was at this gathering?" Gabby said to Kera, who was distracted. "Kera?"

"Yeah?"

"How big was this party?"

Kera shrugged. "Fifty people, maybe more."

"Let me guess. None of our missing subjects were there?"

Kera shook her head. "No. But there were a few interesting sightings. Rafael Bolívar, the media mogul and tabloid sensation—"

"Hold on. Rafael Bolívar was there? At this basement party?"

Kera looked up. That this, of all things, should capture Gabby's attention was peculiar. She nodded. "He was. So was Natalie Smith."

"Who is she?"

"A filmmaker. That's an ad right there for her new documentary." Kera pointed out the window at the giant *America* billboard across Times Square. She added, almost to herself, "Canyon said the studio is planning to drop the film. I think I left that out of my report."

"Wait, you *spoke* to him?"

"He spoke to me."

"How do you explain your decision to fraternize with a person of interest in a classified case?"

"I told you. I made a judgment call. It was an opportunity to see what our surveillance network can't."

"Maybe on your second date, he'll tell you where all the bodies are. You're bordering dangerously on operational malpractice. Both of you. I want another briefing tomorrow morning. You have twenty-four hours to learn something that impresses me about this case."

Gabby pushed back to stand, plucked her tablet from the table, and set off toward the hallway. Her movements were a little too exaggerated, Kera thought, almost as if she were enjoying this.

"Did you know that ONE hired seven people from the NSA this week?" Kera said to her, still looking out the window. She heard Gabby stop in the threshold. In her periphery, Kera saw Jones lift his eyebrows.

Since she'd been called to Rowena Pete's town house, promoted to agent, and then assigned to the ATLANTIS case, Kera had nearly forgotten about ONE and the twelve Wall Street quants they'd hired. But her computer hadn't. In preparation for the meeting with Travis Bradley, she'd programmed the computer to run an automatic, daily analysis of news stories and other indicators linked to ONE, looking for patterns or new behavior. It was an entirely routine practice. The new alert had hit her in-box overnight. Two NSA data analysts and five cybersecurity experts had jumped ship to ONE. "That whistle-blower you sent me to meet with last month was right. It looks like the ONE case is heating up."

"There is no ONE case," Gabby said, glaring at her. "And until you locate these people, you don't have the luxury of thinking about anything else—not ONE, not what you want for lunch, not whether you need to go to the ladies' room, nothing."

Kera acknowledged this with a nod, but she didn't turn to look at Gabby. A few seconds later, she heard the deputy director's heels clapping down the hallway away from them.

"Are you all right?" Jones asked.

"Yeah," she said softly. "I didn't sleep much last night."

"What was that thing about ONE?"

"Just something she had me look into before all this. I thought it was nothing. Now I'm not so sure." Kera exhaled heavily, feeling suddenly exhausted. "What?" For a moment, Jones looked as though he'd been about to say something, but then he glanced at the open door and seemed to think better of it.

"See you back in the Control Room?" he said.

Kera nodded. She'd spent most of the last twenty-four hours either in the Control Room or out tailing Charlie Canyon. She hadn't been in her office since before lunch the previous day. She went there now and stood at her desk, studying the four note cards on the wall, each displaying the name, age, occupation, and alleged fate of the missing people. Meeting Canyon had not helped in the way she thought it might. He was different from what she'd expected. And now the case felt even murkier to her than it had before. She couldn't tell if she was overthinking it or not using her imagination enough. If she were back at the agency, she'd go to Lionel, and he'd help her talk it through. But here, she was on her own. Gabby was no mentor; the only communication Gabby had with her was to give her deadlines.

Kera switched on her laptop. The photo she'd taken in the bathroom stall at the party had synched up with the others. She looked at the photos, four of them now, like echoes of each other across the city: *Have you figured it out yet?* She tapped the screen and the photos disappeared. They were a distraction. This case was booby-trapped with distractions—the basement party, the artist known as It, maybe even Canyon. She made herself read each note card again, straining to see a pattern she hadn't noticed before.

When she was done, she sat at her desk and looked out the window. It was that brief time of day when the midday sun was high and bright enough to diminish the flashy advertisements that walled Times Square. It was only a matter of time, she thought, before advertisers found a way to block out the sun and give their brand-buzzing wattage a round-the-clock advantage. She panned across the commercial thicket and then up to its apex, finding the ONE billboard. The population clock was difficult to read under the sun's glare, but she could see the digits clearly enough to understand that the number was getting larger and larger. More potential consumers coming into the world every second.

Lowering her gaze, Kera's eyes settled on the *America* billboard and she thought of Canyon's comment about the film—that the studio would pull it from theaters. It had struck her then as an odd comment for him to make to her, and she hadn't been able to shake the feeling that he'd been trying to tell her something. Or maybe she was reading too much into nothing, and this was just another distraction. The *America* billboard was still prominently displayed over Times Square. Clearly, the studio was charging full speed toward the film's release.

The studio. Even as she spun toward her computer to check, she knew that the studio distributing *America* would be owned by ONE. The search engine confirmed this for her a few seconds later. But so what? ONE owned at least a third of all major films. It wasn't even a coincidence. It meant nothing.

· · · · ·

The Fredericksburg High School yearbooks were in a package outside her front door when she got home that evening. She'd ordered three of them—1996, 1998, and 2000—so that she'd have enough material to work with over the range of years she estimated Jones could have been in high school.

Taking advantage of the fact that Parker wasn't home yet, she sat on the couch with the yearbooks and flipped directly to the index pages. There were listings for students named "Jones," but after looking at the corresponding photos, she eliminated these as possible matches—or even relatives—of the man she knew to be J. D. Jones. With this obvious tactic out of the way, she grabbed the 2000 book and began flipping through each page, looking for a familiar face among the male students.

She did her first double take when she got to the sophomores. There was a picture of three male students, two of them wearing football jerseys, posing in the aisle of a bus. The luggage racks above them were stuffed full of sports bags. Kera stared at the face of one of the boys wearing a jersey. The dark eyes, the shape of the nose— perhaps it approximated a resemblance, but was it anything more than that? Nearly halfway through the thick volume, she'd already studied hundreds of faces and began to wonder if her eyes were playing tricks, seeing what she wanted them to see. The caption said the student's name was Sean Carr. She made a note of it on her tablet, but kept searching.

She finally found him among the juniors. He was not in any of the photographs depicting members of sports teams or other extracurricular groups, but there he was near the end of the pages that featured rows and rows of head shots. She had no doubt that it was Jones. The held-back smile, the dark-brown hair that encroached upon his face; this was the teenage version of the man she knew. Under the picture was the name James Carr.

She glared at the name, surprised to find that the rush she'd expected to feel at this breakthrough was offset almost entirely by the confirmation that Jones had indeed kept the most basic thing from her: his name. Given their line of work, this was a small, impersonal betrayal. But a betrayal nonetheless.

So be it, she told herself. Now she had a name. It was time to find out who James Carr was.

SEVENTEEN

When Kera returned from a late lunch the next day, Jones was down in the pit, where a hushed debate was in progress between a group of analysts standing over their monitors. They were as she'd seen them on her first day in the Control Room, gazing up at a giant map that filled the big screen. Their faces shifted in unison as a dot on the screen jumped in short pings from one location on the map to the next.

Kera walked to her workstation as quickly as she could without drawing attention to herself. Once she was logged in, she swiped aside the ATLANTIS case files she'd been working on and pulled up a database that she'd accessed only once during her time at Hawk. On that occasion she'd run a search for her own name, curious to see what information was available about her background. Since the appointment of a director of national intelligence following the September 11 terror attacks, the US intelligence community had been forced to improve interagency communication and cooperation. One of those improvements had been the creation of this massive, classified database that contained the employment records of people working in each of the seventeen US intelligence agencies. Kera knew from her previous search that her security clearance did not grant her unrestricted access to individual files. But a search here was worth a shot. It was a hell of a lot better than Googling the name "James David Carr."

After she entered an additional set of security codes, she opened a new query field and typed in Jones's real, full name. She glanced up as she tapped the search button to see that Jones was coming up the stairs out of the pit. Her first thought was to abort the search and try again the next time he was away from his workstation. But when would that be? The decision was made for her when she turned back to the screen and saw that the results had already displayed. There was a hit. James David Carr had an employment file with the NSA. She tapped on the link, fighting an urge to look up at Jones, who she could see approaching out of the corner of her eye. She still had a few seconds before the screen she was looking at would be visible to him.

The file for James David Carr was marked RESTRICTED. The only information that displayed was the dates of his employment. He'd been with the NSA from late 2001 to early 2007. Kera's eyes tripped up on the word beside the latter date. TERMINATED, it said. Kera committed the information to memory, and then with two swift taps, she was back to studying her ATLANTIS case files.

"What's that all about?" she asked Jones, who had arrived at his console but did not sit down. He had paused to study the big screen above the pit.

"The Gnos.is case," he said.

"There's still a Gnos.is case? I thought we'd shuttered that."

"It's back. The director himself is overseeing it."

"Is there new intel? A threat?"

"Not that I know of. They just want to ID whoever's behind the site. Those are our orders."

"How's that coming?"

"It's not. As we discovered the first time around, whoever is running Gnos.is doesn't want to be found." He nodded at the map on the big screen. "They've figured out a way to bounce the site's host server around faster than we can trace it."

Jones finally sat down. He had not looked at her screens once. After a few moments, Kera returned to her work, though not without that word—TERMINATED—scrolling through the back of her mind. So Jones had worked at the nation's electronic spying agency. And then he'd been fired. And then he'd changed his name. And though he hadn't explicitly lied to her about any of that, he'd certainly left it out of their conversations. But why? Was he embarrassed? Was he just being private? Or was he trying to hide something else?

To push that distraction aside, she forced herself to return to her work. Each day, one of her routine tasks was to check the overnight news bulletins that the computer had flagged for her. An algorithm used patterns from her recent computer activity to prioritize the alerts. This was how she'd learned about ONE's hiring of NSA technicians. Today there were about two-dozen hits—a pretty average day. Usually, she read through them first thing in the morning, but the day had gotten away from her. She tapped the link to the first alert, which mentioned Rowena Pete. It turned out to be nothing new, just a follow-up news report about mourning fans growing restless for information. She returned to the list, scanning it without optimism.

Her eyes stopped on a headline that mentioned Rafael Bolívar. She tapped the link. The article amounted to little more than a gossip column about "Rafa's" $8 million apartment overlooking Central Park. It described Bolívar as "the extraordinarily successful businessman (and the city's most eligible bachelor) who has guided the Alegría media empire out of obscurity and established one of the fastest-growing television networks on the air." Beside the column was a picture of Bolívar coming out of a SoHo restaurant with a young Russian model on his arm. He was wearing dark glasses. Kera couldn't see his eyes.

She skimmed over the other bulletins, her brain quickly categorizing them as either irrelevant or old news. Then she got to one that made her say aloud, "No."

Jones glanced up at her.

She clicked the link, and her eyes tore through the copy, struggling to process whether she'd interpreted the headline correctly. Was it possible? The article was accompanied by several images of colorful paintings.

"That little shit."

"What?" Jones said.

"The paintings at that basement party. They were stolen." She picked up the phone. "Manhattan, please. AM + Toppe."

"You're calling him," Jones said, knowing there was nothing he could do about it.

"Charlie Canyon, please."

"May I ask who's calling?" said the secretary who answered.

"It's—" Kera hesitated. She hadn't given Canyon her name at the party. "I'm a journalist. We spoke the other night about an artist who I believe is one of Mr. Canyon's clients."

She thought the woman paused, as if confused, but then hold music came over the line. The next voice Kera heard, thirty seconds later, was Canyon's.

"You work slow, Ms. Mersal."

Kera bit her lower lip. She hadn't been sure how well Canyon would remember her. She didn't think it was a good sign that he not only knew it was her on the phone, but had figured out her name.

"What's going on?" she said.

"Two ad pitches, prepping a commercial shoot. Some days I feel like I'm just making a living. Others I make a killing."

"Cut the bullshit. You know what I'm talking about. Would you like me to read it to you? 'Art thieves strike Chelsea gallery. Eight oil-on-canvas paintings by the painter Marybelle Pickett have disappeared from the Waterford Gallery, including a ten-by-ten-foot piece known as "Vibrant Night" done in black and white.'" Kera remembered seeing the painting at the basement party.

"I think that one is my favorite," Canyon said.

"The paintings were *stolen*. They went missing after hours last Thursday. *Thursday*, Charlie. Your party was Friday."

"Mm-hmm," Canyon said, which infuriated her.

"You stole them. Why?"

"I didn't. I helped the artist remove them from a gallery that was doing nothing to get them any attention."

"That isn't the way the gallery sees it. Or the police. We're talking about ten thousand dollars' worth of art."

"Ten thousand? Is that all they say it is? It's going to be worth ten times that when this is over."

"When what is over?"

"Why did you call me and not the police?" Canyon said.

"How do you know I haven't?"

"The bluffing routine is unbecoming. Why don't we level with each other?"

"Excuse me?"

"Kera Mersal. Born June 1984, exact day unknown. Adopted, raised in Seattle. Graduated Dartmouth 2007, moved to DC, allegedly to work at ComPlex Technologies, which, it turns out, is an empty office in Alexandria. Ms. Mersal then leaves abruptly to become a journalist at the *Global Report*, which has as venerable a reputation in journalism as you do. Which is to say that *TGR* did not even exist until two weeks before you were hired. Does that sound right?"

"That's right. We're a start-up, and we're doing pretty well for ourselves." Kera glanced at Jones through the gaps between their workstations. If he was paying any attention to her conversation, he wasn't letting on.

"Pretty well? You have the smallest newsroom I've ever heard of."

"Lean. That's how we like to think of it."

"And not a single scoop in two years that's made national news. Only twenty thousand hits a day. No paid subscribers and ad revenue that couldn't outfit a Little League team. I'm sure your investors are thrilled."

"We'll be fine."

"I wonder, though, about those investors. What are they getting out of it? It looks almost as if the mission of the *Global Report* is to keep as low a profile as possible."

She had to get off the phone. She was on the secure line at her workstation, and her conversations almost certainly were recorded and stored by Hawk's internal security. That had never concerned her before. But if Gabby—or Jones, for that matter—thought her cover had been blown by someone on the outside, she could be expelled. Disavowed.

"I'm sure your talents at redirecting a story make you good at your job," she said. "But I'm pretty good at mine too. I called to get your comment on the stolen paintings, and I'm not falling for your spin routine."

"Get your pen ready," Canyon said. "This is my comment: 'Ms. Pickett is a talented and important young artist. As you can imagine, she's quite distressed about the theft of her paintings. We hope they will be recovered and returned to the gallery in short time and in perfect condition.'"

"You're kidding. That quote will look laughable in an article that reports extensively on how you showed the paintings at a private, star-studded event the day after they were stolen."

"It would. But you won't publish that. It would ruin your chance to get the story you really want."

He was taunting her, and it made her face flush. She could feel it like sunburn on her cheeks and forehead. She cupped her free hand against the side of her face so that Jones wouldn't notice.

"You're arrogant, Charlie. And that's just the start of your problems. Thank you for your time."

She hung up and took a deep breath. Then she thought, *What am I doing?*

EIGHTEEN

A day later and no break in the case. A day closer to their next meeting with Branagh. To ward off her feelings of helplessness, Kera paid another visit to the auto body shop, whose owner still insisted he'd never heard of Charlie Canyon and that no art show had taken place in the basement of his garage.

Heading back uptown, Kera paused in front of a newsstand on her slow trudge down the subway platform. She didn't touch any of the periodicals, just stared at them, her eyes going blurry at the rows of headlines. From the gossip mags to the newspapers, they all professed to know something about the world, as if the world were something that could be known in such declarative truths.

The day had shaken her more than she wanted to acknowledge. To settle her nerves, she kept telling herself that this was a test. The rapid promotion, the ATLANTIS case. Gabby was testing her—testing her commitment, her resourcefulness, her instincts. The solution was to solve the case. Complete the mission: find the missing people, alive or dead, and figure out what happened to them. That was what she was expected to do. After this initiation she'd be reassigned to more important cases, cases that fell within her expertise and within Hawk's charter as it had originally been laid out to her.

There was also the matter of Jones and how she should interpret the fact that he'd withheld his NSA history from her. Of course, she hadn't volunteered much about where she'd come from either, but with Jones, the red flags seemed to be accumulating. Her caution had only deepened after other searches for "James David Carr" on the Internet and in the obvious public databases turned up no consistent record of him.

Stumped on where else to look, she'd turned her attention to Jones's brother, Sean, who had been the first familiar face she'd come across in the yearbooks. Her research efforts there proved much more fruitful. Sean Carr had been an accomplished high school football player and track champion, but he'd turned down scholarship offers and had instead enlisted in the army. After multiple deployments to Afghanistan, he was discharged and wound up back in Kabul working for a West Virginia–based private security contractor. The records stopped abruptly after that, and those that did exist all listed Sean Carr as deceased. She'd come across a sole reference to a self-inflicted gunshot wound, but otherwise, she found no detail about the circumstances of the incident that had ended his life. The date of death, she noted without assigning any specific significance to the thought, had come just three weeks before Jones had been terminated from the NSA.

A burst of warm air preceded the screeching arrival of a train on the opposite track and blew her hair across her face. The cars made their exchange of passengers and accelerated noisily into the dark uptown tunnel. Kera understood that this was how the city stayed alive. Just like in It's Tribeca mural. Train after train, watt after flickering watt, flush after flush, twenty-four hours a day. Not so much a triumphant pursuit of anything worth pursuing as a relentless grind.

When Kera returned to the Hawk building, it was a gloomy late afternoon. From her office window, the flickering commerce of Times Square seemed forced and depressing, like an amusement park trying to beckon tourists on a rainy day. She'd come here with a cup of coffee, delaying the inevitability of another long evening in the Control Room double-checking old leads that went cold no matter which trail she followed them down.

Outside, across Times Square, workers erected flights of scaffolding over the sidewalk. She watched them drag metal pipes up through the structure and lock them into place, the whole operation telescoping up the side of the building eight feet at a time. She envied the skeletal simplicity of their work, the way each piece fit into its proper place, reinforcing the others. If only her investigation could come together with some of that orderly logic.

As always, the population clock on the ONE billboard dominated her view, its number increasing at twice the pace of a heartbeat, reminding her that she was one of 7,375,077,224 humans on the planet. The word "ONE," swooping across the company's futuristic logo, beamed proudly over the clutter of competing brands. Kera struggled to articulate what irritated her about the clock. Maybe it was the device's inorganic precision. It was impossible that the world's net population rose so consistently. Twins, even triplets, were born. Busloads of people died at once. These things made a simple, steady count impossible. The ad misstated the neatness of the world, and in that way, it was no different than any other ad.

She lowered her gaze. The assembly of the scaffolding was complete, and the construction workers were now elevated like Jack on his beanstalk into the commercial stratosphere. She inhaled sharply when she realized what they were doing. The platform had risen to even with the top of the *America* billboard, and now the workers crawled like spiders across its broad face. She knew what was about to happen, and still she winced when she saw the first corner of the ad sag away like old wallpaper. The announced release date, visible below Natalie Smith's name, was still five days away. Kera turned to her computer and ran a search. Sure enough, dozens of news headlines announced that the studio, a subsidiary of ONE, had bowed to pressure from right-wing religious groups and had decided to pull the film from the market.

As she watched the workers roll away the decommissioned ad, she fumed silently, cursing Charlie Canyon. Finally, she got up and went to the Control Room to find out where he was spending his evening.

NINETEEN

The warehouse was easy to spot. White light poured from two open loading doors, spilling onto the quiet street. A gaff truck backed up to the dock was being watched over by a bored PA wearing a headset and playing with his smartphone. He looked up at Kera, mildly curious as she stepped past him, but then he only nodded hello before returning to his phone. On her approach she'd counted three cameras with coverage of the street and sidewalks along the block. She spotted a fourth now, this one trained on the loading dock from a perch twelve feet up the building's exterior wall. She turned her face away from the camera as she passed beneath it and slipped into the warehouse.

For all the powerful lights, the shoot was a lean operation. A single camera sat on a cart at the center of the vast room, aimed at the minimalistic set. In the foreground a mattress bed lay on the floor beside a standing lamp. Next to these was a turntable. Behind the turntable, and suspended only a foot or two off the ground, was a massive, curving rack of stadium speakers, the kind she'd only seen hanging from the rafters at major concerts. Up close the speakers threw off the whole scale of the set. Behind them the background was cluttered with large, graffiti-tainted objects made of concrete and steel.

She didn't see Canyon, but no one seemed suspicious of her presence, so she stayed out of the way and waited for him to appear. She watched a lighting crew at work on a platform high up the warehouse wall. Using lights and reflectors, they created white and blue shafts that added texture to the scene below. Two men and a woman approached the camera cart and stood behind it, fine-tuning the frame on a large monitor. A girl, her head clasped in a headset, began calling for people to find their places.

Charlie Canyon came through a doorway with two men, one shirtless in jeans, the other dressed in a casual jacket. The half-nude actor strolled onto the set, his bare torso glistening in the shafts of light as if he'd been sweating. He stood at the turntable and put large headphones around his neck. A woman ran up to him and adjusted his jeans, pulling down the waist so that the denim seemed to hang there, precariously at the mercy of the contours of his hips. He'd looked a little thin when he walked out, Kera thought, but in the stage lights, which threw shadows that carved out the muscles across his abdomen, chest, and shoulders, he looked like the live-action version of a magazine cover. Colorful concert lights began flashing and dance music boomed from a speaker system off camera. A half-dozen figures wielding cans of spray paint and wearing all black appeared in the background and went to work defacing things.

Someone called "rolling" and the busy crew settled. Canyon and the man in the jacket stood off to the side watching. The woman behind the monitor yelled "action" and the actor's body moved, feeling the beat. As the scene progressed, the graffiti artists advanced from background to foreground. They painted lines across the speakers and the bed and then, as the camera pushed in, across the actor's body.

Mesmerized by the production, it was a minute, maybe two, before Kera looked over again at Canyon. When she did her breath caught. He was staring at her, a sly grin playing at the corners of his mouth.

The director ended the take and barked a few crisp instructions at the crew, who began to set up the shot from a different angle. Kera waited until Canyon was alone before she crossed the room to him.

"You're less predictable than I thought," he said, smiling.

"It wasn't safe to talk on the phone. Do you have a second?" she started to say, but Canyon put a hand on her upper arm to turn her toward the actor, who had come up behind them.

"Kera, this is Daryl Walker, my star client."

"Hi. That was . . . what *is* all this?" she said, indicating the set.

"We're shooting a commercial," Canyon said.

Kera looked at Daryl Walker. He had a sturdy, stubbled jawline and walnut hair. If anything, it was his eyes, marbled green and brewing with a mix of earnestness and confidence, that elevated him from the merely attractive. She meant to direct the question to his face, but when she spoke her eyes had lowered to his abdomen. "For what?"

"Fashion. Jeans," Walker said, giving himself a playful pat on the ass. He walked away and disappeared through the door where she'd seen him enter.

"The designer is over there. He goes by X." Canyon pointed at the man in the jacket.

"That's his name? X?"

"That's his brand. They are one and the same."

Kera smiled politely. "I'm sorry to interrupt you here. I don't think this will take long. I only have a few questions."

"Have you figured it out yet?" he said.

She had rehearsed a few questions she wanted to ask him first, but his words threw her. "Wait. Why did you say that—that phrase?"

He shrugged, revealing a sly grin. "It's just a saying. I think it's growing on me."

"It doesn't make any sense."

"Lighten up," he said and then changed the subject. "Did you mean that the phone wasn't safe for you or for me?" he asked.

"I think speaking in person is better for both of us. How did you know about *America*? That the studio would pull out at the last minute?"

"Oh, that. When you see the film, you'll understand."

"I guess now I won't get that chance," she said.

He shrugged. "I wouldn't be so sure. Natalie Smith isn't the kind of woman who backs down from a fight. That stubbornness is both a strength and a weakness when it comes to her career."

Kera didn't know what he meant by that, and she was mildly curious, but she hadn't come here to talk about Natalie Smith. She pulled her tablet from her shoulder bag and turned it on, angling the screen so that Canyon could see. She began swiping through the head shots. "I don't know how to preface this. I assume these people are familiar to you?" Canyon stared at the screen. For the first time, Kera felt the sensation of having the upper hand on him. "Charlie?"

"Yeah. They look familiar."

"Friends of yours?"

"Acquaintances." He touched her arm and guided her underneath a flight of metal stairs that led to a loft overlooking the room. Apparently, he didn't want anyone overhearing this conversation.

"Acquaintances? Nothing more than that?" she said. He looked at her, sizing her up, but did not respond. "Any idea where they are?"

He shook his head. "I don't think I can help you."

"I think you can. You're aware that these people are missing? They vanished."

"I'm aware of that, yes."

"And I'm aware that you met with them—*all* four of them—in the months before they disappeared. In fact, you were the only person to meet with all of them. And now they're gone."

"I don't understand. Are you accusing me of something?"

"Not necessarily. But now that I know you're capable of grand art theft, it occurs to me to ask."

"That wasn't theft."

"It was. But that isn't the point. Forget the paintings. I'm asking you a simple question: Where did these people go?"

"Who's asking?"

"I am."

She saw his eyes lighten with interest. "Oh? Has this become personal for you?" he said.

"Four people are missing, people who you knew. Shouldn't you care a little more about that?"

"You don't know a thing about what I care about."

This was truer than Kera was willing to admit. She'd watched Canyon virtually around the clock for two weeks, and the man was still a complete mystery to her.

The director called out to Canyon from across the warehouse floor. Kera thought Canyon might hold up a hand to indicate he needed a minute so that they could finish their conversation, but he just shrugged and smiled and said he needed to get back to work.

"What do you know about It?" Kera called after him. Canyon turned and flashed her an amused look, as if they'd been playing a card game with quarters and she'd just dropped a few twenties into the pot.

"What?" he said.

"The artist they call It. What do you know about that?"

Canyon smiled. "You have an interesting story on your hands. I look forward to reading it." And then he walked off.

"Hey, Charlie," she called after him. He stopped and turned. "I'm going to find those people. Things will be easier for you if you help me."

"We'll see."

She watched him walk toward the director as a graffiti-coated Daryl Walker, now wearing only underwear, emerged flanked by the artists with their spray cans. Kera started across the room. She wanted to leave before they called rolling again.

She got as far as the loading dock when a movement from the darkness of the sidewalk caught her eye. Her feet stopped beneath her. The man had his hands in his pockets. His features clarified gradually as he approached and hopped up onto the loading dock in one fluid, athletic leap. A thought formed sharp in Kera's mind and dragged out over the next few moments like an echo: *here is Rafael Bolívar.*

Their eye contact was brief, but she was certain she had not imagined it. In an instant he was past her, and she could no longer see his face. She watched him stride into the warehouse and then, knowing he would not look back, she turned for the street.

TWENTY

"Two kilo alfa, you are clear for takeoff."

The Hawker 900XP with four souls on board accelerated obediently down runway nineteen and tipped upward, nudging into the clear morning sky.

"Two kilo alfa, turn east heading zero eight five. You're free and clear climbing to twenty-two thousand feet."

"Copy that, Teterboro. Two kilo alfa is free and clear."

The continent of North America sank from view until it was a flat, distant surface shooting west. When the aircraft banked east, the sight that loomed through the cockpit window was one of nature's most startling boundaries—not between earth and sky, but between land and sea. The abrupt, brown-to-blue exchange formed a continuous seam along the edge of the continent, like two puzzle pieces that interlocked perfectly even though they'd come from different puzzles. Dwarfed by these tectonic features, the tiny fuselage glided across the seam eighteen thousand feet above the coast, and then there was only the Atlantic, ahead and below.

The flight data recorder, once it was recovered by the NTSB, clearly illustrated the sudden pitch, led by the nose, that occurred seven minutes later, and the subsequent, irrevocable dive. No further audio communication from the crew was recorded. The final words had already been spoken: free and clear.

Very soon after the steep dive, the remaining instruments went quiet, and then there was only the Atlantic, in every direction.

TWENTY-ONE

Kera was in the shower, her face taking the full force of the stream, when she heard Parker enter the bathroom and pull back the curtain. She finished rinsing her hair before she opened her eyes. Parker was standing before her, naked and smiling. He always smiled when he was naked. It had been one of the most comforting things about him when they started living together. In those first few months, when they made love, or didn't, even as they just slept beside one another, he was never ashamed of his body or hers. Before and after sex, he would pad naked through the apartment, to the toilet, to get her a glass of water, always with an uncontainable smile on his face. It was a nervous, happy, vulnerable smile, one that made her feel less self-conscious.

He stepped into the shower and embraced her.

"What are you doing?" she said.

"Call in sick."

The way she smiled reflected the impossibility of that, but not in a way that rejected him. She put her hand on the back of his neck and pulled his mouth to hers. They kissed in the downpour until he shut off the water and led her, both of them dripping, back into the bedroom. They fell onto the bed. *I love you*, he whispered in her ear when his hips brought him as close as he could be to her. *I'll love you forever.*

Afterward, they lay for several minutes, their thoughts drifting apart in the silence. The night before, after speaking to Charlie Canyon at the commercial shoot, Kera had gone back to the office. It was late by then, late enough that even Jones wasn't there. The time stamp on her access record would show that she was in the Control Room from 2335 hours to just before midnight. She had never initiated a surveillance order in HawkEye, but she'd seen Jones do it for Charlie Canyon.

She hadn't been after information about either Jones or Canyon. When she keyed the final stroke, there was an odd beat of stillness on-screen, as if to signal that a point of no return had been eclipsed. In fact, it was nothing as philosophical as that. It was simply a staggering amount of data that the computer was processing. That's what it was: a stagger. The system staggered briefly under the computational weight of her inquiry, and then there it was. The HawkEye surveillance map for Rafael Bolívar.

She lay lazily in bed now, listening to the city outside the window. The city was awake and sunny. It was out of character for her to postpone the start of the day like this. She knew she had to get up. When she came out of the bathroom after a second shower, Parker was in bed with his tablet in his lap.

"ONE announced the acquisition of another company this morning," he said.

"What's that, three this month?"

"Something like that. Their corporate mission is to destroy as many souls as possible."

"Only the souls of the willing," she said.

"Come on. Give people some credit."

"ONE produces the kind of crap they produce not because they're evil, but because it works."

"You're defending them. Are you feeling well? Maybe you should call in sick after all."

She smiled. She was enjoying herself. "I'm not defending anyone. Just pointing out that the way people spend their free time and money is a choice."

"Well, if ONE gets their way, there won't be very many choices left."

"What kind of company did they acquire?" Kera asked, getting dressed.

"It's a PR agency. I've never heard of them. AM + Toppe."

Her face whipped toward him.

"What?" he said.

"Nothing. I just—I know someone who works there." She walked from the bedroom to the kitchen table where she'd left her phone, but then decided that it was too risky to call Canyon with Parker in the next room. She'd try him on her way to work.

"What are you doing?" Parker said in boxer shorts from the doorway of the bedroom.

"Is it possible we don't have any coffee in the apartment?" she said. She was standing before the open cupboard, staring hopelessly at cans of tomatoes and beans and boxes of sugar, macaroni, and baking powder.

"I'll go get some," he said.

"Don't be ridiculous."

"Really, I can run down to Starbucks. Be back in under ten minutes."

"Parker," she said, but he had already disappeared back into the bedroom. "I can wait till I get to work," she called after him. "I have to leave now, anyway."

She opened the freezer. Nothing there but a blast of cool air. She shivered, feeling baffled and irritated by the way Parker attended to her. It wasn't just his insistence on this particular coffee errand, but the way he was in a more general sense—so reliable, so perfect. Had she given some indication that she expected this sort of treatment? She had not. And it made her more aware of the fact that she rarely reciprocated his displays of thoughtful behavior. She wondered briefly, before closing the freezer door and turning to go, whether this inequity had begun to forge a widening gulf between them, one that would only grow more challenging to bridge.

·   ·   ·   ·   ·

She dialed Charlie Canyon's extension from the street as she walked to the subway, expecting to leave a message with his secretary. He snapped up the phone himself on the second ring.

"Can you meet for a drink?" she asked.

"It's barely nine in the morning."

"After work, I mean."

"No. Not today," Canyon said. "Haven't you heard?"

"Just now. What happened?"

"Money. Power. Destruction. Same thing that happens every day in this city."

"Do you want to talk about it?"

"Some other time. This week is a wreck. Let me give you my cell."

She noticed in his voice an instability that she hadn't heard before. She hung up and was swallowed into the subway station. The stairs were like the esophagus of a creature that was eating too quickly, a morsel or two shy of choking itself. And then she was in the train, the digestive tract, a mush of humanity barreling through the bowels of the beast. The interior of the car was walled with LED screens that had been sold, fifteen seconds at a time, to the highest bidder. Ads assaulted the captive audience frantically, tempting eye-balls with humor, fear, sex, and beauty. Kera tuned out all of this, as well as the thirty-second news report—sponsored by ONE—that monopolized the screens once every five minutes. The president was on a trip to South America. The stock markets were opening up. A private plane had just crashed into the ocean off the southern tip of Long Island.

TWENTY-TWO

TWENTY-TWO

Every panel on the main wall of the Control Room flickered with images from news networks covering the crash. Workstations around the room glowed with blue-tinted light. The image on the big screen appeared to be a piece of metal floating in water. Kera spotted Gabby pacing by the pit, her phone clutched against an ear. She did not look calm.

"What's going on, Jess?" Kera said to the analyst manning the workstation closest to the door. She knew by name almost everyone who worked in the Control Room—after all, they spent more hours together in a single room than any of them spent with anyone in their personal lives. But the woman looked up from her screens only briefly to give Kera a you-know-better-than-that glance. An unspoken rule discouraged agents and analysts from inquiring about the top-secret cases their colleagues were working on. It was a courtesy Kera supported and respected. It was just that it hadn't occurred to her that what was unfolding on every major news network might be related to one of Hawk's cases.

She made her way across the Control Room and came up behind Jones.

"What's all this?"

"Plane crash," he said.

"Big plane or small plane?"

"Small plane. Corporate jet. Took off from Teterboro at 8:53 this morning carrying a pilot and three passengers. Air traffic control's last contact with the plane was at 8:58. They were in the air for another fifteen minutes. The wreckage is a few miles off Montauk. This is all according to what I can see on the FAA system."

"Botched terrorist attack?"

"It crossed my mind, sure. But it doesn't pan out. The tail number is clean. I checked with DHS, CIA, FAA, the works. No red flags."

"Can I ask the obvious question? Planes crash sometimes. Why all the commotion around here?"

"I haven't figured that out yet."

"What do you mean you haven't figured that out? What did Gabby tell you?"

"Gabby hasn't told me anything."

"But you said you ran the tail number? Who asked you to do that?"

"No one. I got curious about all the excitement. You might be interested in what I found out."

"Try me."

"The tail number is registered to the ONE Corporation," Jones said. "Guess who was on board?"

"On the plane? I wouldn't begin to know."

"Members of a band. Background Noise Pollution."

That name meant something to her. She struggled to recall why. "Background Noise Pollution," she said, sitting down at her workstation to Google it. "A band. Rough month for the music industry, huh?"

"Rough month for ONE," Jones said. "The band was signed to the same label as Rowena Pete. It's owned—"

"Owned by ONE. I know. What isn't?" Then Kera remembered where she'd heard of the band before. It was at the basement art show. The group of smokers on the stairs had been talking about Background Noise Pollution. She scanned through the search engine results on her monitor. She recognized some of their music, she realized. It was indie rock with a stripped-down sound anchored by the lead singer's sturdy, melodic voice.

"The whole band was on the plane?"

"Yes. I checked the surveillance tapes from Teterboro. All four were on the tarmac this morning."

"One of them is a pilot?"

"Apparently." There was an obvious joke about him not being a very good pilot, but neither of them made it. They were both distracted, their minds working to assemble this new data into information. Then suddenly, Jones turned back to HawkEye and began tapping and swiping at the touch screen without explanation.

Kera logged in to her own workstation and found a fan site where she learned that the band members lived—or had lived—in the East Village and occasionally played impromptu gigs in the neighborhood. They'd stopped touring recently to record a new album, which by online accounts appeared to be highly anticipated.

"Bingo," Jones said. Kera looked up. "At least two members of Background Noise Pollution visited the bar at the Empire Hotel in the past month. Guess who was there at the same time?"

Kera lifted her eyebrows. "That's no coincidence. So ONE has lost two of their top-selling musical acts in as many weeks."

"And they each had contact with Canyon," Jones said.

"It doesn't look like the band was traveling to a performance." Kera nodded at her screen. "There are no scheduled tour dates listed on their website. Why were they up there?"

Jones shrugged. "Nice day for a plane ride, I guess."

She nodded. They were both thinking the same thing. "And maybe a swim. Let me guess—no bodies have been recovered."

"Coast Guard's looking."

"You don't think they'll find anyone, do you?"

"Nope," he said. "I think we have missing persons numbers five through eight. HawkEye has already started generating maps."

Kera nodded. But something didn't make sense. "Wait. Only a handful of people know about ATLANTIS. Why is everyone else in here so interested in that plane—?"

Jones cut her off with a glance. She understood why a few moments later, when Gabby appeared behind him, her thumbs pounding away on her phone.

"Where are we with Rowena Pete?" she said, not looking up.

Kera and Jones glanced at each other. When neither of them answered, Gabby lifted her eyes. They went first to Kera.

"Still missing." Kera braced for a dressing down.

"That's all we know?" Gabby said, but her attention was too divided to land the comment with any sting. Her eyes kept drifting between her phone and the footage of the plane crash on the big screen. For a long moment, she watched an overhead shot of the wreckage. Then she said, "Christ, what next?" and walked away.

Kera sat in front of her screens thinking. She pulled up the HawkEye dossier on Rafael Bolívar, careful not to let Jones see what she was doing. She hadn't told Jones about speaking with Canyon at the commercial shoot, and she didn't know how to explain why her interest in Bolívar warranted full HawkEye surveillance. She wasn't sure there was a good explanation for that.

Bolívar had left his apartment building at 0815 hours and had gone directly to the headquarters of Alegría North America, the company of which he was chairman and CEO. She watched surveillance footage of him walking into the building. Then she watched it again. She resisted a temptation to watch it a third time and instead closed down his dossier and opened the profiles that HawkEye had started to assemble for each member of Background Noise Pollution.

Christ, what next? Gabby's words played across her mind like an echo. There was something about the incident with Background Noise Pollution that was different from the other disappearances. Before there had been improbable suicide notes and bicycles left tethered near clichéd jumping points. This, though, was more audacious. Had this been a grand finale? Or did it mark the beginning of a new trend? She pondered this as Gabby's words ricocheted through her mind.

Kera felt suddenly restless, on the verge of a breakthrough but unable to pull it into focus. She should have been poring over the HawkEye data, looking for the first lead to follow. Or should she? The computer would spit out more data than she could ever read, but what would it tell her? What she really needed to see was what was going to happen next. If she was going to do more than tally up the growing number of missing people, she needed to alter her approach. She needed to find a way to connect the incalculable variables. Charlie Canyon. Rafael Bolívar. It. ONE. There are 7,375,248,777 people in the world. Soon they will all be connected. Christ, what next?

What next?

She stood up quickly. There was a ONE artist, she realized suddenly, who was similar in quality to the missing artists, but who was still known to be perfectly alive and well. Now, with ONE's purchase of AM + Toppe, Canyon would have direct access to him. Could he be next? How had she not considered this until now, when an image of the artist's billboard in Times Square flashed across her mind? She waited until she'd slipped out of the Control Room before she broke into a run, sprinting down the hallway and through the threshold of her office, where she stopped finally, standing before the floor-to-ceiling windows overlooking Times Square. There it was. Below the domineering ONE ad, and above the place where the *America* ad had been—was a vast billboard hit by the full glare of the late-morning sun.

JW. New music from Jalen West.

TWENTY-THREE

Jalen West, international pop star, rose through the center of the ONE Corporation's Midtown Manhattan headquarters. He wore a white T-shirt, black vest, and black jeans, the cuffs rolled up and stuffed partially into the tops of silver high-top sneakers. At ground level, one of his managers had pressed the button for the forty-third floor and the elevator music changed to an R&B tune recorded by a ONE artist.

Jalen stood smiling, surrounded by the three managers and a bodyguard. He bobbed his body to the music the way most people's lungs processed air: a subtle, intimate dance that occurred without thought. The paparazzi cameras and screaming teenagers who had formed a channel between the limo and the building's glass revolving doors fell away as he savored the thrust of the elevator hoisting him further above Manhattan. His mother used to say his head was always in the clouds. It was just the way music made him feel.

The hallways and the corner executive suite on the forty-third floor were lined with photographs of musicians and recording artists and the industry executives who had profited off them throughout recent decades. The photos reminded him of home, of the hallway in his mother's house in Detroit, which was much darker and narrower than this but was lined with photographs of four generations of relatives. They were all his family in a sense, he thought, these musicians and executives and blood relatives. They all were the people who came before him to lead him to where he was today.

Now a month before his twenty-sixth birthday, Jalen had recorded two megaselling pop albums and sold out stadiums on four continents. It was for these reasons that ONE Music had been interested in Jalen West. Jalen, for his part, had expressed no interest in deserting the only label he had known and the manager who had first invested in him. He had not wanted to relinquish control of his astronomical career to a conglomerate that possessed a much more crowded list of artists. His original label had given him the opportunity to make music his life; conglomerates had other concerns, like insatiable shareholders who demanded year-over-year growth. So Jalen, through his manager, had told ONE he wasn't interested in their offer.

ONE's response was to simply acquire the entire label that controlled Jalen's contracts and absorb them into the fold. ONE already had a deep stable of music talent. They did not need to absorb another record company. But if that was the only way to get Jalen West, well, there were worse problems for a multibillion-dollar media empire to have. This one cost them only $180 million, and they expected to earn that back within the next presidential term.

Jalen found it easy to detach himself from all the fuss during the transition. He buried himself in the process of writing new music, even as the gossip sites churned out alleged details of his private life and produced photos that hinted, just enough, at their possibility. The latest rumor was that he had started dating the action film star Scott Michaels. It was true that they had met months earlier at a party, at which photos of them were taken. But by the end of the night, the actor had made such a little impression on Jalen that

Jalen had needed to see the photos online himself to be reminded of the supposed heartthrob he was supposedly sleeping with. The un-tabloid-worthy truth was that Jalen had found it impossible to hold down a boyfriend since the success of his first album. So he'd focused on his music and had emerged only recently from his writing and recording frenzy to discover that he now had three managers, a major upcoming album release, and a tour planned under the care of ONE Music's marketing division.

Flanked by this new entourage, Jalen West was escorted toward the plush corner office of the president of ONE Music.

A half-dozen people had gathered for the meeting. He shook hands with Ford Dillingham, the president of ONE Media and Entertainment, and Tom Barkley, a holdover from his previous label and the man who had discovered him, if any man can claim that about another. The other execs stepped forward one by one to greet him. It was a homogeneous, dull-looking troupe. There was one woman, not of his generation, nor even of an adjacent one. The rest were men. White men. Jalen was the only person of color in the room (the bodyguard waited outside). Not that that mattered. He was used to that now—ever since the video. After the video, life had changed for him overnight. Now, whenever his career or money—especially money—were being discussed, it was typical to be in company like this.

He shook more hands. He was pleasant and charismatic. These were not traits that had helped him on the streets of his neighborhood growing up, but they seemed to provide him with a limitless advantage now. He finished shaking hands. The only person whose face he would remember, whose name would leave an imprint in his mind, was the young marketing consultant who, during their introduction, was praised as the brains behind the rollout of his album's promotional campaign.

"This is Charlie Canyon. He's just joined us, and we think he'll be the best person to oversee your campaign. We have some innovative ideas about the promotion of the *JW* album. We're excited to get you out there."

Jalen shook hands with Charlie Canyon, and their eyes met.

The first thing Jalen had noticed when he stepped into the room, even before the stunning view that looked south down the spine of Manhattan toward the tip of Battery Park and west over the Hudson to New Jersey, was the baby grand piano in the corner. He wanted to go to it now, to slide his fingers over the ridges between the keys. The feeling came to him like a phantom itch on a limb he didn't have. With a piano, his ten fingers became eighty-eight keys, and those keys became an infinite combination of chords and notes—all of it an instant extension of himself, as accessible as the words of a first language rolling off a tongue.

"People love your story. They feel a part of you now." The head music mogul was still talking. Jalen couldn't remember the man's name. "People respond to your bravery, your courage, your faith."

"I don't believe in God." He did not say it as a confession but as a simple matter of fact, to correct a misunderstanding. The misunderstanding that most worried him was unrelated to his theological leanings. The real danger was that these people were trying to shape him. They were trying to create an image of him that would sell the music they wanted him to make. He intended to be clear that there were certain activities in which he would not take part.

The young marketing consultant looked up. The one named Charlie Canyon. Jalen wasn't sure why he noticed that. He'd stopped noticing all of the other executives. They looked and acted and wanted the same. But the young marketing consultant had sharp eyes that pinged deep with curiosity. Curiosity was sexy. Or maybe it was just rare, and rare was sexy. He wanted to write lyrics suddenly. He wanted to sit at the keyboard and put lyrics to music. The boredom this meeting inspired was excruciating. When would it end?

Ford Dillingham had smiled sourly at the God comment. To Jalen, Dillingham was no different from everyone else who assumed he was Christian and assumed this was a virtue. They permitted themselves to assume this because of Jalen's gospel music background and, of course, because of the video. And then they spoke of it in complimentary or adoring terms that he found bizarre and unbecoming. He did not believe in God. He believed in religion even less. He didn't recognize the good in devoting oneself to contrived, abstract principles about the world when all around him there were things that were real and meaningful and true. Things like music.

The men and the woman started shaking hands again, and it appeared the meeting was winding down. Tom Barkley looked over at him and, as a courtesy, or perhaps even just as a figure of speech, asked if he had any questions.

"Are we gonna talk about the music? I already have a few songs for the next album. Want me to play one for you?"

"Yes—" said Charlie Canyon, who had said nothing through the duration of the meeting.

"No, that's all right," said Dillingham, looking at his watch. "Some other time. We're about to release this album of yours. We need you to focus right now on promoting that."

"He wants to play," Canyon said. "I want to hear it."

There was suddenly a great tension in the room, a white-hot buzz forty-three stories up in the air. Canyon's was not quite an insubordinate request, but certainly some very polished toes were being stepped on by the young gun with the sharp eyes. Jalen felt a rush of gratitude and respect for Canyon, his coconspirator in music. Music that urgently needed to be played, right here in this room, for these people who couldn't wait to make a killing off it but couldn't be troubled to sit through a song.

"If you'd like," Dillingham conceded, gesturing toward the piano.

They stood around, the executives, and listened to his song. If there is any proof that certain human beings are put on this earth for a reason, it was a plain fact that Jalen West was born to sing. The first note, when he opened his mouth, was as sturdy and pitch-perfect as the last. As he played, he imagined the music reaching into their chests and massaging their souls. That's how it felt whenever he heard music that mattered to him. That was why he wrote music and why he couldn't stop himself from singing it. He just wanted to create that over and over for anyone who would listen.

When he finished and turned around on the bench, the only pair of eyes that were looking at him belonged to Charlie Canyon. The others had already turned for the door.

TWENTY-FOUR

Parker was home from work by seven. He hated being in the apartment alone. It made him think too much of who and where he was, in this city, in this endless transitory stage of his life. When he was home alone, there was never more than one light on in the apartment. He preferred the stand-up lamp he'd fixed with the energy-saving bulb that Kera despised. She thought it glowed yellowish green and turned the walls the color of an alien's fingernails. She said it had tiny imperceptible pulses that caused depression. "What are you talking about? I don't see any pulsing," he had said. Im-per-cep-ti-ble, she had replied and proceeded with her gluttonous consumption of light and water.

He switched on the lamp and undressed. He sat in his underwear in the dim room and opened his computer. He checked his in-box, the headlines on his home page, the weather. Nothing had changed since he left work. It was still work mail and junk mail, death and corruption, hot and humid.

Kera said she had to meet with a colleague before she came home. They were meeting over drinks, she said. Meeting over drinks could mean almost anything. City people were meeting all the time for drinks. They never had barbecues, they never had people over to their apartment, they never built campfires on the beach. They met for drinks, grabbed drinks, had drinks, got drinks, did drinks. Sports bars with eight-dollar drinks next to lounges with twelve-dollar drinks next to dives with one-fifty cans and four-dollar pitchers. Suits and ties and fraternity sweatshirts and high heels. Pool and darts and video games. Two-for-one glasses of wine before eight. Free drinks for anyone named ____ (never "Parker"). Three-fifty pints before seven. Parker went out for drinks with guys from work once or twice a week. Tonight he'd forgotten that Kera had her meeting—her drinks. He'd come straight home, and now he wished he'd gone for a drink of his own.

He refreshed his in-box, his home page, the weather page. Another junk e-mail, no new headlines, the temperature a degree cooler, the wind shifting direction.

He put on jeans and a T-shirt, clothes he'd worn on the weekend, and went down to the street. The sun was low, the city was in shadows, but it was still sticky warm. He crossed the street and walked in the direction of L@Ho. Just one drink.

The same bartender was there. He doodled on a napkin when he wasn't mixing a beverage. Something about the way he returned to the napkin at every free moment, as if escaping, made Parker think bartending was only his temporary job. When Parker asked, the bartender admitted to being a writer. He wrote novels. He had a novel coming out soon. Parker asked him what it was about. It was about love. It was about whether we have to know someone before we can fall in love with them or if we must love them in order to ever really know them. It was about a pilot and his wife, said the bartender. Those were the main characters. But love, that's what it was *about*. Parker wished him luck. Said he looked forward to reading it. Said he'd take another gin and tonic.

A table of jersey-clad soccer fans celebrated a goal. Parker watched the final minutes of the match and then paid his bill. On the street he came across one of the population clocks that had started popping up on the sides of bus stops and on billboards across the city. *There are 7,375,331,951 people in the world. Soon they will all be connected.* He didn't feel connected. He felt small and lonely, just one of seven billion strangers who lived on a planet. He walked the streets and felt as if the world were moving too fast, as if he were surrounded on all sides by those ticking counters, reminding him of how relentlessly humanity was expanding.

He walked three blocks to the grocery store, and then he walked up and down the aisles. He hated grocery shopping in the city because the aisles were too narrow. The people were too rushed or else they were in his way or they were too cold and inhuman-looking. He hated the lights that were lit twenty-four hours a day, the freezers and refrigerators that worked overtime to maintain regulation temperatures.

He found spinach, mushrooms, tomato, garlic, salmon, heavy cream, Parmesan, and bacon. He went back to produce for red onions and a lemon, and then he went back to dairy where they kept the fresh OJ. He carried the groceries home in the dark. In the three blocks between the store and the apartment, he saw four homeless men, a police cruiser (lights not flashing), a deli cashier smoking, three Asian deliverymen on bicycles, an ambulance (lights and siren blaring), a homeless woman, a couple kissing, three black men standing at a bus stop, two Hispanic deliverymen on bicycles, a white SUV limousine, too many taxis to count, a restaurant entrance crowded with smokers and people waiting for tables, a restaurant with dark windows and SPACE FOR LEASE, and a dog on a leash sniffing a puddle. Humanity.

When he got home, Kera wasn't there. He turned on the lamp with the energy-saving bulb and opened his computer. His home page was set to Gnos.is. He opened a bottle of wine and drank a glass as he browsed the website. He read a review of *America*, the documentary film that had lost its distribution because of right-wing protestors. The reviewer said the movie was clichéd and cynical and unpatriotic. Parker gave the critic a bad rating and read another review that said the film was brilliant and emotional and hopeful. He searched for independent theaters that might show the film. There were only two. It opened in eight days. The film would show in LA and New York and at film festivals in Toronto, Aspen, and Barcelona. Nowhere else. He viewed this as one bright spot in the dimness of city life.

Kera still wasn't home, though she hadn't sent word that she'd be too late. He poured another glass of wine and drank it as he prepped for cooking. He rinsed the spinach, diced the vegetables, salted the salmon, and peeled the potatoes. He was trying to replicate a meal they'd had on a date. The salmon wasn't as good as he could get in a restaurant, and he wouldn't be as good at cooking it, but the effort would be worthwhile.

Kera called to say she was coming home. Even with two glasses of wine—almost three glasses of wine—he was not safe from the awful flutter inside his stomach, his chest, his throat. It was not isolated in any particular organ. Dull regret broken by an occasional flutter of fear. Dull regret, flutter of fear. It had been a week since Dubai. He was afraid every time she came home, every time she called, when he held the door for her, told her a joke, when he entered her and she pulled him close.

How could she not know?

He heard the key in the lock. His lungs, bowels, esophagus. Flutter flutter flutter.

TWENTY-FIVE

The world knew Rafael Bolívar as the handsome, Venezuelan-born playboy who, at just thirty-three, had transformed Alegría North America from a fledgling Latin American TV network into the fastest-growing media company in North America. Only ONE controlled more TV networks and radio stations. Bolívar's father founded the company in Venezuela and had discovered in his only son the man who could turn it into a successful enterprise on an international level. Since his college years at NYU, Bolívar had based himself out of Manhattan, maintaining his status in the country with a work visa until he gained dual citizenship. He owned apartments in New York and Miami and houses in Los Angeles and Aspen. He traveled frequently. His net worth was hard to estimate, given his family's Caracas-based business holdings, but previous years' US tax returns suggested he was good for at least $1.4 billion.

Kera's glimpse into Bolívar's private life revealed a man not altogether dedicated to the lifestyle portrayed in the tabloids. His success with Alegría had earned him respect in the business community, even if it did leave people scratching their heads. How did he run this business so masterfully when he spent so much of his time entertaining the young, social elite at the city's hottest drinking establishments? Kera was surprised to discover that, away from the spotlight, he carved out time twice a week to play a pick-up soccer match at Pier 40. And though he made evening appearances at trendy restaurants and nightclubs in the company of attractive women, these were, in fact, rather brief excursions selected for the benefit of the photo op they provided.

He spent his nights alone in his apartment, where the lights were often lit well into the early morning hours. Then he'd be up at six or seven, an hour that clearly challenged his playboy credentials, even though he didn't walk into view of the surveillance camera aimed at his office building's front entrance until nine or nine thirty.

That was his daily routine. In addition, HawkEye dove deep into Rafael Bolívar's past and surfaced with a trove of personal records and documents. There were minutes from Alegría board meetings, citizenship application papers, and library records listing books he'd checked out in college (when people still did such things). It was too much to absorb. Kera flagged a few interesting things for later reading. There wasn't time for that now.

She was consumed in her screens. Both Charlie Canyon and Rafael Bolívar were at work. She watched the video clip from that morning of Bolívar walking from his apartment building to the waiting car. He was wearing dark dress jeans and a white button-down shirt open at the collar. She switched to the next clip and watched him step onto the curb and stride into the front doors of the Alegría building. He would likely remain at the office engaged in meetings until twelve thirty, when he would be met outside by a town car and be driven to his lunch meeting. She wondered whom his lunch was with today.

Charlie Canyon's morning had been equally uneventful. He was already set up in his new office at ONE's headquarters building. Ever since the acquisition, Canyon had been spending less time at the

office. He usually went home at six and stayed in all evening. She
had no idea what he did at home alone. She wondered about that
and about what he thought of his new role at ONE. She had learned
a great deal about both Canyon and Bolívar, but this knowledge had
only produced a seemingly endless list of questions about what she
did not know.

She put in a call to Charlie Canyon. He called her back two minutes later and agreed to drinks that evening after work.

• • • • •

She spotted him at a round booth deep within the restaurant's belly,
his face slanted down at the pages of a book. It was a physical, paper-
back book, the kind she never saw people reading anymore. She was
a few minutes early and immediately resented him for being earlier,
for beating her, just as she would have resented him for being late.
She had picked the venue. It was a subterranean Russian caviar bar
she and Parker favored for the cocktails, since caviar was, in general,
out of their league, and here, where the prices were obscenely displayed on tiny menus, their only practical use for the caviar was to
make the twelve-dollar drinks seem like a hard bargain.

He looked up from his book as she approached, taking care
first to dog-ear his place. As he set the book aside, she saw that the
cover was blank. There was no title or jacket design, just plain, white,
heavy-stock paper binding the interior pages together.

Canyon stood to greet her and then leaned back casually against
the booth. He'd loosened his tie and unbuttoned his shirt one button
more than was really necessary. His style was superior to Parker's,
she thought, though she couldn't pinpoint why and had never
thought of her fiancé as particularly unfashionable. She suspected
the difference had something to do with Charlie's broad shoulders,
the subtle but unmistakable plains of pectorals split by the V of his
open collar. It was a well-fitted shirt. On the cushion beside him was

a lightweight green and white jacket. The tag was visible at the collar, but the only marking was a simple black X.

"Your jacket. Is that the designer you were making the commercial for last week?"

"Yes."

She pictured the shirtless actor, Daryl Walker, dancing at the turntable while the small army of graffiti artists climbed around the bizarre warehouse set. "How did the spot turn out?"

"It's great."

"Will we be seeing it around the city soon?"

"No." Canyon's eyes dimmed a measure or two.

"Does that have anything to do with the merger with ONE?"

"Acquisition. It was not a merger. And yes, the X campaign was dropped because there's no room for small fish anymore. Not even the most promising."

"But you still have your job?"

"I was promoted," he said without emotion. "My first role is to manage the Jalen West account."

"Congratulations," Kera said, using extraordinary control not to react to this news. He was doing it too, she realized—not reacting. "What are you reading?" she asked.

He looked down at the book as if he'd forgotten it was there. "A novel by Lazlo Timms."

Kera winced apologetically. "Haven't heard of him." She made a point to commit the author's name to memory.

"You will. It's about a pilot who slowly discovers his wife's fear of flying."

"A metaphor," she said. "I don't read much fiction."

"I only read fiction."

"Really? No news sites? No blogs?"

"Only to look at the ads. The rest of it is trash."

Was this small talk? She couldn't figure out why Canyon had agreed to meet with her. He seemed detached, his eyes distant. "Is something wrong? You seem preoccupied," she said.

"I lost Daryl today."

"The actor?" How had she not seen that coming? She had to text Jones to get a dossier going.

"He was up for a big role. Major motion picture. The good kind, though. Quality screenplay. We found out yesterday that he didn't get it. He should have. They're making a monumental mistake. But fuck them. And fuck Daryl. He's decided to become useless. Don't get me wrong—this role would have been huge. But rejection happens, you know? It's not like his career's over. He's what, twenty-seven? And he hasn't eaten or showered or left his bed since I called him with the news. A little dramatic, don't you think?"

"Wait, he's OK?" Kera felt heat in her cheeks. "I mean, he's not—he didn't disappear?"

Charlie laughed at this, but in a way that was neither funny nor happy. "No. He wouldn't do that." She waited for him to say more, but he slumped back into the booth. He had finished his drink, and Kera hoped the waitress would bring him another.

"He's an actor. Maybe you just need to give him some time," she said.

Canyon shook his head bitterly. "He's better than this victim routine, and he knows it. That's the worst kind—" Canyon stopped suddenly. His gaze tilted upward, and she could see in his eyes that he'd forgotten she was there.

"What is it?"

Canyon pointed up, indicating the music coming from the speakers. Kera hadn't even been aware of it before. But now she recognized the song.

"Jalen West," she said. Canyon's eyes had gone glassy. She let him listen to a few bars, studying him. "Is he next?" she said, seeing her first opening and taking it.

His face was stony for a moment, his mind off somewhere else, but then he shook his head. He repeated the word tentatively. "Next."

"Look at me, Charlie. There are now eight people who are missing, and they all have exactly two things in common: they were signed with ONE and they met with you. You just said yourself that you're working on the Jalen West account at ONE. That's not a coincidence, is it?"

He took a gulp of the new drink the waitress had put before him. "If it was, would you believe me? Don't take this the wrong way, but you seem like the kind of girl who has lost her ability to appreciate a good coincidence."

Kera ignored this. "What happened to them, Charlie? Eight people."

"Is that what you came here to ask me?" He smiled. "I can't help you with that."

"I'll find them, with or without your help."

"You know, you just might."

"This isn't a game. You could be subpoenaed. It's a felony to withhold evidence to a crime."

His eyebrows arched. "Has a crime been committed?"

"Until this week, I wasn't sure about that. Before vanishing each of them made preparations to avoid default on any financial or legal obligations—although I suspect ONE would dispute that on contractual grounds. Either way, fake suicide notes are one thing. But an airplane? A full-fledged search-and-rescue effort that, aside from wasting tens of thousands of taxpayer dollars, put the lives of first responders at risk? Yeah, I'd say a few crimes have been committed." She watched for his reaction, but he had none. "I want to hear your side of the story, and I want to believe you. But I won't overlook a crime any more than I'll ignore the truth, once I uncover it. What about Rafael Bolívar?"

For a moment he seemed to be weighing the subject, how much to say. But then he stretched out his arms across the back of the booth, richly enjoying the suspense.

"You and Bolívar were classmates in college," she said. "Are the two of you friends now? Are you working together?"

"I'm going to make Rafa famous. Don't you think Rafa should be famous?"

"He's already famous."

"I don't mean in that way. All that is just a diversion. Rafa is a genius. It's people like him, people with the ability to change the world—they are the ones who should be famous, don't you think? Not vacuous celebrities or quitters like Daryl Walker."

"What does being famous matter?"

"It matters a great deal. Ideas are valuable to society in proportion to the extent that they are popular. When people go unheralded, their work is wasted."

"What about people who disappear? Would you say their work is wasted?"

He permitted, in fact seemed to enjoy, the prolonged cross-table stare-down that followed this challenge. "You know what your problem is?" Canyon said in a way that made her imagine stabbing a fork through his cheek. "You think too small."

"Eight people. What happened to them?"

"Why are you so interested?"

"I told you. I'm doing a story."

He glanced at the clock on his phone and then leaned back, looking directly at her. "I don't have a lot of time. And I'm getting bored with that pretense. We both know you're not a journalist."

"I'm sorry?" she said, staring at him. He stared back with steady eyes. They both knew that she'd heard him.

"What is Hawk?"

Paralysis seized her. The effect was most devastating for her lungs, which could not move air. Those three words—*What is*

Hawk?—could end everything. Protocol in this situation required her to tell Gabby immediately that she had been compromised. Hawk would be turned inside out in a hunt to discover the source of the leak. She would be disavowed, possibly Jones, possibly others. They would evaluate whether the breach was catastrophic. If it was, all of the mission's resources would be redirected to damage control. Hawk would be shuttered and everyone involved would lose their careers in the intelligence community.

"I don't understand," she managed to say.

He smiled. "The look on your face suggests otherwise. I didn't mean to alarm you. But I feel entitled to a few answers. What I've been trying to figure out is why a shadowy intelligence contractor would send someone like you to spy on someone like me. It seems like a waste of both your time and mine."

"You don't know what you're talking about," she said. It came out as a whisper.

"The answer, of course, is so boring and predictable as to not warrant a discussion: somebody must see a profit in it. Hold on, this is my favorite part."

"What?" But then she understood. Jalen West. Canyon had closed his eyes, savoring the vocals as they built up to the final chorus. She had to get out of here.

"Wait," he said when she started to get up. "I thought you wanted to trade information."

She hesitated, then sat. What more did she have to lose?

"Where is the profit in this for Hawk?" he asked. "Who are they working for?"

"I told you, I don't know what you're talking about."

He stared at her for a moment. "Maybe I was wrong about you. I didn't think you were involved. You seemed . . ." he shrugged, "better than that."

"You don't know anything about me."

"I know you're paid to spy on private citizens."

"Whatever you think about journalists, it's not like that," she said. "I investigate. I analyze. And I've accumulated a great deal of knowledge about cybersecurity. That's my area: computers and networks. But sometimes I'm assigned to stories that fall outside of my primary expertise. That's why I'm here. I'm not used to investigating humans. Especially domestic extremists," she added, with an edge. "But I'm trying to learn."

"Bullshit. You know as well as I do that it is humans who turn computers into cyberthreats. If you weren't good at analyzing humans, you wouldn't be very good at your job. Can I ask you a personal question?"

"No."

"It's also a professional question. One that is particularly relevant." With her silence, she gave him permission. "Do you ever examine something not for its potential as a threat, but for its potential to do good?"

"It's my job to see threats."

"Even when they aren't there?"

She didn't answer.

"You have gotten one thing right about me," Canyon said. "I am an extremist. But I'm not a threat, nor am I some kind of terrorist. My objective is to enlighten."

"By making people vanish?"

"By making an argument."

"I think you're delusional."

"We'll see."

"When?"

"I can't tell you that."

She put a twenty on the table and slid out of the booth. It startled her when he put his hand on the cash and pushed it back across the table.

"My treat," he said. When he lifted his hand, there was a piece of paper on top of her twenty-dollar bill.

"What's this?" She picked it up.

"I put you on a guest list for a party that I think you should attend. Those are the details."

"What party?"

But he wasn't listening. He was lost in the final measures of the Jalen West song.

· · · · ·

She wandered onto the darkest street she could find and leaned against a wall. The tears came then, and she could not stop them. It was a moment of weakness, as inevitable as it was resented. But it was better to ride it out here, to let it destroy her in the privacy of this alley with her head thrown back against a brick wall, than to try to bury it and simply carry on. It took many minutes, maybe half an hour, until her breathing evened and she began to reclaim her mind.

There was a pay phone two blocks away. She'd noticed it one morning on her commute soon after she and Parker had moved into the neighborhood. The cameras on that corner were privately owned, trained on storefronts; they didn't capture pedestrian or vehicle traffic. The pay phone there was safe. Unsteadily, she straightened and stepped away from the wall, surprised at how much she had relied on it to keep her from collapsing to the sidewalk. It was very clear to her what she had to do. One foot in front of the other for a little while. That was all. And then pick up the phone. She moved through the streets anonymously. The city was cool and apathetic.

She had not used a pay phone in years.

"Bright speaking." Lionel answered on the fourth ring. There were voices in the background. He was at a dinner or cocktail party. Her lips parted, but not even a breath slipped out. A beat of silence made the round trip from her end of the line to his and back again. Then another. The background noise grew fainter, and then it was gone completely. He'd moved to a quieter room. She could almost hear his breathing.

"Who is this?" he asked.

On the street behind her, a large delivery truck whooshed through the intersection. In response to her silence, she could feel Lionel thinking, gathering intelligence, analyzing what the call could mean. Her vision blurred suddenly. She blinked until the moisture hit her cheeks and she could see clearly again. She was careful not to breathe. She was afraid to make a sound. She was afraid that if she did, she would break down.

Rather than admit failure, she hung up.

She was only five blocks from home, but she couldn't go there. There was too much to do. At Houston she flagged a cab and gave the driver the address for the office.

After tapping her badge in the lobby and again in the *TGR* waiting room, and then clearing the retinal scanner at the security checkpoint outside the Control Room, she went directly to the on-duty surveillance clerk. He sat at a console behind a counter in a small, adjacent anteroom.

"I need to process a target," Kera said, exposing her eyes to another scanner. This one would attach her security clearance and case assignment to the intercept request. It worked like a filter, the idea being that not just anyone should be able to look at any private citizen's correspondence. The agent making the request had to be cleared at the classification level of the intercept he or she was requesting to access, and the intercept had to be crucial to an open case. That wouldn't be a problem. "Name is Canyon, Charlie. Here's his social and DOB. Case code name: ATLANTIS. I need metadata of the target's phone calls." She hesitated. "Transcripts too. I need his e-mails. I need VoIP packets. Everything."

HawkEye was useful for location tracking and collecting some transactional data, like credit card purchases, incoming and outgoing phone numbers, search engine queries, and e-mail header details.

But it didn't capture the actual content of private correspondence, which is what Kera needed now.

The young man keyed in her command. "Starting when, ma'am?"

"Uh, I don't know. A month ago."

He glanced up at her, but then obediently processed the order. There was no need to specify that the request was urgent. Everything was digital and therefore virtually instantaneous. By the time she walked to her office, all the requested files that were classified at or below her security clearance were accessible to her on one of the Hawk servers. After she retreated to the kitchen for a cup of coffee, she sat down at her desk and started to read.

TWENTY-SIX

"I'll introduce you to her," Parker was telling the bartender at L@Ho. "I'll bring her in sometime." He'd been talking about her again. He didn't know why the urge to talk about Kera was so persistent, especially here. He didn't know why he felt himself nudging closer and closer to saying aloud the thing he'd convinced himself never to mention to anyone. It was buried forever. It had to be.

Except it was getting worse. He was fatiguing. Forever was an impossibly voluminous amount of time, whereas just saying the words would get it over within moments. He could wrap his head around the latter; maybe that's why it kept creeping up on him like an itch that needed relief. He'd thought it would go away. Of course he'd thought that; it *had* to go away. He'd learned his lesson, and the best thing was to move on. Dragging it on like this served no one. "She works a lot. Too much, I think. That's how it is at the start of a career, I guess, right?"

The bartender wandered down the bar to attend to a new patron. Parker fiddled with his phone. He checked the half-dozen social networking accounts he oversaw at work and then switched over to have a glance at his own personal profiles. That was how he learned about the new It piece, a sculpture in Central Park. His fingers swiped and tapped, eager to learn more.

The piece of art, as described by a blogger, was discovered in a wooded area near the Metropolitan Museum of Art. Once it had been "excavated" from the shrubs, the piece was revealed to be a slab of granite into which had been carved, in bas relief, a mock magazine cover. The magazine's name was *Renaissance Man Quarterly*, and the cover image was Michelangelo's David, but distorted to mimic an unnaturally thin model with enhanced abdominal muscles, airbrushed pectorals, and facial features that betrayed the symptoms of a little surgical work. Having not defaced any public or private property this time, the piece was merely hauled away by authorities like disowned furniture left on the curb.

"Did you hear about this?" Parker asked the bartender, showing him a picture of the sculpture when he returned.

The bartender chuckled. "Is it It?"

"No one else has taken responsibility," Parker reported. "That's one of It's trademarks."

Displaying uncharacteristic interest, the bartender took Parker's phone and scrolled through the entire blog report.

"The other trademarks are there too."

"Like what?" Parker said, surprised. The bartender rarely engaged him in conversation. He usually just listened.

"The way it required discovery. The 'excavation.' And the way the sculpture was trucked away so quickly by city officials, as if in a panic. It's art is always destroyed within hours of completion."

Parker took a long pull from his gin and tonic. He'd had a few already and could feel the dreamy buzz in his skull.

"You know what they say about It?" said the bartender.

"What?"

"That he's the freest person alive."

"What do you mean by that?"

"He has no obligations. Not to family. Not to society. He exists as he wishes. *If* he wishes. I envy that, in a way." After a pause, he added, "But I can't decide if it's courageous or cowardly."

TWENTY-SEVEN

The video opened on the casket. After a few seconds the camera panned slowly to the left, and there was the choir, about twenty strong, singing "Till We Meet Again" in purple robes. There were a few rows of parishioners, visible from behind, between the camera and the choir. These men and women were subdued, their heads bowed in respect or heartbreak. Ninety-seven seconds in the first chorus ended, and a young man stepped forward to sing the second verse. The image jerked and zoomed tighter before it steadied on the soloist. At the sound of his first notes, the total grief in the room became palpable. The first few bars were overwhelming in their pain and beauty. Even viewed on the YouTube video uploaded from a smartphone camera, the pain and beauty were utterly overwhelming.

Sorrow gripped her by the throat. Chilled goose pimples rose in waves along her arms. Kera was on the couch with her laptop and her earphones, a forgotten glass of wine on the coffee table beside her. Parker had long since nodded off and then come to just long enough to shuffle away to bed, mumbling incoherently. This was the first time she'd seen the video, which put her far out of step with most of America. The video had more than 180 million views. It was the first time she'd seen one of these viral videos and thought, *I get it. It is worth spending a few minutes of my short time on Earth watching this.* The soloist was unnamed in the video. He was just a young man, a boy, really, who stepped forward for a solo and unleashed a voice so full of innocent hurt and courage and beauty that the first record label would call within hours of the video's posting.

That was five years earlier. Now Jalen West, the thin Detroit boy whose pop music career began at his best friend's funeral, was on top of the world.

Kera hadn't slept more than three hours in the last forty. Exhaustion dulled her judgment and played with her emotions like puppet strings. *Bedtime,* she told herself. *That's an order.* The night before she'd remained in her office until shortly after four AM, poring over the intercepts of Charlie Canyon's private correspondence. She discovered exactly what she'd hoped to find: nothing. Not one mention of Hawk to anyone. Not even a mention of the *Global Report.* However Canyon had learned of Hawk, he either wasn't very interested in it or he was being very careful not to discuss it with anyone. Both of those scenarios favored her. Though nothing excused her of her duty to report that her cover had been compromised, with each minute that passed without her world crashing down around her, she became more tempted to wait just a little while longer. Just until she could complete the case. Then she would come forward and acknowledge that someone on the outside had blown her cover.

As though it was against her brain's nature to shut itself down, her mind created a sudden memory of the slip of paper Canyon had passed her at the restaurant. It was zipped into the pocket of her shoulder bag, within arm's reach of the couch. She reread it. The note provided a Midtown address along with the day and time: Tues., 8:00 PM. That was six days from now. Below these practical details were the words DON'T MISS THIS.

In an act more of due diligence than hope, she Googled the address, date, and time. The event, to her surprise, was promoted widely. It was a fund-raiser gala called the Annual Celebration of Media Industry Pioneers.

Don't miss this. Her detestation of Charlie Canyon had blossomed healthily. She despised him not just because he refused to admit his connection to the missing people, nor because he had compromised her undercover identity and thus her career; the thing that drove her most infuriatingly toward insanity was his ability to tell her just enough. Just enough to beckon her a little further into his world.

TWENTY-EIGHT

Charlie Canyon peered up at the hotel through the tinted windows of the limousine. The black stretch lurched forward in Park Avenue traffic and slid into an opening that was even with the hotel's revolving doors.

Gray Heller, ONE Music's VP of Marketing and Canyon's new boss, had won two near-shouting matches in the last five minutes: one with the limo driver, who had failed to nudge them close enough to the entrance because of curbside traffic, and the second with the hotel's doorman, who was irritated with the driver's solution, which was to double-park in the right lane of Park Avenue. For the moment Heller had convinced all relevant parties that the vehicle wasn't moving until they had their guest on board.

Canyon offered to go up to get Jalen West, and he jumped out of the limo before Heller could suggest otherwise.

He knocked on the suite door at the end of a plush hallway on the twelfth floor. The eyehole darkened for a moment, and then light filtered through again. After a long beat of silence, the door opened and Jalen West, wearing only basketball shorts, stepped back to let him in.

They walked a few steps into the suite before pausing awkwardly. It was the first time they had ever been alone with each other.

Canyon whistled. "You know, the cost of this room comes straight out of my salary."

Jalen smiled and looked down, as if embarrassed. The suite featured a bilevel living area, bedroom, and sprawling bathroom and changing room. Pulled forward by the view of Midtown, Canyon stepped around Jalen to approach the large windows. As he did, he cut close enough that the fabric of his shirt grazed Jalen's naked torso. A few seconds later, Jalen came up beside him.

They both looked out at the city, though neither was aware of anything but the few inches of space between them.

"I should get ready—" Jalen started. But Canyon reached out and gripped his forearm before he could turn, an act that echoed into one continuous motion that neither of them resisted. Canyon shut his eyes. First, he felt Jalen's mouth on his, and then Jalen's open hand on the back of his head. They never made it to the bedroom. Undressing each other in stages, they stumbled as far as the living area until Canyon, sliding out of his underwear, pushed Jalen to his back on the couch.

"We have somewhere we're supposed to be, don't we?" the pop star said when they'd finished.

"Yes. The limo's double-parked downstairs."

"Shit."

They laughed hard, and then they got dressed.

"You think I should go to this nightclub?" Jalen said, checking himself in the body-length mirror before they stepped into the hall.

"I think you should do whatever you want to do."

Jalen shrugged. "I want to work on my next album."

"Then do that. It's only the publicist who wants you to go to the nightclub."

"Why?"

"To get your picture taken." Canyon paused. He was standing behind Jalen, looking over his shoulder at him in the mirror. "Scott Michaels is going to be there."

"I'm not interested in Scott Michaels. Do you have his number? I'll call him and explain."

Scott Michaels was the star of *Apocalypse*, ONE's tent-pole action movie due out a week later.

Canyon considered that for a moment. The thought amused him: Jalen West, ever the gentleman, putting in a call to Scott Michaels to tell him that it wasn't personal, it's just that neither his conscience nor his intolerance for boredom would permit him to spend all hours of the night at a hip club just for—especially for—a shameless publicity stunt.

"I'll take care of it," Canyon said. He wanted to kiss Jalen on the back of his neck. So he did. He pressed his lips to the firm tendon that descended from the pop star's hairline and disappeared into his collar. The skin there smelled like Jalen West. It was magnificent. "How about the basketball game? The car's still waiting."

"You better believe we're going to the game," Jalen said. "Pistons–Knicks in the playoffs at Madison Square Garden? There's only one thing I'd miss that game for, and we already did that. Let's go."

TWENTY-NINE

The news came in the late afternoon. Parker sat in stunned silence while his bosses, the firm's cofounders, expressed their excitement and outlined the details of the transition. Despite the celebratory atmosphere, Parker could not trigger those feelings within himself. To him, there was something crushing about the news, something that gnawed on his conscience as he walked the streets of the city. Helplessness mounted quickly, not like pressure building in a volcano or a gas line that could be relieved with the release of a valve, but a kind of depth pressure, like sinking under hundreds of feet of water. There was no release. He would drown or be crushed if he wasn't rescued.

He wanted to talk to someone who would understand—or at least listen. He walked into L@Ho and planted himself at the bar. He had come here ready to unload about the work situation, but instead, as soon as he'd swallowed his first sip of gin, he began to tell the bartender what he'd done to Kera. It bubbled out of him irrevocably. He could not stop it.

He'd been in Dubai for four days. Four. An insignificant length of time for someone who had lived thirty-one years. He had always been a man in control of himself, deliberate and rational. He and Kera had dated a full month before sleeping together. He'd waited a full year to propose to her, even though it was apparent long before where things were headed. Deliberate and rational Parker, the furthest thing from self-destructive.

In Dubai it had taken the length of the post-keynote cocktail hour for a young woman, a slim Dutch start-up consultant with a charming take on the English language, to invite herself up to his room. She was not particularly persistent, though she was absolutely attractive—blond hair, sharp but playful eyes, the whole package managed with a businesswoman's confidence. Still, she was no more attractive than women he'd politely declined before. He always managed to sidestep trouble discreetly, disposing of any errant urges or fantasies later, in a few harmless moments with himself. He'd never *actually* intended to go through with sleeping with anyone other than Kera.

But then he was in Dubai. On the other side of the world. The cliché of it all made it, in retrospect, almost laughably pathetic. One of the most frustrating characteristics of this brand of regret was Parker's inability to understand why things had been so different in Dubai. It wasn't oversimplifying it to say that it had just happened.

He paused his confession, trying to recall what it was that the Dutch consultant at the cocktail party in Dubai had first said that made him want to keep talking to her. Had he been jet-lagged? Had he approached her, or was it the other way around? He could only remember her saying, not long after they were acquainted, "We can lay together in your room?" At first he hadn't even understood what she meant, and then somehow it was too late. They were upstairs lying together in his hotel room, and the poisoned logic of the moment permitted him to go through with it.

In the cab ride home from the airport, Parker had been afraid to face Kera, afraid that she would know and that he would make everything worse by not telling her before she figured it out on her own. What if he'd contracted something? Was that a burning sensation when he urinated? He had never been any good at keeping secrets. Secrets ate away at him. But when he walked in the door and saw the way they slipped so comfortably and safely back into each other's lives, it occurred to him that it would be worse now to introduce trouble. It was over and done with. He started thinking of his mistake as a blessing, a wake-up call. Kera was, without a doubt, the woman of his life. Chastened by his brief failure of judgment, Parker had begun to feel more than ever that he was up to the task of deserving her.

But then, how could she not know? He couldn't let that question go. It was all he thought about, even when he was thinking about other things. He spent hours in his head trying to make it go away. Since it wouldn't go away, he tried to make it better. Often he longed to come home and find her hurrying a shirtless stranger onto the fire escape. He wanted to surprise her at lunchtime and catch her kissing a coworker. He wanted that power back, the power to grant forgiveness. He did not have the balls to ask to be forgiven.

The bartender said little while Parker spoke. On a few occasions, the moments when Parker outlined his lowest acts, the bartender looked up from his doodling. And once or twice he nodded sympathetically. But otherwise, he kept his face down, offering nothing harsher than ambivalence in judgment of his customer. *He's disgusted by me*, Parker thought, and ordered another drink.

Hours later he approached the door to his apartment. He had trouble with the dead bolt and made a stumbling mess of his entrance. Kera was on the couch with her laptop. For a moment they both looked at each other.

"What's wrong?" she asked. She sounded concerned, also maybe a little judgmental about his drinking.

I cheated on you! For a brief moment, he could imagine in sensational detail the words forming at the back of his throat and then dislodging, existing, those words in that order, floating across the air between them. He had no idea what would happen next. Tears, a slap, bitter silence, a great weight lifted from his chest? What did it matter? The words would not come out of him. They sat undigested in his gut like something heavy eaten too fast. Guilt, he thought, must be the most useless human emotion. Fear alerted one to danger and therefore saved lives. Love alerted one to living and therefore improved lives. But guilt—guilt was so uselessly after-the-fact, so absent as a tool of prevention and yet so powerful as a tool of misery. Guilt rotted men in cells and suburbs and churches. Guilt destroyed lives. Following that orgasm on the other side of the world, he had slumped against the foreign sheets, paralyzed with a sickening stillness of emotion. He smelled the strange girl beneath him and knew, as he should have anticipated ahead of time when they were downstairs talking, vertical and clothed and among chattering colleagues wearing name tags, that everything was ruined.

"Tomorrow morning my boss will announce that our company has agreed to be acquired by ONE," Parker said.

Kera's expression was blank for a moment. And then finally she said, "Why?"

This question annoyed him. She wanted facts. What why who when how. It wasn't enough that his job was fucked; she wanted all the gory details. That's how she was, *who* she was. Who he'd fallen in love with. He loved that idealism, that pure trust in the idea that situations improve automatically if you uncover all the facts. "That's a really excellent question. They're calling it a 'strategic acquisition.'"

He could feel her watching him as he sat on the arm of the couch and bent down to untie his shoes. He wanted another drink. He did not want her to watch him pour it.

"Will you go and work for them?" she asked.

"No." That felt good to say. He felt principled. He liked the little surge of power that came from feeling principled.

But then what? He knew the alternative. He could search for a new job. The thought was at the same time exciting and exhausting. It had been one thing searching for a job after he'd first arrived in the city, when naïveté sheltered him from noticing the struggle. Now he was painfully aware of what a job search would entail. The résumés, the unanswered cover letters, dressing up for interviews, shamelessly e-mailing his network of friends and acquaintances—horrible, inhumane things he'd not had to do the first time around, thanks to the friend of his father's whose son had gone to business school with the founder of his firm. No, he didn't think he could put himself through all that.

"What will you do?" Kera said.

"What will *I* do? When did this not become about what *we* will do?"

She raised her eyebrows. "Babe, that isn't what I meant."

"Oh, it's not? How am I supposed to know what you mean? You work all day, all weekend. You work constantly. Do you ever think about our wedding? Or no, forget the wedding. Do you think about me? Am I as important to you as work? Do you wonder what your job does to me, what this city does to me? That's what I want to know: What will *we* do?"

The next few moments would have been more difficult to get through but for the convenient fact that he was wasted. It made it easier for them both to dismiss the things he'd just said. They became silent partners in this conspiracy, together excusing the pain and brutality that lived in those words.

"Drink some water, babe. Take a shower. You're not yourself right now."

Rotting rotting rotting. He felt thirsty. They had gin and vodka and scotch in the apartment. He imagined mixing himself a drink. Three parts rotting, one part self-loathing guilt.

Later, she lay next to him in bed and told him that there wasn't any shame in keeping his job. "You're successful. It's a good job. If you find you can't stand it, then you'll know it's time to look for something else."

He didn't respond to this. He just lay there, hiccupping at odd intervals, his body turned from hers. Finally he said, very quietly, "I wish we could just go away together. There's a place somewhere where we'd be happier." And then the next thing she heard was the deepening of his breaths into light snores.

THIRTY

When the young man slid unnoticed into the black waters of the Hudson, it was twilight, still cocktail hour up on deck. He had excused himself from a conversation, descended to the lower cabin, and walked out onto the aft viewing deck. Without hesitation, he had swung one leg at a time over the railing and had taken a long step away from the vessel.

The water was many levels more uncomfortable than he'd expected. Not just the cold, seeping temperature, but the foul taste and smell. The boat's propellers churned the surface of this soup into a white froth.

Soon the wake settled, and the raucous atmosphere of the boat died away. The darkness stretched deep below him, clasping tightly around his neck, compressing his chest and weighing his clothes like blocks of ice. He had not anticipated such a moment of humility: he had not thought he would actually feel death in this way, its isolation, its irrevocability. He shed all but the closest layer of clothing and tested a few strokes in the direction of Manhattan.

His fear dulled gradually. A spectacular view of the city rose before him. The lights of the west side seemed to have been tilted forward and *dipped in the water, leaving blurred imprints of color dancing on the surface. He thought he could hear laughter from the distant boat. He liked the sound of that. It meant they were not coming back for him. He wouldn't be missed until the group took their seats for dinner. And by then it would be too late.*

He started swimming.

THIRTY-ONE

The next day was a busy news day, even by New York City standards. A bomb scare shut down the 1 train, a major airline declared bankruptcy, and the UN was hosting a special session on global trade that was being protested enthusiastically by PETA and Greenpeace, both of whom had sent activists scaling the sides of Midtown buildings to unfurl billboard-sized slogans. The headline that caught Kera's eye, though, in the business section of the *New York Times*, was a short article about an unnamed ONE employee who had gone overboard on a dinner cruise the previous evening. The company's top executives and their staffs, including Ford Dillingham, ONE's president of Media and Entertainment, and Gray Heller, the music arm's VP of Marketing, had been on board. The occasion, apparently, was a welcome celebration for new executives who had been corralled under the ONE umbrella in recent acquisitions.

Kera was reading this on her commute to work when a conversation between two girls near her on the train suddenly got her attention.

"The Internet is fucking genius."

"What?"

"You know that actor, Daryl Walker?"

"What was he in?"

"Nothing major. But you'd recognize him. Look." The girl passed her tablet over to share a series of photographs.

"Oh, him. He's hot."

"Right?"

"What about him?"

"Gawker just posted this. It says that if people make donations that reach a million dollars, Daryl Walker will make a naked video and post it online."

"I'm in. What's he raising the money for?"

"For himself, I guess."

"That's genius."

"Right?"

"I can't believe no one else has thought of this."

"He says the video will be five minutes, and it's not porn. It's just a nudie vid of him—oh, yeah, get this. Everyone who contributes five bucks or more has voting rights."

"Voting rights?"

"Yeah. You can vote on what he'll do in the video."

"What he'll *do*?"

"Not like that! The options are showering, performing house-hold chores, and lifting weights."

"Definitely household chores. Is there a way to pitch other suggestions?"

"Vacuuming."

"Changing the oil in his car."

"Cleaning toilets."

Nearby eavesdroppers cracked smiles.

"How many people would it take to reach a million dollars if everyone pays five bucks?"

There was a brief silence during the computation.

"Two hundred thousand."

"Wow. That's a lot."

"There's no way he'll get to a million, right? Otherwise, every-one would be doing this."

"I don't know. It's possible."

Kera put her earphones in. Over the last week she'd listened to *JW*, Jalen West's new album, so many times that certain phrases looped continuously in her head. She listened now with her eyes shut, opening them only to watch for her stop. Aboveground in Times Square, a pedestrian backup on the sidewalk brought her march toward work to a halt, and her eyes drew upward. In the spot where the *America* billboard had once been, there was now a new advertisement for the action movie *Apocalypse*. She put her head down and waited for the foot traffic to flow again.

When she got to her workstation, she read through the day's alerts, which included mentions of the ONE employee who had fallen into the Hudson while on the company cruise. There were also more and more articles, she noticed, dwelling on the fact that both Rowena Pete and the members of Background Noise Pollution—both ONE Music artists—had gone missing. Kera felt a flutter of urgency course through her. It would complicate her investigation if the disappearing artists became a media obsession.

She reached for her cell phone to call Canyon. She wanted to apply a little pressure on him, to see what information he was willing to give up in exchange for her attending the event he'd told her not to miss on Tuesday.

"May I ask who's calling?" An unfamiliar secretary answered the phone.

Kera said she was a friend. Her policy was to reveal as little as possible to secretaries. Canyon always seemed to know it was her.

"I'm afraid I can't give you any information," the secretary said.

"That's all right, I'll call back later."

She was logging in to HawkEye to see what she'd missed in the life of Rafael Bolívar when the secretary's words struck her. *I can't give you any information?* Kera dialed the number again.

"May I ask who's calling?"

"My name is Kera Mersal. I'm a reporter—"

"Hold, please."

Kera exhaled, relieved to be getting somewhere. She half expected Canyon's would be the next voice on the line.

"Are you there, ma'am?"

"Yes."

"I'm going to read you the official statement. 'The disappearance of Mr. Canyon is currently under investigation, and all employees of the ONE Corporation are cooperating fully with the NYPD. No further statement will be made until the investigation has reached its conclusion.' Do you have an e-mail address you'd like me to send this to?"

"Wait." The only other thing Kera could say was, "He's gone?" It was unthinkable. She'd been sitting across from him just a few nights before. After a moment, though, she began to see that it was entirely thinkable. Perhaps even inevitable.

"You all right?" Jones said through the monitors between them when she'd hung up. His responsibilities on the Gnos.is task force had kept him busy over the past few days, and she had not had much interaction with him. Ignoring his question for a moment, she brought up Canyon's HawkEye map. She'd last glanced at the map around 1800 hours the previous evening. She started the playback there to see what she'd missed. Canyon had boarded the corporate cruise around 1830. Over the next ninety minutes, he'd used his phone three times to make routine business calls while the yacht looped down around the tip of Manhattan before making its way back up the Hudson. At 2014 the dot vanished. It had not reappeared since.

"We have number nine. It's Canyon."

THIRTY-TWO

The Annual Celebration of Media Industry Pioneers was held in a ballroom on the sixty-third floor of a Midtown skyscraper. Kera gave her name at a podium in the ground-floor lobby and was ushered onto a dedicated elevator. She rode up with a man dressed in a suit and tie who never took his eyes off his BlackBerry, a paparazzo, an underdressed but stylish man who tapped his foot to the elevator music, and two couples gossiping about a colleague who edited a pop culture and entertainment blog.

When Kera entered the ballroom, the first thing she saw was the view: the dark green carpet of Central Park stretched north, framed by neighboring skyscrapers. At this dizzying height, it was easy to imagine the slow roll of the earth, forcing the distant New Jersey horizon up to block out the sun, which was reddening more and more by the second, like cooling steel. Because she didn't yet know why she was here, and also to position herself to get a good read on the crowd, she crossed the room and stood before a large window, silhouetted against the city. She wore a blue dress and a silver necklace and bracelet that matched her heels. The outfit had raised

Parker's eyebrows, first because he said she looked beautiful and then because the only explanation she gave him for where she was going was, "It's a work thing, babe."

The room swelled from half to three-quarters full. She got a glass of champagne and circled the floor slowly, then strolled through the adjacent hallways and anterooms. Canyon must have known all along that he'd be gone by this point and that she would be here alone. The question was, what did he want her to see? She listened closely to the chatter of guests as she weaved back through the ballroom.

In one circle the topic of conversation was Daryl Walker.

"Won't it ruin his acting career if he makes this video?"

"Are you kidding? Before a week ago, half of us had never heard of him. Now his career will take off."

"And if it doesn't, so what? He's a millionaire."

"There are already hundreds of people promising copycat videos," said a young man with meticulously crafted hair. "And some are willing to set the bar way lower than a million dollars." His peers laughed.

"I think he's going to do it. He's already a third of the way there."

Flashbulb bursts exploded suddenly behind Kera. She turned in time to see the proud figure of Rafael Bolívar stride into the room and be swallowed immediately by a circle of gawkers, some of them his media-industry peers, others reporters and photographers.

"Rafa, can you comment on the rumors that Alegría plans to launch a cable network dedicated to reality television?"

His reply was, "Stay tuned."

"Rafa, look this way."

He did.

"Rafa, do you have a comment about Daryl Walker?"

"He's a pioneer," Bolívar said with a smooth smile. This generated a round of laughs and raised glasses.

He spotted her then. Their eye contact was a small moment, at least as measured in the arbitrary units of time, but in that moment the mind that lay behind those eyes had distinguished her from everyone else in the room.

"Rafa, are you concerned about the growing number of artists who are disappearing? Just an hour ago it was announced that a painter named Marybelle Pickett has vanished."

This was news to Kera, and her reaction was as it had been with Canyon's disappearance—first surprise, almost disbelief, followed after a moment of thought by the understanding that it had been inevitable.

"You know what I'll say about that?" Rafa began. He spoke easily and confidently. "I think the future of our culture has never been brighter. We live in an age where the average person's contributions online can be far more influential to the culture than the contributions of the greatest painters or writers of previous centuries."

The crowd gulped his words thirstily. At least most of them did. Someone thought to point out, "Those paintings, the ones by Marybelle Pickett that had been recovered, they were just auctioned for more than one hundred thousand dollars."

"What's a hundred thousand dollars?" Rafael Bolívar said. "It's nothing. Painting is irrelevant. It has no more value to pop culture. And pop culture is the only culture that has value anymore."

If this was what Canyon wanted her to see, she'd seen enough. Bolívar had not looked again in Kera's direction. When he began to move about the room, she backed out of the crowd and made a cut for the exit. A man in a suit stopped her before she could get to the elevator. She noted the clear wire that curled behind his ear and disappeared down the back of his jacket.

"Will you come this way, ma'am? Mr. Bolívar would like a word."

The bodyguard led her to a small conference room and then disappeared. Kera walked to the window. The room faced east, but the vista stretched south as far as the Brooklyn Bridge, which looked as delicate as two strings of lights draped across the void of the East River. She turned when she heard the door. Bolívar entered. It was, to her knowledge, the first time he had looked at her openly, without averting his eyes.

"Would you like to sit?" he said. His voice was different from how it had been with the reporters in the ballroom, only minutes earlier. The contrast caught her off guard.

"I'll stand."

"What are you doing here?" he said.

"I was invited here. By Charlie Canyon." She let him register what she'd said and decided from his expression that he had not known or expected this. "What happened to him?"

"He drowned. Isn't that what the police are suggesting?"

"Do you believe that?" she asked.

"I have no reason to form a belief on that matter one way or the other."

"You and Canyon were friends?"

"No. He—" Bolívar hesitated, tacking mentally in a different direction. "Canyon wanted to work for me. I wasn't hiring people like him."

Without thinking, she said, "Why do you say those things? About mindless culture? About web videos?"

"I've made a fortune off those things."

"You already had a fortune."

"You seem to know a great deal about me."

"You're a public figure."

"Ms. Mersal, I don't want to waste your time, and I don't intend to waste my own. Let's cut to the chase. Why are you here?"

"I told you, Canyon asked me to come here. I didn't even know that you'd—"

"Drop the act." His words interrupted her, but it was the look in his eyes that had stopped her midsentence. "What was Hawk hired to do to me?"

The room tilted. She put a hand on the back of a nearby chair. "Did Charlie tell you that?" she whispered.

Bolívar looked confused. "No. I told Charlie about Hawk. In your defense, he seemed to think you weren't in on it. But the fact that you're here seems to suggest otherwise."

"In on what?"

"Ms. Mersal, given the amount of money Hawk has at stake here, I don't believe they sent an incompetent agent into the field. We're both here now. Can't we be straight with one another?"

"I don't know how else to say that I don't know what you're talking about."

"Very well. If you refuse to engage with me, perhaps you can at least deliver a message. Tell your client that they're wasting their money. Whatever they're after, they can't have it. I will never let them touch me."

"My client?"

"ONE."

Kera shook her head. "There's been a misunderstanding."

"I don't think so." Bolívar looked at her. "But I'm beginning to think you're being played worse than anyone. In your field, I can't imagine that's an enviable position to be in."

"You don't know a thing about me or what I do."

"Oh? Kera Mersal. Born, like me, outside of this country. Adopted. Shall I skip ahead to the relevant part? You had a promising but brief career at the CIA before you jumped to the private sector, apparently at the first chance you got. Now you're a hired spy."

She started to tremble. To hide it, she gripped tightly the back of the chair where her hand was resting. "You have some gall, suggesting that I'm some sort of a sellout. Have you listened to yourself? Ten minutes ago you were standing out there spewing a bunch of mindless crap to the press about pop culture being the only culture that matters. I don't know why Charlie thought you were better than that."

"The difference between you and me is that in my career I've never claimed to be better than that. I don't have a security clearance and a badge to wave around that tells everyone I'm serving my country. When I want to improve the world, I set out to do it."

He was making it easy for her to leave. "While this lecture from you on my patriotism has been quite an unexpected diversion, I do actually have better things to do. Good night, Mr. Bolívar."

"Very well. Please pass along my message to your friends back at Hawk. Whatever they want with me, they're wasting their time. I would personally destroy everything I've built rather than allow ONE to get their hands on it."

"Hard as it is for you to imagine, none of this has anything to do with you." She studied his face for as long as she thought she could get away with it. He was beautiful. She understood him less now than she had after watching his every move for two weeks, but she knew this: he was beautiful and extraordinary. "I'm sorry about your friend," she said. And then she felt her legs carry her to the door. She did not wait for him to open it for her. She let herself out and devoted all of her concentration to not looking back until the elevator doors closed and she was dropping out of the sky in a cherry wood-appointed aluminum cage that would deliver her to the streets of the city and back to her life.

THIRTY-THREE

Parker stood at the edge of the wide plaza at the base of ONE's Midtown headquarters, sipping a box of orange juice. He had stopped without warning, suddenly unable to join the continuous ant-like march of people who came up out of the subway tunnels and streamed into the building. A curved driveway funneled taxis, black cars, and the occasional limousine to within feet of the tower's front entrance. Pedestrians veered off the adjacent avenue and lined up at doughnut and coffee carts before crossing the plaza to take up their loyal positions in offices or cubicles on one of the building's seventy-nine floors. Parker felt particularly resentful of the narrow, landscaped slivers of green that dotted the plaza, audacious in this island metropolis where anything that wasn't concrete or vertical steel was inherently a waste of space. He looked up at the ONE tower and then quickly looked down, shielding his eyes from the bright morning sun reflecting off its glass facade. It was 8:20 AM on his first day of work at ONE, and he was hungover. He crushed the juice box in his fist and tossed it in a waste can.

The lobby of the ONE tower was a massive atrium that opened to two separate banks of elevators. The atrium's exterior walls were made of glass panels that allowed broad views to the plaza and the churning city beyond. The interior walls were lined with screens of varying size that displayed a collage of ONE programing—news programs, reality contests, music videos, feature films, and prime-time sitcoms and dramas. The lobby's main attraction, however, was the giant employee clock that hung above the security turnstiles. The clock was the first thing Parker saw when he stepped through the revolving doors and found himself inside. It ticked up from 118,094 to 118,095, almost as if acknowledging his arrival. Then it continued on: 118,096 . . . 118,097 . . . 118,098. Above and below the digits, sleek type read: ONE HAS 118,099 EMPLOYEES CONNECTING THE WORLD.

He was relieved, after he was issued a temporary employee ID card, to board an elevator and leave behind the visual chaos of the lobby. But he remained unsettled. The car's upward motion stoked his nausea. He felt terrible inside and out. There was no point on the horizon of his future on which to steady his vision, no reason to believe anything would soon become better. Why had he done it? "We can lay together in your room?" No! We cannot! He wanted to fly halfway around the world just so that he could be put in that situation again. *No, no, no,* he would say. It would be the easiest syllable he'd ever utter. But there was no more flying to Dubai. They'd dumped those clients in the acquisition. Now he was the associate social media consultant to the president of Digital Information and Entertainment at the ONE Corporation. He was glad he didn't have to see that on a business card. He had declined business cards on the grounds that they were environmentally unfriendly and made him look like a Luddite in the digital landscape of social networks.

The first thing he did in his new role was sign a ten-page nondisclosure agreement. The people in his department got off on secrecy in a big way. They threw around phrases like "proprietary products" and "sensitive consumer data." They were, he was assured during a large orientation with other new employees, developing technologies that would revolutionize the consumer's role in the digital space.

After the orientation meeting, Parker found his way to his new office, only to be told by a temp secretary—he would get to hire a permanent replacement soon—that Mr. Lawson, his boss, wanted to see him in his office.

An LED screen built into the closed door of Lawson's office, about eye height, read STEVEN LAWSON, PRESIDENT OF DIGITAL INFORMATION AND ENTERTAINMENT. When Lawson's secretary ushered Parker inside, he expected to find Lawson as he'd always found him in his limited experience to date: a pale, overfed man who delivered everything he said with an arrogant scowl, as if his audience was wasting his time. Alone with the man in his office, though, there was no sign of this trademark scowl. Lawson made eye contact and spoke in a friendly tone. Parker realized that this man saw people as being either inside or outside his sphere of influence, and Parker was now an insider.

"How are you liking it here so far?" Lawson said, half sitting on the edge of his vast oak desk and leaning toward Parker as if he had something to confide.

"It's great," Parker said. "It's only been a few hours. It's a little overwhelming, I guess."

"Forget whatever other shit you've been told. That's not what any of us is really here for."

Parker wasn't sure whether he was meant to react to this or not. He couldn't think of a suitable thing to say and began to sweat. Then the fear of becoming nauseated in this man's office made him sweat even more. But Lawson didn't appear to want to test him; he was merely setting up his next point.

"All of our key employees here at ONE have two jobs: the first is to carry out your duties related to your established media specialty. This is how we excel in the present and keep the shareholders off our backs. In your case, you'll be overseeing the social campaign for the release of *Apocalypse*, our first big film release of the summer."

Parker nodded cooperatively. He'd been told about this in one of the many interviews ONE had conducted after the acquisition to determine whom they wanted to keep. Eager to impress, Parker had already come up with a few ideas for the campaign to present to the team. But Lawson didn't seem to want to talk about that.

"The second job," Lawson continued. "Now, that is the fun part. It's what sets ONE apart from every other company on earth. It's our commitment to the future. As president of Digital Information, I am responsible for maximizing ONE's access to information. And you are going to be a key player in that strategy." Lawson, apparently concerned that Parker did not appreciate the gravity of what he was being told, leaned farther forward and continued as though trying to close a sale. "Some ONE employees work years to reach this level of responsibility, Parker. But you work in a field—you're an *expert* in a field—that is crucial to ONE's future.

"Social media is where the consumer becomes a part- ner with us in creating value from information. Most consum- ers already have an intuitive sense that the future is a place where everything—everyone—will be valued digitally. Our task is to show them that embracing that future is beneficial for everyone. The obvi- ous place to start is in the social landscape. That's where you and I are going to make history here. You up for that?"

"Yeah," Parker said, feeling for the first time that working for ONE might be a better opportunity than he'd first thought. "Yeah," he repeated, more enthusiastically.

"Good. Then let's get you credentialed with Information Security, and I'll introduce you to the bunker. Why don't you take a few minutes to settle into your office. Meet me down in the B7 lobby in, say, ten minutes?"

"B7. You mean, 'B' as in basement?"

"Yep. Ten minutes."

The basement has a lobby? Parker thought.

· · · · ·

Parker took the elevator to B7, which was located beneath P1–P6, and found the promised lobby, where he waited on a leather couch. Lawson joined him a minute later and led Parker through two separate doors that required a tap of the ID card Lawson wore on a lanyard around his neck.

They walked down an empty concrete hallway. "We'll get you set up with your credential in here," Lawson said, tapping his card to enter yet another locked door, this one with a narrow horizontal screen that said INFORMATION SECURITY.

Two humorless men issued Parker his own ID card, which displayed a regrettable head shot under his name, department, and the words LEVEL 4 ACCESS. "I got you access at a level higher than you need, strictly speaking. It should minimize the red tape," Lawson said, scowling at the IS men, who had clearly been on the losing end of that battle. "Your background check kicked off a little debate around here. You sailed through, of course. But the issue of your fiancée was something none of us had encountered before."

"My fiancée? Kera? What about her?"

"Nothing to worry about at all. Just the opposite. In the end I convinced everyone that, if anything, your association with her was a strength. You're already accustomed to navigating the usual insecurities that professional secrecy can sometimes create for couples."

"I'm not sure I understand. What does any of this have to do with her?"

The IS men looked concerned, but Lawson found a way to turn it into another victory. "See. Exactly. It has nothing to do with her. And she'll understand that. Just like you understand that there are things about her work that she can't tell you."

Baffled, but afraid to challenge Lawson further in front of the IS men, Parker followed his boss back into the hallway.

"What I'm about to show you is the very core of our information mission. Its existence is kind of 'need to know,' you know? But ONE is desperate to carve out a more dominant market share in the social space. So you need to know. You also need to know that this is the most confidential thing you will work on at ONE. You don't discuss it in the presence of anyone who isn't credentialed at Level Three or higher. You already signed the NDAs about this. I'm just reminding you."

Parker nodded.

The next door they went through opened into a small glass-enclosed control room that overlooked a massive chamber full of long rows of what looked like futuristic refrigerators, each with a few blinking lights on its outward-facing panel. A dozen technicians looked up from their consoles in the cramped room. "Everyone, this is Parker. He's working Information with me. Anything he needs help with is top priority."

Parker waved lamely and was greeted by friendly nods from the men and women looking back at him. Lawson guided him to the glass where they had the best view of the chamber.

"Those are all servers?" Parker asked.

"Yes. But this is only the local relaying station. These servers encrypt requests sent out to the bunker and then accept and distribute all the data that comes back."

"The bunker?"

"Yes. The bunker is about ten times this size, or so I'm told. It's where the real computing happens. Only a handful of people have seen it or even know where it is. I'm not one of them." Lawson walked Parker through the control room, explaining how the technicians monitored cybersecurity, bandwidth, temperatures, electricity usage, and a host of other variables. "As I was saying upstairs," Lawson said when they were walking back to the elevator. "Your role will be to help develop new social networking platforms that will engage more intimately with consumers' moment-to-moment lives. This will allow us to collect necessary data and merge it with the bunker's existing stores."

"What do you mean by 'necessary data'?" The onslaught of ambiguous jargon, the internal security clearances, the revelation that he actually had two jobs here—it all sent Parker's head spinning.

"Oh, that's just the way Keith Grassley, our CEO, refers to all data. It's all necessary. Transparency won't fully pay off for everyone until it's universal," Lawson continued. Parker couldn't pinpoint what about Lawson's smooth advocacy of the company made him uneasy, but the feeling poked at the back of his mind, even as he nodded agreeably at Lawson's words.

Lawson stopped at the end of the hallway before exiting through the lobby doors. "Think of it as the Big Bang, but in reverse. The data we are interested in is like all the matter in the universe, which is expanding. We want to know what is contained in all that matter. The bunker, then, when it's complete, will be like the whole of the universe at the moment just after the Bang. It will contain a complete copy of all the information that has ever existed, even information that was not represented as data until people like you and me found a way to turn it into digital bits that can be meaningfully calculated. As Grassley likes to say, that bunker contains the end of secrets."

THIRTY-FOUR

Lieutenant Commander William Farris of the US Coast Guard Rescue Command Center returned Kera's call late in the morning, just before she was about to walk into a meeting with Gabby and Director Branagh—a meeting she wasn't entirely confident her career would survive. They had long since run out of promising leads and were now struggling to imagine even the most out-of-the-box possibilities.

Over the past few weeks since the Background Noise Pollution plane crash, Kera had put in dozens of calls to the Coast Guard, NTSB, and FAA, none of which had advanced their understanding of why the plane had gone down or whether they should expect any bodies to be recovered. Now, over the phone, she explained to yet another Coast Guard man that she was a journalist researching a story on the aviation tragedy. He sounded surprised that she'd obtained his direct number and tried politely to transfer her to a spokesperson, but Kera somehow kept him on the line, assuring him that her questions would only take a moment.

"Am I right that the search-and-rescue effort has been called off?"

"That's correct. I don't know how to put it tastefully, ma'am, but after a week in those waters, there's very little to recover."

"And no serious injury or loss of life to your crew, I hope?"

"No, ma'am. We're used to doing SAR missions in some pretty hairy weather. This was all sunshine and calm seas."

"Do you know if there were any boats in the area when the plane went down? Are records kept for something like that?"

"As I said before, I don't have any information that hasn't already been released to the press. I'm happy to transfer you—"

"I understand. Maybe, if I could, just one more question. Do you think you could estimate for me the cost of the Coast Guard's search-and-rescue mission?"

"It was eighty-seven thousand dollars."

Kera nearly laughed. "You just happen to have that figure at hand?"

"Only because you're the second person to call about it, and then just the other day, we—" The man cut himself off.

"I'm sorry, I didn't get that," Kera said. Across her workstation she could see that Jones had shut down his screens. He looked over at her as he rose, indicating that it was time to go. She held up a finger in Jones's direction. "Just the other day you what?"

"Well, it's not classified information. A pretty remarkable thing. Two days ago the United States Coast Guard Rescue Command Center received an anonymous cash donation of eighty-seven thousand dollars."

Kera sat up. "Lieutenant Commander Farris, this is very important. You said you received another call about the expenses? Do you know who that call came from? Do you have a name or a number?"

"I'm afraid I don't, ma'am. Didn't think anything of it at the time. And then, I'll be damned, that pile of cash turned up."

She thanked him quickly and hung up. Then she ran down the hall to the conference room.

Director Branagh and Gabby did not look up immediately when she entered. Jones had found a way to stall for her by walking them through some data on his tablet. Kera took her seat and listened quietly as they finished. They were talking about Gnos.is.

"We need to discuss ATLANTIS," the director said, reclaiming the agenda after he'd heard enough from Jones. His tone did not leave room for hope that this would be a pleasant meeting. "I'm going to be as blunt as I possibly can. This case came to us as a minor priority, a bullshit little side gig to bolster our reputation and take in a few extra bucks. I expected to have this thing sewn up and forgotten by now. And yet, somehow, we have half a dozen more disappearances linked to this case than when we started—and not a single fucking corpse or a hint of an explanation."

Kera opened her mouth but was silenced immediately by a look of warning from Gabby and by the director, who raised a scolding finger.

"No. I don't want any more excuses. Gabby put you two up for this, and you fucked up. The way you've managed this case makes you look incompetent, and that reflects poorly on Gabby. And what reflects poorly on Gabby reflects poorly on me. Listen to me very carefully. None of us can afford to look incompetent. Not right now. Not ever. All of our futures here are at stake. Nod if you understand me."

Jones nodded. Kera did not. Everyone looked at her.

"If I may, sir. There might be a new development," she said.

"A development?" Gabby was furious. Kera could feel Jones looking at her.

"Well, I have a theory."

Gabby started to protest, but the director stopped her. "Go ahead," he said, as Kera had hoped he would. He'd said it himself—the outcome of this case reflected on him. He was as desperate to solve it as anyone. But he wouldn't pretend to be patient.

"I believe that the circumstances of the disappearances suggest that all ten of the missing people are alive and well." Kera took a few minutes to outline the brief law career of Caroline Mullen, the twenty-nine-year-old woman who had abandoned her bicycle on the George Washington Bridge and supposedly leapt off. It had been Caroline Mullen's career track—as an associate attorney, not an artist or writer—that had set her apart from the other missing. And that had led Kera, early in the investigation, to the offices of Milton & Booth to talk to Raymond Booth, the estate attorney who spoke so highly of Caroline Mullen's skill and passion. Booth had also spoken to Kera about the legal rights of missing persons.

"In most cases of pseudocide," Kera explained, "the subject is motivated by financial troubles or a failed romantic relationship. They fake their death to collect on a life insurance policy, to avoid a debt, or to flee an abusive spouse. None of our subjects appear to be motivated by such circumstances. In fact, it's quite the opposite. All were current on their taxes and credit cards at the time of their disappearance. And none of them were married, which means no spouses have been left in the lurch with respect to their legal marital status."

"I'll stop you right there," the director said. "Are you suggesting that these people are not only alive, but that they've gone missing *by choice*?"

"I am, sir."

"Jesus Christ," he said, and seemed to be considering the implications of this. But then he shook his head. "It's impossible. Putting aside for the moment the question of why they would even want to do this, I don't see how it's practical. A person faces hundreds of obligations that cannot simply be abandoned. What about bills, lease agreements, car payments?"

"I checked. Those obligations are real, and in every single one of these cases, arrangements were made in advance to avoid legal default. I thought that that was what Caroline Mullen might be helping them with, but I couldn't be sure. Until today." Kera paused for effect. "An eighty-seven-thousand-dollar payment was made to the US Coast Guard to cover the expense—the *precise* expense, it turns out—of the search-and-rescue mission after that plane crash last week."

There was a long silence.

"That's true?" the director asked.

Kera nodded. "I believe that the members of Background Noise Pollution created an aviation disaster to fake their deaths, and then paid the US Coast Guard for their troubles, in effect."

"Why?" Gabby said.

"Because they want to avoid legal trouble."

"Please. If a cash payment is all it took to clear people of legal trouble, that would happen more often," the director said.

"I think this case might be unique," Kera said. "If the only crime here is wasting taxpayer money, well, this solves that. There's no longer any victim."

The director did not appear convinced of her legal expertise, but his silence indicated that he was at least starting to consider the possibility that she was right about the missing band members. Gabby wasn't quite there yet. "Why would someone who's dropping off the grid care about legal trouble? That seems like the least of their worries."

"Because they plan to come back."

"But why?" Jones said. It was the first time he'd spoken, and for this reason he got everyone's attention. He was looking at Kera, and not kindly. She'd stuck both their necks out with her theory, and she hadn't consulted him first. Challenging her now was his way of showing Director Branagh and Gabby that Kera was alone in this hypothesizing. "You're forgetting the most basic problem with this case: there's no motive. Why choose to vanish? What do you imagine these people are trying to accomplish by disappearing—by faking their suicides—if they intend to come back?" He had chosen the word *imagine* deliberately to make her sound like a lunatic. She might have expected him to be annoyed with her, but this cut much deeper.

"I don't know," she admitted.

"Say there *was* some motive to vanish—which there doesn't appear to be," Gabby said with an edge in her voice. "How do you explain all the references to suicide? Why fake one's death so elaborately? Why not just walk away and disappear with no trace?"

Kera thought about this. "I don't know the answer to that. But if I had to guess—"

"I'd prefer we keep the guessing to a minimum," said the director.

"I think the elaborate suicide scenes are a key part of the message they're trying to send."

"The message?" the director asked.

"Yes. Each of these people was passionately committed to what they were doing with their lives, whether it was art, or the law—whatever. They were highly unlikely candidates for suicide, and the way they went about staging their departures was so outlandish, so . . . creative, I think it was their way of sending a message to the people who knew them. Like that phrase that's left behind at all of the scenes: 'Have you figured it out yet?'"

"What is that about?" Gabby said. "I hear people saying it to each other. What does it *mean*?"

"I think in the case of these missing people, it's their way of saying, 'I'm OK. But I'm gone. You won't find me unless I want to be found.'"

"Do you have proof of any of this?" the director asked.

"I've told you what I know."

Jones leaned back in his chair. He was not supporting her here.

"So, no," Gabby said.

Jones was silent. Kera would have liked the opportunity to step aside and apologize to him. She knew he felt blindsided, and she hated the way he was looking at her now.

The chance to confer with him would not come, however, at least not now, because just then Director Branagh's assistant burst through the conference room door unannounced to say that something urgent had happened with VINYL.

Director Branagh, Gabby, and Jones stood immediately. Kera, who did not understand what was happening, looked up at Jones. "VINYL?"

"The Gnos.is case," he said, and then they all hurried away.

THIRTY-FIVE

At 1150 hours a cryptologist at an eight-screen array in Hawk's Control Room leaned back in his chair and whispered to himself, "Holy shit." For the past three months, his workstation had been tethered to a supercomputer buried fifteen stories under Manhattan. The computer, a Cray XK7 owned by the NSA, had been working around the clock to try to break Gnos.is's 192-bit encryption key. The cryptologist had estimated that, if they got lucky, this brute-force attack on the site's encryption key would take a few years. But luck wasn't a strategy of any Hawk operation. So while the computer churned away its calculations at more than seventeen million billion operations per second three hundred feet underground, the cryptologist sat at his workstation and studied what little anyone knew about Gnos.is's back-end operations, trying to come up with a faster solution that wouldn't make him appear less useful than a computer.

The audible obscenity was on account of the fact that his job had just become exponentially harder. At midnight early that morning, Gnos.is had switched to a 320-bit encryption key. He was one part impressed—320-bit encryption keys were nearly unheard-of—and one part fucked. It would take a dozen supercomputers like the one he was using twice as long to crack a 320-bit key. They didn't have that kind of computing power, and they didn't have that kind of time.

The cryptologist's discovery was the first new information the VINYL team had collected on Gnos.is in months, and for that reason it was of analytical interest. The heightened encryption level could mean that Gnos.is was undergoing a major system upgrade or data migration, and that might leave the site vulnerable in other ways. If Hawk was waiting at the right place at the right time, they might pick up on something that would help them identify whoever was behind Gnos.is.

Thirty minutes later an analyst monitoring Gnos.is's live site came forward to report something odd: a sharp decrease in the site's routine maintenance. "Gnos.is basically looks the same on its face, but they've halted all back-end maintenance. For the past twelve hours, the site's been running on autopilot."

"Isn't it designed for that?" Gabby asked. Director Branagh stood back, quietly taking everything in.

"Yes, in some respects. But the site is still growing. Glitches pop up almost constantly. Without a team at work to fix bugs, these glitches will start showing on the front end within a few days."

"Maybe they lost their funding," someone suggested.

"And then upgraded their encryption? I don't think so. Jones, what's happening with hosting?" the case officer said.

Jones, already at a workstation in the pit, had anticipated this question. He'd tried to get a step ahead, but then he had to backtrack to check his work. Not because he thought he'd been sloppy, but because he almost didn't believe what he was seeing.

"We've got increases here too, sir. Hosting's shifted to almost double the previous rates."

"Put it on the big screen."

A dozen pairs of eyes looked up at the wall-size display in unison. Gnos.is relied on the encryption key to remain anonymous. But the thing that kept the site live and out of danger from saboteurs or investigators was the way the site bounced quickly from server to server, staying ahead of pursuers. Gnos.is accomplished this by constantly making complete copies of itself, storing them on multiple servers, and switching randomly between them. By the time anyone could pinpoint where the site was being published at any one time, the live site had moved to a different server, usually on a different continent. Even if Gnos.is could be shut down on the right server at the right time, the site would just pop up on another server almost instantaneously.

What Jones put up on the big screen illustrated that Gnos.is had improved the speed of this random scramble of host servers. Before, the live site jumped from server to server at a rate of once every 90 to 120 seconds. Now the dots on the big screen were staying lit for less than a minute.

"The only reason they'd do all this is if they're getting ready for something," the case officer said. "Judging by how serious they're taking their encryption, I'd say it's got to be something big."

Jones waited for his first chance to leave the pit and climb the steps to his own workstation. The Gnos.is discoveries—and what they implied—created a feeling among the task force that they'd learned something new about the site. Jones suspected that that feeling would deflate quickly into helplessness as they began to realize that, in fact, all they had learned was that it would now be more difficult than ever, if not impossible, to actually learn anything about Gnos.is that Gnos.is didn't want them to know.

"I'm sorry about the meeting," Kera said when he approached. She'd been standing at his workstation with a good vantage of the action unfolding in the pit below. "I didn't mean for—"

"Sit down." Jones had said this so calmly that she almost hadn't heard him. She was standing behind his chair, her body turned toward the big screen above the pit, which was still displaying a map of all the Gnos.is hosting sites the task force had identified.

"What's going on?"

"Don't look up there. Sit down."

Kera sat and tapped the touch-screen keypad. Whenever her workstation was inactive for sixty seconds, it locked into sleep mode. It was an annoying and perfectly sensible security mechanism. The first time she entered her log-in passcode, she got it wrong and had to start over with the print scan. Jones's tone had thrown her.

"Can you hear me?" he said. She glanced over at him. "Don't look, just listen. Do you remember what Gabby said when you told her that ONE was hiring people from the NSA?"

Kera looked at him and then remembered he'd told her not to, and she steered her eyes back to her screens. Her fingers resumed the detached motions of opening programs as if she were getting back to work.

"I remember. What's going on?" Gabby was down in the pit with the Gnos.is team, which meant she was out of earshot as long as they whispered.

"We can't talk about it here," Jones said and fell silent. When Kera finally stole a glance over at him, she saw that he was hunched over his desk writing something on a napkin. A few minutes later, he stood up and strolled over to her workstation. He was holding a coffee cup and, beneath it like a coaster, the napkin. He nodded at the ATLANTIS dossiers Kera had opened on her center monitor.

"Interesting about that Coast Guard donation," he said. His voice was casual, as if nothing else had happened.

"Jones, I would have told you. That phone call I took just before the meeting—that's when I found out about it. I had to mention it in the meeting. The director wanted to shut us down."

"Look, I gotta get back to work," he said abruptly. Then he wandered off in the direction of the men's room.

Kera stared at the coffee cup and napkin resting on the edge of her desk. The cup was one of the disposable paper amenities from the Control Room kitchen. There was a half inch of tepid black coffee in the bottom. She lifted the cup. When she was done reading the instructions, she ripped up the napkin and shoved the crumpled remains into the coffee dregs before tossing it all into her wastebasket.

THIRTY-SIX

THIRTY-SIX

After work she rode the F train to Broadway-Lafayette, her usual stop. She walked three blocks in the direction of her apartment before she stopped at a spot she knew to be out of view of any surveillance camera accessible by HawkEye. She flagged a cab and told the driver to take her to Eleventh Avenue and West Twenty-Seventh Street. There were no cameras there either. She got out on Eleventh and walked around the corner onto West Twenty-Sixth. She waited for another cab and told the driver to take her uptown and then cross over to Central Park West when they were in the mid-Seventies.

After they'd cruised several blocks north of the Museum of Natural History, which was monitored heavily by surveillance cameras, she asked him to stop. For a block in either direction, the only visible cameras were trained on the entrances of co-op apartment buildings across the street. She stepped out of the cab and took the nearest path into the park.

She found Jones on a bench at the south end of the Great Lawn.

"Did you switch cabs?"

Kera nodded. "What are we doing here?"

"You initiated a HawkEye dossier on Rafael Bolívar," Jones said. The anger in his voice startled her.

"He's connected, Jones."

"How?"

"I'm working on that." She checked the sight lines around them. If anyone other than Jones had been waiting for her, it wasn't obvious. "You wanted to come all the way out here to talk about Bolívar?"

"No. This is about you. You got too close to Canyon, and you were lucky he took a swim in the Hudson before he made you. But now Bolívar? You shouldn't have snuck into the Control Room behind my back to set up a dossier on him. And you shouldn't have gone to that ridiculous media pioneers event."

"You have surveillance on me now?"

"Fuck you, Kera. Your privacy is not high on my list of concerns. You're being reckless."

"I'm being resourceful. I'm trying to solve this case. You might have noticed if you spent less time marveling at Gnos.is."

"I spend my time exactly where I'm supposed to be. And it's where you're supposed to be too."

"Sitting in front of our screens all day? That's working out well so far. Look, I'm sick of watching people disappear and not being able to do anything about it. I had to try something new. What happened in the Control Room today?"

"No. First we settle this. Convince me that tracking Bolívar is worth the risk. Because if he finds out we have surveillance on him, we're done. Can you imagine the ratings bait that would be for his TV news and talk shows? If he gets one whiff of us, it will be everywhere."

She'd imagined that a lot, in fact, and now she wondered again why Bolívar hadn't gone public with his knowledge of Hawk. She didn't mention that to Jones, though. She just nodded.

"Give me a sign that I can trust you," he said. "Let me in on where you intend to go with all this."

Kera thought of Lionel. *Don't trust anyone. Throughout your entire career, you will trust perhaps two or three people.* J. D. Jones did not qualify as one of those people, not by Lionel's standards nor her own. But her instinct told her that Jones was at least an ally. She believed they were working toward the same end, even if they went about it in different ways. Her instinct also told her that she needed him. Jones was respected at Hawk, and without him she'd be isolated. That is, if she wasn't already. It was not encouraging that Jones thought it necessary to leave the most secure room in Manhattan and rendezvous on a park bench to have a conversation.

She began to talk and found that it felt good to do so. She focused mostly on Charlie Canyon and their bizarre exchanges—from the art show with the "stolen" paintings to confronting him about the missing people at the commercial shoot.

"In person Canyon was, I don't know—odd. Philosophical at times," she said. "At first I thought he was just aloof, but he missed nothing. Sometimes I felt like he was three steps ahead of us." She brought Bolívar into the picture by mentioning how she'd spotted him at the commercial shoot and had left with the impression that he and Canyon were working together. On what? Well, that was still the open question. "I didn't intend to keep any of this from you. I was waiting, I guess, until I'd connected the dots. Because the truth is that I had evidence of nothing. It wasn't until that phone call today, right before the meeting, that I felt like I might be getting somewhere. And the timing ended up blindsiding you. I'm sorry for that."

When she was finished, Jones sat in silence for a full minute. Then his eyes swept from one periphery to the other. He was checking for company, she realized, and it gave her comfort to see that he, too, expected them to be alone. Finally he said, "The reason I acted the way I did in the meeting is because I didn't want Gabby and Branagh to think that you and I are working too closely together."

Kera looked at him, openly confused. "Why?"

"They're watching us."

"Hawk is?" She shrugged. "OK. I guess I assumed as much. But so what? We haven't done anything wrong."

"What was the ONE case?" he said suddenly.

"What?"

"The thing Gabby was upset over."

"Oh, that. I don't know much. Like I told you before, Gabby sent me to meet with a source. The guy had been a quant on the Street, and he said ONE hired him and some other math whizzes to work on complex consumer behavior models. Real invasive, data-mining-type stuff, and then selling off the information to the highest bidder. I'm a foreign cyberthreat analyst, Jones. It wasn't my area. But I asked her if she wanted me to look into it. I was mostly just kissing ass; I didn't want the case. Though I guess it wasn't a total dud. Think of it this way: if a foreign government was spying on American consumers the way ONE is, we'd go after them with everything we've got, right?"

"Did she want you to look into it?"

"No. She told me to leave it alone."

"Then what happened?"

Kera shrugged. "Rowena Pete happened. Gabby assigned me to ATLANTIS with you, and ONE never came up again."

"But you didn't let it go."

"Sure I did. It wasn't my responsibility, and it's not my area. What could I do?"

Jones looked confused. "What about the thing with the NSA hires? You brought that up."

"That was a coincidence. I had alerts set up in the system. Same as I do for any case. I hadn't turned them off because I got swept into ATLANTIS and forgot all about the stuff with ONE."

"So you got an alert that ONE had hired some NSA guys."

"Yeah. It was just a news report, if I remember."

"You knew it would shake Gabby, though. That's why you brought it up. Why?"

"I was mad at her for treating me like an idiot, especially in front of the director. I was acting out; I just wanted to show her that I knew more than she thought I did." Kera tried to think of anything she'd left out about the meeting with Travis Bradley. She'd told Jones everything. Now it was his turn. "What are you dancing around? You think it's more than that? You think there actually *is* a ONE case?"

Jones had been looking up the Great Lawn. Now he looked at her. "I think it's much worse than that."

"What do you mean?"

"Why do you think Gabby sent you to meet with that source?"

"Apparently, the source had come to us—well, he'd approached the *Global Report*, anyway. He was a whistle-blower looking for a journalist. Gabby told me to find out what he knew."

"What he knew? Or what he was prepared to talk about?"

"What's the difference?"

"You know the difference. You're assuming Gabby's interest in this guy was to find out whether ONE was doing something illegal. What if she really sent you to find out if the quant was in a position to give ONE any trouble?"

"You mean, was he someone who needed to be silenced?"

"Something like that."

"But why would Gabby—" Kera stopped herself and took a long moment to process this, first rejecting the thought multiple times before expanding her mind enough to accommodate what she thought Jones was saying. Not just Jones. Both Charlie Canyon and Rafael Bolívar had suggested it too.

"We're working for ONE, Kera."

She shook her head.

"Yes," he said. "I'm certain of it."

"Why do you say that?" She was still shaking her head.

"VINYL."

"That's the Gnos.is case?"

"Yes. About three months ago, Branagh formed a team to root out whoever is behind Gnos.is. I thought, 'Here we go again,' right? Because we'd already been through that. Didn't you say you worked the Gnos.is task force the first time around?"

Kera nodded.

"We got back into it, and at first I forgot about how strange the assignment seemed. After all, Gnos.is's influence has only grown, and we still know virtually nothing about who runs the site or what their intentions are. Iran, China, Russia—we're not sure whether they're capable of something like this, but what if they are? It seemed like a natural precaution for the intelligence community to want to keep an eye out. And why not use Hawk? We're the best, right? Plus, I have to say, on a personal level, Gnos.is has always kind of needled me. It keeps me up at night, you know? How are they doing this? They don't take in any revenue, which means they don't have to file with the IRS. They just exist. But why? What are they getting out of it? Why can't we crack it? My point is, I was eager to be back on the case, and because of that it took me some time to notice something was off."

"Off how?"

"The mission of VINYL doesn't make sense. We aren't looking for encrypted codes in Gnos.is news stories; we aren't looking for signs of foreign political influence or espionage or even evidence that Gnos.is is storing users' private data. We're not really looking for threats at all. From the beginning this whole op has been laser focused on one aim: finding the people who run Gnos.is. Just ID 'em. That's the basis of every order I've received. It's crazy. Who's interested in intel that myopic?" He was looking at her as if what he'd just said implied something obvious.

"I think you lost me. What are you saying?"

"Our client for VINYL isn't coming from the intelligence community. It's ONE. ONE ordered the intel on Gnos.is, and I think they're contracting everything else we're doing at Hawk too." He let this sink in.

Kera shook her head. "That's impossible. When I got to Hawk, I worked on Iran. I've worked on China. Most of what I've done here was on real, hard intelligence targets."

"I know. But then that stopped, right? When's the last time you looked at a string of code from a Chinese computer virus or a satellite image of an Iranian nuclear plant? Kera, everything we've worked on in the past six months, I can connect it all back to ONE. VINYL, the meeting Gabby sent you on with that source, and now even ATLANTIS."

"It can't be."

"It can. I confirmed it."

"How?"

"I got curious. It's a problem I have. My background isn't military, and it isn't government. I mostly don't give a fuck about rank. I believe in questioning orders. Call me disrespectful, but I didn't have much of an internal dilemma before I decided to use my security clearance and some computer gymnastics to get a peek at where these intel orders were coming from."

"And you found what?"

"Contracts. A lot of them. From what I could see, Hawk has contracts with ONE worth more than a hundred million dollars."

"Those could have been planted." Kera was indignant. "It doesn't make sense."

"Sure it does. I'm not CFO, but I suspect a hundred million dollars is double what Hawk was making from government contracts."

"That's not what I meant. What's ONE's interest in ATLANTIS?"

"You heard the director today. It all comes back to money. To hang on to these contracts, Hawk needs to keep ONE happy. ONE has this little problem creep up—all of a sudden, a handful of their artists start vanishing. They want to know what's going on, and they want it to stop. And in the meantime they want to keep it out of the press. So they turn to us to figure out what's going on, since we're already working on other, bigger cases for them."

Kera couldn't quite spot a hole in his argument, but she wasn't sure she was convinced. "And what about Gnos.is?" she said. "Why would ONE be so interested in finding the owners of Gnos.is?"

Jones looked at her as if this should have been obvious. "So they can make them an offer."

The brashness of it, the simplicity—she didn't have to think about it for long before she saw that his theory was plausible. Gnos.is was a formidable presence in the online media space. Acquiring them would eliminate an unpredictable and powerful adversary. And that wasn't even Gnos.is's greatest potential value to ONE. From her own work on the first Gnos.is case, Kera was very aware of the site's elegance and efficiency. The coders and designers behind Gnos.is— whoever and wherever they were—were the best in the world. They would be valuable to ONE. Perhaps even valuable enough to hire the best intelligence contractor ever assembled to find them.

The prospect that Jones was right about all of this finally hit her. But there was one problem with Jones's theory. "We weren't for sale," she said softly.

"Everyone in this business is for sale. Hawk might have originated at CIA in partnership with NSA, but it was structured as a private contractor."

"That was supposed to be part of our cover."

"Welcome to the intelligence business."

His condescension infuriated her. "I swore an oath. Christ, Jones, I didn't come here to be a corporate spy."

"Your oath meant something at Langley, and I believe it still means something to you. But we didn't swear anything to Hawk. We signed contracts to analyze computer intelligence. At the end of the day, ONE was willing to pay more for that service than our government."

Kera looked up the Great Lawn. It was a warm evening. A half-dozen softball games were in progress. People lay on blankets reading. Shirtless men threw a Frisbee. She saw little of this, though. Her vision was turned inward. "You discovered this today?" she asked.

"No, weeks ago."

"And you didn't tell me?"

"I had nothing to gain by telling you." She felt sure the chill in his voice was intentional. He was making it clear that they were in a business where the only way to survive was to watch your own back. Which raised her next question.

"Why are you telling me now?"

"Because I need your help bringing them down."

"What are you talking about, bring them down?"

"Expose them and destroy them. They are using us, Kera. They've stolen some of the intelligence community's best resources, including people like you and me. And for what? To spy on other Americans for their own profit? I'm not comfortable letting them get away with that, and I'm certainly not comfortable being a part of it. I'm telling you now because they don't yet know what I know about them. But they will. They're watching everything we do. We have to bring them down before they catch on to what we're doing."

"What makes you think I want to bring down Hawk?"

He looked her in the eye. "Because the alternative is to keep working for them."

She turned away. On the field immediately in front of them, a pair of corporate softball teams were battling it out. A batter knocked a foul ball that bounced off the backstop. "Why did you come to Hawk?"

"We're not talking about that now. Listen to me, Kera. We have to assume ONE is controlling Hawk now. All of it. All of us."

"How do I know you're not working for ONE?" she said. "How do I know everything you've just told me isn't a test that Gabby put you up to?"

"How do you know anything?" he said.

She stood up. "I have to go."

"Can I ask you something?" he said. Kera turned and waited. "Where do you think they are?"

"Who?"

"The missing. The people in hiding, or whatever we're calling them. I think you're right about ATLANTIS, Kera. I couldn't say that in there today. But you're right. They're alive, and they're planning to come back. But why? What are they getting out of this?"

"I don't know," she said. And it was the truth.

THIRTY-SEVEN

Lionel Bright was sitting at his desk, presiding over a weekly intel coordination meeting for the China division, when he noticed the postcard on top of the new mail in his in-box. His eyes kept coming back to it as the meeting droned on around him.

The purpose of these meetings was to facilitate a line of communication between the cyber guys, who were antisocial, and the case agents, who were secretive to a fault. They needed each other and wouldn't admit it. So he'd had the idea to force them to sit together in a room for an hour each week and make sure they hadn't withheld anything crucial from one another, out of negligence or ego. It was important work, despite its tedium. Most weeks Lionel just sat there, interjecting only occasionally and growing bored out of his mind. By the end of the hour, he was usually second-guessing why he'd agreed to waste part of his day on this level of redundancy. Gazing out the window for too long sent a signal that he wasn't paying attention, so he'd kept his eyes facing forward where he could let his mind wander more covertly.

That's when he'd noticed the postcard. It was a picture of the New York City skyline on a glorious day, the crown of the Statue of Liberty sparkling in the sun in the foreground.

A sinking feeling tugged at his insides.

If it's blank . . . , he thought, already knowing that it would be but unable to confirm it until all of the men and women had filed out of his office. When he was finally alone, he stood looking down at Lady Liberty for a second before he lifted the card between thumb and index finger and flipped it over. There was nothing on the back but his address and the postmark. The card had been mailed from Manhattan the previous day.

Lionel left Langley around five and exited the freeway one ramp earlier than normal so that he could swing by his neighborhood's small public library. He parked ten minutes before closing time and jogged to the entrance against a light stream of departing foot traffic, mostly parents fetching energetic children from after-school programs and slower-moving elderly patrons who still liked to check out books on tape.

Ignoring a librarian's warning about the time, he went directly to one of the public computers and logged into the Yahoo account he had established for this purpose. The in-box was empty, but there was a single message saved to the drafts folder. The subject was WORK FROM HOME! DOUBLE YOUR INCOME! He clicked on it and scrolled quickly through the scam's tacky, boldface promises and testimonials. At the bottom of the message, below a copyright line, was a block of generic legal disclaimers in a much smaller font. He had to squint at the words to read them, but eventually he found what he was looking for. Inserted into the legal paragraph were six sentences that didn't belong there:

HAWK COMPROMISED. FOREIGN TARGETS ABANDONED. WARRANTLESS SURVEILLANCE OF US TARGETS & CORP ESPIONAGE, POSSIBLY ON BEHALF OF MAJOR US CORP. ADVISE NEXT STEPS ASAP.

THIRTY-EIGHT

The quant emerged from his Tribeca condo building at 10:25 A.M. She let him walk half a block before she got up from the bus stop bench. He stopped at an intersection to wait for the light. She hung back, watching. She knew there was no HawkEye coverage on his block, but she didn't want to approach him too close to home. Instead, she waited until he dropped down to the subway platform at Canal. The surveillance cameras on the uptown platform had been out of order for a week, creating a temporary blind spot. It was just the place to talk to Bradley without setting off any scenario alarms that Gabby or Branagh might have programmed HawkEye to recognize.

She slipped through the turnstile, closed the gap between her and Bradley, and came up on his right side. It must have been some time since the last train; there were more people than usual on the platform.

"Not returning calls these days?" she said in a voice only he could hear.

He turned toward her, not understanding at first that she was talking to him. But then recognition flooded his eyes, succeeded quickly by fear. He stepped away from her and looked down the tunnel, desperate for a train. She approached him again.

"Take a hint, huh? I can't talk to you," he said, angling himself away from her. He swiveled his head around as if scanning the platform around them. Then he looked down the tunnel again.

"There have been developments with ONE. I need to talk to you." There would be cameras on the train. She had to talk to him before it arrived.

"Yeah, there have been developments. I get threats now. People follow me. I can't use my phone; I can't sleep at night." He scanned the platform again, and this time she thought his eyes caught on something. She tried to follow his gaze, but there were too many people. Then the rumble of the train rose up, echoing through the station.

"When did the threats start?"

He said something, but his voice was drowned out by the screech of brakes.

"What?" she yelled.

He looked at her when the train stopped.

"The threats started after I met with you," he said. He glanced over her shoulder and she spun around to see what he was looking at. At first she saw nothing out of the ordinary, just people crowding toward the open train doors. But then she caught sight of him. The man was halfway down the platform. Unlike the others, he wasn't shuffling toward the train. He was holding a telephoto-lens camera to his face. It was pointed right at Kera and Bradley.

"These are the people following you?" Kera said, turning back. But Bradley had already retreated to the center of the car. She let him go. When she turned around, the man with the camera was gone.

She was climbing out of the subway station when her phone buzzed with an incoming call from an unsecure line. The ID display said it originated at Alegría North America. She hesitated. *It can't be him*, she told herself, prepared to let the call go to voice mail. But after two rings another urge took over. *What if it is?*

"Hello," she said. She was up on the street now and had to cover her other ear in order to hear.

"Ms. Mersal." It was his voice.

"How did you get this number?" she said.

"I'm resourceful. I didn't know how else to reach you."

"Why would you need to reach me?"

"I'll be direct. Small talk feels ridiculous when we both know other people are listening." That was probably true. It was unlikely that Hawk monitored her calls live, but she didn't doubt that they were all recorded and stored in case an investigation of her behavior became necessary—which, eventually, it would. She wondered whether Jones would notice the call in Bolívar's dossier.

"Go on," she said. There would be a record of the call either way; she might as well find out what he had to say.

"Will you see a film with me?"

"I'm sorry?"

"I'd like to take you to a movie."

Kera nearly laughed. "That's why you're calling?"

"It is."

Was he talking in code? If he was, she had no way to decipher it. She said, "The other night you insulted me. And now you want me to spend an evening with you?"

"You're not saying no?"

"I'm saying it's very unusual to receive a call like this. I don't know what to say."

"Aren't you supposed to tell me that you're engaged?"

"I—" Was he testing her to see which she would throw under the bus first, her fiancé or a new opportunity to crack the case? Did he really know about either, or was he bluffing?

"There will be no press," he said. "If you are looking to get your picture with me in the tabloids, you've missed your chance."

"Do I need to state for the record that this will not be a date?"

"I think you just did. I won't give any of the details over the phone. I'll have them sent to you. Keep your Thursday evening open." And then he hung up.

She did not try very hard to think of a reason not to go to the movie with him. It was reason enough that he had something to say and that it could not be said over the phone. But that wasn't the main reason she would go. Her confrontation with Bolívar at the media pioneers event had been bizarre and unpleasant, but that hadn't stopped her from thinking, almost constantly, about when she might see him again.

THIRTY-NINE

The car Rafael Bolívar sent for her wound its way uptown. Kera wore a blood-orange dress and had arranged her hair in an elegant heap at the crown of her head. From the backseat, she enjoyed the evolution of city blocks as they moved across her window. She could not remember the last time she had ridden in a car and just looked at the city, free of distractions from her phone.

Against Gabby's warnings that Kera must always have the phone on her person, Kera had left it behind—intentionally—when she'd gone home from work early to get ready. Any phone could be an accurate way of tracking the location of its owner. But a phone issued by Hawk, she suspected, might have even more invasive monitoring capabilities than that. This evening she wanted to be alone. And so the phone was in her work bag by the coffee table in their apartment where, she hoped, it might seem she'd simply forgotten it if it ever became necessary to explain herself.

Kera did not know the car's destination, and she did not ask the driver. Not knowing added to her feeling of exhilaration as the vehicle lurched through the city. Some blocks shot past out of focus;

others rolled along at a pedestrian's pace. She sat up with interest when the car pulled over on Fifty-Ninth Street at the entrance to two glass towers that rose up over Columbus Circle at the southwest corner of Central Park. It was his building, where he lived. She recalled reading about his apartment in a tabloid piece, and, of course, she had watched surveillance footage of him coming in and out of these doors daily.

She was surprised to see Bolívar himself emerge from the building's entrance to open her car door. The way he moved—fluid and confident—made his custom suit seem less formal somehow, as if he would be just as natural in sandals and shorts as he was in a suit on Fifty-Ninth Street. Through the hours she'd watched him, she'd grown familiar with this comfortable way he had in his own skin, his intrinsic Bolívar-ness. But that description had never been adequate. She realized now what had eluded her about his presence: he did nothing casually; everything was intentional.

"Good evening, Ms. Mersal," he said, and guided her inside with a firm hand at the small of her back. She thought about that hand a few moments later when she watched him reach with long, slim fingers to push the button to call an elevator. As she removed her sunglasses, which she had worn to throw off facial-recog software, she could still feel the spot on her lower back where he'd touched her.

An elevator whisked them skyward and opened to a lobby on the fifty-sixth floor. The room hummed with conversation. Dozens of people stood sipping cocktails and talking in groups. Bolívar led her outside to a bar on a balcony that jutted out from the room. There was not a bad view of the park from any vantage, inside or out. The only interior camera she'd spotted had been in the elevator. She hoped it was a firewalled, closed-circuit feed isolated to the building's security monitors and not accessible by Jones or anyone else in the Control Room.

When they'd stepped from the elevator, it had been impossible not to notice Natalie Smith among the crowd. She stood, as ever, like a magnetic pole that pulled on the flow of traffic through the room. Her skin was radiant, her smile warm, her eyes sharp. She had noticed their entrance.

"You two dated," Kera said, leaning against the balcony railing and looking inside.

Bolívar did not need to ask whom she was referring to. "We experimented. I think we both concluded that it was a valuable and enjoyable mistake." His voice was so free of regret that it caught Kera off guard. Her motive for bringing it up had been jealousy, and that now seemed low in the face of his honest response.

"The movie we'll see; it's hers, isn't it?" Kera said.

"Yes. After *America* was pulled by the studio, I offered to pay to distribute it to every movie theater in the country. She declined. But I finally convinced her to let me host this small screening."

"Why did she decline?"

Bolívar smiled. "You should ask her that yourself."

Kera waited and observed the crowd while Bolívar went to the bar. When he rejoined her, she said, "What do you really think about Marybelle Pickett?"

"What?" he said. "Oh, that."

"I saw you at that basement art show for her work. But at the gala the other night, you completely dismissed her."

"I was asked a ridiculous question. I gave the answer they wanted."

"I find it hard to believe that you've gotten to where you are by giving other people what they want. Do you like her paintings?"

"Very much. I tried to buy them that night at the art show."

"Which painting?"

"All of them."

Kera laughed. "How much did you offer, if you don't mind my asking?"

"I was prepared to pay twenty thousand dollars on the spot. But I was told that they weren't for sale."

"Right. Because at that point they were stolen."

"I didn't know that then. I only learned it later that night," he said. "The artist, those paintings—the whole thing was another one of Charlie's stunts."

"Stunts?"

Bolívar nodded. "He thought stunts like that were important, to draw wide attention to something deserving. I see things the other way around, that if people can't recognize value in art, they aren't deserving of it. It was an ongoing disagreement we had."

"It worked," Kera said.

"What?"

"The stunt. The paintings were auctioned for eighty thousand more than you would have paid."

"If the stunt proved anything, it's that the value of paintings has little to do with their price at auction."

When they were each holding a drink, Kera led them several steps away from the crowds.

"I have to ask you something," she said. She knew he expected her to ask why he'd invited her here. So instead she said, "How did you find out about Hawk?" She did not want to reprise their first conversation, but the chance to learn the answer to this question was one reason she had agreed to come here tonight.

Bolívar seemed unafraid of the topic. "It was because of the *Global Report*. When *TGR* launched two years ago, I assumed it was a competitor, so I started doing my homework. The more I researched, the less *TGR* seemed to be what it first appeared. Eventually, I figured out that *TGR* was just a cover for a private security contractor. So I let it go. Or I would have. But then you showed up."

"You mean, at the media pioneers event?"

"No, before that. At the art show in that basement."

"You thought I was following *you* there?" Kera said. "Is that why you left so suddenly?"

"No. I didn't know who you were then. I left because I was angry with Charlie. That was the first time I'd seen him in years. And let's just say his little stunt with the stolen paintings did not amuse me. It wasn't until we left the art show that I heard about you. Charlie and I were having it out, and he mentioned that a journalist was at the party. He said you worked for *TGR*. I knew enough about *TGR* to know that that meant you weren't a journalist. I guess I assumed that it was me you were interested in."

"It wasn't."

"I know that now. But I still don't know why you were following Charlie."

"He didn't tell you?" she asked.

"No. What did you want with him?"

"I'm sorry. I can't say."

Bolívar nodded. He watched her take a sip of her drink. "I'm sorry for the way I spoke to you the other night."

"You were protecting yourself. But Rafa—" It just came out. It was the first time she'd called him that. "Why do you think Hawk is after you?"

"I can't say."

"You can't say or you won't say?"

He shrugged. "I think Charlie was right. You're not in on it. That's what matters to me."

"In on what?"

He did not answer, and she did not have a chance to prod him because they were interrupted by an announcement that the film was about to begin. He led her into the theater, and they sat side by side. Kera had not anticipated caring much about the movie one way or the other. But at some point in the first few minutes, she became completely engrossed. Natalie Smith was relentlessly self-critical of herself and her career, but also of American culture. She used discomfort as a weapon against complacency—revealing in devastating, often drily humorous interviews the unflattering disconnect between what most Americans proclaim to be American values and how those Americans actually behave. But the takedown was only the setup. The film's principal achievement was driving home, artfully and without didacticism, the notions that we shouldn't be so offended to have our flaws revealed, and how it is only through honestly identifying those flaws that it becomes possible to correct them and advance.

There were several moments during the film when Kera was aware of Bolívar next to her. Once she felt him watching her and turned to face him. She was startled to find herself wanting to see desire in his eyes—and then was terrified to find it there.

Afterward Bolívar introduced her to Natalie Smith. They were standing in a large group, and Natalie was fielding questions from people electrified by what they'd just seen.

"Where did you get the idea for this film?" someone asked.

"A critic of my last movie declared that I would never be a commercial success because I was out of touch with the average American."

"So you made this film as a rebuttal to a critic?"

"No. I made this film to expose why we shouldn't care a damn about the average American."

"What do you have against the average American?" someone asked, a little self-consciously. "Some people are bound to be average. Isn't that a statistical certainty?"

"My understanding of what it means to be average has nothing to do with statistics. The average American is truly average only in the ways he falls short of his own potential, particularly when he is motivated by the expectations of others. There is always someone more to the right or left of you, someone more or less attractive than you, someone richer or poorer, someone who claims to know how you should live your life better than you know it. People are average when they are driven by a motivation to fit in. The American challenge, then, is to be oneself—only, exactly, and totally."

"Why is that American?"

"Because of our freedom to pursue life, liberty, and happiness. People assume the most important word in that sentence is 'freedom,' when, in fact, it is 'pursue.' If we don't pursue life, we are just as free to waste it. Our averageness is the degree to which we fail to attempt that pursuit. It is also the degree to which we accept the status quo. The status quo beckons us in not because it's evil, but because it's the status quo. That's its nature. Our culture's failure is not that we have a status quo—that fact is perfectly unavoidable in any mob. Our failure is that we actively resist people who fall outside the status quo and especially those who reach beyond it on purpose. An average American is one who cannot overcome his instinct to view the honest aspirations of others with suspicion."

Kera realized that Bolívar was not by her side. He had excused himself at some point and had not returned. She glanced around, looking for him, but continued to listen in on the conversation.

"Didn't the studio claim that your film was unpatriotic?" someone asked.

"Yes, but only after certain interest groups characterized the film that way, which is their right. And which, as I've just explained, makes them average." A healthy ripple of laughter spread through the group. "Average—not because they didn't like it, but because their reason for not liking it was dishonest."

"Don't they have a point, though? The film *is* more of a criticism, rather than a defense of, America?"

"I believe patriotism requires a clear understanding of who we are. How do we defend ourselves if we don't know what about us is worth defending?"

"Do you doubt that parts of this country are worth defending?"

"I don't view the question itself as blasphemy, if that's what you're implying."

Kera slipped away to go in search of Bolívar. He was not in the main room. She checked the park-facing balcony where they'd stood talking before the film. No sign of him there either. She cut back through the crowd and stepped through a door onto a long, narrow terrace that stretched along the south side of the building. Darkness had settled over the city while they were in the theater, and the balcony was lit with dim, infrequently spaced fixtures.

She almost didn't see the two figures. The terrace contained a series of benches and ashtrays arranged into groups separated by iron planters that sprouted trimmed hedges. In the dark she at first confused the two men with silhouettes of foliage. She had paused to look south at the view of the city, and as she did, her eyes must have adjusted to the relative darkness. When she turned back to the door to go inside, she spotted them, just barely distinguishable from the shadows.

Bolívar was seated on a bench at the very far end of the balcony. He had his back to her and was huddled next to another figure who wore a hat and dark jacket. They were talking in low voices, and she would not have interrupted except that Bolívar turned. A few seconds later, he stood and came toward her. The person he was with never looked back in her direction.

"Who was that?"

"It's nothing," he said. But when they were back inside, she saw that his face had drained of its color. She studied his eyes; behind them, his mind was off somewhere faraway.

"Do you feel well?"

"I'm fine. But I think I'm ready to leave. Would you like to come downstairs with me?"

She could not be certain exactly what he was asking her. But she voided any chance that there had been a misunderstanding when she said yes, and they stepped together into the elevator.

FORTY

The building's floor plans had clearly illustrated a two-bed, two-bath unit with a central living space that provided park views and opened to a large kitchen with a center island and bar. What Kera did not know from studying the plans was how he'd furnished the space or, more importantly, what he did in there alone when the lights were lit into the small hours of the morning.

When Bolívar opened the door for her and she stepped inside, her first thought was that it was larger than she'd imagined. The ceilings in the main living area were very high. The rooms throughout, from the closets on up, were of a different scale than the residential Manhattan she knew. There was real space here. The floors were concrete and wood, decorated tastefully with rugs. The walls were concrete and clean white plaster, decorated boldly with contemporary paintings that hung in minimalist steel frames. All of the paintings were originals. If Bolívar was a heavy reader, as Kera suspected he must be, he read e-books. There were no bookshelves or stacks of physical books lying around. The furniture was minimalist but less bold than the paintings and, she thought, less tasteful than the rugs.

Also of note were the screens of varying size built into the walls in each room, installed in places that were convenient to control the lighting or music or to display videos or Internet access.

She took three or four steps into the living room and laughed.

"What's funny?"

"I heard you tell a whole room full of people that paintings have no value to pop culture and that pop culture is the only culture that has any value anymore. And look at this place. It's like a gallery."

"I've said a lot of things. I wish you wouldn't pay so much attention to all that."

"Don't you think it matters, what we say?" She forgot to listen for his answer because she was distracted suddenly by one of the paintings. It was not one of the prominent works that hung on the big walls of the living room but a smaller canvas, about the size of a poster, centered on a small wall in a recessed area that led to the two bedrooms.

"Where did you get this?" Kera said, walking toward it.

An odd look of thoughtfulness crossed Bolívar's face when he saw which painting she meant. He hesitated before he said, "Someone gave it to me."

"It's . . . it's by that artist they call It?"

Again, a hesitation. But then he shrugged. "That was painted by a classmate of mine in college."

"But look at it!" It was obvious. The painting was of a young man reclined on a rooftop. His face had no features, yet it seemed clear from the way he lay on his back with his hands behind his head that he was looking up at the stars, thinking rather than sleeping. The artist had not needed to give the subject eyes to express this. Every stroke of paint said it. The lines were graceful and confident; not one of them was unnecessary. The colors were harsh, a little rebellious. There was no mistaking it—there was only one artist she knew of that created art like this.

Kera was tempted to press Bolívar further on the artist's identity, but he stepped in to give her a tour of the place.

"What's in there?" she asked, nodding at a closed door across from the master bedroom. She knew from the floor plans that the space was intended to be the second bedroom. But the door she was looking at was metal and had been outfitted with a serious-looking lock controlled by a keypad.

"Just some work stuff." He did not offer to show her. Instead, he detoured to the bar in the kitchen to pour two glasses of wine. She trailed behind, noting the cleanliness—or was it barrenness?—of his home.

"Is something wrong?" Kera said. Bolívar had fallen silent and was looking over at the small painting again. He seemed entranced by it, as if he hadn't noticed it hanging there in a while.

"No, I was just thinking," he said. "Have you ever created art?"

"No." She almost laughed. "I wouldn't even know where to start."

"I always wanted to be an artist," he said. "Not because I was very talented as a painter or writer, nor because I thought I had anything important to say. You know what it was? It was because of the commitment an artist must make in order to have even a chance to succeed. It was something I admired. It's incredible, if you think about it, for someone to be so passionate about one small corner of our world that it drives him to give up everything else—to forgo a stable career, to spend hours by himself in thought, to approach the word processor or easel or instrument every day with the discipline of an Olympic athlete. And for what? No certain reward. Merely for the opportunity to try to convince his peers not just that there is beauty in the world, but that paying attention to that beauty might lead to a greater understanding of ourselves. That motivation, that drive to create art, is so inherently optimistic, it's so for the cause of human progress, that it has always been startling to me that most artists fail."

Kera stood perfectly still, watching him. She felt almost as if he didn't know she was there. She did not want to make any move that might startle him and interrupt his thought.

"I was never going to be an artist," Bolívar said. "But I thought if we could figure out a way to integrate that artist's drive for human progress into our most basic cultural infrastructure, we would be . . . better, I guess. It's strange, there isn't a word for what I'm trying to describe. In the business world, it's called 'profit.' But we don't have a word outside of the commercial realm for prioritizing human betterment. Happiness, maybe, comes close. But that refers to an individual's state of mind, and the problem I've always wanted to solve is on a larger scale than that." As he spoke, he had taken a few steps into the living area so that he could look up at the canvases on his wall. Very softly, almost to himself, he said, "And now I've solved it."

"What?" She thought she'd been following him, but now she had no idea what he was talking about.

"I solved it. You're the first person I've told. Don't worry, I don't expect it to mean anything to you." He turned back to her. "I'm being a terrible host. I'm sorry."

"No, it's fine," she said. She did not know him—this was only their second conversation—but she felt certain that something about him had changed, right here, tonight. It had happened at some point after the film, when they were upstairs. "Who was that person you were talking to on the balcony?" she asked.

Bolívar closed his eyes and shook his head. And Kera knew suddenly that he would say no more. He looked beautiful, she thought. He was standing with the large windows behind him, and through the glass she could see the peaceful, meandering lights of the park and the abrupt line where the park met the wall of Midtown. Bolívar, she realized, had retained a youthfulness that was absent from other successful people in this city. Because he was known as a precocious businessman, she had always assumed that he was cunning and conservative. But looking at him now, as he stood in his apartment with his walls of paintings and something troubling his mind, she saw he was none of what he appeared to be to the world. He was, when he was most himself, a fearless dreamer. Upon naming this in her mind, her first feeling was of deep admiration. And then, without warning, she felt a new fearlessness of her own. She moved toward him. If he was surprised, he did not show it. He welcomed her, his eyes on hers, steady as a heartbeat.

She had to have his hands on her. Those hands. It hadn't occurred to her until that moment that this kind of creature desire was something she needed in her life. She had never needed it before. Not like this. She let him press her against the dizzying glass of the living room window as they kissed. And then his hands and lips weren't enough, and she started to undo the buttons of his white shirt.

$$\cdot \quad \cdot \quad \cdot \quad \cdot \quad \cdot$$

They were lying naked on his chair and ottoman later when Kera thought of a question. It was one she'd promised herself she wouldn't ask, but suddenly felt entitled to.

"Will you tell Natalie? I think she's in love with you."

She expected Bolívar's body to tense up in defense or anger, but he was still. He said simply, "She knows."

She knows. What made Kera shudder was the idea that this was already so deep. It had not merely been, as she'd told herself, a sudden urge to put her mouth against his. There was a grander scheme, already in motion before tonight, and it was undeniable enough to have been noticed at the very least by Natalie Smith.

Kera thought suddenly of Parker and felt very lonely. She did not feel guilt, at least not a guilt she assigned specifically to herself. It was more like a heavy sadness for what the human species was capable of, the relentless burdens of emotion that balanced the risk of feeling love with the pain of falling short. All of a sudden, she was furious with Rafa Bolívar. Why was he allowed to do this to her? Didn't he know that there would be consequences? And if he didn't, then had it even meant anything to him? This frustration did not stop her from running her hand gently back and forth across his chest.

"What do you do in your free time?" she said.

"All of my time is free. My family is enormously wealthy." He said it without shame or pride. "My father owns Venezuela's largest media conglomerate. I suppose you know about all that. He threatened to cut me off when he learned I'd become an American, but then I started making him more money from the US market than he'd ever made in South America."

"But you continue to work, even though you don't need to."

"Work isn't the right word for it. Work is what people do to survive. That kind of work is rarely interesting, least of all to the people who are doing it. The things we choose to pursue in our own time are what matter."

"And for you that's proving something to your father?"

"No. But that keeps people from speculating about the real reason."

"You have interesting views about work for someone who doesn't really need to think about it at all." She didn't know what to make of what Bolívar was saying or the way he was acting.

Who were you talking to up there? she wanted to ask him again.

But then he rose from where he'd been lying on his back, with her hand rising and falling with his chest. He went to the window and stood with his naked body silhouetted against the city. He was quiet for so long that Kera felt again like she was no longer there. Then suddenly, he turned to face her.

"You have no reason to trust me, so I won't ask you to. Just as I have no reason to trust you," he said. "In a way, we are both undercover, and that makes trust impossible. I hope someday we can meet again when the circumstances are different."

"Meet again? I don't understand you."

"You will," he said.

She got up to put on her clothes and to wrap her head around the idea that she had to get on the subway now and go home to Parker. In the elevator, as she descended alone to the lobby, she braced herself for a wave of regret that didn't come, but was hit with an even more grotesque emotion: the consequence of not feeling regret for what she'd done.

• • • • •

Kera Mersal stepped out of the elevator at 0234 hours and was visible to three of the small cameras that were hidden inside small reflective-glass domes mounted to the lobby ceiling. Like the thousands of hours of footage being collected around the world every second, this surveillance was fed through HawkEye's filters on computers a dozen blocks south and two blocks east. As soon as Kera's face was visible to the nearest camera, HawkEye's facial-recognition software identified her, which triggered an alert on the only workstation still lit in the Control Room.

J. D. Jones looked up.

He'd planned to leave the office hours ago, around nine. But then, in a moment of weakness as he was preparing to leave, he'd checked HawkEye to see whether Kera was still at home. That's when he discovered something strange. The computer indicated that her phone was at her apartment, but a camera on Fifty-Ninth Street had flagged her as a partial/probable match. Jones watched the tape. It was her all right, wearing large, dark glasses to throw off the recog software. His curiosity turned to shame when he recognized the man who greeted her and escorted her inside. Bolívar.

Angry with himself for spying on her, he'd ordered himself to log off and go home. But he couldn't bring himself to do it. It was like an addiction he'd grown to hate and still couldn't quit.

Finally, just after two thirty in the morning, he watched her come out of Bolívar's building, and his self-loathing reached its climax. It seemed an appropriate punishment, he thought. At least now he'd gotten what he deserved: the knowledge that Kera was out of his league.

FORTY-ONE

FORTY-ONE

Parker had never been busier with work, and he'd never wanted so badly to keep taking on more. Everything he touched at ONE fascinated him. The data he had access to when formulating target demographics for the *Apocalypse* release was breathtaking. His team was knowledgeable and responsive. Only a week into the new job and he'd already taken over a pet project of Steven Lawson's: a smartphone app called LifeCoach that mapped out everything users did throughout the day and, after a month of intense scrutiny, began offering daily pointers on how to increase their efficiency, whittle away at bad habits, and even connect them to other users who might make suitable workout partners, dates, or fellow hobbyists.

Parker was reviewing film from a focus group on LifeCoach when his phone display lit up with a call from Information Security. When he answered, the voice on the other end was Lawson's.

"Can you come down here, Parker?"

"Yeah, sure," Parker said. He'd wanted to catch Lawson for a few minutes anyway, to give him an update on LifeCoach. It wasn't until he was in the elevator, sinking underground, that he fully registered the grave concern in Lawson's voice.

Down on B7, a uniformed IS woman escorted Parker from the room where he'd first been issued his Level Four badge and down a hallway into a small conference room. Lawson rose from the circular table and motioned to the chair across from him. Also present was one of the two IS men whom Parker had met on his first day. Parker looked around nervously, though there wasn't much to look at. The white, cinder-block walls were bare but for mounted screens, all of which were dark.

"Is something wrong?" he asked.

"We sure hope not," Lawson said. The female IS employee closed the door behind her on her way out.

The IS man opened a file folder and removed a photograph, which he slid in front of Parker. "Do you recognize this man?"

In the photo was a man around Parker's age, dressed in jeans and a sweater, descending the front steps of a residential building. Parker shook his head.

"That man is one of the original engineers of the software that runs the bunker. Unfortunately, he is the only Level Five employee to have resigned from his position at ONE. We're not sure whether he presents a risk, but we've taken precautions, just in case." The IS man looked to Lawson, who nodded for him to continue. "Two days ago one of our men on the street captured this."

Parker glanced down at the new photograph as it was put in front of him. At first he registered only the setting—a subway platform. The man at the center of the picture was the same as the man in the first photo. He appeared to be about to board a train and he was talking to—

Parker recognized her in a flood of confusion.

"What's going on?" he said, first looking up, then down again at the photo. There was no doubt it was Kera.

"We were hoping you might be able to help us with that."

The men looked at him. Parker stared back blankly. His mind was racing, and he couldn't think of a thing to say.

"Any idea why your fiancée has taken an interest in this man?" Lawson asked.

"I—" *What the hell were they implying?* "It must be related to a story."

"A story?"

"She's a journalist. She's never mentioned this man, but she can't discuss her stories with me before they've been published—"

The men exchanged glances in a way that made Parker stop himself.

"A journalist?" the IS man said. "Is that normal, for journalists to be so cagey about their work?"

Parker had never had warm feelings for the IS department, but now he suddenly hated them.

"Parker." Lawson leaned forward. "We're just trying to protect ONE. You understand how sensitive what we do here is, don't you?"

"Yes, of course. Look, I'm sure it's nothing. I should talk to her. There's probably a very simple explanation."

"I don't think that's a good idea," Lawson said. "Have you spoken to her about work? Does she know what you do here? I don't mean your normal job, but on the Information side."

"No, no. Of course not."

"And you don't know what she does either?" the IS man asked, incredulous.

Lawson held up a hand as if to let the man know his tone wasn't helping, and then he looked at Parker. "Is there any way she could have accessed any of your work files?"

"*No.* This is crazy. She wouldn't do that. And she wouldn't look to me as a source, in any event. It would be a conflict of interest."

The men again shared a look of confusion.

"Parker, I don't know how to put this. Has it occurred to you that your fiancée might not be who she says she is?" Lawson asked.

The IS man produced several more photos. There were additional photos of Kera talking to the ex-ONE employee in the subway station, as well as a photo of her, taken from a distance, as she was led by an unidentified man into the lobby of a glass tower. Then there were photos of her exiting that building hours later, well after midnight, according to the printed time stamps in the corners. "These are all in just the last few days. Is this the behavior of a reporter?"

"Are you suggesting Kera isn't a journalist?"

"I'm sorry, Parker. I thought you knew. We never would have brought it up like this, except for her association with this man," Lawson said.

"Now we have to assume the worst," the IS man said.

"The worst? You people don't live in reality, do you? You've taken this too far. Everything's not a conspiracy, OK? Kera is an investigative reporter. Have you heard of the *Global Report*? You might have searched for her byline before following her around the city with a camera." He stood. "Now you've checked into it, and everything's fine. Pat yourselves on the back. And please, stay out of my personal life."

Parker surprised himself with this uncharacteristic show of—what was it? Courage? Loyalty to Kera? For a few brief moments, pride and adrenaline coursed through his body. And then he saw Lawson's meaty face, glaring up at him with that arrogant scowl for the first time since he'd been officially brought aboard. Brought *inside*.

"It's too late to worry about your privacy, Parker. I thought showing you this would remind you that you have your own career to worry about. Be careful who you let get in the way of that."

FORTY-TWO

The evening after she'd seen Bolívar, Kera, exhausted from a short night and a long day, made her way from the subway to her apartment. As was her habit, she took a route she hadn't used in four or five days, winding two blocks farther north than she needed to before crossing west and then south to approach her street. Just as routinely, she took inventory of the activity on her block. There was a man in an oversized hoodie seated by himself on the steps of a brownstone across the street, his face turned down toward the sidewalk and obscured by the hood. There was a woman walking her terrier at the far end of the sidewalk. And, midblock, a ConEd truck was backed up to an open manhole. Two men loitered at the back of the truck, occasionally peering down at their subterranean colleague. Kera absorbed these details without altering her stride or her train of thought, which all day had veered recklessly to the situation with Rafael Bolívar. Actually, the situation now encompassed more than just Bolívar; it had expanded to intrude upon her entire life as she knew it.

She was halfway across the street, heading for the entrance of her building, when the man seated on the steps said her name.

"Kera." His voice was low and gravelly but sharp.

She stopped. Her fastest escape was around the end of the block in the direction she'd just come from. Then she could either sprint down the short blocks to busy Houston Street or dash into one of the alleys. But before she could take flight, the man lifted his face, and under the hood she saw glasses straddling a sharp nose. Then she saw his eyes. Her calves and fists relaxed.

"Lionel," she said. As he rose, glancing up and down the block, she studied him. It occurred to her that she'd never seen him in anything other than slacks and a button-down shirt. It was easy to forget that Lionel Bright had spent most of his career as a chameleon in the field.

"Can we go somewhere and talk?" He grabbed her elbow to lead her back toward Houston and Lafayette.

"Not that way. Too many cameras."

Kera took him to a diner on Bowery, and they slid into a rear booth away from the windows facing the street. Lionel tugged off his hood. She decided that he looked ridiculous in a sweatshirt.

A waitress brought them coffee, which Kera stirred but had no intention of drinking. She needed to sleep tonight.

"What the fuck's going on?" she said when the waitress left them.

"I got your postcard."

Kera had been checking the Yahoo account for his response. She had not expected him to appear in person. "Did you know Hawk was compromised?"

"Tell me what you think is happening." His eyes were steady, revealing nothing.

"Gabby sold us out to the private sector. And she's betting she'll get away with it because the agency protects its secrets above all else," Kera said.

"Slow down. What makes you think that?"

Kera lowered her voice. "At first we thought Hawk had simply picked up a few side projects with corporate clients. You know, the highest bidder here and there, a way to turn Hawk's technology and computing power into some extra cash. Maybe not quite on the level, but nothing dangerous. Now, though, it's gotten way bigger than that. In a matter of six months, all of Hawk's cyberintel work on foreign targets has stopped. You must have noticed it dry up on your end." She paused, inviting him to acknowledge this. He nodded very slightly. "I'm spending all my time now on domestic projects that violate surveillance laws and have nothing to do with national security."

"Projects for who?"

Kera couldn't tell from his eyes how much he already knew and how much he was learning from her now. "We think it's probable that all of Hawk's active contracts originated with a single, corporate client: ONE. ONE has effectively bought Hawk."

"Who's 'we'? Where are you getting all this?"

"I have a colleague helping me."

"Helping you? Jesus." Lionel shook his head, but it was his eyes that troubled her most. She saw real fear in them. "Kera, listen to me. I need you and your colleague to stand down. Just go back to doing the work that's assigned to you."

"Why?"

"Please. Give me a chance to handle it."

"How high up does this go, Lionel?"

"How high does what go?"

"You showed up on my street dressed as a homeless person. Don't pretend you're clueless. What's really going on?"

"I'm sorry, Kera. It's all classified."

"Bullshit, it's classified. There's not even a record that Hawk exists. I deserve to know what's going on. Am I right about Gabby? You can just nod if I am," she said, staring at him as he brought the coffee mug to his lips. After he set it down, he nodded.

Her anger took the form of more questions. "Does it go higher than Gabby and Branagh? Was this the plan for Hawk all along, or did they outsmart the agency, and you're too embarrassed to admit it?" She tried to pull back her last comment, but it was too late. "I'm sorry. I didn't mean that." Lionel said nothing. "I trust you, Lionel, but I'm starting to think I've been cut out. Let me help you bring in Gabby and Branagh. I'm closer to them than you—"

Lionel jumped in. "Bringing in Gabby and Branagh is too risky."

"I don't understand. You can't be suggesting they'll get away with this."

"It's not about them. If we make it about them, things could get messy. The damage that would do to the agency is unacceptable."

"That's really what you're worried about?" she said.

"You're too caught up in it, Kera. I have the bigger picture to think of."

"Have you tipped off the Feds yet? They should be in on this."

"No, they shouldn't. It's more complex than that. Everything has consequences. Some aren't worth bearing."

Kera smiled bitterly. "Is that what you came to tell me, that I'm supposed to keep my mouth shut so that Gabby can't embarrass the agency? That's exactly what she's counting on, you know?"

"I came here to warn you that you're in danger if you pursue this."

She glared at him, but it didn't hold. Lionel wasn't the person she should be mad at. He was, perhaps even more than Jones, the ally she needed most desperately.

"This isn't what I signed up for," Kera whispered, almost to herself.

"I know. But please sit tight. Will you do that, Kera? Give me a chance to handle this."

She thought of Jones. No way he was going to sit tight while a bureaucrat in Langley tried to cover his own ass. But Jones didn't know Lionel like she did.

She nodded.

Lionel pulled his hood back up and laid a twenty on the table as he stood.

"I'll send you word when I know more," he said. "In the meantime we can't communicate. If we talk by phone, they can hear us. If we use the e-mail account too much, they'll eventually intercept it. You've seen what that Control Room is capable of. Kera?" She looked up at him. "I'm sorry."

She sat still until she heard the diner's front door swing open and shut. Then she got up and walked home alone.

FORTY-THREE

Kera entered the apartment with her mind still back in the diner, replaying everything Lionel had said—and what he'd failed to say. She stopped and looked up before she could pull the key from the lock. Parker was standing in the center of the living room, looking as though he'd been waiting for her for some time.

"Can we talk?" he said.

"What's wrong?" She shut the door and walked toward him until she could see that he was shaking. And then she knew: he'd found out about Bolívar.

Without warning he wrapped his arms around her.

"Babe," she said, "is everything OK?"

"Yes, I think so. But . . . you're a journalist, aren't you? Not . . . something else."

"Of course." She was not proud of how naturally this lie came out of her, faster than she'd even been able to think.

"If not, I need to know the truth. I won't ask anything more about it. I just need to know."

"What's this about? Why are you even saying these things?" She guided him to the couch.

"Today at work I was questioned by our Information Security department."

"Your what?"

"Never mind that. They're like—they're just security guys. But well funded, apparently. It was creepy, babe. They had pictures of you, like you're some kind of criminal. Talking to some man in the subway, coming out of a building late at night."

When he looked up at her, she felt certain that now he was going to ask her who she'd been with so late at night. It was about Bolívar, after all. At this realization she felt a calm pass through her. She would tell him the truth, at least about that. She could only take so much of the empty feeling that came with lying to him. But he didn't ask.

"They said you aren't who you say you are, that you're not really a journalist."

"Why? How come they were following me?"

"The man you were talking to—the one in the subway—he used to work at ONE. They're worried about things he knows, I guess. Company secrets. God, listen to me. It sounds crazy to even say that."

"If it helps, I can just tell you. The man I was talking to is a source," Kera said. The way he looked at her compelled her to go on. "It's for a story I'm working on about quants. You know, the Wall Street guys. I did a short piece a while back about how some of them had been hired by ONE. This is sort of a follow-up. Not just to understand why a company like ONE would want these math geniuses, but also to see how other industries, besides finance, are finding these guys useful. I contacted that guy from ONE because I thought he'd be willing to talk to me now that he's no longer involved with the company."

"Was he?"

"Not really, no."

Parker looked hopeful. "So he didn't tell you anything about ONE?"

"No. In fact, he seemed terrified to talk. Parker, what's going on? What does he know that's so dangerous?"

"Honestly," Parker said. "I don't know."

He fell silent, and she didn't like the troubled look on his face. "Parker," she said, "did they threaten you?"

He hesitated.

"Babe?"

"No," he said quickly. "It wasn't really like that. The whole thing just shook me, that's all. It's probably me who's overreacting."

FORTY-FOUR

Kera waited for Jones to come off the elevator. From the Starbucks in the ground floor of the building, she watched him cross the lobby and turn left on the sidewalk. She checked her watch. It was ten after seven. She tailed Jones down Seventh Avenue toward the Forty-Second Street subway station, just as she'd done on four of the five nights since their conversation in the park. For the first two nights, she'd noticed ONE's man drifting a block behind her with the telephoto-lens camera. She could tell from his movements that he didn't much care whether she knew he was there. They were sending her a message.

Then he'd stopped showing up. She figured Bradley was their priority, and the clumsy resources they'd dedicated to her were seeing diminishing returns.

Tonight she stuck on Jones after determining that the ONE goon wasn't in tow. Jones's routine was to take the train to his neighborhood in Brooklyn. There, he would usually get takeout from a local eatery and disappear into his apartment building for the rest of the night. Once he ate dinner by himself in a restaurant before turning in. She didn't know if he lived alone, but she couldn't imagine otherwise.

Tonight, though, she did not intend to track him all the way to Brooklyn. At a spot she'd picked for its lack of HawkEye coverage, she closed the gap between them and came up beside him a block short of the subway. He didn't notice her until she spoke.

"We need to talk. Can I buy you a drink?"

He seemed more pleased to see her than she'd expected he would be. *Maybe he's just lonely,* she thought. *Maybe he's in love with me.* Then he grew tense, and she knew he was thinking of the cameras.

"This way," she said. The sidewalk on Forty-Fifth Street was covered for construction for a full block. This allowed them to skirt west with little risk of being picked up by HawkEye.

They found a bar on Ninth Avenue. The place didn't really matter, only that it wasn't too loud or too bright. Jones ordered a scotch. Kera could tell he'd gone with the eight-year because she was paying; she told the bartender to make it a twelve-year. She ordered a vodka with soda for herself and paid in cash.

"Jones, I have to ask you something."

"What's that?"

"Why did you come to Hawk?"

He looked both relieved by and suspicious of the question. "I assume it's the same reason you're here. I was asked to serve my country."

"That's it? That was enough?"

"Enough to quit my fourteen-bucks-an-hour job so I could work in that Control Room for ten times the pay? Yeah, it was more than enough."

"Before Hawk, why were you working in Austin?"

"I told you. I was married. I was trying that lifestyle out for a little while."

"'That lifestyle'? Installing security software you could have cracked in under a minute? You seem like the kind of guy who needs more of a challenge."

He studied her. "If you're implying something, why don't you just come out and say it?"

She stuck her tongue in her cheek. She was asking him to level with her; it was only fair that she do the same. "OK. Why were you fired from NSA?"

Jones's eyes sharpened with caution, warning her off. Seconds earlier, he had seemed relaxed. The contrast was stark. Kera forced herself to return his gaze, growing more uncomfortable by the second. But then, just as suddenly, something new came into his eyes. An exhaustion. She recognized it immediately: he was tired of all the secrets.

"So that's why we're here," he said. He tipped his glass on one edge, gazing down into it as he rolled the ice cube around.

"Why were you forced out?"

He hesitated, but finally answered. "I broke the rules."

"What rules?"

"All of them I could. I took that to be the purpose of my job. That's what a hacker is supposed to do, isn't it? Question everything. Disrespect boundaries. Live by the idea that security doesn't come through self-congratulation; you're safe only if you catch your flaws before anyone else does." Jones shrugged. "They didn't like how good I was at exposing their flaws."

"What broken rule, specifically, got you fired?"

He shrugged. "I used NSA equipment to hack into the e-mails of executives at a private security contractor."

"That have anything to do with your brother?" Kera said.

His eyes darkened in a way that made her wonder what he was capable of. But it was brief, only a reflex. He seemed to have brought it under control a moment later when he released an amused chuckle.

"Some other time you'll have to tell me how it is you know so much about me."

She smiled. "We all leave a trail, right? Isn't that the premise that makes HawkEye possible?"

"You didn't use HawkEye on me, though."

"That's true. I had to go much more low tech than that. I took advantage of your weakness: the world that can't be controlled with keystrokes. So, your brother?"

He nodded slowly. "Yeah, it had something to do with my brother."

"What happened?"

"You weren't able to learn that?"

"No. I know the outcome but not the reason. I'm not doing this for my entertainment, Jones. I need to understand your motivations here."

He took a long pull of scotch. "Sean was working for this contractor over in Afghanistan. I'd been e-mailing with him regularly. And then suddenly his e-mails stopped. I had a bad feeling about it, so I went looking for answers."

"And that's how you found out he'd died?"

He nodded. "I found out he shot himself when I read it in an e-mail between his commander and the firm's CEO. You should see the e-mails these fuckers write. Men like my brother aren't soldiers to them; they're business expenses. After he died, they just wrote him off and passed his weapon along to the next vet fresh off the PTSD plane from Afghanistan. That's their business model. They put guns back into these guys' hands, pump them full of steroids, and profit off the fact that war had turned them into monsters. They killed him, Kera. He might have pulled the trigger. But they killed him." Jones stopped himself, embarrassed by the state he'd worked himself into. "Sorry."

"It's OK," Kera said. She wondered if he'd ever talked about this to anyone. "And you got caught stealing these e-mails?"

"Sure. I wanted to get caught. I wanted to expose a flaw in the way we were fighting our wars. Clearly, they weren't amused."

Kera sucked back a large gulp of her drink to keep pace with Jones, then ordered them another round.

"How did you first get into the NSA?" she asked.

"The way my brother and I were raised, if there's a war on, you fight it. I thought that's how everyone in America was brought up. It wasn't until I got out in the world a little more that I understood that most Americans don't even know a single vet from the Iraq or Afghanistan wars. Most of the country just goes about their lives as if the wars aren't even happening. Not in our house. I'd grown up thinking that I'd be army like my father. But the truth is, I wouldn't have been much help to anyone on a battlefield. I was a wimp. A geek. Sean knew that and so did my parents, even though no one would say it. I didn't want to let everyone down—most of all myself. So, out of desperation, I guess, I took some tests for the NSA. Turns out they were the only people in the world who thought the hours I spent alone in my room throughout junior high and high school were well spent. They hurried me off to Fort Meade like I was late to the party."

"And you were there for six years?"

"Yeah."

"And then you were forced out and went back to Texas to live the American dream?"

"Something like that."

"Who recruited you to Hawk?"

"One of Branagh's guys. I led them right to my doorstep. Mind you, I had a lot of free time back then. My days consisted of coasting through a bad marriage and showing up for my menial job. I spent every second of my spare time on my computer, mostly fucking with the NSA. Finally they noticed. The surprise was that instead of sending FBI agents to haul my ass to jail, I was at a coffee shop one day, and Branagh's guy just sits down across the table from me." Jones smiled. "They were a little pissed that it was me."

"They didn't know?"

"No. When I hack, I stay anonymous."

"What was Branagh's pitch to you?"

"I was getting a second chance to serve my country. It was going to be elite, top-secret stuff, vital to national security, blah, blah, blah."

"Sounds familiar."

Jones shook his head. "In retrospect, I should have been suspicious that they wanted me back. I wanted it too bad."

"Given your past at NSA, they knew it was a risk to take you," Kera said. "And yet they still wanted you more than you wanted them."

"Yes. But Hawk is being more careful with me this time. They're watching closely. That's why it's taken me so long to figure out their connection to ONE. And don't kid yourself, Kera. They're watching you too."

"Then we'll just have to do this right under their noses."

He shot a hopeful, questioning glance at her.

She nodded. "I'm in. I'll help you take down Hawk. If we can."

He nodded but did not thank her. There was no reason for that; they both knew that she wasn't doing it for him. This would only work if they were each looking out for themselves.

"But just so we're clear," Kera said. "We're in agreement that Hawk has become a rogue operation of the CIA and the NSA. I still have a contact at the agency I trust and who trusts me. I'm guessing you're no longer on good terms with your former colleagues at NSA?"

"That's correct."

"OK, then we'll feed whatever we can get on Hawk back to my guy at the agency, and let them clean it up internally."

"Kera, I—I don't think it's that simple. What if they don't clean it up internally? What if it's too messy for that, and they opt to do nothing?"

A part of her knew that Jones was right. Lionel didn't want her and Jones to succeed at exposing Hawk any more than Gabby, Branagh, or ONE did. That was the problem with classified secrets that were kept classified for the wrong reasons: only the people who were keeping them knew if they were the sort that ought to be revealed. But if she couldn't bring this to Lionel, who she hoped could help her get her job back at Langley, then she couldn't even imagine what she would do next.

"What other choice do we have?" she asked. "Everything related to Hawk is classified. If we take it to anyone else, we'll violate our security clearances, and our careers in the intelligence community will be over."

Jones thought about this, though she suspected he'd already thought about it plenty. Finally he nodded. "OK. We can give it a shot your way. But I won't let this just disappear. If the agency tries to bury it, I'm going public. I don't think I was cut out for an intelligence career anyway."

"Fair enough," Kera said. "One more thing. It isn't just Gabby and Branagh who are watching us. It's ONE too."

Jones eyed her. "Since when?"

"A few days ago. When I contacted Bradley, I was careful to slip past HawkEye, but ONE has men on Bradley. They made me. And then yesterday Parker was asking questions about my job."

Jones looked away, and at first Kera thought he was angry. But he just nodded, and she realized he'd only been thinking about how this changed things. "It's better that they're watching us. Let them. Allow them to think that they're a step ahead. Parker, though," he said, looking her in the eye. "I need to know right now. Will he be a problem?"

Kera had already made up her mind about Parker—perhaps she'd made it up weeks or even months ago. But it was still difficult to actually take the next step. "No," she said. "I'm going to handle that." Then she moved the conversation forward to more practical matters. "We'll need to keep working ATLANTIS until we walk out of that Control Room for the last time."

"Of course. It would look suspicious to Gabby if we didn't."

They went over the remainder of the evidence they would need to collect on Gabby, Branagh, and ONE, and how they would collect it without being detected. It was not a long conversation. What they needed to do was remarkably simple, given the consequences. When they had covered everything, Jones looked at her.

"Kera, why are you doing this?"

"It's like you said. The other option is to keep working for them." She got up and, in a tone softer than she was accustomed to using, she said, "Jones? I'm sorry about your brother."

FORTY-FIVE

Kera had not been to Parker's new office, and she looked around when she entered. It was nicer than she might have imagined. The furniture was attractive, if cold. Film posters for several ONE-produced movies hung on the walls, which seemed like a quaint touch for someone so dedicated to digital media. But Parker was sentimental; that wasn't a revelation. His desk showcased framed pictures of the two of them and, amusingly, of his parents. There was not a single photograph of his parents at Kera and Parker's apartment. If he'd perceived that she didn't care for his parents, well, he would have been right, but she wouldn't have objected to his hanging a picture of them. None of this, of course, mattered. It only confirmed for her how little of her own attention she'd devoted to her fiancé.

"What are you doing here?" Parker said, standing. He seemed anxious as he watched her take in the room.

"I figured you would still be here," she said.

"You shouldn't be here. Not after—"

"I know. I'll only be a minute." She heard the quiver in her own voice. Parker must have heard it too because he stopped midsentence with his mouth agape. "Parker," she said. The room swayed. She felt outside her body, as if she were hearing herself speak. *Just a little while longer,* she thought, *and the worst will be over for both of us.* "I can't marry you."

All he said was, "What?"

"I'm sorry I didn't know it sooner." Strangely, it was not Hawk or ONE or the agency that had pushed Kera to this point. They were factors, of course, along with the lying that was required just to avoid losing her job. But the real shift had occurred in the basement of that auto body shop when she'd first seen Rafael Bolívar. Even if she had never seen him again, his existence had shown her that Parker was not enough. It was a brutal realization, coming out of the blue like that, but there was no denying it. There would be no kind way to explain that to Parker, even if she'd wanted to. Nor was there any way to explain what she and Jones intended to do to Hawk and that, whether they succeeded or not, her life as she knew it was about to flip upside down.

She couldn't just walk out on Parker, though. She owed him this conversation. Whether she owed him more than that was not something she could consider right now.

"I don't understand," he said.

She didn't say anything.

"Can we talk about it?" he said.

"Sure."

"I mean, if you're questioning things—"

"I'm not."

"What I meant was it's OK to have doubts. About the wedding, I mean. We don't even have to set a date right now. We can wait until it makes sense."

"No, Parker. I'm sure."

Parker sat down and was silent for a full minute. Kera imagined that he was thinking, beginning to understand that perhaps they both should have seen this coming. But then he said, "This has to do with what I brought up the other night, doesn't it? I knew I shouldn't have said anything."

"No, not really."

"They have no right coming between us like this."

"Please, Parker. It's not that simple. I'm sorry I didn't know any sooner. I'm telling you now because now I know. It's over."

A horrible sadness came into his eyes then, and she knew that his powerlessness had finally sunk in. It was the worst moment of the conversation for her, seeing that. She felt sorry for him. She felt sorry that something he'd wanted so badly had come within sight and then slipped away, out of his control.

"What will you do?" he said.

"I'm going to the apartment to pack things. I'll find a hotel tonight."

"No. I mean after that. What will you *do*? What do you want to do with your life, without me?"

She wanted to tell him not to do that to himself. But what was the use? He would do it, sentimental Parker. Instead, she told him the truth. "I'm probably going to have to go away for a while."

And then, within a few seconds, she was gone.

·   ·   ·   ·   ·

Later, at their apartment, Kera was in the bedroom gathering the last of her things. She had tackled the chore systematically, like a one-woman evidence-collection team, beginning in the kitchen and working through the living area to the bedroom and bathroom. She had not meant for the packing to be so thorough, but with each drawer opened, with each new item she touched, she became more powerfully drawn into the task. It was now eleven and Parker, to her relief, had still not come home. She pulled her large suitcase from the closet, the oversize kind she had used only once or twice, for moving, never for travel. She had believed it was the last of her stored possessions in the closet, but as she freed it, she saw a file box pushed back into the farthest dark corner. Seeing it was enough to remind her of what it contained. She had to get on one knee and duck under the thick, soft row of Parker's work shirts in order to slide it out.

She opened the box on the bed, ignoring the dust that smeared on the comforter. Inside were some effects from college, a diploma and a few essays she thought at the time were worth saving but that now embarrassed her to reread. She had no intention of going through the entire box now. This wasn't that kind of cleansing, reflective move. She already knew that this box would be packed into storage with her other belongings and she could sort through it later, or perhaps never see it again. But there was one thing in this box she wanted. She found it quickly, pressed between manila file folders that contained tax returns and bills from a time when such things were printed on paper.

The adoption file contained detailed information about Kera's adoptive parents and the date they had taken her into their possession. There was very little documentation of her journey into existence. An agency form listed the name of a coastal town in El Salvador. A crude birth certificate bore a doctor's illegible signature and a date she had taken as her birthday, though the agency paperwork stated clearly that they could not independently verify the precise day she had come into the world.

What she was after was the photo. And there it was, almost to her surprise. It seemed remarkable to her that so much about her origins were unknowable, including the most basic details about her birth mother. And yet here was this photo, a fading four-by-six, the only copy in existence. Paperwork seemed natural; the existence of the photo, though, seemed miraculous. A single photo of an infant in a faceless woman's arms. So much could have gone wrong. The film could have been exposed or never developed. The print could have been left on a table or shelf in her mother's small house. Everyone who had touched it might have had a conceivable reason to throw it away. Except her. Except now. It had survived, and it had found her.

She got her phone and took a picture of it, rescuing the photo from its precarious physical existence and committing it to digital permanence. Then she grabbed what of her belongings she could carry with her and left Parker's apartment.

FORTY-SIX

Parker did not move for several minutes after Kera's visit. When he did, it was with the foolish idea of returning to what he'd been doing before she'd arrived. He looked at his computer screen and brought his hands to the keys. But he couldn't will himself to soldier on any further than that.

He'd been enjoying something like peace before she appeared. Lately he worked past nine nearly every night. His days filled up quickly with meetings, and he found he enjoyed the quiet evening hours when he could sit at his desk alone with the windows darkening behind him. Almost as bizarre as the incident with Lawson and Information Security was how ever since, Lawson had treated him as if it had never happened. He'd given Parker lead roles in two new projects and hadn't seemed at all hesitant to invite him to high-level meetings where sensitive information was discussed. Parker wanted to believe that this was because Lawson trusted him, though he couldn't help but feel that he was being tested.

But at a quarter to nine, in the nighttime office quiet, such thoughts had seemed more like standard workplace paranoia than anything darker. He'd been reading through the day's freight of e-mails when the evening lobby attendant rang to tell him that a woman named Kera was there to see him.

Now work was unpalatable. No, impossible. He needed a drink.

He walked to the elevators and stood there, feeling numb, while he waited for the soft chime. The numbness, he knew, was his mind's way of coping. It was denial, an unwillingness to put Kera's decision in the context of reality. And also a buoy to salvage him from the deepening comprehension of his utter helplessness. It seemed unjust that anyone would be expected to face this without a second chance to make it better again, but there was nothing—nothing—he could do.

The elevator doors parted. He blinked at the panel of buttons, forgetting for a moment what he was doing. And then everything came into focus and the numbness drifted away. He stared for a long second at the bottommost button. B7.

Finally, he reached out and pressed it.

FORTY-SEVEN

Kera woke up in a Midtown hotel room, disoriented for an uncomfortable moment until she remembered how she'd ended up there. Not that those circumstances were very comforting. She'd slept past eight, late for her. Most of the night she had sat at the window, looking out at the city and thinking, planning. The hotel was within walking distance of the office. As she left, she stopped by the front desk and paid cash for an additional two nights. She hadn't worked out yet where she would stay after that, but for now it was convenient and clean enough.

The night had delivered another name to the list of the vanished. Lazlo Timms, a novelist/bartender, had left his shift at closing time two nights before and had not been heard from since. According to the police report Kera accessed from her workstation, a handwritten note had been found in Timms's small Brooklyn apartment. The words were scrawled on the back of a ONE Books contract, which the novelist had not signed. The note said: *Have you figured it out yet?*

Kera spent the morning studying up on Timms, who, unlike the other missing, was almost completely unknown. He had no prior novels, no literary reputation. She had heard his name only once before, from Charlie Canyon, who had been reading a bound manuscript of Timms's novel in the restaurant where they'd last met. Kera stared at the police photo of Timms's note. It fit neatly—almost too neatly—with the pattern that had been established by the others. There were still two things that every single one of the missing artists had in common: their disappearance amounted to a rejection of ONE, in some form or another, and that phrase had been found written among the belongings they'd left behind.

· · · · ·

Later that afternoon Kera was at her workstation scanning through headlines on Gnos.is when she came across a report about Daryl Walker. Pledges for contributions to his million-dollar exhibition video had reached $750,000. She didn't know why she desperately wanted the actor not to raise the million dollars, nor why she felt certain that he would. It made her think of something Charlie Canyon had said during her last conversation with him. Kera had asked him whether Daryl Walker would be the next to disappear, and Canyon's response had been a short, "No. He wouldn't do that," and a dismissive laugh. And maybe he was right. There was a difference between Daryl Walker and the other artists who had vanished. A qualitative difference, a seriousness, maybe, about their creative pursuits. Something like what Rafael Bolívar had spoken of in his apartment.

Kera glanced at the HawkEye maps she had running on three of her monitors. The private *America* screening and the encounter that had followed in Bolívar's apartment had occurred the previous Thursday. It was now Tuesday. In the days since she'd seen him, Bolívar had maintained his usual daily routine with prompt predictability. Just that morning, Kera had watched him enter the Alegría headquarters building at nine fifteen and then go out for a scheduled lunch. He'd returned at two, and she had expected him to remain there until the end of the business day. HawkEye, though, told her that he was now somewhere else. She leaned forward in her seat, at first thinking she was looking at the wrong map.

"Hey, Jones. What do you make of this?"

Jones glanced up. It was the first they had spoken to each other all day. A few seconds later he came over, and Kera slid her chair to one side so that he could get a better look at the screen. But when she looked up at him to gauge his reaction, he was eyeing her instead.

"You OK?" he asked.

"Yes," she said, a little too quickly. "I'm fine. Please, look at this."

He studied the screen for few moments, long enough to orient himself to what he was looking at. "Rafael Bolívar is at the ONE building?" he asked. Kera nodded. "What's he doing there?"

"I don't know."

Jones shrugged. "It could be anything. He could be meeting a friend or just making a courtesy call. What makes you think it's not a business meeting?"

"He's never been there before. The two companies don't have business together."

Jones lifted his eyebrows. "You mean, they don't have business together *yet.*"

"Rafa wouldn't do that," she said, staring at the blinking dot on the map. She realized her mistake only after it was too late.

"Rafa?" Jones said. Kera tried to ignore this, but she couldn't stop her face from flushing. "Think about it. Alegría is a major player now. Why wouldn't ONE be interested in them?"

"I'm telling you, Bolívar would never let that happen."

"All right. You know him better than I do," Jones said, his implication heavy.

This made Kera self-conscious, and that made her doubt herself. She thought again of the small painting hanging in Bolívar's apartment near the metal door with the keypad lock on it. Had she been fooling herself thinking she knew who Bolívar was?

She picked up the phone. If ONE and Alegría were truly contemplating a merger, as Jones was suggesting, there was only one place Bolívar could be in that building. She asked the ONE operator to please connect her to the office of Keith Grassley, CEO of the ONE Corporation.

"Oh, hi. This is Audrey over in Mr. Bolívar's office at Alegría," Kera said, using the name of one of his secretaries.

"Yes?"

Kera couldn't tell if the man sounded guarded or just suspicious. She hadn't done much research into this Audrey character. For all she knew, the girl had a Southern accent or was British.

"Mr. Bolívar was running a few minutes late," Kera said. "I just wanted to warn you in case he hadn't made it there on time."

"Thank you. And no need to worry. I showed him in a few minutes ago," the man said, though he sounded a little hesitant, like the wary victim of a prank call.

"Oh, wonderful," Kera said.

There was a strange pause on the line. When the young man spoke again, it was in a different tone, more personal, almost as if in confidence. "You OK?" he said.

"Yeah, of course." Kera had to get off the phone.

Another pause. "Drinks at seven still, right?" he said.

"You got it. See you then." She hung up and exhaled. "I think I just confirmed drinks on behalf of a total stranger."

Jones nodded. "So their secretaries are fucking. I'd say there's a good chance ONE and Alegría are about to be in business."

· · · · ·

Kera waited at her workstation until she saw Bolívar emerge from ONE's headquarters and slide into the waiting town car. She expected the car to cut across Midtown and return to Alegría's headquarters, but instead it turned north and let him off at his apartment building.

It was only 4:45 PM, early for him to be home on a weekday. A live surveillance feed provided a view of him exiting his car and walking into the lobby. She watched him closely, aching a little at the familiar spring in his step. He had not contacted her since she had left his apartment five nights earlier.

When he'd disappeared inside, she switched over from the HawkEye map tracing his movements to the digital dossier on his background. After seeing the contrast between Bolívar's public persona and the person she'd witnessed in private, she was curious to review his file more closely.

She spent an hour reading what was available about Bolívar's childhood in Caracas—his early school records, information on the members of his large family, and articles about his father's ties to key Venezuelan politicians, connections that no doubt had aided in the spectacular growth of his media empire, securing the family's wealth.

It wasn't until she got to Bolívar's college years that Kera began to read with interest. At NYU Bolívar had been working toward a double major in computer science and philosophy. That was news to her. She'd assumed he'd studied business, though she hadn't really thought much about it before. Computer science seemed too technical and specialized to interest someone bent on scaling the corporate ladder as swiftly as Bolívar had; philosophy seemed too abstract and impractical. Kera wondered what it meant that Bolívar's college studies didn't fit the man he had become.

Scrolling through Bolívar's NYU transcripts, Kera noted the As he'd been awarded for each course. *Epistemology 3420 . . . The Future of Computing . . . Value Theory.* At the bottom of the list, she stopped, puzzling over the dates of the final courses he'd taken. She scrolled up and down a few times, thinking she must have missed something. But she hadn't. His academic records stopped midway through his senior year, as if he'd simply walked away from his formal education a semester shy of graduation.

Searching for an explanation, Kera turned to other records that were contemporaneous to the incomplete portion of the transcript. As usual, HawkEye was a prolific source of information. The dossier included parking tickets, travel documents, credit card statements, academic calendars, and electronic library transactions. She scanned through most of these quickly, performing a swift triage. One area she lingered over was the library data, which was voluminous. Bolívar's literary interests had ranged from highbrow novels to books on philosophy and economics by authors she'd never heard of. In his senior year, he had added to these a dozen or so titles related to journalism. Nothing, though, that seemed to foreshadow his eventual turn toward pop culture and mass media.

A few minutes later, she came across a change-of-address request Bolívar had filed with the Post Office. She scrolled through it, looking to understand the chronology of where he'd lived when. For his first two years of college, he'd resided in a brownstone in the Village, and then he'd moved to—her breath caught when she saw the SoHo address. It was familiar. Switching to a new screen, she pulled up Charlie Canyon's dossier to confirm it, though her memory was clear. The address was for a large flat in SoHo and, a week earlier when she'd done a similar review of Canyon's dossier, the apartment had stuck out in her mind because it didn't seem like the sort of thing Canyon would have been able to afford. Bolívar, however, could have afforded something twice as lavish.

She leaned back in her chair, thinking. She'd been aware that Bolívar and Canyon had attended NYU at the same time and that they were at the very least acquaintances, but neither of them had mentioned living together. Bolívar had, in fact, brushed aside the implication that they were friends. For a few moments, she wondered whether their being roommates a decade earlier was significant, and then, even though she couldn't think of a particular reason why it was, she scolded herself for not drawing this link between them sooner.

How had she not seen it? *Grew up in Caracas . . . studied at NYU . . . moved up the ranks at Alegría.* She realized that before today, she had only familiarized herself with a broad sketch of Bolívar's biography, and her mind had lazily filled in details that, while far from unlikely, happened to be wrong. People dropped out of college all the time, didn't they? Maybe, but not people pursuing double majors, not people who go on to climb the corporate ladder in the most calculated of ways.

She returned to Bolívar's transcripts, and this time she studied the names of the professors who had taught each course. She wasn't looking for anything in particular, just a name or a course that inspired a feeling stronger than the others. What she found was much more straightforward than that. There was one professor who had taught Bolívar in four different courses over his three-and-half years at the school. Carl Tierney, professor of Computer Technologies and Society. She checked the school's current directory and found that he was still listed as a professor.

FORTY-EIGHT

Professor Tierney welcomed Kera into his office the following afternoon. The room was small, but it had a large window overlooking Washington Square Park. Peculiarly for a man who carried the banner for the digital future, the cramped office was overrun by physical books and paper files. The inescapable burden of academic bureaucracy, she supposed. She thanked him for seeing her and sat in a chair wedged against the wall, where she had to keep her legs tucked under the seat to avoid brushing against his feet beneath the desk.

"I looked you up, Ms. Mersal," Professor Tierney said. "I confess, I wasn't familiar with the *Global Report*. It seems they have you covering quite a wide range of subjects."

"A sign of the times, Professor. The news is not what it once was."

"That's very true. But you know, in my courses I encourage students never to bemoan the changing times. There's always good reason that the past has gone away, and in any event, no amount of hand-wringing will bring it back. Better to approach any criticism of the present with the future in mind. I think that's saying something from an old guy like me." As if catching himself being professorial in front of a young woman who had not enrolled in his class, he frowned. "But I understand you are, in fact, here to discuss the past."

"That's right. As I noted in my e-mail, I'm preparing a piece on Rafael Bolívar, and I've run into a dead end. It appears that Mr. Bolívar's academic records are incomplete. They simply end a semester shy of graduation. Maybe it's nothing, but I noticed that he'd taken several of your courses. I was hoping you might know what happened?"

Professor Tierney looked at her from across his desk, perhaps weighing whether it was ethical to get into a conversation about a former student's records. "I'm afraid I do, Ms. Mersal. Mr. Bolívar dropped out."

"Voluntarily?"

"Yes."

"Why?"

"Because I gave him a D on his final assignment in my Digital Innovation course."

"He dropped out of college because of a bad grade?" Kera was now familiar with all of Bolívar's transcripts. He'd received straight As in everything else. Dropping out over one anomaly seemed extreme.

"Obviously, it must have been more complicated for him than that. I'm not sure I understand it myself. I won't lie; it's bothered me over the years."

"What was the assignment?"

"The assignment, which I still assign to classes each semester, was to design an Internet-based innovation, such as a website or an application, and write a thesis to defend its originality and societal importance. He presented his theory on paper quite passionately, but he was unable to complete a functional prototype. You see, he made the engineer's crucial flaw—he overreached. The thing he was striving for was impossible. Frankly, I was charitable in giving him the D instead of an all-out failing mark."

"Were you surprised when he dropped out?"

"At first, yes. But I shouldn't have been. You see, Rafael Bolívar was not motivated by a need to adhere to social conventions, like getting good grades or earning a diploma. Not because he didn't care. In fact, I suspect he cared too much. I think he probably thought that if he didn't drop out, it would be a sign to himself, if no one else, that he didn't believe deeply enough in his theory."

"You keep saying 'was' and 'didn't.' Are you referring to him in the past tense intentionally?"

"Ah, yes. Well, there was the man who wrote that thesis and put everything on the line to defend it. And then there's the man who got rich selling reality shows and infotainment programs through his television networks. These cannot possibly be the same man."

There it was, she thought. The same contradiction she herself had noticed in Bolívar—his public persona versus the man she had witnessed in private.

"When was the last time you spoke to him?" she asked.

"That's easy. The day he learned I'd given him a D on the assignment."

"Just like that? You haven't heard from him since?"

He shook his head. "I won't pretend I have a clear conscience about it. When you've been a professor as long as I have, you see a lot of promise go unfulfilled. Rafa Bolívar's, though; that was a real loss. I know, anyone will say he's gone on to do just fine for himself without the approval of a passing grade in my course, but that incident has always remained a little unsettling to me."

"Do you still have the thesis he wrote?"

"I'm sure it's saved in my e-mail archives. But I don't keep it laying around, if that's what you're asking."

"I've imposed plenty on your time, Professor Tierney. But if you find a moment to dig it up, I'd be curious to have a look." She passed him her card, then pulled out her tablet. "Just one more thing, and it's probably a stretch. Do you recognize this young man? I don't think he was in any of your classes, but he was a roommate of Bolívar's at the time."

Professor Tierney looked at the photo of Charlie Canyon on Kera's tablet for long enough that by the time he answered, she had grown hopeful. "Yes. I wouldn't know his name. But he was one of Bolívar's friends. I saw them together often. With another boy too."

Kera's phone rang in her bag. The volume was low but audible, and she reached down to silence it. When she did, she noticed the call was coming from an unfamiliar number with a Manhattan prefix. "Another boy?"

"Yes, outside of class. Whenever I saw Bolívar around campus, he was with these friends. Always the three of them."

Kera thanked him again and invited him to e-mail her if he found Bolívar's thesis or thought of anything else.

Outside she reached for her phone to call Jones and noticed the previous caller had left a voice mail. The display said that the message was over a minute long. She brought the phone to her ear as she waited to cross the street into Washington Square Park.

"Kera. Kera. It's me," the voice mail began. It was difficult to hear clearly over the traffic, but she could tell it was Parker. "I didn't want to use my phone, just in case. I got it for you. It's big. You can use it for a story. Come by the apartment. Can you do that . . . today? It's important. Right when you get this. I'll show you everything. They'll fire me for this, but now I know what they're doing with the bunker and why it has to be stopped. I'll have to quit, just like the quant did. But I'm not afraid of them. Not if you can write a story—"

Kera stood frozen on the curb, straining to listen. When his voice cut out, she pressed the phone harder against her ear. Nothing. The message had terminated far short of a minute. What had he been talking about? She brought the phone down to try to play the message through again, and that's when she noticed something was wrong.

Her voice mail in-box was empty.

Then she ran.

FORTY-NINE

Parker had decided to wait to hit rock bottom before he quit drinking. This surely was it. But there was some relief in that—knowing that in a day, or perhaps a week or a month, things would get better again.

He'd spent the entire night at a terminal in the basement, and then he'd spent the day at his desk, working as diligently as a sleepless night allowed. If anyone noticed anything amiss, they didn't let on. He just needed to get to five o'clock and get out of the building without drawing any suspicion. Once he handed everything over to Kera, once it was all out in the open, he would be untouchable.

Heading downtown, he pulled up his jacket collar against the wet chill. Dusk stalked the city several hours ahead of schedule. The light that managed to seep through the clouds was the sort that sucked color from everything. Buildings were indistinguishable. Glass, metal, concrete—all the same shade of ashy gray.

On the way to the subway, he kept seeing women who he thought for an instant were Kera. Confident, purposeful women navigating the damp city in long jackets, their dark hair tucked under hats or sheltered by umbrellas. The whole city seemed to be filled with women like this. But on second glance, none of them were Kera, none of them even close.

He told himself not to hope that she might reconsider leaving him.

He called her from the pay phone outside of L@Ho. As her phone rang and rang, he recalled the first time he'd wandered into the bar and how he'd liked the feel of the place immediately. Now he craved it almost as much as he craved sleep, even though it no longer satisfied him to sit and chat and think about the day. His favorite bartender was no longer there. Parker had read in the news that morning that the man had disappeared along with the other missing.

Hearing her voice on the recording had stung him more than he'd expected, as if she'd been gone for years. His message rambled. He wasn't sure how much to divulge over the phone.

He walked the remaining four blocks and climbed the steps to their—his—apartment. It had been nearly thirty-six hours since he'd been home. The keys were in a pocket of the leather courier bag he carried to work every day, a gift from Kera the previous Christmas. He retrieved them and let himself in.

Two men were sitting on the bar stools at the kitchen counter, and they said they just wanted to talk.

FIFTY

Kera threw a twenty over the seat and slid out of the cab as it was still rolling to a stop in front of the apartment building. She took the stairs two at a time and put her ear to the door before knocking. She heard nothing.

She knocked four times and listened again. Silence.

Using her own key, she tested the dead bolt, which she and Parker both had a habit of always locking, even when they were home. It was not engaged. The door knob, which locked automatically, clicked loudly when she turned the key. As soon as the door swung on its hinges, she could smell burnt gunpowder in the air. The odor was unmistakable; it reminded her immediately of the firing range at the Farm. She threw herself flat against the hallway wall, a safe distance from the door, at first bracing for gunfire and then, when it didn't come, crouching to strike low at anyone who emerged from the apartment. Between breaths, she strained to hear any movement that would give away a threat.

But there was no rustling of clothes, no creak of the floorboards, no voices. Just a terrible silence that hung heavy with the acrid odor.

Moving cautiously, Kera entered the apartment and leapt for the shelter of the kitchen, which she could see was clear. The living room, just on the other side of the bar counter where she had ducked for cover, was still. She tested a few glances into the open space and then, staying low and against the wall, crept out far enough to see that the living room was also clear. The bedroom was next. Again, she approached it as though it contained a shooter, and again she found herself alone, the only sound her pulse thumping in her ears.

By the time she reached the bathroom, she knew what she would find.

She expected it to be bad, and it was far worse. She had an overwhelming urge to run to him and touch him, to shake him and haul him out of the bathtub. He didn't belong there. This was all wrong. A wave of nausea stopped her. For all her training, she had never seen a corpse in the field. There was nothing but the real thing, she thought, that could prepare anyone for the first time they see what a bullet at close range can do to a skull and the matter it holds. What had not been contained by the walls of the tub had soiled the lower half of the curtain and part of the tile wall. She spun away and then shielded her eyes to avoid looking at herself in the mirror. It seemed indecent to be seen like this, even by herself.

For several moments Kera concentrated on getting her breath back. This was a crime scene, she realized. She had to pull herself together. She had to think clearly.

She turned and took a few steps toward the tub, keeping her eyes on the bathroom floor. Then she drew them up carefully. The gun was in his hand, which had fallen across his chest. She couldn't bring her eyes up any higher to look at his face, and was glad of that in the moments that followed, when she needed to be very careful and not make any mistakes.

She called 911 and heard herself tell the operator that her fiancé had shot himself in the head. Her words felt disconnected from herself, a voice faraway and down a tunnel. While she answered the operator's questions, she retraced her steps through the small rooms, this time looking in closets and behind furniture. Everything was almost exactly the way Parker would have had it. Almost. There was one thing amiss: Parker's work bag was not in the apartment.

She kept looking for it until she could hear sirens. Then the operator said it was OK to hang up and she did. She sat down on the side of the couch that was farthest from the bathroom and hugged her legs against her chest. There was nothing more she could do now; it was OK to start letting go. Her sobs came in awful, desolate bursts, seizing her chest until she could hardly breathe.

FIFTY-ONE

One Week Later

That week was the worst of her life. Not just the frequency with which her mind replayed images of Parker's body slumped in the bathtub, but also of the funeral, two hours north of the city in Connecticut, and the wild, accusatory looks from his parents, when they looked at her at all. What was the appropriate role for an ex-fiancée in that situation? That week Kera felt, more than at any other point in her life, that she had no friends. Her parents were consoling from afar, but they were also a chore, with their own worrying and their demands that she either fly home or they would fly out to meet her.

Gabby, impossibly, infuriatingly, had attended the funeral. She stood in the third row of pews with a blank expression, looking once or twice at Kera and staying only long enough afterward to tell her that she couldn't imagine what Kera was going through and that she should take whatever time off she needed.

Hawk had paid to put her up in a more comfortable Midtown hotel so that she wouldn't have to go to the apartment until she was ready. Besides at the funeral, she spoke to virtually no one for a full week. She instructed the hotel's front desk to give no one her room number and to forward no calls. Occasionally, she collected messages from them or checked for messages on her phone. Her parents called and e-mailed daily. Jones had come by once. Even Lionel had called, breaking protocol to leave a message, which said he was sorry about what had happened and to let him know if she needed anything.

On the eighth day, she got dressed and ventured as far as the hotel's café for coffee and oatmeal. The continuity of the city's awful human machinery, the way it just went on, was ludicrous. She could see it outside from her window table. And from the television on the nearby wall, which broadcast one of the cable news networks. It just went on and on. To what end?

She had played a key role in Parker's death. That is what she had dedicated the week to reminding herself. Her role in his death was not the one his or her parents thought she'd played—breaking up with a man more troubled than anyone could have known. She knew her real role. As did Gabby and the people at ONE who had been asking Parker questions about her. Kera was not innocent. If only she'd convinced him not to accept the job at ONE, or if only she'd left him earlier. It was Parker's ties to her that had got him killed.

Kera looked up when the news anchor on the television announced that Natalie Smith, the filmmaker, had vanished. That this, of all things, should be the event that compelled Kera to action after a week of seclusion was not something she dwelt on. There wasn't time for that. She felt suddenly that she had to get to Jones before he gave up on her, if he hadn't already.

Yes, it had been Parker's ties to Kera that had gotten him killed. But she hadn't killed him.

FIFTY-TWO

Gabby greeted Kera with uncharacteristic interest in her well-being, protesting Kera's return to work as premature. "I saw there was another missing person," Kera told her. "I need to be back. I'm not doing anyone any good alone in that hotel room."

Gabby finally conceded with a cautious smile that made Kera wonder how long either of them would be able to keep up this charade.

Jones, of course, was at his workstation when she arrived. He gave her a hug and did not ask her any questions. "Let's finish this," Kera said, nodding at the ATLANTIS files open on his screen, but meaning everything else they had discussed before Parker's death. All else that needed to be communicated between them was done with their eyes.

One of the strangest things about her week away, Kera realized, was how isolated, almost helpless she'd felt without access to HawkEye. She spent the rest of the morning and afternoon reorienting herself in the case. Bolívar, oddly, was at home. He'd been there for almost two full days. It was the first time since Kera had begun tracking him that he'd not gone into the office. Next she reviewed Natalie Smith's final forty-eight hours and found nothing surprising. The filmmaker had left behind a video of herself stepping off the roof of her eighteen-story apartment building. On the pavement below was the chalk outline of a body that wasn't there. The words were scratched out in chalk by the ghost corpse's feet: *Have you figured it out yet?*

Late in the afternoon, after the novelty of having her back had begun to wear off for her colleagues and they seemed to be paying her less attention, Kera discreetly used HawkEye to look at something else. Without opening an official dossier, she checked the archived footage from the camera that she knew to be closest to her old apartment. Working forward from the approximate time Parker had last called her, she reviewed the footage until she spotted him. She only needed to play the clip once. There he was, walking down the sidewalk, in no apparent danger. The leather courier bag was slung over his shoulder.

Kera quickly closed out of the camera's viewer window and brought up her ATLANTIS notes. The first thing that caught her attention was Bolívar's meeting with the CEO of ONE, more than a week earlier. It bothered her now, as it had when she'd first learned of it. The man she'd studied for weeks was a man of habit and routine. But ever since that meeting with ONE, his behavior seemed to have changed. She squinted at the HawkEye screen. The dot representing Bolívar's most recent activity hovered over his apartment. It was the middle of a weekday, and he was still at home.

Moving through her notes, Kera was reminded that the last thing she'd done was meet with Bolívar's college professor. Picking up where she'd left off, she started to sift through both Bolívar's and Charlie Canyon's NYU records to see if there was any mention of a third roommate or friend, as the professor had suggested existed. For the first time in a week, she became lost in thoughts that didn't end with Parker's head ripped open in a bathtub. She worked nonstop until a few seconds after six PM, when a murmur rising from the analysts in the pit pulled her out of her work.

Kera looked immediately to Jones, who was at his workstation. When she saw the bewilderment on his face, she stood up and walked around their desks to look at his screen.

"What's happening?" she said.

"I don't know. It looks like Gnos.is is down."

He refreshed the site's home page and got the same screen. He tried retyping the URL. Again, he was directed to the same bizarre page. In the place of the familiar Gnos.is home page were six black digits separated by two colons at the center of the screen. It took Kera a few seconds to understand that it was a digital timer counting backward.

In a moment of confusion, a technician in the pit keyed a combination of commands that pushed the Gnos.is home page onto every screen on the Control Room's main tactical display. The sight of all those ticking digits plunged the room into an eerie silence. Gnos.is—one of the most popular sites on the Internet—was gone. The page that replaced it contained no hyperlinks. Just the clock, counting backward from twenty-four hours. There was no explanation for the countdown, nor what would follow when the digits reached 00:00:00.

The VINYL team, Jones included, huddled over the bank of consoles in the pit for a half hour until they'd determined that there was nothing else unusual about the site. All of its content had simply been replaced with this clock. Eventually, Director Branagh made an appearance, spent a minute glaring at the digits as they ticked toward the unknown, and then told the VINYL case officer to keep an eye on it.

FIFTY-THREE

The man in the black leather jacket waited at the very end of the plat-form for the train. When it came, tearing past him with a piercing screech, he stood back and watched people crowd the ledge as if it were worth risking an accidental shove onto the tracks for a shot at being the first to squeeze through the doorway. After the train accelerated out of the station, there was a short period during which the platform was empty. It would begin to fill again in moments, but for a few seconds, it was deserted. The man did not look directly at the security camera at the end of the platform, but he could feel it watching him as he jumped down to the tracks. He walked into the downtown tunnel and wondered, though it seemed beside the point, whether he was breaking any law.

He squinted, straining for the first glimpse of light thrown toward him from the headlamp of the next train. His eyes played small tricks on him, but the tunnel remained dark. The number 6 trains could always be counted upon to be few and far between.

Deeper in the tunnel were rats. He heard them first and then felt them at his ankles and shins. The ball clattered in the spray can as he shook it. Then the paint hissed against the wall. He formed each letter carefully and doubled back over each line until the letters were thick and bold. The rats began to retreat, and he glanced down the tracks. The tunnel became illuminated around the near bend, growing brighter with a low rumble. He pushed harder against the head of the spray can. He had to finish. The rail he stood on vibrated through his soles. Air began to flow uptown, lifting his hair, blowing cool particles of paint across his bare knuckles. At first it was only a draft, carrying a lifting sensation that made him feel like a dolphin riding the bow wave of a boat. But then the currents grew stiff and wild, the stale air desperate to escape the path of the train. When he looked again, the headlight curved into sight. He had one letter yet to finish.

He no longer felt the rats scratching at his ankles. They had all taken cover.

Cowards, he thought.

FIFTY-FOUR

Kera might never have received the envelope had the receptionist not called out to her as she crossed through the lobby.

"A delivery?"

"Came by courier just after I got in. It's on your desk."

She was already late getting into the office, but what were a few more minutes? Instead of clearing directly through to the secure zone within Hawk, Kera went to her desk in the *TGR* newsroom—the desk she never sat at, the desk that looked like it belonged to a rising young journalist who found time to balance her work and family lives. What first caught her attention were the pictures of her and Parker displayed around the cubicle. She had steered clear of the apartment for the past week and had thus avoided moments like this, which exposed the stark cleavage between the innocent before and the horrific after. Thinking it was safe now to look at photos of him, she picked one up—a shot she'd taken of him in Battery Park, smiling, a ferry pulling away in the background—but all she could see was his body in the bathtub. She set the photograph down, fighting the feeling she so often had had in the days since he'd been killed, of wanting just to lie in bed, unable to face even the most ordinary tasks.

The sight of the envelope on top of her in-box rescued her from this spiral. It was thick. There was no return information, just an ink stamp from the courier service. Mail addressed to her came regularly, but it was mostly paranoid letters professing news tips from people too suspicious or too old to use e-mail. No one she could think of would mail her anything important, not here, not addressed to the *Global Report*. She assumed, then, that the envelope likely contained a rant from a more aggressive breed of conspiracy theorist, one with cash to spend on a courier that delivers before nine AM.

She ripped away the seal. Inside were sheets of paper, perhaps twenty or thirty pages, clamped together with a binder clip. It wasn't until she pulled them out and had a look at the cover page that she began to understand where the package had come from. She looked around. No one seemed to have noticed her lingering in the newsroom. She put down her bag and sat in the unfamiliar chair. The top page was a printout of a *TGR* article that she'd become very familiar with: RISING I-BANKERS DECAMP FOR ONE. Her byline beneath the title was what had originally caused Travis Bradley, the ex-Wall Street quant, to contact her. And that had led to the meeting with Bradley that Gabby had sent her to.

The pages beneath the article were less revealing. She flipped through them quickly, passing over grids of dense data. At first glance page after page looked the same—columns of dates and rows of numbers. And then a folded pamphlet fell out from between the final pages. It was a tourist map of Central Park, the kind purchased at sidewalk kiosks. Because a map was more interesting than pages of endless numbers, and because she didn't think the map had gotten in there on accident, she unfolded it. She noticed immediately that there was a mark beside a path near the park's southwest corner, a small X inked in red pen. The ex-Wall Street quant, it seemed, was trying his hand at tradecraft. But what was he trying to tell her?

She returned her attention to the packet of papers and flipped back to the first page of data. This time she looked more closely and discovered there was a different name, age, address, and phone number on the header of each page. The name on the first page got her attention. She flipped through only three more names before she shoved the packet back into the envelope and hurried for the Control Room.

.   .   .   .   .

After she'd cleared the retinal scanner and entered, she crossed through the familiar glow of digital maps, databases, and surveillance imagery. This morning she noticed that several of the screens above the pit displayed the Gnos.is clock, which ticked backward through 10:28:45 as she approached Jones's workstation. Director Branagh and Gabby hovered over the VINYL case officer in the pit, each of them attached to a phone and a cup of coffee. A familiar crew of analysts cycled by. But no one seemed very busy. That clock was headed to zero and there was nothing more anyone in this room was going to learn about Gnos.is before it got there.

"Jones," she whispered, coming up behind him. She suddenly didn't know how she should proceed. What she had to say was not something they could discuss with Gabby and Branagh in the room. "I heard from our source. We have—"

"Kera—" he said, cutting her off. He stood up and glanced down at the pit to make sure Gabby and Branagh weren't paying any attention to them. "Come with me."

He guided her into the small kitchen just off the Control Room floor. There was no one else there. For the moment, they were alone and out of earshot—at least out of range of human ears. "We can't talk about this in here," she whispered.

"If we're quiet, we can." He must have read the skepticism on her face. "It's clean. No bugs."

"How do you know?"

"I looked for them. There are ceiling devices in most offices and conference rooms. And the cameras in the Control Room also pick up audio, though I can't imagine they pull in anything more than a steady din most of the time. But the bathrooms, kitchens, and hallways are clean."

"I think they skipped over all that during my orientation," she said. "I suppose sweeping rooms for electronic devices is normal behavior for you NSA guys?"

But Jones was not in the mood for dry humor. In fact, he seemed to be struggling to look her in the eye.

"Jones?"

He exhaled. "There was an alert. It came in just a few minutes ago." A hesitation. "Bolívar's gone."

"Gone?"

"Right now they're saying he's dead, Kera."

"What happened? Is there a body?"

"Kera—"

"Answer me. Did they find a body?"

Jones looked away. Finally he shook his head, as if resigned to what was coming. "It's too early to say. It happened in one of the subway tunnels. They found his jacket, his phone. NYPD is still investigating whether he could have been clipped by a train—or worse."

"What, a hit-and-run by a train? And one where the body does the running? Jesus, listen to yourself. You can't believe that."

"It doesn't matter what I believe."

Kera made a move to leave. She needed more information; she needed to see for herself.

"Kera." He was blocking her. "Stay focused. I need you today."

"Bolívar is one of them, Jones. He's part of it, whatever it is."

"I believe you. But we have to stick to our plan."

She tried to slide past him. "I've got to get to his apartment."

"No. Kera, look at me. You have to stay here. If you're not at your workstation today, Gabby will know you're up to something. We can't give her any reason to keep a closer eye on us. Not right now."

Kera was thinking of the locked room in Rafael Bolívar's apartment. But Jones was right. Deserting her post right now would be a red flag for Gabby. The fact that she'd even considered it made her wonder if she was more shaken by Parker's death than she imagined. She couldn't afford a stupid mistake. Both her own life and Jones's depended on it. She nodded. "So you knew?"

"Knew what?"

"About . . . Bolívar and me."

He said nothing. He looked at her for a moment more and then turned to leave.

"Wait," she said. She pulled the packet of papers from the envelope and handed it to him.

"What's this?" he said.

"It's data on surveillance targets. But look at the names. Senators, foreign ambassadors, even the secretary of defense. They have phone records, purchases, location data—everything. It's these people's lives, broken down into numbers and formulas."

"Slow down. Where did you get this?"

"From Bradley. This is what ONE is doing."

He looked up at her. "Why?"

"Because it's information they can sell. It's a product. You don't have to stretch your imagination to figure out what sort of consumer would be interested in this. Look at the last page."

Jones flipped to the end of the packet. The note was scrawled in unruly handwriting:

I have more examples like these. By tomorrow I will have a list put together of everyone they're selling to. It won't take them long to discover the breach. I'm leaving the city for a while. If you want a copy of what I've managed to gather, meet me at noon tomorrow.

"Meet him where?" Jones asked.

Kera held up the map.

"Are you up for going?"

She nodded. "This is what we've been waiting for. We have the link between Hawk and ONE. Bradley, let's hope, comes through with the rest."

"All right," Jones said. "Tomorrow it is. I'll copy the ONE contracts and Gabby's and Branagh's e-mail files before I leave tonight, and we'll have to hope it doesn't set off any alarms before noon tomorrow. Why don't we meet later, outside, to go over everything?"

She nodded. "McKinley's scotch bar in the Village? Meet there at nine?"

"It's a date."

FIFTY-FIVE

News came in the early afternoon that ONE had acquired Alegría North America. An elaborate press conference had been planned to announce the multibillion-dollar deal, but it was scrapped hastily after Rafael Bolívar was first reported dead—reports that were revised throughout the day until the final consensus was that he, like the others, had gone missing. ONE executives, fearing for the company's valuation on the NYSE, rushed to assure investors that the deal had been finalized the day before Bolívar's disappearance and that, though they were hopeful for Bolívar's safe return, Bolívar's absence would not present any lasting complications.

Given Bolívar's recent behavior, news of the acquisition did not come as a surprise to Kera. But it still didn't make sense. Selling out to ONE seemed to contradict everything else she knew about Bolívar.

In any case, the Alegría acquisition seemed destined to be overshadowed. By the end of the day, no one was paying attention to anything other than Gnos.is.

• • • • •

Theories had developed throughout the day that the clock wouldn't last to the end, that in the final minutes too many people would be watching, too many browsers would be burdening the servers, and the site would crash under the weight of anticipation. But the site's infrastructure held.

At six PM Eastern Standard Time, the city was gripped in its predictable commuter chaos. Trains thundered underground at full capacity, people fought over cabs that inched through gridlock, sidewalks clogged with crisscrossing pedestrians. But the people of New York weren't so far from a phone or computer or television that, at precisely the top of the hour, they could not spare a few seconds to cast an eye on the nearest screen. And it seemed that any screen capable of connecting to the Internet was tuned to Gnos.is.

When the final few seconds slipped away, all the digits came to rest at zero. And then, as if after a breath, the Gnos.is home page was restored.

"It's back," Director Branagh said, his head tilted back so that he could look up at the wall screens. "What are we looking at?"

Everyone at a console went to work. Jones, who had been standing next to Kera near their workstations, sat down in front of his monitors. Kera had no official duty in that moment, so she lingered where she stood, watching the display on the main wall.

The new Gnos.is home page was a clean, simple design. There were only three words on the entire page. At the top was the word Gnos.is, the letters slanting in their recognizable font. The other two words opposed each other in the middle of the screen. On one side was the word /FACT. On the other, /TRUTH.

The analyst in control of the big screen selected /FACT, and the page slid to the left, revealing a large cloud made up of bubble-like spheres floating in a clump. The sizes of the spheres varied widely. Each sphere was wrapped in a skin of transparent, rotating graphics that included a headline, photo and video images, and descriptive text highlighting the content of the story within.

"It's news, sir," an analyst said. "Like before, but . . ." he trailed off, unable to articulate yet what about the site was so different. Kera scanned the most prominent headlines: FAMINE FEARED WITHIN A DECADE, CLIMATE CHANGE ACCELERATING, PROGRESS SEEN ON AIDS VACCINE.

After a few more minutes, a different analyst spoke up. "Sir, it looks like they've altered their sorting algorithms."

"Their what?" Gabby said.

"The way each news story is prioritized. Before, on the previous incarnation of Gnos.is, headlines were more or less ranked based on how many people clicked on them. That's how most news sites work."

Kera had been studying the spheres as she listened, and suddenly she understood what the analyst was about to say before he said it.

"Now, though, the stories are prioritized according to their real global impact. See the larger bubbles there? They are news stories that affect a greater number of people than the smaller bubbles. Well, that's an oversimplification. It has to do with more than just the number of people affected. It's a little early to say, but it looks like the algorithm is factoring in several other variables too. Things like financial impact, health implications, and historical significance. Basically, it's calling out the stories that have the most tangible impact on the population's quality of life."

What was not factored in, Kera noted, was each news story's entertainment value. That, more than anything, differentiated it from other news sites.

"What about the bar on top?" the director asked. Above the cloud of spheres was a small bar with the word GLOBAL in it. "Does that change?"

The analyst tapped the bar, and it expanded to offer two other options: NATIONAL AND LOCAL. He selected them one at a time. Each time he tapped a new region, the cloud vanished and then reappeared with a different set of spheres. Similar to the GLOBAL cloud, the size of each sphere was proportionate to the story's respective impact on the lives of people in that region. As such, while famine, violence caused by religious conflict, and climate change stood out in the GLOBAL cloud, things like subway and sewer failures, tax and zoning laws, and severe weather patterns dominated the local cloud. Neither featured any headline about a politician's extramarital affair, a roller coaster disaster at a distant county fair, or an actor's exhibitionist video.

Kera felt the gentle pulse of her smartphone as it received an incoming e-mail. She slipped it out of her pocket and looked at the screen. The e-mail had been sent to her *TGR* account. It was from Professor Carl Tierney.

SUBJECT: THESIS

HE'S A DECADE PAST THE DEADLINE, BUT I THINK HE'S JUST COMPLETED MY ASSIGNMENT. PLEASE SEE ATTACHED.

Kera reread the message three times. *What was he talking about?*

She put her phone back in her pocket and looked down at the activity in the pit. That's when she saw it.

"What is that?" she said aloud, pointing to one of the analyst's screens below her as she descended the stairs into the pit. A few people looked in her direction, including Gabby, whose first reaction was a territorial glance, as if to warn Kera against butting into a case that wasn't hers. But what she saw in Kera's eyes stopped her. "That!" Kera said. "What's that?" She was directly behind the analyst now, hovering over his shoulders.

"This is the /TRUTH side of the site," he said.

In the background across the top of his screen were the words HAVE YOU FIGURED IT OUT YET? The letters were red on a black background, stylized like graffiti. Below them a video played of a singer, a young woman, performing alone on a stage. At first Kera had only noticed the familiar phrase, but now she studied the singer.

"Put that up on the big screen. Do we have audio?" Kera said.

The analyst had never met Kera before, but since Gabby wasn't objecting to Kera's demands, he did as he was told. The audio came over the speakers as the image appeared on the wall display. Kera froze at the sound of the first notes. She had never heard the song before, but she recognized the voice immediately.

"Is that—?" Gabby said.

"Rowena Pete," Kera whispered. Then she looked down at the analyst. "This is coming from the new Gnos.is?"

"Yes. This is basically what the /TRUTH side of the site contains. Here, look." He swiped the video away, and it seemed to fold itself into a sphere and recede back into a cloud, just like the spheres did on the /FACT side. In this cloud, though, all of the spheres were wrapped in images of performing musicians, artwork, and text from books. "It's just a bunch of entertainment and art stuff, see?" the analyst started to explain.

But Kera was walking away from him. She moved toward the big screen, gazing up at the spheres. They were all there—all of the missing subjects from the ATLANTIS case: Rowena Pete and Background Noise Pollution, the musicians; Cole Emerson and Natalie Smith, the filmmakers; Craig Shea and Lazlo Timms, the novelists; and Caroline Mullen, the estate attorney.

And there was a new one. The largest sphere of all featured the art of It.

Gabby turned from the screen and looked at Kera. "Alive and well, indeed," she said. "It looks like your theory came pretty close."

Kera nodded, acknowledging the compliment, but she was thinking the same thing as Director Branagh, who voiced the question aloud.

"Where *are* they?" None of the analysts had an answer for that. "They're on here, publishing all this content—but where did they go? *Why?*"

Kera reached suddenly for her pocket and pulled out her phone to read Professor Tierney's e-mail again. This time she thought she was starting to understand what he was talking about. *Was it possible?* She climbed up out of the pit and sat down at her workstation, but instead of logging into the computer, she reached for her tablet. She pulled up the e-mail Professor Tierney had just sent to her and opened the attachment. It was a sixty-three-page Word document titled *Fact and Truth: The Link between Knowledge and Meaning*. The author was Rafael Bolívar.

She read it through in a half hour. By the time she reached the end, she had forgotten about everything else that was happening in the room around her.

"What did you say?" Jones said, looking over at her. She'd been unaware that she'd said something aloud.

"He did it," Kera repeated.

"Who did what? Why are you smiling?"

She looked over at Jones. Then she whispered so that only he could hear her, "Meet me back in the kitchen in five minutes."

· · · · ·

Jones stalled for a minute or two, and then, after an innocent-looking detour to the men's room, he slipped into the Control Room kitchen and filled a paper cup with coffee. Kera made her move to join him when she could see that Gabby was tied up with the director.

"Read this," she said, keeping her voice low despite Jones's previous assurances that the kitchen was free of eavesdropping devices. She extended the tablet toward him, already cued up to the key page.

"What is it?"

"It's something Bolívar wrote."

Jones shut his eyes. "Kera, this isn't the time—"

"Trust me. Go on, read it. Just this one page."

Jones looked over his shoulder at the passage to the Control Room. His face didn't even try to disguise the fact that he thought she was crazy. But because arguing would have taken longer than reading a page of text, he took hold of the tablet. At first his eyes scanned quickly, as though he was merely going through the motions to appease her. She smiled when she saw his eyes catch and then sweep back to the beginning to read it more closely.

A clock does not innocently measure minutes and hours; it imposes on us the bias of time. A clock can give us free time, for example, just as surely as it can imprison us from nine to five. But in a world with clocks, one cannot opt out of time.

There are other examples of such man-made "mediums" that, once created, fundamentally alter human existence. Take, for instance, the written word, demonstrated here, which does not innocently record what would otherwise be said aloud, but instead insists upon structured, logical thought—a higher level of thought than is otherwise possible.

The most powerful of these mediums, though, is currency. Currency does not innocently transfer value; it imposes on us the bias of profit, and in doing so insists that profit is itself the highest value. The result, not surprisingly, are markets—and humans—that exist solely to maximize profit, often at the expense of living (though such "expense" is never accounted for on the balance sheets).

We cannot unwind our attachment to profit any more than we can cut ourselves free of time or logical thought. But there is room for more. There is room for a new medium, a medium that is as self-interested as currency, but that insists not upon an accumulation of profit, but a deepening of our understanding of the meaning in our lives. If your first thought was to try to understand this in the context of market-like incentives or to ask yourself, "Will it be profitable?" then you can begin to understand that our largest barrier to advancing human understanding is mostly a problem of human imagination.

We have the capacity for so much more. We need only to realize that "more" contains whole worlds that have no relationship to "profit." The clock is ticking.

"Bolívar wrote this?" Jones said, still staring at the tablet screen. Kera nodded. She saw him read aloud the title of the thesis, which was displayed in the margin at the top of the screen. The words came out as just barely a whisper. *"Fact and Truth: The Link between Knowledge and Meaning."* He looked at her. "Gnos.is is Bolívar's."

"Yes," she said. "Gnos.is is not just a website. It's his attempt at this new medium he talks about."

Jones checked the door again with a glance. "So this is what ONE is after?"

"If they weren't before, they will be now. A few missing artists is a nuisance for a media company like ONE. But the new Gnos.is is real competition."

Jones nodded. "Where did you get this?"

"Bolívar's college professor."

"Who else knows about it?"

Kera shrugged. "Who knows? Although I doubt anyone other than me has asked the professor about it in over a decade."

"They'll be asking now. Does Gabby know you have it? Does anyone else in there know?"

Kera shook her head. "No. But it will get out, Jones. And as soon as it does, Gabby will come directly to me. The professor e-mailed it to my *TGR* account."

Jones thought about this. "All right. If it comes up in the next twenty-four hours, play dumb. We just need to buy a little more time. See you tonight?"

She nodded and turned back toward the Control Room.

"Kera. Be—"

"I know," she said. *Be careful.* She didn't need to be reminded of that.

FIFTY-SIX

She did not go immediately to the hotel. First, she took a cab to Columbus Circle and got out on Fifty-Ninth Street, across from the entrance to Rafa's complex. Three cruisers and an FBI truck were parked at the curb in front of the glass towers. The lobby doormen inside, well aware that they'd lost a famous resident, were taking their duties as seriously as ever. She gave them the line about being sent from the mayor's office and said Detective Hopper was expecting her. He was not, and he was not pleased to see her when she stepped off the elevator on the forty-eighth floor. But it was the end of a long day for Hopper, and his fatigue and indifference earned her a quick, self-guided tour of Bolívar's apartment.

"You have five minutes, Ms. Mersal."

"I only need three."

The kitchen and living room were neat and tidy, just as she remembered them. Her eyes lingered for a second on the chair and ottoman where she and Rafa had fallen, intertwined. She couldn't decide which was more surreal, her memory of that evening or the idea that he was gone and that his apartment now crawled with cops taking photos and dusting surfaces.

The painting was missing. She noticed it as soon as she turned for the bedrooms. For a moment she stood there with her head cocked slightly, looking at the place where it had hung. She swept the room with her eyes. There were no other gaps that would have suggested another missing canvas. There must have been hundreds of thousands of dollars hanging on these walls. And the only one missing was the small oil-on-canvas that had been painted by one of Bolívar's college classmates, or so he'd claimed. She walked toward the recessed area where the painting had hung and ran her fingers over the thin black screw protruding from the wall.

From that vantage she got her first look into the room she had come here to see—the mysterious second bedroom with the heavy, locked door. The door was open now, and there were signs that the task of unlocking it had been an indelicate one. The frame was bent and twisted, and dark scorch marks flared around the keypad.

She stepped through the threshold. The room had been gutted of everything but harsh, overhead fluorescent lights. The smell of electrical sparks and plaster particles hung in the air. A row of outlets, many of their covers dangling from braids of multicolored wires, lined the walls at one-foot intervals. There must have been fifty outlets. She noted the marks on the floor where furniture—shelves or desks, maybe—had been positioned, anchored over small bolt holes in the concrete. But there was not a single object in the room. It was bare enough for her footsteps to echo.

However, the first thing she had noticed upon entering were the words sprayed in red paint across one wall. She faced them now. At a few points, the paint bled in streaks where the spray can must have lingered too long. The writing said: *Have you figured it out yet?*

"You guys stripped this whole room today?" she asked one of the nearby cops. They were taking photographs of the furniture marks on the floor.

"No, ma'am. Once we blasted through the door, this is the way we found it."

FIFTY-SEVEN

Jones did not like the look of the figure loitering on the sidewalk a half block from the entrance to his condo building. It was dusk now, an hour and a half before he was to meet Kera, and he'd left the Hawk offices in time to go home and change. He had not picked up a shadow on the street or in the subway, but if anyone was watching—including via HawkEye—he intended to make this trip home appear as if he would be in for the night. He was paranoid; that was all. Things had been going too smoothly, and that was making him overly cautious. Still, even though he couldn't be sure, he thought he'd seen this same man outside the Hawk building when he'd left work.

The man was not looking in Jones's direction. He was dressed plainly in dark jeans and a dark shirt with a baseball cap low on his forehead, so he might have been anyone. There were at least even odds, Jones reasoned, that a man standing nearby on a Brooklyn sidewalk represented absolutely no danger.

He waved to the doorman, who was out on the curb looking to hail a cab for another of the building's residents, and went inside. The man on the sidewalk hadn't taken any interest in him, after all.

Inside the building's lobby, Jones checked the mail. He tossed the coupon pamphlets and takeout menus and sorted through the credit card offers, a bill, and a *Rolling Stone* as he waited for the elevator. He was alone when he stepped into the car and lit up the button for the fourth floor, reading the teaser headlines on the magazine cover. He looked up, just before the closing panels met, in time to see a man fill the narrow opening and extend his hand to trip the sensor. The doors jerked back obediently, and from underneath the low bill of his baseball cap, the man looked Jones directly in the eye.

FIFTY-EIGHT

Kera left the hotel from an exit she'd never used before and switched cabs twice on her way downtown. None of these maneuvers exposed any shadows. When the first cab hit a mysterious snarl of traffic, she waited it out for a few minutes before asking the driver to take an alternate route. It wasn't until she was riding in the second cab that she learned the cause of the traffic jam. A newscast coming over the small flat screen attached to the back of the driver's seat reported that there was a new piece by It. In the last hour, a billboard in Midtown had been commandeered by the artist and was delighting fans as much as it was inconveniencing motorists.

She was ten minutes late when she approached the double glass doors of McKinley's. Just inside, she scanned the crowd. Jones was seated at the bar, his jacket draped over the empty stool to his left. Most of the other seats were taken. He wore a white button-down shirt, which for him was unprecedented. Kera had only ever seen him in black T-shirts and jeans. He was touching a glass in front of him lightly with one hand, his eyes pointed down into it. *People do this in bars,* she thought. *They look into their drinks as they sit alone.*

She was just about to approach when she saw his head turn to the right and his lips move.

He was talking to the man next to him.

Before she could skirt around the high-top tables to get a better view, the man got up and started to cross the room. Her first thought was that he was headed to the men's room. But then she noticed the twenty-dollar bill on the bar next to the empty glass he'd left behind. She swung her gaze back just in time to see him push through one of the rear exits by the kitchen.

She started after him, picking her way through the crowd calmly so that she wouldn't draw attention. He'd gotten a head start, but when she opened the back door and found herself in an alley, he was still in view, walking quickly away.

"Charlie!"

Even from a distance she could see the small hiccup in his step, the slight shift in the position of his shoulders at the sound of her voice. But he did not stop or glance back to acknowledge her. Then, in the next instant, he reached the end of the alley and the start of the city, and he was gone.

She went back inside, where Jones did not seem to be aware that she hadn't come in from the main entrance. In fact, he didn't seem to be aware of anything going on around him.

"Jones," she said softly. He looked almost surprised to see her, as if he'd forgotten that they'd planned to meet. "That was Canyon, wasn't it? Just now, leaving through the alley."

Jones did not respond. After a hesitation he moved his jacket so that Kera could sit down.

"What's going on? He was talking to you, wasn't he?" Kera said. "What did he tell you?"

Jones gestured for her to sit, but she ignored that.

"What did he say to you, Jones?"

He made a point to look her in the eye, as though to reassure her. Finally he said, "He offered me a job."

Kera stared at him. "With Gnos.is?" She took a step back. "How long have you been talking to them?"

"I haven't been," Jones said quickly. "I'd never spoken to Canyon in my life until just now."

"How did he find you?"

Jones shrugged. "Bolívar, I guess. He said that Bolívar had become curious about the *Global Report* after it launched. He was interested in news sites that aggregated data from the web to create original news content, like Gnos.is. He figured out pretty quickly that *TGR* wasn't a real news site."

Kera nodded. Bolívar himself had told her that on the night he'd hosted the screening of the *America* film. But this reminded Kera of something that had never made sense to her. "So Bolívar knew about Hawk for one—maybe two—years? Why not expose us? He knew we were tracking him. And he runs a media conglomerate. He could have ruined Hawk in less than a news cycle."

"Canyon said we'll know that tomorrow."

"Tomorrow?"

"Yes. Something to do with ONE's acquisition of Alegría. He said that deal was very important to Bolívar, and he didn't want to jeopardize it by rocking the boat with Hawk."

"That sale never made sense to me either. Why get so friendly with ONE all of a sudden? Bolívar built Alegría North America on his own. It was taking off. You heard all the talk lately, analysts saying that Alegría was the only company with a chance to rival ONE. He certainly didn't need the money."

"No, he didn't. And, according to Canyon, he despises ONE."

Kera looked at him, confused.

"Come on, sit down. I'll tell you everything." He glanced up at the bar. "Besides, I got a new job. We're celebrating. What would you like?"

She looked up at the shelves of amber-colored liquor and, overwhelmed, just ordered whatever he was having. They were silent while the bartender poured each of them a finger of eighteen-year Macallan.

"So that's it. You're going to join them," Kera said. "What's the job?"

Jones nodded proudly. "I'll head cybersecurity for Gnos.is."

"Well, that's at least a full-time job. Congratulations." Their glasses met. Kera felt the liquor's initial bite soften as it descended down her throat. "So I was right. Bolívar and Canyon are working together."

"They are now, yes. But not all along, according to Canyon. Back in college Bolívar had discussed the early concepts of Gnos.is with him. It wasn't called Gnos.is back then; I don't know what they were calling it. But Bolívar was obsessed with the project and sought out Canyon's help. There were two problems, though. The first was that Bolívar couldn't figure out how to complete the actual design."

Kera nodded. She recalled Professor Tierney's words when he'd explained to her Bolívar's failure to deliver a functional prototype to correspond with his thesis. Bolívar had been ambitious to a fault, the professor had said. The thing Bolívar was striving for was impossible.

"The second problem was more of a philosophical disagreement," Jones continued. "Bolívar envisioned Gnos.is as a new way to understand things that are—or ought to be—important to us, but that cannot be quantified in financial terms. He thought that people, if given the opportunity, would recognize the value in that. You know that part. It was in his thesis."

"Right."

"Canyon, though, was more pessimistic about how Bolívar's idea might be received. He thought it would, at best, remain completely obscure. At worst, it would just become another participant in the race-to-the-bottom entertainment culture. Anyway, it was a chicken-or-egg argument, and they disagreed stubbornly on which came first. Then Bolívar left NYU, and the two of them drifted apart."

"But Bolívar eventually completed his design for Gnos.is," Kera said.

"Yes. The first version was launched. And it turned out that Canyon had been right: Gnos.is did not fail to become popular, of course. In fact, it became wildly popular. And that was the problem. The more popular it became, the more the site was reduced to an exchange of superficial content. It was quickly overrun by the cultural fixation of the minute rather than becoming the platform for deeper understanding that Bolívar believed it could be."

She nodded to let him know she was following.

"Canyon and Bolívar had fallen out of touch, but as soon as it launched, Canyon recognized where Gnos.is had come from. He remembered it all from their discussions back in college. He could see that Bolívar had finally solved the design problems that had prevented him from launching the site earlier. And he could also see that the remaining problem was exactly the one he'd predicted."

"That the content Bolívar most wanted to receive attention would be crowded out by more trivial entertainment?"

"Exactly. That was the paradox Bolívar faced with Gnos.is from the start: how to make a worthy idea popular without compromising it in order to appeal to a lower and lower common denominator. Canyon understood that the problem with Gnos.is wasn't in the coding or with any other technology issue. It was a human problem. Bolívar might be a genius at designing the code, but he couldn't control how artists and their audiences and people seeking out news would decide to use Gnos.is. Canyon, though—his passion is manipulating human behavior."

"The stunts," Kera said, beginning to see where this was headed.

"The what?"

"Stunts. That's what Bolívar called them. Marybelle Pickett's stolen paintings, for example." She paused to allow a few more pieces to fall into place. "And the artists disappearing. The whole thing is an advertising gimmick."

"Sort of," Jones said. "On the surface, anyway. Canyon began to develop his plan without even telling Bolívar what he was doing. He figured they'd argued about it plenty in college and got nowhere. He wasn't going to do that again. Instead, he was just going to make it happen. So first, Canyon approached Caroline Mullen, a young lawyer he'd met through a friend, looking for advice about how one might minimize the legal fallout of faking a suicide or simply disappearing. Mullen, it turned out, was much more receptive to Canyon's plan than he'd expected. She wanted in, and she wanted to go first, to see if it could be done."

"Wait. What about It? It's art had already begun appearing anonymously before Caroline Mullen disappeared."

Jones shrugged. "I know. I asked him that. Canyon wouldn't talk about It."

"What do you mean?"

"He just wouldn't. All he said was that It would remain anonymous, even after the other artists rejoin society."

"When will that be?"

"I imagine they'll each decide on their own when the time feels right. There's no big hurry, I guess. These artists have had more attention paid to their work today than they might have hoped to have in their entire lifetimes. And they don't have ONE execs butting in with the latest data-driven edits that might help them reach a bigger, dumber audience."

Kera shook her head. "But what if that's only temporary? They don't know who they're dealing with. Canyon, these artists, even Bolívar—they're no match for ONE. Especially now that ONE knows they're alive and well and profiting off their art without ONE getting its cut. This isn't a game for ONE. Look what they did to Parker."

Jones nodded. He seemed aware that this was the first time she had spoken of Parker since her return to work.

"OK," she said, changing the subject quickly, "so the artists start disappearing. When did Bolívar get on board with this plan? He told me himself he wasn't a fan of Canyon's previous stunts, like the stolen paintings."

Jones smiled. "Canyon said you might ask that. He said you were there on the night he approached Bolívar."

"No, that isn't possible," Kera said. But then she thought about it and saw that it was.

"The man on the balcony," she said. After the *America* screening. Could that have been Canyon? Kera thought of the evening, weeks before, when Bolívar had rejoined her looking like he'd seen a ghost after talking to the man on that balcony. For a few moments, Kera permitted herself to think of the evening she'd spent in Bolívar's apartment. His strange behavior made more sense now. All but the deal for ONE to acquire Alegría. "Canyon told you all this? Just now?"

"Yes. He approached me at my condo. We would have talked longer, but I told him I had to meet you. Do you want another?"

Kera looked down at her glass. It was empty, as was his, though she hardly remembered drinking.

They were silent while the bartender worked. When he put drinks in front of them and retreated out of earshot, she spoke again.

"Did you get them?"

Jones's eyes widened at her mention of the Hawk files.

"What is it? Was there a problem?"

In their previous discussions, Jones had explained that he'd already located the most sensitive files that existed on Hawk's servers. Given his firing from the NSA, Hawk had been smart enough not to include Jones in the design of Hawk's cybersecurity systems. But whoever had been charged with protecting Hawk's data was no match for Jones, who had found it relatively easy to access Gabby's and Branagh's e-mail accounts and the contracts between Hawk and ONE. The real risk was making copies of all these sensitive files without sending up any red flags. Which is why he'd waited until the last possible moment.

"No. The files were on the servers just where I expected them. And the copies I made are now in a bank box near the office. It's just—there's more than what I'd been aware of before." He lowered his voice. "It goes back to the CIA, Kera."

"What does?"

"The corruption. There are e-mails between Gabby and a contact at CIA. Recent e-mails."

"Who at CIA?"

"Some guy named Bright. That mean anything to you?"

"Lionel," Kera said. It was a whisper. Very slowly, she took a sip of the scotch. The ice cube made the liquid cool against her tongue, but it felt powerfully warm when it hit her chest. By the time she set the glass down, a slight smile had spread across her lips. "I think that's a good sign. I'd say it means he's keeping contact with Gabby, stringing her along until he can squeeze her into a corner."

"No, Kera. Wait till you see these e-mails. Hawk has leverage over Langley. If anything goes wrong, Hawk can put all the responsibility back on the agency."

Kera shook her head. "No. Lionel's smart. He's just drawing them in to see what they're capable of. When we turn all of this over to him, he'll have enough to bring them down."

He eyed her. "So that's your plan? Turn all of this over to the CIA?"

"Isn't that what we discussed?"

"Yes, before we had evidence that they were involved."

"Look, I know that's what this looks like. But I trust Lionel. He's doing this for a reason," Kera said. "What else would we do with the files? We don't have anyone else to turn them over to."

"Sure we do," Jones said. "Gnos.is."

She studied him for any sign that he was joking, but found none. "You want to make all of this public? Jones, no. Don't you see what that would do?"

"Yes, it would destroy ONE and Hawk, and it would expose every foreign intelligence agency that ONE is selling data to."

"And we'd also be breaking espionage laws that come with some very ugly consequences. Leaking classified files to the press? That's jail time or worse, Jones."

"Only if we're around to stand trial."

"What, we're going to flee? Go on the run while our own government calls us traitors? That's crazy."

"Is it?" he said. She could see that he was serious. It frightened her. "I've made up my mind, Kera. I'm taking this job with Gnos.is. That means I'm going underground. And my conscience will be clear. With what we're doing here, stopping Hawk and ONE, no one has any right to question our patriotism."

"Well, if we give these files to the press, that's exactly what they're going to do."

"Let them."

"Give me a chance first, Jones. One chance. I'll have what Bradley gives me tomorrow and what you've pulled out of Hawk. Let me take that to Lionel and give him a chance to do this the right way. Then we can have a clear conscience—and also have a chance of getting our lives back."

He exhaled. "You still want to go back to the agency, don't you? After all this."

She was quiet for a long moment. She realized that she hadn't really known how much she wanted it until just now. Finally she nodded. "I don't know how to do anything else, Jones."

FIFTY-NINE

Jalen West, alone in the back of a limousine, composed music in his head. He was more in his head, really, than he was in any physical place. The vehicle's windows were tinted and his eyes were half-closed, so at first when he became aware of the familiar, irregular flashes that signaled a waiting mob of teenagers, he thought little of it. A few seconds later, though, when he straightened and prepared to exit the limo, he realized something unusual. There was a crowd, but they were not waiting for him. The band of excited onlookers was huddled across the street, their heads tipped back. Jalen ducked toward the window to peer up through the glass.

And then he saw it. Mounted high on the corner of a building was a large LED billboard, the kind that could be programmed to cycle through a variety of advertisements. The screen was lit, but not with an ad. Not exactly. Jalen thought first of an ad, but then, looking closer, he could see it was something else—a swimming collage of many ads, or recognizable components of them, but deconstructed in a way that excluded any specific product or brand. The result was a meld of stunning landscapes, perfect flesh, pleasant colors, and other appealing photography that warped slowly, hypnotically, in and out of one another.

Jalen watched with his face pressed up against the glass until the limo door was pulled open and the crushing noise from the street trespassed into his world. He hopped out of the vehicle and turned to look up at the video collage. Some of the onlookers were asking each other what it was for, since there was no brand or product attached. But Jalen didn't wonder that. He knew what it was for: itself.

"There's Jalen West!" someone shouted.

Jalen stayed standing beside the limo's open door, gazing at the billboard. He could not pull his eyes from the screen. It was not until the crowd swelled around him and he could feel people tugging on his clothes that he blinked and turned to face the adoring strangers. He did not dislike moments like this. It felt good to be so wanted. He had to admit, with a twinge of shame, that it never got old, even at times like tonight when his mood was down.

He'd just come from dinner with a group of anxious ONE executives who had spent the meal describing to him a new plan to involve fans in the development of beats and lyrics for his next album. Just wait, they told him. Crowd-sourced collaboration between artists and fans was the future of the music industry—of all entertainment. He should feel lucky, they seemed to be saying. They had chosen him. They were going to dedicate a healthy chunk of the company's resources to perfecting him in the eyes of his audience.

He'd sat patiently through the meal, waiting for any of them to inquire about what he was working on or how he thought his next album should sound. It never happened. It was possible that the executives were right, Jalen had thought glumly on the limo ride back to his hotel. But if they were, he didn't think he wanted to be a part of that future.

He waved to the assembled fans and signed autographs, wondering briefly what the collective input of these teenagers would sound like. What beats and lyrics did the ONE executives expect them to create? And why did they assume that his fans would want to hear that more than the music he could create on his own?

He felt a slight tug on his jacket, which he'd tucked under his arm while he signed digital signatures on smartphone screens.

"May I take this up to your room, Mr. West?"

He turned to face a bellhop who had stepped forward from the hotel's entrance. Except that it was not a bellhop. It was Charlie Canyon dressed as one. Jalen felt his heart stop and then race to catch up. His breath came back a long second later.

"What are you—?" he tried to say, but Charlie cut him off with a look.

"Your jacket? Shall I hang it in your room for you?"

"Of course," he whispered, and gave Charlie the room number and key card. When he'd signed several more autographs than he thought he could stand, he pushed through the lobby's revolving door and rode the elevator to the top floor. He entered the suite to find Charlie leaning against the bar, the city spread out behind him through the window.

"They told me you'd drowned."

"I'm a good swimmer."

"What are you doing here?"

"I always see you when you come to New York. I wouldn't have missed—"

"Don't talk," Jalen said, and, with some urgency, he helped Charlie out of the bellhop outfit.

• • • • •

When they finished and had showered, they lay together on the couch under a blanket. They were reclined so that Jalen's face was pressed against Charlie's chest. Charlie was holding him, and when they weren't talking, Jalen could hear the double thump of his heart, like a pair of cannons going off underwater somewhere far away.

"Are you back now?" Jalen said.

"No. Not till it's over."

"Till what's over?"

After a pause, Charlie said, "You've seen the new Gnos.is?"

"Of course."

"Have you thought about what it could do for your music?"

Jalen didn't respond. That was the first thing he'd thought of after the site had relaunched. The new Gnos.is had made sense to him immediately. It was a service for artists and the people who found art meaningful—not a business for any middleman between them. Consumers paid for the content they consumed, and that revenue went to the artists, who had control over every aspect of their work. There was no demand made on anyone that profits must expand year after year. Some of the music, writing, and art only connected with a tiny audience; some had already connected with millions of individual consumers. The connections mattered, not the numbers. It was like something Jalen had always known, but had not had the words to describe. It had never occurred to him, until he saw it materialize on the screen, that other people wanted that too.

"Has ONE explained to you what they want to do with your next album?" Charlie asked.

"Yes. That seems to be all they want to talk about. What's that got to do with you disappearing?"

"Everything." Charlie got up suddenly and walked to the window. He put his forehead to the glass so that he could look down toward the street. Far below, the colors from the billboard danced across the crowd of onlookers.

"You saw the billboard?" Jalen asked.

Charlie nodded but didn't turn around. He was watching the crowd below. It was still growing. "He's the only person I've ever known as dedicated to their art as you are."

Jalen sat up, supporting himself on his elbows. "You know him? It?"

"His name is Connor," Charlie said. "We went to college together. Our senior year there was a fire in the student art gallery, and there was some evidence that he'd started it. They said he'd killed himself. Arson-suicide, if you can believe that. I didn't, of course, but there wasn't a better explanation. He was gone." Charlie turned toward Jalen. "And then two years ago I came across a billboard in SoHo that had been painted over in a way that I had only seen once before. I knew it was him. I had always loved his art, but this was different. To have it vanish, to think that it was gone forever, and then to have it back—that was very powerful. It made me look at his art differently. And not just me. Other people were looking too. That's what gave me the idea."

"The disappearing artists," Jalen said softly. Charlie nodded. "But doing it that way, doesn't it just turn it into a marketing gimmick?"

When Charlie smiled, his eyes flared with excitement. "Everything else that matters in our culture is peddled with marketing gimmicks. Why not this?"

"Because it requires you to stoop to their level."

"Is that what you think I'm doing? I think I'm just communicating in the common language. Attention-grabbing gimmicks are the way our culture conducts its public discourse, and because of that we have proven ourselves capable of devising an infinite number of ways to draw people's attention. The danger is that there are fewer and fewer things worthy of drawing people's attention *to*. I want to give those things their due."

"But aren't you just manipulating people's emotions?"

"Of course," Charlie said. "Manipulating emotions is the most important function of meaningful art. We cannot grow unless we invest our emotions in an idea. Without emotion, nothing takes hold. I think you know that better than anyone. Music is the most powerful manipulator of emotions that humans have ever created. And you're a master at it."

He stepped toward Jalen, who was still reclined on the couch, and ran a hand down the back of his neck. Jalen was silent, thinking. Finally he said, "So now what?"

"You've thought about what Gnos.is could do for your music?" Charlie asked again.

This time Jalen nodded.

Charlie looked at him and said, "Come with me."

And to Jalen West it sounded like a song.

SIXTY

Though she'd awakened before dawn, too wired to fall back asleep, Kera was careful to arrive at the Hawk offices at her usual time. It had been a month since Gabby had made her an agent and given her access to the Control Room. Kera could remember the private exhilaration she used to feel each time she cleared the retinal scanner, heard the soft click of the lock, and pushed through the doors into the electric din of activity beyond. That feeling had been pride. Now her heart skipped anxiously as she went through the motions.

Kera and Jones didn't speak to each other all morning except for a few benign exchanges related to the ATLANTIS case. Kera's attention was divided between keeping up the appearance of work and watching the time. She had calculated that it would take her fifteen minutes to walk to the meeting spot Travis Bradley had picked out in Central Park. That meant that she would drop everything and leave no later than 11:45 AM.

At 11:20 AM two Hawk security guards came through the Control Room door. When Kera looked over at them, the nearer of the guards tapped his partner's arm. Then they approached.

"Kera Mersal?" one of the guards asked. "Can you come with us? Deputy Director di Palma would like a word."

"Can it wait? I'm in the middle of something important."

"No, ma'am. Follow us, please."

"Really," Jones cut in from his workstation. "I need her help for a little while longer."

"Di Palma's orders. Let's go," the guard said.

Kera gave Jones what she hoped was a reassuring glance, though she wasn't feeling so assured about the situation herself.

They brought her to a room she'd never seen before. The walls were metallic gray. Inset into one of them was a rectangle of one-way glass. The room's only furnishings were a bare table and five chairs. It was a lopsided arrangement—a hard wooden chair on one side of the table that faced four sleek, ergonomic office chairs on the other. Kera was invited to sit on the wood. When the security guards had gone, she turned and tried to look through her reflection in the mirrored glass. There was nothing to see there but herself staring back. For what it was worth, she thought she looked more composed than she felt.

A hurried clack of heels on the tile in the hallway preceded Gabby's entrance. She'd brought three men to fill the chairs on her side of the table. Kera couldn't have named any of them, but their faces were familiar. Two worked the VINYL case, the third was with internal security. Gabby appraised Kera from across the table while the security man set up a laptop where they could all see it. When he was finished, Kera glanced at the image on the screen. Then she looked away.

"You went to Rafael Bolívar's apartment last night," Gabby said. "Why?" Her voice was calm, the curiosity in her question sincere. When Kera didn't respond, Gabby nodded at the security man, who flipped through more images. There were video clips of Kera talking to the doormen in Bolívar's lobby and photos of her at the media pioneers event where she had first spoken to Bolívar. The last clip was of Kera coming out of Bolívar's apartment building the previous week at two thirty in the morning. The security man froze the footage on that image and left it there with the time stamp conspicuously displayed. Gabby leveled her gaze on Kera. "We'll come back to the implications of all this. But first, we need information. Rafael Bolívar vanished yesterday. Do you know where he is?"

"No," Kera said, relieved to be able to tell the truth.

"Then he hasn't contacted you?" Gabby said.

"No. Why would he do that?"

Gabby's gaze slid to the frozen security camera footage and back, but she changed tacks. "Did you know about what Bolívar was doing to Alegría?"

"The acquisition, you mean? I heard about that yesterday."

"ONE acquired Alegría, yes. But that wasn't what I was referring to."

"I don't understand."

Gabby squinted slightly, as if trying to gauge whether Kera was telling the truth. If Gabby was desperate for information and believed Kera had it, she'd dance around things to try to give Kera a chance to cooperate. If she'd already made up her mind that Kera had turned, she wouldn't waste any time. This would be a short meeting—and it would not end well for Kera. "Bolívar never discussed it with you?"

"No. As your surveillance tapes show, I only met with Bolívar on a few occasions. We weren't confidants."

Gabby again eyed the laptop screen and the image of Kera coming out of Bolívar's building at two thirty AM. But again she let that go. "Did you discuss Alegría North America with Bolívar at all?"

"No."

Gabby glanced at the two VINYL men before turning back to Kera. "Then you didn't know that it was worthless?"

Kera stared back at her. "I don't understand."

"Alegría North America is worthless. The company's media holdings were worth barely a fraction of what ONE valued them at."

"That's impossible," Kera said.

"Unfortunately not. The company was, until recently, extraordinarily successful. But Bolívar ran it into the ground before handing it over to ONE—intentionally and in secret."

"How?" Kera asked.

"I don't know the details and don't really care. Apparently, he created millions of fraudulent digital customer accounts and other company assets that existed online but had no real value."

"Didn't ONE do due diligence before acquiring all of that?"

"Of course. And Bolívar had built in mechanisms to deceive them during that process. He's a criminal, Kera. Where is he?"

"I don't know."

"You were right all along about these missing people. You must have some idea of where they are."

"You're assuming Bolívar is with them?" Kera said.

Gabby ignored this. If she had discovered Bolívar's thesis, she was not ready to reveal that. "We're all on the same team here, Kera. You knew something that made you go to his apartment last night. Now would be the time to share that information with us."

"Or else?"

This caught Gabby off guard. She'd clearly expected a confrontation—otherwise, why stage this in an interrogation room? But she hadn't expected the first aggression to come from Kera. "I'm not asking," Gabby said, adapting her tone to the circumstances. "Let me phrase it a different way. Last night you went to the apartment of a suspect in an open investigation, which, I shouldn't have to remind you, makes that a crime scene. There you tampered with evidence and tried to keep it from us."

"That isn't true."

Gabby smiled. "That isn't the point, Agent Mersal. It doesn't matter if it's true. What matters is what it looks like, or can be made to look like. And on this surveillance footage, it looks a lot like you were having an affair with a suspect who is now on the run. It doesn't take much of an imagination to see that you went to his apartment last night, without authorization, to alter evidence in an effort to clear his name."

What she wanted to say was: *Bolívar's not on the run. He isn't a coward.* Instead, she said, "Why are you doing this to me?"

"It's all in the spirit of teamwork, Kera. You want your career. I want Bolívar. We can both get what we want."

"I don't know where he is," she said.

One of the two VINYL men spoke up. "You can still help us. You went there last night. You saw the room?" He did not need to clarify which room he was talking about. Kera nodded. The man looked to Gabby, who nodded her approval for him to continue. "We have new evidence that suggests Rafael Bolívar is the man behind Gnos.is. We think he might have been developing the site out of that heavily fortified room in his apartment. Do you know anything about that?"

What she knew was that they had found the thesis, and that they must not find Bolívar. For the first time, she let herself hope that he was far away. "No," she said. She was eerily calm. She imagined a polygraph needle. It was controlled by her mind and nothing else.

"What *do* you know about him, then?" Gabby said.

"For a brief period, Bolívar was a person of interest in the ATLANTIS case. I arranged for us to cross paths on a few occasions to gauge his involvement. But the evidence was never there. As far as we could tell, he had no meaningful role in the disappearances."

"But you got to know him . . . personally," Gabby said. "You spent time with him. You spoke with him on several occasions. Let me ask a different question. What's your read on him? What do you *think* he's up to?"

"I wouldn't know. This is the first I've heard about this business with Alegría North America. And from what you've just told me, it sounds like Bolívar fed into ONE's obsession with valuing everything digitally. It appears that he played me as much as everyone else."

"What about Gnos.is?"

"You're the ones saying he's involved with that, not me."

The two VINYL men leaned back in their chairs. Both Gabby and the security man leaned forward. Kera looked once at the security man to show him that she wasn't intimidated, then glared at Gabby.

"I'd advise you to do nothing further that undermines this investigation," Gabby said. "And that's just to keep you out of jail. If you want to restore your chances for a career, I suggest you make an effort to pull your weight around here. We're looking for Bolívar. Either you help us or you don't."

Kera stared at the spot on Gabby's neck where her jugular was most vulnerable. After a moment, she said, "Well, he's not in this room. If we're done wasting our time, can I go?"

When no one challenged her, she rose and left.

As she hurried down the narrow hallway, she looked at her watch. It was 11:51 AM. She didn't have time to go back to the Control Room. She headed straight for the elevators.

SIXTY-ONE

Kera spotted the tail the moment she stepped off the elevator. He was seated at one of the small tables in the lobby of Starbucks, reading a magazine. As the elevator doors parted and she made her first hurried steps toward the revolving exit, the man took an involuntary look in her direction. It was sloppy work on his part, sloppy enough that at first she thought she'd simply caught the eye of an admirer. But then, once she was outside on the sidewalk and heading west, she glanced back through the lobby window to see that the man, who before had been comfortably leaning back in his chair, semi-engrossed in the periodical, was now on his feet. She kept her eyes on him long enough to let him know he'd been made.

She turned up Broadway. Two blocks later she saw him again in the reflection of a storefront. It wasn't the camera-toting ONE goon who had followed her in the past. This man was something different and, considering the interrogation she'd just come from, she suspected Gabby had something to do with his presence. This was not good news. Until now, all of Hawk's surveillance of her and Jones had been passive—watching them via cameras, scanning their e-mails, listening in on their phone calls. The only exception had been when the voice mail Parker had left for her had been deleted from her phone seconds after it appeared. Seeing this man on the street, Kera felt the same horrible premonition that she'd experienced then, but this time it was followed by the burst of gruesome images of Parker's body in that tub that seized her mind several times each day.

The man was about twenty yards behind her, wearing a leather jacket and sunglasses. *Dammit,* she thought. She used the urgency of the situation to steer her mind back into focus. She could draw him into an alley, where she would appear more vulnerable, to try to get a read on his intentions. But she didn't have time for that. She walked two more blocks until she saw her best chance to lose him. A cab pulled over to discard a fare, allowing Kera to jump quickly into the backseat. Before the tail could even raise an arm to hail a cab of his own, Kera's driver beat a yellow light and slipped another block uptown. She told the cabby to go east to Park Avenue. When they were there, she told him to cross back across town on Fifty-Ninth Street. By the time they reached Columbus Circle, Kera was confident that she'd forced the tail to give up pursuit.

A few minutes after noon, she entered the southwest corner of Central Park. She was walking quickly, faster than she should have been. In the field it was best to avoid behavior that might attract attention. Speed walking at a near jog in her work clothes clearly challenged that principle. But it was too late to do anything about that. The chat with Gabby, followed by the evasive detour to lose the tail, had spoiled her plan to arrive early and do things by the book.

Under normal circumstances she should have waited to see where Travis Bradley would turn up next and then approached him on her own terms. Bradley was not a professional; he would be easy to find. But she and Jones needed what Bradley had, and they needed it today.

Kera slowed as she neared the rendezvous point and veered onto a path that wound its way over a small rise. From there she could get eyes on Bradley before she approached. He was seated on a park bench overlooking an empty softball diamond. A few large trees provided shade, but there were open sight lines in almost every direction. Bradley wore a baseball cap, large sunglasses, and an overcoat too warm for the weather. He looked like a man trying hard to disguise himself. He had nothing in his hands, but there was a black backpack under the bench by his feet. Kera watched a jogger run by and wished there were more people around. This was a relatively quiet, low-traffic pocket of the park.

She would have preferred to watch him from a distance for several more minutes, but by now she was nearly fifteen minutes late. She couldn't risk him bailing. After a quick 360-degree glance to make sure there was no sign of the tail, she retraced her steps down the rise and turned onto the path that would take her to Bradley. Kera's walking pace was casual now, just a midday stroll in the park to clear her mind. Every ten paces or so, she glanced up at him. She saw him check his watch and look around, away from her first and then toward her. Even though he was wearing sunglasses, she saw the moment he spotted her. He hesitated, registering her before looking forward again, and then he sat waiting for her to close the distance.

She kept walking, checking right and left. There was a woman in running shorts and a T-shirt a hundred meters up the path. Thirty meters to the left, two men stood on the grass playing fetch with a golden retriever. Beyond them another man wearing sunglasses and a Yankees cap strolled along a path, talking into a phone.

When Kera looked again at Bradley, she was no more than twenty paces away from him. He must have been sweating in that jacket. He had the collar pulled up around the back of his neck, as if that could render him invisible. It was then that his throat tore open. Even as she watched it happen, it seemed impossible. After a bizarre second, his head tipped forward, and his chin slumped against his chest where blood from the ragged hole in his neck had started to darken his shirt and jacket. Retroactively, she registered the soft whiz and a dull thump from somewhere nearby, where the bullet had lodged in the ground, finally halted by something more substantial than human flesh. The approaching jogger noticed the blood then too and screamed, drawing the attention of the other onlookers as she ran in the other direction. The two men on the grass looked up and paused, unsure how to react. Kera was too distracted to register the reaction of the fourth onlooker, the man who had been farthest away.

The window to do something would be open for only seconds. The first thing Kera felt was her mind retreating to that bathroom and Parker's mutilated body cradled in the tub. Whenever her mind went there, it shut down. *Not now,* she told herself. She'd arrived too late to that bathroom to discover whatever Parker had wanted to show her. She couldn't let that happen again. In the unpredictable gray area between training and reflex, Kera's mind began to pair things quickly into simple decisions. Either the shooter knew she was here to meet Bradley or the shooter didn't. Either there would be a second bullet intended for her or there wouldn't. Either she had the slight advantage of countersurprise or she didn't.

She turned sharply and ran a dozen steps away from Bradley's slumped body, mimicking the panicked flight of other pedestrians. And then, just as abruptly, she pivoted back and sprinted toward the bench. Bradley's clothes were dark with blood down to his lap, where his sunglasses had fallen. She could see his eyes. A naive glimmer—the very early beginnings of surprise—had been frozen into his retinas as they went dead. She reached for one of the backpack's straps and, without slowing down, swooped up the bag from beneath the bench.

With the pack in hand, she made two sharp zags that took her through the trees providing the nearest cover. Just as she cleared those, her mind processed two thoughts in quick succession. First, she identified the fourth onlooker, the man in the Yankees cap and dark shades. Second, she registered that he was jogging calmly but purposely, not away from Bradley's body, but toward it. He noticed her at almost the same instant, and at first proceeded forward. But then suddenly his head whipped back in her direction, and he stopped. Kera did not linger to see his next move, but she imagined that in the several seconds that passed before she looked back again to see him chasing after her, he had glanced at Bradley's park bench, seen that the backpack was missing, and then confirmed that it was in her hand.

Picturing her location, she sprinted toward a path that she judged to be the shortest distance out of the park. Looking back was costly, speed-wise, and she only permitted herself one strategic glance at her pursuer. The man was up to full speed and had closed the gap to within a few dozen feet. But she must have surprised him as much as he'd surprised her. He did not appear to be armed. His only role had been to retrieve the backpack.

Breaking into a clearing, Kera had a direct shot to Central Park West, where a taxi was idling at a red light. But she could hear footsteps behind her now. She wouldn't make the cab in time. Her eyes began to search the ground, low tree branches, and the arms of pedestrians for a makeshift weapon.

Instead, she spotted two NYPD officers on bicycles, pedaling full tilt into the park.

"He has a gun! He's the shooter!" she yelled at the cops, who braked obediently and drew their weapons on the man she was pointing at. She didn't bother to hang around and give a statement. She was in a cab and rolling away from the curb before the cops even approached the man, who had been ordered to lie facedown with his hands on his head.

SIXTY-TWO

"Where to?"

Through the cab window, Kera could see people running up the paths in search of safety. Some cradled children, coaxed dogs, or yelled into cell phones. She blinked when two police cruisers swerved around the cab and cut into the park.

"Ma'am?"

"Just drive. Toward Midtown."

She tried to focus. What were her options? Going to the hotel was out of the question, as was returning to the Hawk building. *Focus*, she ordered herself. As the cab cruised away from the chaos of the park and drifted into Midtown, where life appeared to carry on as usual, her phone rang. She pulled it from her pocket. It was Jones.

"Are you all right?"

"Get out of there, Jones. Whatever you're doing right now, just walk away."

"I'm out. I left a few minutes ago. They're tracking you, Kera. Gabby and the director. And they have men on the street."

"They killed him. They fucking killed him." The cab driver looked at her in the rearview mirror.

Jones was silent for a moment. "Are you all right? Did you make contact first?"

Kera looked at the backpack on the floor of the cab between her feet. Her fingers were still wrapped tightly around the shoulder strap. For the first time since she'd snatched it from under the bench, she loosened her grip. Her palm was smeared with bright blood. *Christ,* she thought. She looked at the cabby; he was watching the road. She commanded herself to be calm. Then she unzipped the backpack and looked inside.

"Kera?"

"I grabbed his bag. I think the files are here."

"Listen to me. We have to get off the phone. When we hang up, turn off your phone and remove the battery. Then throw them both away. Meet me at the place we went to two weeks ago after you approached me on the street. OK?"

"OK," Kera said, picturing the little bar they'd walked to from Times Square. After she hung up, she told the driver to drive around the block and let her out. She took another cab halfway downtown and then switched to a cab that brought her back up to Hell's Kitchen.

·   ·   ·   ·   ·

Kera arrived at the bar first and used the ladies' room in back to wipe blood from the backpack and wash her hands. Then she sat at the dim table nearest to the back exit and kept her eye on the front door. When Jones came in and she saw that he was alone and unharmed, she rose. Jones had his computer bag slung over his shoulder. He hugged her before she could say anything.

"Are the files in there?" he said, staring at Bradley's backpack, which Kera still gripped in one hand, afraid to let go.

She nodded and unzipped the main pocket. Inside was an external hard drive. Jones took it from her and began to unpack his laptop on the table. Kera stepped to the bar and ordered two Cokes from the bartender, who'd started to eye them expectantly. He made a show of being unimpressed with her order, but what could he do? It was early afternoon on a weekday. To keep him out of their hair, she left him a ten-dollar tip for use of the table. When she returned with the sodas, Jones had tethered the external drive to his computer with a USB cable.

"Let's have a look," he said, clicking the icon as it appeared on-screen.

The drive contained only two folders. The first one they selected displayed seven files. Jones opened them one by one. They were all architectural designs—blueprints and 3-D renderings of a large underground complex.

"What is it?" Kera asked.

"It looks like a series of large, insulated rooms—five stories of them. That's hundreds of thousands of square feet of space. And see these plans for the central air-conditioning system? They're serious about keeping this place cool. I'd say we're looking at a massive server farm."

Kera could see from the elevation drawing that the complex was buried in a hillside. The coordinates in the legend identified a location in semirural New Jersey, some forty miles west of Manhattan.

"You think ONE is planning to build this?" Jones asked.

Kera shook her head. "They already have. At our first meeting, Bradley called it 'the bunker.' Parker's voice mail mentioned it too. What's in the other folder?" The server farm in the bunker was interesting, but this couldn't be the full extent of what Travis Bradley had given his life for.

Jones clicked open the second folder, which contained several dozen database files, all of them enormous. Most of the file names were opaque combinations of letters and numbers. Jones glanced up at her as if to ask where they should start. She shrugged and told him to just open the first file. It was named "Clients."

She felt her pulse thump as a grid of numbers spread across the screen. It looked similar to the printed pages of data that Travis Bradley had sent her the morning before, except that these weren't data files of surveillance targets; they were the names and addresses of all the entities who had purchased such information from ONE. She scanned the grid quickly, noticing that the clients had been given code names.

"Can you search clients by address?" she asked.

Jones clicked to the search field and typed in "Beijing." There were four hits. Kera recognized one of the addresses as the head-quarters of the Chinese government's Ministry of State Security. Next he typed in "Moscow." There were two hits there. "Islamabad," "Riyadh," "Jerusalem," and "London" all turned up in the addresses of clients as well.

"Try Langley," Kera said.

Jones looked at her. Then he typed in the letters. It was a hit. Kera stared at the list of results. There were at least forty-five orders for information on targets in just the last month. In the column next to the date of the order, each request was marked as "Delivered."

"Jesus," she whispered.

Jones spent a few more minutes searching for cities in and around northern Virginia, Maryland, and the District of Columbia, until he and Kera had determined that US intelligence and law enforcement agencies were using ONE's information services as readily as anyone else.

"It's like privatized espionage," he said. "With no national loy-alty. Is this really worth the money to ONE?"

"Apparently," Kera said. "And it probably goes beyond that." She wished now—now that it was too late—that she'd paid more atten-tion to what Bradley had told her at their first meeting. "Bradley said ONE was striving for total transparency, for the end of secrets. But I think what they really want is to *control* all the world's secrets. That would give them more power than any amount of money could buy."

They spent fifteen minutes clicking through each file in the two folders. The last file in the second folder was different from the others. Instead of another database, it was a compressed file that contained thousands of internal ONE e-mails discussing the details and ambitions of the secret data-mining program. In the "to" and "from" fields, Kera recognized the names of several of the conglomerate's key executives.

"Such arrogance," Jones said, "to put things like this in an e-mail and believe that they won't come back to haunt you." He closed down all the files and pulled up a web browser. The bar's Wi-Fi password was written on the bottom of a chalkboard that touted the day's happy-hour specials.

"What are you doing?"

"The last two people who had these files were murdered. We're going to get rid of these before ONE or Hawk finds us."

"What—here?"

"Got a better idea?"

"What about HawkEye? You said yourself they were using it to track me."

"I'll explain in a moment why we don't need to worry about that. But first, where are we sending these? We should get started. It's going to take a while for them to upload."

Kera bit her lower lip. "We can't send them to the agency. You were right last night. They're too involved. They'd want the whole thing to go away, and I'm afraid they'd succeed at that."

Jones lifted his eyebrows as if to say, *Well, then?*

"Do it," she said. "Send them to Gnos.is. But not with our names attached." She watched Jones work and wondered where she would go next. She had passports, whole identities that she'd created for herself for situations like this—though she'd never really believed they would be necessary.

"Want a drink?" Jones said, when the upload had started. "We might as well get comfortable. The Wi-Fi here isn't bad for a bar, but I don't think they had file uploads of this size in mind when they selected their Internet plan."

"I think first you better explain why you're not more worried about Hawk tracking us down here."

"Oh, right. HawkEye," Jones said, and she thought she saw a shade of sadness cast over his eyes. "It no longer exists."

SIXTY-THREE

In the Control Room, Gabby di Palma and Dick Branagh were gazing up at the main tactical display, monitoring feeds from surveillance cameras on the south end of Central Park. This was interrupted occasionally by Gabby's yelling into a phone that broadcast radio signals to Hawk's team on the street. Kera had left the building earlier than any of them had expected and then, infuriatingly, she'd lost the one man who had been in a position to tail her. Then she'd vanished into the park, where there were no cameras.

Twenty minutes later, still with no sighting of Kera, the major news networks had begun to report on a shooting in the park. HawkEye picked her up again when she used her phone while in a cab going south on Central Park West. And then suddenly, all the screens in the Control Room flickered and went black.

"Goddamn it," Branagh shouted—the only time Gabby or any of the rest of them had ever heard him raise his voice. It startled Gabby as much as the blackout. "Now what?"

"The system's down," an analyst in the pit reported.

"Yes," Branagh said drily, control regained. "Now, if you would get it back up, please."

There was a period of frantic activity among the analysts and technicians in the pit until finally one of them reported that it wasn't possible to get HawkEye back online. It hadn't just crashed; a bug had damaged it catastrophically.

"Who was she talking to on the phone? Can we at least figure that out?"

"Jones," Gabby said suddenly. Branagh looked at her, and then they both turned to look up at Jones's workstation.

But Jones was gone.

· · · · ·

An hour passed. In the absence of any input from HawkEye, someone had switched all the big screens over to show the feeds from cable news networks that were covering the Central Park shooting, as well as popular news websites, such as the *New York Times* and Gnos.is. The shooting victim had been a man named Travis Bradley. Gabby did not need HawkEye to tell her that it was the same Travis Bradley she'd sent Kera to meet with a few weeks earlier. As requested, Gabby had passed Kera's report of that meeting along to her client at ONE. In her opinion, given the stakes, ONE had been slow to react. Bradley should have been eliminated immediately. But instead, ONE had fixated on finding the missing artists and, of course, on Gnos.is. The only silver lining was the way that those cases had ultimately exposed Kera and Jones as traitors.

Gabby had no doubt that, HawkEye or not, Jones and Kera would be found—if not today, then tomorrow or the next. They'd been clever, but they should have known better what they were up against. It wasn't only Hawk and ONE that would prevent them from surviving on the run. If this little incident couldn't be contained before the CIA caught wind of it, then the agency would join the ranks of irritated parties who couldn't afford to have them loose either.

While the computer technicians tried to revive some capability that might assist her men in the field, Gabby had been shifting her eyes systematically from screen to screen, scrutinizing the cable and online news images for anything that looked wrong. It was in this way, several minutes later, that she came upon the neglected screen in the lower corner, which was displaying the Gnos.is home page. By design, apparently, the Gnos.is home page didn't change often or arbitrarily, which prevented it from overreacting to breaking news. And so the relatively quick movement of a new sphere popping up and growing in size as it rolled forward toward the front of the cloud caught Gabby's eye. She brought a hand to her mouth, sensing the unfolding disaster even before her mind could assemble a full understanding of what had happened.

As she moved out from behind the consoles in the pit to get a better look at the Gnos.is headline, the CNN feed on one of the larger screens abruptly switched over from coverage of the shooting to introduce another breaking-news story. The screen filled with a live overhead shot of a hillside in rural New Jersey. Outside an inconspicuous concrete facade, a small, tree-lined employee parking lot lay hidden from the public road. The headline running across the bottom of the screen read:

BREAKING: SECRET ONE CORP. FACILITY AT CENTER OF INTERNATIONAL ESPIONAGE SCANDAL; FBI WILL LEAD INVESTIGATION

Gabby was holding her phone in her hand, so she felt the vibrations when it started to ring. It was her secretary. "Keith Grassley at ONE is on the line for you."

Gabby looked over at Branagh and caught his eye. He looked merely anxious, as he had since his momentary loss of control after

HawkEye had crashed. She could see that he'd not yet noticed the report on CNN. Bracing for the fallout, she nodded toward the screen, and he followed her gaze.

"Ma'am?" She could hear her secretary's voice in her ear. "Mr. Grassley sounded upset, but he wouldn't say what he was calling about. Should I put him through?"

Across the room, Branagh suddenly exploded. "What's going on? Can anyone tell me what the fuck is happening?" Above him, two other networks flipped over to cover the new story. Like CNN, they already had their own helicopters arriving in the airspace over the bunker.

Gabby had the phone pressed to her ear, but she did not know if her secretary was still there or if the young woman had gone ahead and put ONE's CEO through. That question was answered a few seconds later when she heard her secretary's voice again.

"Ms. di Palma, I tried to connect Mr. Grassley, but there was some sort of disturbance at his office. I'll see if I can get him back."

Gabby felt the phone slip from her fingers. One of the networks broke into their coverage of the raid on the ONE bunker to show scenes of tactical teams surrounding a Manhattan skyscraper. She recognized the building as ONE's headquarters.

"Abort," Branagh said, seeing it too. And then, shouting, "Everybody out. We're going black."

Gabby didn't move. She'd seen the Gnos.is headline, which mentioned Hawk by name, and knew, with a wave of nausea, where the story had come from and that it was too late. As she steadied herself against the nearest desk, she watched over the heads of her fleeing colleagues as the first of the SWAT men, weapons drawn, filled the hallway outside the Control Room.

SIXTY-FOUR

Kera wore a hat and glasses and was careful to turn away from the cameras in the airports. Even without HawkEye in operation, the cameras were still there, and they still saw nearly everything. Hawk, she'd read on Gnos.is and elsewhere, had been dismantled. Gabby, Branagh, and dozens of ONE executives had been arrested. But the agency would be looking for her, and they weren't interested in a hero; they needed scapegoats. She could see the signs of their work already—in the evolving speculation from media pundits about the motives and credibility of the "anonymous" leaker, which had begun to sour. Common sense dictated that she should stay out of airports and lie low, and that she should not attempt to leave the country. Which was why she was doing just the opposite.

She had another reason too.

In Houston she considered calling her parents' home phone to leave a voice mail and then decided against it. They might be waiting by the phone, even though they would have been at work at this hour on a typical day. Instead, she wrote them an e-mail. She explained, rather lamely, that her work situation had grown complicated, a gross understatement given what her parents would be reading in the news. She added that she needed some time alone for reflection after everything that had happened. This was probably not an adequate explanation to give to a parent, but it was all she had. She knew they would forgive her, whether she deserved it or not.

It had been just before she boarded the flight out of the States that she happened to look up at a television to see a report that ONE's stock price was in free fall. The company was threatening lawsuits, a strategy that seemed increasingly laughable as its top executives, one by one, were indicted for white-collar felonies.

SIXTY-FIVE

Garita Palmera,
El Salvador

Once she was on the ground and through customs in San Salvador, Kera hired a driver to take her into Garita Palmera. There she rented a bike. For most of the afternoon, she pedaled slowly on dirt roads, constantly triangulating the only landmarks she had to go by: the beachhead, a cluster of distant buildings, the ocean farther in the background. It was late afternoon when she finally came upon a small dwelling that seemed to fit all the criteria. She dismounted and leaned the bike against a water pump. A young girl, maybe seven, was playing in the dirt and looked up at her. Two unkempt dogs sniffed for food by a blackened fire ring. Kera mounted the steps to the porch. There was no proper door, just a simple curtain and a bug screen, through which she could see a woman washing dishes. She knocked on the frame and the woman came to investigate.

She removed her sunglasses. The woman looked a few years younger than Kera, but easily old enough to have mothered the child in the front yard. She had skin darker than Kera's, and hair blacker. Kera judged quickly that she and the woman did not share any relatives. She determined soon after that they also did not share a common language.

Kera removed the photograph from her pocket. It was the original print; the digital copy had been abandoned along with her phone. While the woman studied the photo, Kera glanced past her, into the main room. From the photo, Kera recognized the large window in the far wall and the wooden pole in the center of the room, supporting the low ceiling. But the furniture and other decorations had been replaced. The family who had been here then had long ago moved on.

The woman handed the photo back, confused. Kera pointed to the infant in the photo and then to herself. She repeated this motion several times. When understanding came into the woman's eyes, they grew wide and round and then a little damp. The woman became excited and offered Kera a cup of something hot to drink and a chair to sit in. Kera politely declined both. She only needed a minute. She put the picture back in her pocket, and there it was in real life—the view that had become familiar to her from years of studying a creased and faded four-by-six print.

Her affiliation with the present slipped momentarily. Time scoped, refocusing like a giant lens. Over the past few years, and especially with the ATLANTIS case, her identity had morphed to the point that it was no longer definable, even to her. Who was she? Perhaps this had started much earlier than her career in the intelligence community. Who was the infant girl in the photo? This was what she knew: she was a disavowed clandestine agent of the US government. She was an American, born elsewhere, a daughter of someone else's making, an ex-fiancée to an earnest and loving man who had been killed because of his links to her.

She drifted back into the present one layer of awareness at a time, hearing first the distant waves and the call of seagulls, and then a motorbike on the road, and finally, the window curtain in front of her, flapping in a breeze.

Who was the infant girl in the photo?

It had taken a thirty-year journey before she had arrived here to really ask herself that question. She would start over now. And this time she would do a better job of keeping track of the answer.

• • • • •

A few days later, Kera took a trip to the city and picked up a copy of the *New York Times*, which she had been monitoring online in short snatches of time she stole on the hotel's tired, shared computer. Exchanging cash for the paper in a small kiosk on a dusty commercial street, she thought that her father would be proud that they still lived in a world where news was printed on broadsheets and distributed to faraway news shops not unlike his own. He would be less proud of the story on page one that began in a narrow column beneath the fold. FORMER INTELLIGENCE ASSETS INVESTIGATED FOR TREASON, it said. And then her name, right there in the lead paragraph. Though she'd already read it online, it seemed more consequential in print.

Kera Mersal, a former CIA analyst, and James Carr, a former employee of the NSA (who goes by the name J. D. Jones), are wanted for questioning as federal authorities struggle to learn more about the widening ONE scandal that has rocked both Wall Street and the global intelligence community.

Investigators say they now believe Mersal and Carr were behind the massive leak of classified documents published to the website Gnos.is by an anonymous source last week. A CIA official with knowledge of the investigation said that the leaked documents, which at first appeared to implicate the agency in the scandal, were in fact fabricated and planted by Mersal and Carr on behalf of Russian and Chinese intelligence organizations in an attempt to shift the balance of power in global espionage circles. Such charges, if brought, would amount to treason under US law and would ratchet up tensions between Washington and Beijing and Moscow.

The CIA maintains that their involvement with ONE was a carefully planned strategy to infiltrate the corporation and learn about their illegal practices of collecting and selling detailed information on US citizens to foreign agencies. The CIA operation, the agency claims, was badly damaged by Mersal's and Carr's actions. Mersal and Carr are reportedly at large.

Meanwhile, experts predict that the crippled media giant, ONE, which was first at the center of the scandal, is spiraling toward bankruptcy.

Kera sat on the balcony of her hotel room overlooking the beach. She read the article again and again, folding the irrelevant half of the paper back on itself to prevent interference from the breeze that occasionally blew a ribbon of hair across her face. This was another reason she'd come to the tiny Central American country: to wait and see what she was facing. Now she knew. It was part of the game, she thought. It was the agency's way of trying to get her and Jones to resurface on their own and defend themselves.

She sat in silence, thinking, as the sun cooled and dropped toward the line of the Pacific. Finally, she spread out the newspaper on the small balcony table.

Then she got out a pen.

SIXTY-SIX

Langley, Virginia

Lionel Bright was having one of the worst weeks in his career. Six days earlier, his boss, the director of the CIA, had learned on CNN that the agency's most highly classified black operation, Hawk, had gone under. On the list of career low points, having an operation get botched this spectacularly was second only to having an agent killed in action. And that was without it being the lead story coming out of every media outlet in the world.

In subsequent meetings throughout the week, Bright had sat and listened to his team and the FBI investigators as they tried to piece together what had happened—and what they were going to do to clean up the mess. The Feds had not permitted him to talk yet with Gabby, who was being held in a federal prison in downtown Manhattan. But Bright's team had sent word to her through her lawyers that the agency had a crisis management plan that would work if she played along. Bright wished to God they didn't need her so badly to save their own asses; he'd have been content to see her serve real prison time. If anyone deserved to be thrown under the bus, it was Gabby, not Kera.

He'd been furious when he read Gabby's statement, which the agency had written for her and in which she claimed that Kera and Jones had sabotaged the well-intentioned Hawk operation on behalf of Russian and Chinese interests. On its face, given the detailed evidence that had been leaked, that story seemed preposterous to Bright, though it had become less and less so each day the media gave it legs and as long as Kera remained silent.

Since she'd left her duties at Langley for the Hawk assignment in New York, Kera and Bright had communicated only twice—once when he'd approached her in New York after her postcard and e-mail warning, and then when he'd left her an unreturned phone message days after her fiancé's death. He had not heard from her since their discussion in the diner.

Until now. Just this afternoon he'd received a sealed manila envelope that had come by courier. There was no return address. Thinking little of it, he cut into one end with his letter opener and pulled out the contents. When he saw that it was a newspaper, he forgot everything else.

He sat down to study the broadsheet closely. It was a Tuesday *New York Times* from the previous week, the edition that had prominently displayed the story about Kera and Jones facing possible charges of treason. At first there was nothing else notable about the newspaper. But after he turned carefully through a few pages, he saw it. He checked a few more pages to confirm the pattern.

He reached for a pen. On every page of the newspaper, he found two ink dots—one in the vertical margin and one in the horizontal margin. Imagining that the dots were points on two perpendicular axes, he followed them until they bisected on a word somewhere within the copy. Advancing in order from page A1 to page A6, he located the word marked on each page and wrote it down on the back of the envelope. When he was finished, he walked to the window of his office and stood there awhile with a complex smile on his face, part pride, part sadness, and part fear. He'd burn the newspaper and the note in a minute. But for now, for just a little while longer, he wanted them to exist.

Her decoded message said: *Have you figured it out yet?*

ACKNOWLEDGEMENTS

The process of writing a novel requires a suspiciously disciplined person to sit for hours alone, daily, for a year or more, trying to put into words a bunch of stuff he's cooked up in his head. Turning that document into a coherent, enjoyable, publishable book requires the patience, wisdom, and generosity of dozens of people who go well out of their way to offer support and expertise. The following people were crucial in pushing me to make this novel far better than I could have done alone.

Chris is my daily source of support, encouragement, and happiness. And I do mean daily. He goes above and beyond the call of duty in accommodating my writing schedule, and his presence keeps me sane and productive. He also happens to be the love of my life, and on that front I can't imagine being any more fortunate.

I lucked into the most supportive family any human being—and especially a writer—could hope for. Mom and Dad, thank you for your endless support and for sharing in the ups and downs of seeing this through. Kelly and Gretchen, thanks not only for your kind words of encouragement, but also for being so eager to read an early draft and give incredibly useful feedback.

It is not putting too sentimental a spin on it to say that my friends are like my second family. Their support is sincere, their good humor is life-giving, and their talents at their own creative and professional pursuits are inspiring. They'll likely all be household names before I will. Jon Bergman, Eric Brassard, Phil Buiser, Zac Hug, Max Miller, and Marc Valera were particularly helpful in coaching this book along and helping me get it across the finish line.

I'm extraordinarily grateful for Anh Schluep and the rest of the Thomas & Mercer team at Amazon Publishing, as well as Terry Goodman and Jessica Poore, for their passion, professionalism, and for taking a chance on me. Rebecca Brinson copyedited this thing with an impossibly sharp eye; the English language and I are in debt to her for that. And finally, I want to acknowledge David Downing, my brilliant editor, whose wisdom and patience helped me transform the final drafts of this book. Readers will never know the full significance of David's guidance—which, I think, is the point. But it's a shame that the best editors are inherently underappreciated by readers. Take my word for it, dear reader, David has done you all a great favor in the immense value he added to this book.

SOURCES

If I were a clandestine agent of the US government and had acquired firsthand knowledge of actions and details similar to those portrayed in this book, I would be forbidden from acknowledging that here or anywhere else. So assuming I'm not, I'll confess to relying upon a wide array of sources that I found invaluable in my research for this book. The most influential were *The Shadow Factory: The NSA from 9/11 to the Eavesdropping on America* by James Bamford; *You Are Not a Gadget: A Manifesto* by Jaron Lanier; *Amusing Ourselves to Death: Public Discourse in the Age of Show Business* by Neil Postman; and *Priceless: How I Went Undercover to Rescue the World's Stolen Treasures* by Robert K. Wittman. These books are all highly readable, and I recommend them if you have further interest in grappling with the evolving roles of privacy, technology, and conscientious discourse in our culture.

Finally, it is incumbent on me to acknowledge that many readers will recognize in this book key plot devices inspired by Ayn Rand's novel *Atlas Shrugged*. Those similarities are as intentional as the differences.

SOURCES

ABOUT THE AUTHOR

A native of Alaska, Ryan Quinn was an NCAA champion and an all-American athlete (skiing) while at the University of Utah. He worked for five years in New York's book-publishing industry before moving to Los Angeles, where he writes and trains for marathons. Quinn's first novel, *The Fall*, was an award-winning finalist for the 2013 International Book Awards. For more, please visit ryanquinnbooks.com.